Born to be a Heroine

CHRISTINE COMBE

PUBLISHED BY BLACK ROOM PRESS

Born to be a Heroine

Copyright 2022 by Christine Combe

All Rights Reserved

Cover design Copyright 2022 Christina Moore

Cover model courtesy of Period Images

ISBN: 9798815619838

Acknowledgments

I cannot express enough my thanks to all the friends who have supported me through the writing of this book for the words of encouragement, the listening to ideas, celebrating the snippets I shared, and boosting me up when I had difficulties getting the words out.

I also must thank all the wonderful readers at fanfiction.net who read along as I posted there for critique for all the kind words and encouragement, for all their enthusiasm and hopes. Even the silent ones who just selected "Follow Story"—and especially those who clicked "Favorite Story"—gave me much inspiration. You've helped me shape this book as much as any of my friends.

And last, but never least, I once again thank the spirit of a most inspiring authoress, Miss Jane Austen. Without her genius this story might not exist, and when I use her own words in certain places, it is always with the greatest respect, because no one could say it better.

Dedication

To every woman who has risen to the occasion and found the
courage to speak her truth.

Prologue

Mr. Allen of Fullerton, Wiltshire was in Bath with his wife and her young companion for the improvement of his gouty constitution when he very unexpectedly suffered a severe and ultimately fatal apoplexy.

His demise tore Mrs. Allen and young Catherine Morland from their revels in a city ironically known for its healing waters as well as its social scene. The elder of the ladies was too caught up in the grief born of her loss to care, and the younger only the smallest fraction vexed to be taken away so soon from friends newly made there. Thankfully, the better of them—Mr. Henry Tilney and his sister Eleanor—were greatly understanding of Catherine's duty to Mrs. Allen, as well as that of her brother, James, who was in Bath also. Not so understanding were John and Isabella Thorpe, who thought that the Morlands not being related to the Allens meant there was no reason they should quit Bath before their planned departure another six weeks hence, but when even James remained firm in his desire to accompany the grieving Mrs. Allen and his sister back home, they relented in their persistent begging that the two remain.

The Thorpes' disappointment in losing their companions was assuaged by the belief that Mr. Allen, who was very wealthy, would leave some legacy to both James and Catherine. That they were likely to be enriched by their generous neighbor appealed to John and Isabella, whose family had not been fortunate enough to achieve either richness or social status—both of which were greatly desired by the pair. That the two deceived themselves as to the prospects of their friends was entirely unknown to both Catherine and James.

1

In due time, Mr. Allen was laid to rest, and his attorney was soon after at the door of Fullerton Manor to discuss matters of business with his client's widow. Miss Morland, who had called on the lady every day and spent hours with her just listening to her talk of her husband and all their years together, was rather surprised when—having given Mrs. Allen and Mr. Jenkins privacy to talk—she was later summoned to the study to join them. After being offered a cup of tea by Mrs. Allen, which was politely declined, Catherine was eagerly perched on the edge of the damask sofa to hear what the kind older lady had to say.

"My dearest Catherine," Mrs. Allen began tearfully—the poor woman was always on the verge of sobbing of late—"I have asked you here to tell you, in person, what I think we ought to have done some time ago. Though Mr. Allen had no idea of this necessity coming so soon, I am sure we would have done either while we were in Bath or soon after our return to Fullerton."

"What have you to tell me, Mrs. Allen?" Catherine asked, glancing confusedly between her hostess and the attorney.

Mrs. Allen reached for her hand. "Well, you know—of course—that Mr. Allen and I had no children. And I should very much have liked to at least have had a daughter, especially if she were as delightful a creature as you are."

Catherine blushed and looked down at where their hands were joined between them on the sofa. "Mrs. Allen, you are too kind."

"It is true!" cried Mrs. Allen with a squeeze of her hand and more animation than she had shown in all the days since her husband had died. "You are the best of girls to have gone with an old woman like me to Bath, and to do so much looking after me after Mr. Allen…"

Mrs. Allen paused and sniffled, and raised her ever-present handkerchief to her eyes and nose before she drew a breath and said, "In any case, my dear, having no children left my dear husband and me in quite the pickle as to whom to leave our worldly wealth and goods to when it was time to meet our Lord. Mr. Allen has a few nieces and nephews to whom it could all have been left, and he has been kind in leaving them each a small legacy, but the bulk of it has been endowed to another."

Catherine now took on an expression and feeling of alarm. "Oh, Mrs. Allen, do not tell me Mr. Allen was so thoughtless as to leave you homeless! Surely he would not do such a thing—he loved you so much!"

"Oh!" cried the lady. "Oh no, my dear! Mr. Allen was very generous indeed—I am to have my marriage portion in its entirety, for one thing, and could live very comfortably indeed off the interest. As for a home, I am to have lifetime residency right here in the house I shared with my dear husband. But as to the rest of his fortune, my dear... Well, your having joined us in Bath played a part in deciding to whom the rest of it should go."

A frown now furrowed Catherine's brow. "I... I do not understand. How did our holiday help Mr. Allen decide who to leave his fortune to?"

Now Mrs. Allen chuckled. "Oh my dear girl, how can you not understand? Let me put it to you this way... Do you recall that day Mr. Allen said he was to leave Bath and would not return until very late in the evening?"

Catherine nodded slowly. "I do. He said he had some business to see to, did he not?" she said.

Mrs. Allen nodded, then gestured toward Mr. Jenkins as she said, "It was to Mr. Jenkins here that he went. Mr. Allen had decided, and I assure you I agreed wholeheartedly, that *you* should be his heir."

Near a minute passed in which Catherine stared gaping at Mrs. Allen in stunned disbelief. At long last, she began to shake her head.

"No! Oh no, Mrs. Allen, this cannot be true!" Catherine cried. "Why should Mr. Allen leave his fortune to *me*? I am no relation to him!"

She pushed to her feet and paced away, wringing her hands as she said, "But surely I cannot *really* be Mr. Allen's heir. It cannot be possible!"

Mr. Jenkins—who had heretofore remained silent—softly cleared his throat then and said, "Miss Morland, a gentleman whose estate is not legally constrained to be disposed of otherwise, such as by entailment, can dispense of it in any manner he chooses. In fact, it is not at all uncommon for a childless wealthy couple like Mr. and Mrs. Allen to adopt the child of a relative or close family friend and name him or her as heir to the estate."

"And your parents," said Mrs. Allen quickly, "have truly been the best of friends to Mr. Allen and me. We spoke to your mother and father about the matter before going to Bath. They were, admittedly, as much surprised by our consideration as are you. Well, before our holiday it was really but a thought which we had discussed with dear Reverend and Mrs. Morland, but as I said before, our time in Bath secured Mr. Allen's opinion. My own was decided long ago."

Catherine blinked rapidly. "But... But why me? Why not James or

3

one of my other brothers and sisters?"

"Because you are special to me," said Mrs. Allen. "Dearest Catherine, while it is true that Mr. Allen and I have watched all your brothers and sisters grow from infancy, your particular kindness to me over the years has made me think of you almost as the daughter I never had."

"Oh, Mrs. Allen, I..." For a moment, Catherine was suddenly too overcome to continue speaking. "I am so deeply flattered by such a sentiment. But are you truly certain you wish to do this?"

Mrs. Allen smiled. "My dear, it is already done. Mr. Allen's fortune is to be yours outright, while this house and all its contents — save for those things decreed in Mr. Allen's will to be given to his remaining family — shall be yours in their entirety upon my passing. You may even come and live here with me if it is your desire — and though I have no wish to unduly influence you, my dear, I'll not hesitate to say that I should like it very much if you did."

Feeling quite unable to maintain her composure while standing — and secretly afraid of swooning, which she had never before done — Catherine returned to the sofa and sat again. "So basically... I am now an heiress?"

Both Mrs. Allen and Mr. Jenkins nodded. Catherine drew a breath and tried to wrap her mind around the concept of having a fortune, then realized she had no idea just how much of a fortune she had gained.

"Is... is it indelicate of me to ask the amount of fortune I have been given?" she asked tentatively.

After sharing another glance with Mrs. Allen, Mr. Jenkins cleared his throat again. "Miss Morland, you are now the mistress of a fortune the interest of which is five thousand pounds per annum."

Immediately after this declaration, for the first time in her life, Catherine Morland swooned.

Chapter One

"**I do** hope she is a handsome girl."

Fitzwilliam Darcy only just stopped himself rolling his eyes. Caroline Bingley and her elder sister, Louisa Bingley Hurst, had been going back and forth about the handsomeness — or possible lack thereof — of the mysterious Catherine Morland who had inherited the bulk of their great uncle's fortune for the whole of the morning. In truth, the topic had been bandied between the two ever since Charles had read to them the letter which related both his uncle's death and the dispensation of his wealth.

It was only for Charles' sake, as the two of them were close friends, that Darcy didn't make some remark about the foolishness of their curiosity. It mattered not at all whether the young lady was handsome — the fortune was hers. In the back of his mind, from the moment Charles had informed them of the fate of their uncle's money, Darcy believed his friend's sisters more disappointed that they had not received a greater share of it than the hundred pounds he had bequeathed each of them than they cared whether Miss Morland was handsome.

"I should think, Caroline, that you would wish her to have warts and a leer," said Charles Bingley cheerfully. "Then she would be less competition for you in next Season's marriage mart."

"Oh Charles, do be serious!" Miss Bingley cried with exasperation. "How could she possibly be competition for me when she will surely be married by next Season?"

Her brother looked up from his book, and though Darcy did not, he found himself surprisingly curious as to his friend's response to the question.

"And what, pray tell, makes you think the young lady will be married before the next London Season?" Bingley asked.

Miss Bingley glanced at her sister, then at her brother with a smile. "Because I have decided we should invite her to join us here at Netherfield, and surely you—with your propensity for falling in love with pretty girls wherever we go—will be so struck by her beauty, should she have any at all, that you simply won't allow any other man to have her."

Bingley laughed heartily. "Oh, I see what you are about now! You think to marry Miss Morland off so that her newly acquired fortune—which I understand is equal to my own—does not attract all the eligible gentleman of Town, like Darcy here!"

Darcy allowed himself a soft snort, then said, "Perhaps you ought to wish Miss Morland plain as the day is long, Miss Bingley, for should she accept your invitation—providing your brother allows one to be sent to a young lady we have none of us ever met—I might find myself as taken with her as Charles. In such a case, we would engage in an increasingly foolish competition for the young lady's affections that could only end in a round of fisticuffs, with the champion being allowed the honor of claiming Miss Morland's heart."

He rarely engaged Miss Bingley in conversation directly in order to discourage her obvious interest in him, but Darcy had found himself compelled to tease, for surely it was only her own vanity she hoped to satisfy rather than any genuine desire to see her brother happily settled. If Miss Morland was indeed handsome, then if Caroline could marry the girl to her brother, she would sate both her need to eliminate the competition as well as not be embarrassed by having to claim a plain girl as a sister.

Bingley laughed again, then said, "That was well said, Darcy! Imagine—you and me fighting over a girl. I almost hope to see it come true, though I know full well I should lose that round of fisticuffs most soundly."

He sighed then, and added, "However, Caroline does have a fine idea. If it is not disagreeable to you all, I should like very much indeed to invite Mrs. Allen and Miss Morland to stay with us here at Netherfield for a time."

Darcy at last looked up from the newspaper he had been reading to regard his friend. "Did you not say your mother was not close with this uncle of hers, and that you had not met him since childhood?"

Bingley nodded. "That is true enough. But surely the lady—our aunt, I mean—would like to get away for a time. Her home must be full of bittersweet memories of my uncle, as I believe my mother once said that they genuinely loved each other. And a change of scene and society can only do both Mrs. Allen and Miss Morland good in any case."

Darcy conceded the debate with an incline of his head. "A good point, my friend. And as this is your house and I merely a guest in it, whom you invite to take up residence with you is entirely your choice. I will admit that I should not mind greater society even if it is two ladies, for surely we will not find much intelligent conversation among the denizens of this little hamlet you now live in."

His host laughed a third time as Miss Bingley rose gracefully from her chair and started toward Darcy. "How readily you and I agree, Mr. Darcy—I wonder at Charles very much for choosing an estate so near to such vulgar society."

Bingley scoffed. "Fiddlesticks, Caroline! How can you say such things about people you've not yet even been introduced to?"

He gave his sister no time to reply, for Bingley laid his book aside and popped up from his seat. "I shall write to Mrs. Allen immediately," said he as he made for the writing desk across the room. "If she and Miss Morland should accept and come straight away, they will be here in time to join us at the assembly!"

Darcy again refrained from rolling his eyes and returned his attention to the newspaper. Bingley was far too eager for his comfort that they should all of them attend the local market town's monthly assembly. The younger man greatly enjoyed such gatherings, where he could converse and dance to his heart's content—neither of which were activities Darcy enjoyed in the least. Well, in fairness he did enjoy intelligent conversation and could find himself as pleased as his friend perpetually was to dance with a graceful partner. But much unlike Bingley, Darcy had never been comfortable in a room full of strangers and was more likely to offend with his reticent manner than recommend himself.

At times, he truly envied Charles Bingley his ability to easily converse with those he had never met before. How he was to get through the evening of the assembly without making himself appear either too proud or utterly foolish Darcy could scarcely begin to imagine.

Bingley's letter to his great aunt soon received a reply. Mrs. Allen accepted the invitation to visit at Netherfield with all due politeness and gratitude, remarking as he had suspected that she had been "in want of an excuse" to travel, though her mourning period was still some five months from being complete. Miss Morland was, she relayed, also gratified by the invitation, and agreed to the journey to Hertfordshire.

They were to arrive on the Tuesday before the assembly, giving both ladies time to restore their constitutions from the rigors of travel. When the day came, the whole party was surprised to receive not only Mrs. Allen and Miss Morland, but also the latter's elder brother James.

"I do beg your pardon at my unexpected arrival, Mr. Bingley," said the young man after he had been introduced. "My coming was rather a last-minute decision. But I found that I could not, in good conscience, allow Mrs. Allen and my sister to travel alone, even to visit distant relations."

"But of course you could not!" Bingley cried. "It is most gentlemanly of you, Mr. Morland, to be so conscientious. You are most welcome, sir—the more the merrier, I say! Now come, let us all go inside."

Darcy observed as they went that Mr. Morland was young and fit and that Miss Bingley had eyed him with an appreciative gaze. Mrs. Allen was a handsome woman in her own right, and Miss Morland a very young—and yes, pretty—girl. They were all of them dressed fashionably (to Caroline and Louisa's obvious relief), and it was quickly disseminated between the ladies as they sat to tea that the Bingleys' great aunt was younger than either recalled—only in her early forties, some seventeen years younger than her husband had been. James Morland was but one-and-twenty and Miss Morland would be eighteen that very Thursday.

"My mother was, thankfully, only a little disappointed that I should want to go away again, especially with my birthday soon to come," said she.

Miss Bingley's brow rose. "Again, Miss Morland?" she queried.

Miss Morland glanced sidelong at Mrs. Allen and then her brother, the former of whom drew what seemed a fortifying breath; Morland merely swallowed and looked down at his hands. She sipped her tea again before saying, "Well, I have already holidayed in Bath this year."

Mrs. Allen sighed. "No need to be delicate on my account, my dear," said the lady, reaching over with one hand to pat Miss

Morland's leg. To the others, she said, "Mr. Allen was ordered to Bath for the waters, as our physician had hoped they might clear up or at least greatly relieve his gouty constitution. We had no idea, of course, of his being soon to suffer apoplexy. Anyway, as he was always wishing to see me happy, he suggested that I should have dear Catherine join me for company."

It was more likely the gentleman had little inclination for traipsing about the shops in Bath, Darcy mused silently. He then also surmised that it stood to reason he would invite along on such a trip the young woman he was considering naming his heir.

"Did you enjoy your time in Bath, Miss Morland?" ventured Mrs. Hurst.

"For the most part I enjoyed it very much," Miss Morland replied.

Mrs. Allen chuckled. "There are shops to be visited and money to be spent, I recall Mr. Allen saying."

Miss Morland smiled. "Yes. It was most kind of you and Mr. Allen to purchase me so many fine things. I had no idea then of his having made me his heir."

"And I told you, dearest Catherine, that we had every intention of telling you our decision 'ere long," said Mrs. Allen.

Mr. Hurst, Louisa's husband, spoke up for the first time as he observed, "Must stick in your craw, Morland, that you sister was chosen to inherit such wealth over you."

Morland frowned as he glanced back at him. "Indeed not, sir. I am very much pleased for my sister that she now has much greater prospects than she might otherwise have had. General Tilney, for instance, would certainly approve."

Here Miss Morland blushed. "James, please. It has been many months since I have even set eyes on the Tilneys."

"But you correspond with Miss Tilney regularly, do you not?" retorted her brother, "And should your acquaintance with her brother ever be renewed, I am certain the general would approve of you. He certainly seemed very concerned that his children should marry well."

"But of course, Mr. Morland! What good society father would not wish his children to marry to best advantage?" said Miss Bingley. "I assume, of course, by your words that the Tilneys are a wealthy family?"

"Indeed, Miss Bingley," said Miss Morland. "I have heard both Mr. and Miss Tilney speak often of their home, which is called Northanger Abbey."

"An abbey sounds like a splendid home, I am sure," rejoined Miss Bingley. "But I am sure it is nothing compared to Netherfield. Could you imagine yourself as mistress of such a fine house as this, my dear?"

Miss Morland looked around her. "Oh, I can hardly think of such a thing! I have been taking instruction from my mother and Mrs. Allen on the running of a household, which I have been informed is essential for a lady of my new station, and can hardly picture myself as the future mistress of Fullerton Manor, let alone such a grand house like this one."

"Well, I am certain you could learn, Miss Morland—do you not think so, Charles?" said Miss Bingley.

"I am sure she could," Bingley agreed. His sister smiled in apparent victory, though her expression faltered when he added, "But then, I am quite certain any young lady could learn to manage a large house, given the proper instruction."

An awkward moment of silence followed, broken by Mrs. Allen asking about the local community. Bingley sat forward and eagerly began to describe the sights he had seen and the gentlemen he had thus far met. He declared he would most happily introduce the ladies and Mr. Morland around at the upcoming assembly.

Catherine Morland brightened. "There's to be an assembly? Does that mean dancing?"

"It does indeed, Miss Morland!" Bingley cried. "I love a good country dance myself—I take it you are fond of dancing?"

James Morland snorted softly. "Cathy loves to dance, Mr. Bingley."

Bingley grinned, then lifted one eyebrow as he asked, "Do I mistakenly assume you are less fond of dancing than your sister?"

"Don't mind him," said Miss Morland with a dismissive wave of her hand. "James loves to dance—he is merely disappointed in love."

"Catherine!" Morland cried.

"What? Brother, you have been moping about ever since I read you that letter," Miss Morland declared. "I am sorry to pain you by talking of it yet again, but you really must get over it if you are ever to be happy. I, for one, and quite glad to be rid of her."

Morland frowned. "Cathy, do not be unkind about Isabella."

"And why should I not be?" she challenged. "That deceitful witch broke your heart by giving her affections to another almost as soon as we had quit Bath!"

"And what of your regard for the wonderful Mr. Tilney, hmm? I daresay you've not had one word from him since our departure," Morland argued.

Miss Morland colored deeply but lifted her chin as she said, "Of course not—it would be inappropriate for us to exchange correspondence as we are not betrothed or otherwise related. But if you must know, Miss Tilney has spoken of her brother. We are still very good friends. Besides, did you not yourself say how awkward it would be for me to be more deeply connected to the family when their brother is responsible for Miss Thorpe's infidelity?"

It was her brother's turn to blush, and Darcy watched the younger man withdraw into himself a little.

Miss Morland then looked about the company that surrounded her, her own blush deepening slightly as she said, "Do forgive us quarreling. As I am sure you have guessed, any discussion of Bath brings up memories both pleasant and painful."

"This Mr. Tilney you spoke of," began Miss Bingley. "Did you like him, Miss Morland?"

"I liked him well enough," Miss Morland replied. "He was very kind and amusing, and he was a fine dancer. I could talk of books with him and his sister, and we took long walks in the country whenever we could."

"And he understands muslin ever so well!" piped up Mrs. Allen.

"Do your friends know of your good fortune?" pressed Miss Bingley.

Miss Morland nodded and glanced at Mrs. Allen. "I did write to Miss Tilney and told her of Mr. Allen's extraordinary generosity. She replied that she and Henry—that is, Mr. Tilney—were stunned indeed, but not altogether surprised, for they had seen for themselves how much Mrs. Allen doted on me."

Miss Bingley and Mrs. Hurst shared a look and twittered, then the latter said, "All your new wealth, and yet Mr. Tilney has not suddenly offered for your hand?"

Miss Morland frowned and looked down at the teacup in her hand. "We have spoken through his sister, I suppose you might say, but no. I have not seen him since our quitting Bath."

"Well! I always say that the best way to mend a broken heart is to find someone new," said Miss Bingley cheerfully. "And here you have already done so—Charles is someone new to you."

"Caroline, please!" cried Bingley softly. "Can you not see that you are making our guest uncomfortable?"

He set his teacup on the tray and stood. "Let us move on from my silly sisters' marriage-minded machinations. You have been shown your rooms but not the rest of the house—allow me to make up for my failings as a host and take you on a tour of the house and grounds."

"Why, a tour sounds delightful, Mr. Bingley," said Mrs. Allen. "What little I have seen of Netherfield still speaks of it being a very beautiful home. I should like to see more of it indeed."

"And so you shall," replied Bingley with a grin. He moved to stand beside his aunt-by-marriage and offered his arm. She smiled up at him as she set her teacup aside and stood to take it.

"How very gallant, Mr. Bingley," said she. "Just like Mr. Tilney when we first met him. He found us a chair at the Lower Rooms, you know."

Bingley smiled again. "He sounds like a fine gentleman, Mrs. Allen. Miss Morland, Mr. Morland—would you care to join us?"

"Mr. Bingley, I should be delighted," said Miss Morland as she set her teacup aside and stood. She turned and looked at her brother, "James, are you coming?"

Morland shrugged and stood as well. "Why not? A tour should certainly keep me from getting lost in this place."

Bingley laughed as he led the small group toward the door. "Mr. Morland, if you think Netherfield is a grand house, you have clearly not seen Darcy's palatial estate at Pemberley. Netherfield is nothing to it at all!"

Chapter Two

"**Lizzy, you** made it!"

Elizabeth Bennet smiled and held out her hands to her dearest friend. "Now Charlotte, you know very well that Mamma would not pass up the chance to meet the mysterious Mr. Bingley and his friends."

Charlotte Lucas laughed as she glanced to where Elizabeth's mother now stood talking to her own. "How much do you want to wager that they are discussing the fortunes of the gentlemen at Netherfield?"

Elizabeth feigned shock and gasped dramatically. "Charlotte Lucas, I am surprised at you! Gambling is an unladylike activity — whatever would Lady Lucas say if she heard you?"

Charlotte snorted softly — also an unladylike thing to do — before she replied, "I have no doubt my mother would not only make a point of saying how extraordinarily fortunate I would be should I catch the eye of one of the single gentlemen, but also the unlikelihood of my actually being so fortunate because I am a plain old spinster next to the likes of Jane and Elizabeth Bennet."

Jane Bennet, Elizabeth's elder sister, stood nearby and turned at the sound of her name. "Oh, dear Charlotte — how I wish you would not disparage yourself so! You are as handsome as any of us and you know it."

Charlotte smiled. "It is most kind of you to say so, Jane, but I am seven-and-twenty and have not had a single offer of marriage."

Elizabeth frowned. "If only 'wife and mother' weren't the only respectable occupations for a young woman of genteel birth," she groused. "Then those of us with more intelligence than the average society debutante could be appreciated for more than our ability to bear children and host dinner parties."

"Lizzy!" cried Jane. "How can you say such things?"

"Very easily, Jane," Elizabeth rejoined. "I would much rather be recognized for who I am and what I can do to better my community than simply as Mrs. Edward Smith."

Jane only shook her head in apparent dismay; Elizabeth grinned and returned her gaze to scanning the room for their younger sisters. Mary, who was next after Elizabeth, sat primly in a chair by the wall, while the two youngest girls—Catherine and Lydia—were already engaged in dancing, each one paired with a young officer from the militia that had recently encamped in Meryton for the winter.

Elizabeth suppressed a sigh. Ever since the militia had come to town, there had been nothing but red coats and officers in her sisters' heads. Kitty and Lydia were wild about them, always running off to talk to one or the other of the militia anytime they went into Meryton. And their mother! Rather than curb such inappropriate behavior, she encouraged it!

She was just considering going to have a word with Lydia about her forwardness when the atmosphere in the ballroom changed perceptibly. Conversation all but stopped entirely, leading even Elizabeth to turn her head in the direction much of the crowd was now looking.

A large party had just entered, and she knew instantly they must be the new residents of Netherfield, for she had seen none of them before. There were an equal number of men and ladies—four of each—though one of the latter was a matronly lady dressed in a dark lavender gown trimmed with black lace that hinted of her being still in mourning.

Leaning close to Charlotte, whose father was now approaching the group with a wide, welcoming smile, Elizabeth asked in a low voice, "Your father was to meet Mr. Bingley this morning, was he not Charlotte?"

Her friend nodded. "He did, yes—and returned with a *very* thorough report."

"Can you tell us who they are?" asked Jane.

"If I have Papa's descriptions correct, I believe the young one at the front with the older lady on his arm to be Mr. Bingley, and the lady must be his great aunt, a Mrs. Allen—who I understand lost her husband very unexpectedly earlier this year."

Elizabeth nodded, having guessed as much. "And the others?" she queried.

"The tall fellow should be Mr. Bingley's friend, Mr. Darcy. Beside him are Mr. Morland and his sister Miss Morland, whose family are very close friends of Mrs. Allen; in fact, their father is the vicar at Fullerton, where they are from. Next is Miss Bingley, Mr. Bingley's younger sister, and Mr. and Mrs. Hurst, who are Mr. Bingley's brother-in-law and elder sister."

Mrs. Bennet was bustling over then, and almost pushed her way between Charlotte and Elizabeth as she said to them, "Girls, girls! You'll not *believe* what Lady Lucas has just told me. That tall gentleman has a greater fortune than Mr. Bingley—*ten thousand a year!*"

Embarrassment flooded through Elizabeth—not only was her mother gossiping about Mr. Darcy's fortune, but she was "whispering" quite loud enough for the whole of the Bingley party to hear.

"Now, here is what the two of you must do," her mother was saying. "Jane, as the eldest—and the most beautiful girl in the county—you must do everything you can to secure Mr. Darcy, for he has twice the fortune of his friend and a grand estate in Derbyshire. And you, Elizabeth, ought set your cap at Mr. Bingley."

"Mamma, please," said Elizabeth, trying to keep the exasperation out of her voice. "You know very well I've no interest in matrimony at present."

It was a statement that could turn into an argument—and had, several times. And though she knew the risk of bringing it up in the midst of a crowd of people, Elizabeth could not help herself reminding her mother she just wasn't ready to be married.

"Oh, Lizzy, don't be ridiculous," admonished her mother. "You just haven't met the right young man, but you will have once Mr. Bingley is introduced to us."

"Which I believe he will be, presently," spoke up Charlotte. "Papa is even now leading the gentleman this way."

She was right—Sir William Lucas, smiling widely as he perpetually did, was escorting Mr. Bingley and the lady Charlotte believe to be his aunt over to them. They were followed by the two believed to be Mr. and Miss Morland.

"Mrs. Bennet, how do you do this evening?" asked Sir William.

"Oh, very well, Sir William, very well indeed!" replied Mrs. Bennet with a flutter of her fan. "And you, sir?"

"Oh, I am quite well, as you can see," the gentleman replied.

"Now, I beg your pardon for interrupting, but our newest neighbor has asked for an introduction to your family. May I present Mr. Bingley of Netherfield, his aunt Mrs. Allen, and their friends Mr. and Miss Morland."

Each person bowed or curtsied as they were introduced. "We are very pleased to meet you, Mr. Bingley," said Mrs. Bennet. "All of you are most welcome to the neighborhood. Might I introduce my daughters to you?"

Bingley blinked, and Elizabeth was forced to temper the brilliance of her smile, for his eyes had fallen on Jane the moment the party walked up, and had not moved from her sister's face.

"Of course, ma'am," he managed. "Please do."

In moments, Mrs. Bennet had introduced her and Jane, and pointed out their younger three sisters.

"Five daughters in one family!" cried Mrs. Allen. "I could scarcely imagine it, were I not so intimately acquainted with my dear friends the Morlands."

Elizabeth looked to the Morlands and asked, "Is yours a large family then, Mr. Morland?"

He looked to his sister and the two shared a smile. "I should say, Miss Elizabeth. Catherine and I are two of ten children—I was born first and she fourth."

Mrs. Bennet's fan fluttered faster. "Good heavens. Ten children? I wonder your mother had the constitution, for I barely survived five!"

She leaned closer, peering at them with narrowed eyes. "How old are you, sir?"

Mr. Morland grinned. "I shall be two-and-twenty in December, ma'am."

"And I turned eighteen only yesterday," added Miss Morland. "Our youngest brother is four years."

Elizabeth laughed. "Well, a belated happy birthday to you, Miss Morland. I am sure yours is a fine family, when you have heads and arms and legs enough for the number."

"Oh indeed!" cried Miss Morland. "I very much love all my brothers and sisters, though I must admit that at times they do try my patience—especially the younger girls."

Here Elizabeth shared a knowing look with Jane. "In that, Miss Morland, Jane and I can very much empathize."

"Miss Bennet!" said Mr. Bingley, perhaps louder than he intended, as his cheeks grew rosy. "May I have the pleasure of the next dance? That is, if you are not already engaged."

Jane's smile was warm as she replied, "I am not engaged, sir."

"Excellent!" said Bingley with enthusiasm. He turned to the young man next to him and said, "Morland, are you going to dance?"

Mr. Morland blinked. "Um, I should be delighted, as soon as I have myself a partner. Miss Elizabeth, are you engaged for the next dance?"

Elizabeth was delighted to be asked, for she'd been longing to dance and there never seemed to be enough partners—Meryton's monthly assemblies always drew more young ladies than young men.

"I am not, sir. Thank you, Mr. Morland," she replied.

"I want to dance, too!" cried his sister. "But I've not been introduced to any young men yet—perhaps I'll go and talk Mr. Darcy into dancing."

Bingley laughed. "I wish you luck, Miss Morland, for you shall need it. I'm afraid my friend Darcy doesn't dance unless he is already intimately acquainted with his partner."

Elizabeth was amused by the other young lady's wide grin. "I accept your challenge, Mr. Bingley," said Miss Morland, before she twirled away and headed over to where Mr. Darcy stood in brooding silence next to Mr. Bingley's sisters.

The two gentlemen and Mrs. Allen laughed and shook their heads, though as the next set was about to start, their attention was drawn to their chosen partners. Elizabeth and Jane accepted the arms that were held out to them and went to join the other couples.

While they waited for the dance to begin, Elizabeth roamed her gaze over her partner as surreptitiously as she could. He was taller than herself, with large, expressive eyes and a mop of curly dark hair. His figure was well formed and he wore his fashionable jacket well, but it was his posture and his expression that captured her attention most.

It was as if he both wanted and did not want to be there.

Not wanting their time together to be awkward, Elizabeth asked him, "Is this your first visit to Hertfordshire, Mr. Morland?"

He nodded. "It is, yes. Mrs. Allen and my sister were invited by Mr. Bingley to come for a visit, as he thought Mrs. Allen might appreciate the distraction."

Elizabeth lifted an eyebrow. "Only they?"

Morland grinned sheepishly. "Technically speaking, yes. But ever since my sister came into her inheritance, I've felt rather…protective of her. Well, I have always looked out for her, of course, but now that she's so rich..."

His voice trailed off and it was clear that he'd not meant to reveal so much. Elizabeth could sympathize with trying to keep things to oneself, but if Miss Morland had a fortune...

"Sir, I fear that whatever the amount of her dowry," she began slowly, "your sister will be the object of desire in the eyes of men and of jealousy in the eyes of other young women—and the mothers trying to marry them off."

Morland snorted softly, then bowed to her curtsey as the dance began. "That's what I'm afraid of, Miss Elizabeth. Especially that first part."

They moved apart and were unable to speak for a few moments due to the moves of the dance, and when they came together again, Elizabeth asked, "You fear she will be prey to fortune hunters? Your father must be a wealthy man indeed if he can so well endow the number of daughters he has."

Her partner laughed. "My family are not rich at all, Miss Elizabeth," said he. "There are ten of us, after all—twelve when you include my mother and father. No, my father is simply a very respected clergyman with more than one very good living. All four of my sisters were to have three thousand each upon their marriage, but since Cathy was named Mr. Allen's heir, she has since said that Father should divide her portion equally amongst our sisters."

The dance separated them again, though when they were next together, Elizabeth naturally took up the conversation where they had left off. "Your sister is very generous. Mrs. Allen's husband must have left her a great deal of money if she is so willing to part with three thousand pounds."

"Have you an idea of Mr. Bingley's fortune, Miss Elizabeth?"

"Not that I purposely sought the information, but yes, Mr. Morland, I do. The size of a gentleman's fortune is often bandied about when he is new to a neighborhood, especially by the mothers who have daughters to see well-settled." She cocked her head to the side and eyed him with one eyebrow lifted. "Why do you ask?"

Mr. Morland scowled briefly. "Then I've no doubt my sister's will soon be as well," he said. "In that case, I may as well tell you as not, for you're sure to hear of it anyway."

"Hear what, sir?" Elizabeth asked.

"Why, that the fortune Catherine inherited is equal to Mr. Bingley's."

For the first time in all her life, Elizabeth was so distracted she missed the cue to move on her next turn—it was not until Mr. Morland moved ahead of her that she realized she'd been woolgathering. She performed the required steps and turns automatically, her mind still very much amazed by what she had heard.

A few minutes later the dance ended, and still Elizabeth had not gathered her thoughts together enough to speak. For a man to be in command of five thousand a year was common enough, but for a woman to be so was unheard of! At least, she had never personally met such a lady.

Her musings were interrupted by the approach of the subject of them—and with her was Mr. Darcy. Jane and Mr. Bingley came upon them from the opposite direction, and Miss Morland smiled triumphantly.

"Do you see, Mr. Bingley? I told you I would get Mr. Darcy for a partner," she said.

Bingley laughed, then performed the office of introducing his friend to the Bennet sisters. "Were you not standing together before my eyes, I should not believe you," he replied to Miss Morland. "Tell me, how did you convince him to dance?"

"I simply told him that you were quite sure he would *not* dance, and that I had determined to prove you wrong."

Elizabeth found herself suddenly enraptured by the face of the gentleman in question as Mr. Darcy smiled, revealing the most endearing pair of dimples.

"Having heard this," said he, taking up the narrative, "I could not in good conscience allow Miss Morland to lose your challenge by my usual taciturn refusal."

"Certainly not, sir—that would be scandalously ungentlemanly of you," Elizabeth heard herself say.

Darcy's brow furrowed as he turned his gaze to her, but before he could speak, Miss Morland said, "Oh, indeed it would, Miss Elizabeth! So you can imagine how very much I appreciate Mr. Darcy not allowing me to stand before him looking foolish."

"I can imagine how much, Miss Morland, but he could still have made you look very foolish if Mr. Darcy did not actually know how to dance," quipped Elizabeth.

"Lizzy!" said Jane with a gasp.

"I assure you, Miss Elizabeth, that I am well educated in the common dances," Mr. Darcy said archly.

"Oh, indeed he is!" chirped Miss Morland. "I can assure you as well, Mr. Darcy is a very graceful dancer."

Elizabeth smiled at her cheerful disposition. "Well, I shall have to take your word for it, or try to catch a glimpse of you during the next dance."

Even as she spoke, the caller was announcing the second dance of the set. The pairs of partners moved to take their place in line, and for a time Elizabeth's attention was once again commanded by her partner. James Morland was also well educated in the common dances, and the glimpses she stole of his sister and Mr. Darcy said that neither had been exaggerating.

"You are examining the competition, I see," said Morland. "A poor clergyman's son like me hasn't a chance in the world with rich men like Darcy and Bingley around."

"I merely looked to see if Mr. Darcy's claim was true, that is all," said Elizabeth. "Though even were I so inclined, such a man as he would hardly take notice of me. As a gentleman's daughter I may be Mr. Darcy's equal, but without a fortune to make him richer, I would not be handsome enough to tempt such a man. My father's income, you see, is enough to make us comfortable while he lives but not enough to secure men of consideration in the world for his daughters' husbands, nor to maintain us when he is gone as his estate is entailed. And I've no one to leave me a grand fortune as was done for your sister. In that manner, she has great advantage."

Mr. Morland scoffed. "You mean to say that she's more attractive because of her inheritance."

"It is the simple truth, Mr. Morland. Even my sister Jane, who is obviously a great beauty, has little chance with such a man." Elizabeth sighed. "Having an independent fortune—or so I assume it to be from what you have said—means Miss Morland will have her choice of suitors, and for both your sakes I do hope there will be no fortune hunters to try and swindle her out of it. I commend you for your desire to see her protected from the like. Being independent, she has the liberty of taking her time to choose a husband. My sisters and I have only a little beauty and our charms to recommend us."

Morland smiled. "And what charms you possess, Miss Elizabeth," said he. "Ready wit and a brilliant smile go a long way with some gentlemen, I can assure you. And I can sympathize with your plight, to an extent."

"Oh? Pray tell, sir," Elizabeth prompted.

"I recently learned that I am to have a living of a four hundred pounds a year," Morland replied. "There are few young women willing to marry a poor clergyman."

"You are to be a clergyman?"

He nodded. "I am. I have been studying at Oxford, but as a result of the Clergy Ordination Act of 1801, I cannot take orders for another two years."

"What do you intend to do in the meantime? Will you search for a wife willing to live on four hundred a year?"

Mr. Morland's expression darkened. "I thought I had already found such a woman, but... I was wrong. She wanted to be rich, and I could never make her so."

"I am very sorry to hear it, Mr. Morland," Elizabeth replied sincerely.

Morland drew a breath and blew it out. "'Tis of little matter—as Cathy would say, I am better off, knowing her true nature now instead of learning it after we married. But to answer your question, I intend to assist my father in carrying out his duties in whatever ways I am able, that by the time I am of age to be ordained, I shall be fully educated in the profession for which I am intended."

"It is a noble course you have set for yourself, Mr. Morland," said Elizabeth with a smile. "And I am sure you will yet find a young lady willing to marry a man of only four hundred a year, for when one considers the average yearly salary of a housemaid, four hundred is no trifle."

Mr. Morland returned her smile. "You are very kind to say so, Miss Elizabeth. And really, I shall eventually have eight hundred a year, for my father told me there is also an estate of at least equal value to the living that I am assured of as a future inheritance."

"And a sure eight hundred a year was not enough for this girl you spoke of?" asked Elizabeth. Her partner nodded, and she scoffed derisively. "Then she is a fool, and you most assuredly are better off, sir. Eight hundred pounds a year may not equal your sister's newly inherited five thousand, but it is not to be laughed at. If I may be so bold, sir, your plan to learn all you can about your intended profession is an intelligent one. Concentration on improving yourself will surely reward you with your heart's desire in due time."

Her partner studied her countenance earnestly for a long moment, then he smiled. "Thank you, Miss Elizabeth. You really are very kind."

A few moments later the second dance of their set ended, and Elizabeth was prepared to join her sister Mary, and perhaps also Charlotte, for a round of sitting out the next set to watch others enjoying themselves. She and James Morland were again approached by Miss Morland and Mr. Darcy, the former saying cheerfully, "I have convinced Mr. Darcy he should dance again!"

"Did you really?" asked Bingley as he came upon them with Jane on his arm. "And who shall your partner be this time, Darcy?"

Elizabeth was greatly surprised when Mr. Darcy turned his gaze to her. "I should be very much obliged if Miss Elizabeth would do me the honor."

Chapter Three

Miss Elizabeth looked back at Darcy with a startled expression, and for a moment, he thought she might actually refuse him.

He found that possibility astonishing—no society daughter he'd ever been forced to meet had refused to dance with him. But then, Miss Elizabeth Bennet had not been born and bred in the first circles of society, and he had only asked those girls to dance when forced by his Aunt Frances to "appear amiable."

"Oh, Miss Elizabeth! Surely you do not mean to refuse him!" cried Catherine Morland when the lady's hesitation lasted longer than the pace of a heartbeat. "I can assure you that Mr. Darcy is a very fine dancer."

Miss Elizabeth blinked and looked to her with a smile. "Certainly not, Miss Morland. I was merely surprised that Mr. Darcy asked me, given that he and I are not *intimately* acquainted."

"Miss Morland and I are hardly intimately acquainted, Miss Elizabeth, and I have danced with her," Darcy said. "I have known her but two days."

Elizabeth lifted a hand to her chin and tapped it with her forefinger, her gaze narrowing as if in thought. "It *was* very gallant of you to spare a young lady you've known but two days from the embarrassment of failing Mr. Bingley's challenge. It would be unthinkable for me to decline an offer to dance with a man who has behaved in so gentlemanlike a manner."

"Splendid!" cried Miss Morland, who immediately let go his arm and reached for Elizabeth's, that they might switch places. "Now, I shall dance with Mr. Bingley, if he will ask me, and James, you must dance with Miss Bennet."

"Cathy!" admonished her brother. "You can't just tell people who they ought to dance with!"

Her cheeks filling with color, it appeared to dawn on the girl just what she had done. "Oh! Oh, I am so very sorry! Do forgive me, I pray you all," she said as she glanced around her. "It's just that I have already been having such a happy time, I want everyone else to enjoy themselves as well."

"It's quite all right by me, Miss Morland," said Bingley with a genial smile. "I should be delighted to dance with you, if you will have me."

James Morland turned to Jane Bennet. "And I really would be delighted, Miss Bennet, if you would do me the honor."

Jane Bennet blushed, but nodded. "Thank you, sir."

The caller was just then announcing the next dance, so the three couples took their places. Standing across from her, Darcy got his first good look at Elizabeth Bennet, and was a little disturbed to find himself appreciating her fine, dark eyes; when he had met her before the last dance, he had scarcely allowed her to be pretty.

"Must be something in the water," Darcy mumbled.

"What was that, Mr. Darcy?" asked Elizabeth.

He just stopped himself flinching, as he did not think he'd spoken loud enough for her to hear. "I was just reflecting on the oddity of my dancing with two young ladies whom I barely know. You see, I haven't the ease in conversing with strangers that my friend Bingley has."

Miss Elizabeth chuckled. "Or Miss Morland," she replied.

Darcy inclined his head. "Or she."

The dance began then and for a moment neither spoke. "I do not think you can say you *barely* know Miss Morland," Elizabeth began. "After all, you did admit to knowing her two days."

"I did, yes," Darcy agreed. "Miss Morland and her brother arrived with Mrs. Allen on Tuesday. Bingley invited them on something of a whim; he is a relation of Mrs. Allen by marriage, you see."

"Let me guess—he and his sisters were eager to see for themselves the young lady to whom Mr. Allen left a fortune," Miss Elizabeth said. "Mr. Morland told me of his sister having been made the heir of your friend's uncle, as he is concerned she will be prey to fortune hunters."

Darcy thought of one fortune hunter he would be loath to see try and attach himself to an innocent girl like Miss Morland. "I am afraid

Mr. Morland is right to be concerned," said he. "When it is known hereabouts that she has command of as great a fortune as Bingley, I've little doubt that Netherfield will be inundated with young men coming to call."

"Indeed. I do not think Mr. Bingley has considered just how much his peace will be disturbed when it is known," Elizabeth said. "But I cannot condemn him entirely, for he has done a kindness to his aunt in providing distraction from her grief, and even to Mr. and Miss Morland in introducing them to greater society."

Darcy scoffed, as he did not think the society he had so far observed was much worth knowing. He then amended the thought to making an exception for his partner and her elder sister, whose manners thus far were much more genteel than those of their neighbors.

"You do not agree, Mr. Darcy?"

"On the contrary," he replied immediately. "It is a kindness indeed what Bingley has done for his aunt. And I do not know that the local society is much different than that of the Morlands' home of Fullerton, which both Miss Morland and Mrs. Allen have spoken of with some little frequency."

"So it is a small market town, then?"

Darcy nodded. "I gather it is a small village, yes. Miss Morland was thus quite eager to take her leave of it again, despite having holidayed in Bath with the Allens in the first part of the year."

A moment of silence passed as they danced, then Elizabeth said, "I understand Mr. Allen passed unexpectedly—was it during their time in Bath?"

Again Darcy nodded. "As I understand it, his passing occurred about halfway through their intended stay, and Mrs. Allen is just past half-mourning. And yes, Miss Elizabeth, my friend's sisters were eager to see Miss Morland for themselves."

The expression that now came over her face gave Darcy the impression that she considered the sisters' motivations to be somewhat in line with his own; she no doubt thought them vexed that Mr. Allen had chosen a stranger to inherit his fortune rather than his own relations, which Miss Bingley and Mrs. Hurst certainly had been.

"Was your friend not also eager to meet her?" his partner asked.

"I expect he was curious about her, but his reasons differ from theirs," he replied, and the grin Elizabeth offered told him she understood his meaning.

Again there was silence for a time, and Darcy took the opportunity of evaluating the young woman he danced with. Miss

Elizabeth's head just reached his shoulder, and her person was well-formed; she was also a very graceful dancer. Her gown was a few seasons out of fashion, but then he did not imagine she had much opportunity to shop at the warehouses in London, let alone the money to visit a good modiste.

How unfortunate, he found himself thinking. Her prettiness would surely be elevated to the natural beauty of her sister Jane were she in a properly fitted, high-fashion gown of silk or chiffon.

"So..." said Miss Elizabeth. "You do not converse easily with strangers? Is that why I observed you wearing such a dark, brooding expression when your party came in?"

Darcy raised an eyebrow—she was a bold one, to ask such a question, or at least to phrase it as she did. "In part, yes. The gathered company here is... much more boisterous than such a party would be in London."

Elizabeth laughed. "You mean to say that our country manners are more vulgar and uncouth than those of your rich friends."

"Do you think it wrong to value refined manners and proper conduct?" Darcy countered.

"No, indeed, Mr. Darcy," she replied. "I do, however, have a strong dislike for stiffness of manner and false politeness. I'd much rather remain in the country forever among my neighbors than to live in a place like London and be forced to pretend to like someone just because their rank and wealth benefited my own social status. I prefer being allowed to laugh and smile as much as I choose without being censured for being 'unladylike.'"

"I could never wish you to smile less," said Darcy, realizing too late that he had spoken the thought aloud.

Miss Elizabeth's eyes widened in surprise and color came to her cheeks. Hoping to eliminate the sudden awkwardness of the moment, Darcy said, "I... I find it difficult to take or even pretend an interest in the affairs and concerns of persons I have never before met, and speaking of trivial matters tends to bore me. That is a large part of why I have a general dislike of being in a room full of people I do not know, and thus tend to avoid such gatherings as this."

"Then this is a special occasion indeed, that you have deigned to grace us with your presence," said Elizabeth.

Darcy frowned. "Do you mock me, Miss Elizabeth?"

She blushed again. "Not at all, sir. I meant only to tease. Forgive me, I only thought to ease your discomfort, not add to it."

He drew a breath and released it slowly, turned her about as the dance required, then said, "Forgive *me*, Miss Elizabeth. I have matters on my mind other than my discomfort amongst strangers which have a tendency to depress my spirits, as well as the fact I am not used to being teased. At least, not by a lady. My cousin Theodore long ago made a sport of poking fun at me."

A moment passed, and then, "I am sorry to hear you are troubled, sir. I can imagine that such grievances as the kind which dampen your spirits would serve to make anyone undesirous of attending an assembly, even if you were to know every single person in the room."

"Indeed, madam," Darcy replied.

Miss Elizabeth then asked him his impression of Bingley's aunt and her friends, and Darcy gave her his honest opinion. Mrs. Allen was knowledgeable in the areas of flowers and fashion, and had some skill at embroidery, but was otherwise more than a little silly and excitable. She liked to talk, and he imagined her prone to participating in gossip.

Mr. Morland he judged to be a sensible young man, though perhaps a little too easily persuaded to follow others' lead—but then, so was Bingley. However, having been passed over by an adventuress hoping to score a rich husband in Bath earlier that year, Morland might have learned to be a little wiser. The only real difference between the two younger men was the amount of their fortunes, and the fact that Morland was by necessity to take up a profession.

Miss Morland, Darcy said, was a pretty girl, full of eagerness to please and be amiable—again, much like Bingley. She liked to read, which was a trait he admired, and though she allegedly could work a needle and thread to mend a garment, and liked to play around with watercolors, she was no artist and had no other accomplishments to speak of. He also thought her more than a little naïve. The newness of her fortune made her rather nervous, and she still had some trouble grasping the full import of what possession of such a fortune meant for her. Her father, though a vicar, was also a gentleman; she, once a mere gentleman's daughter, had been raised above even her father's station due to the amount of money now at her command.

"Miss Morland is young yet, that much is true," his partner observed, "but her brother means to protect her from fortune hunters until he is old enough to take up his promised living, by which time—or so I suspect—he hopes to pass the office to another. Preferably a husband worthy of her. And as she is to stay some time with Mr. Bingley here at Netherfield, perhaps his sisters can be of some use in teaching her more about the position she now holds in society."

Darcy scoffed. "My own sister would be a better teacher, I should think," said he. "The Bingleys, though well-intentioned, are themselves still relatively new to their elevated status, as their fortune comes from trade."

Miss Elizabeth frowned. "Of that I am aware, but I see nothing wrong with such origins. The money was honestly earned, was it not?"

"As far as I am aware, yes."

"Then what does it matter where their fortune comes from? I know, of course, that a fortune inherited is more respected by high society than one earned, but I've two uncles that earn theirs—one is an attorney here in Meryton, and the other owns a warehouse in London—and frankly, I have a higher level of respect for a man who earns his fortune through a life of honest labor than one who sits idly at home spending money that was merely handed to him. A man who has worked for that which pays for his comforts appreciates them more."

Darcy was more than a little stunned at the passion of her speech—and being honest with himself, was more than a little impressed. Miss Elizabeth not only spoke well, but was strong in her beliefs and quick to defend them.

"Yours is a very decided opinion, Miss Elizabeth," said he. "But do you truly believe that a man who inherits his fortune does not labor to keep it? If a gentleman does not properly manage his lands by seeing to the needs of his tenants, if he is not kind to those who work for him and those who pay their rents to him, then he will lose them and his fortune will suffer."

"True enough, Mr. Darcy," Elizabeth conceded. "But then, I do not suppose that I have met such a man—until you, perhaps. My father's fortune was inherited, and is a trifle compared to your own, but he prefers to spend his time in his book room and leaves the management of the estate to our steward. Mr. Howard does his job well enough, but I always wonder if my father's fortune might not be greater if he took more of an interest in the management of his property.

"In any case, I believe Miss Morland would benefit from exposure to ladies of her new station whose experience and wisdom will better teach her the significance of her place in society. If you think Mr. Bingley's sisters not equal to the task, regardless of the origin of their fortunes, then perhaps you ought to ask Mr. Bingley if your sister may also join you at Netherfield that she may present to Miss Morland a better example."

Darcy smiled—it wasn't a terrible idea. In truth, some of the darkness of his mood was due to guilt. He had been given charge of his sister's future upon the death of his father yet he spent so little time with her, often being away with this friend or that. Even when he was at home she was not, for Georgiana was for months at a time at school. His neglect of her was, he was certain, the sole reason she had been vulnerable to the attentions of a man who had sought hers solely to gain access to her fortune.

It should not have taken the observation of an impertinent country miss to make him see that he needed to do better by Georgiana.

Of course, if he followed Elizabeth's advice, he would be exposing his sister to the kind of country manners which Bingley found "charming" but that he considered vulgar and unrefined. Pemberley was a country estate, but the denizens of the villages over which he was patron behaved better than this.

A glance down at the expectant, waiting gaze of his dance partner reminded Darcy that his judgment was not entirely fair. Clearly there were those in the neighborhood who not only understood proper conduct but practiced it—perhaps Meryton's populace thought an assembly reason enough for loosening the cravats and dress ties a little. The Morlands also hailed from a small country village, and they, too, exercised proper decorum.

With a sigh and a smile, he inclined his head and at last replied, "Miss Elizabeth, I may just do that."

Chapter Four

That the Miss Lucases and the Miss Bennets should meet to talk over a ball was a matter of course; the morning after the assembly brought the former to Longbourn to hear and to communicate. That their comfortable coze should be joined by two of the residents at Netherfield was rather unexpected.

Charlotte and her younger sister Maria, who was the age of Elizabeth's sister Kitty, had just sat down in the drawing room at the invitation of their friends when Lydia—who was perched at one of the windows—spied a carriage coming up the drive.

"I wonder who can that be?" she said, pressing her hands and face to the glass.

"What is it, my dearest girl?" queried Mrs. Bennet.

Lydia looked briefly over her shoulder. "Do you not hear it, Mamma?"

About then, Elizabeth did take note of the sounds of an approaching carriage coming across the gravel that led to their door. She glanced at Jane and Charlotte with an arched eyebrow as both her mother and Kitty raced to join the youngest girl at the window. Moments after the carriage had stopped, Kitty exclaimed,

"It's that rich girl staying with Mr. Bingley! And someone else— her brother, I think he is."

Mrs. Bennet scoffed as she turned away from the view. "She's a pretty little thing, I grant you, but I will despise her to the ends of the earth if Miss Morland and that fortune of hers should get in the way of my girls attaching Mr. Darcy and Mr. Bingley."

Her youngest daughters remained for a moment at the window.

"That fellow is a fine one," said Lydia, "but he would be even hand-somer if he were in regimentals. I overheard him talking to Mr. Nelson last night, and he said he is to be a clergyman!"

"Who gives tuppance for clergyman?" said Kitty, the two girls turning away from the window just as the front bell was rung.

"Sisters, do sit down," Elizabeth admonished softly. "Let us all welcome our visitors properly."

Her sisters each rolled their eyes, but followed her direction nonetheless. Moments later, Mrs. Hill was announcing Mr. and Miss Morland.

The whole party stood to greet the new arrivals, and if her eyes did not deceive her, Elizabeth took note of a very pointed glance from Mr. Morland toward her sister Jane. *Oh my*, she thought. *Whatever will Jane do with* two *admirers?*

She knew what her mother would have Jane do. Mr. Bingley's income was only half what Mr. Darcy could claim, but he was still a very wealthy young man, and Mr. Morland's future income was not even a quarter of what Bingley had now. Mrs. Bennet would insist that Jane accept the suit of the richer man even if her preference was for the poorer one.

As everyone took to their seats again, Elizabeth reflected on the ball, bringing to mind her observations of Jane with each of her partners—Bingley and Morland were not the only men her sister had been fortunate enough to dance with, but the both of them did stand out in her mind. The former gentleman was lively and smiled a lot, while the latter was somewhat reserved. Yet Jane had spoken more with Mr. Morland than she had with Mr. Bingley, and of all her partners, he was the only one with whom she had danced a second set.

Though not for lack of trying on Mr. Bingley's part, Elizabeth reminded herself. She had been next to Jane when he had asked her to dance again, but the last open set on her card had been claimed only moments before by his guest. Bingley's disappointment had been clear, but he had nevertheless smiled and congratulated Morland on securing a second set with the handsomest girl in the room.

"I do beg your pardon for intruding on the Miss Lucases' visit," Catherine Morland was saying, "but I thought myself very fortunate to have met so many amiable young ladies last evening, I could not help but pay a call on you."

"You are very welcome, Miss Morland," said Jane.

"Maria and I do not mind at all sharing the Bennet sisters with you, Miss Morland," added Charlotte. "As you can see, there are plenty of them to go around!"

Laughter followed this comment, then Mrs. Bennet said, "I understand you have recently inherited something of a fortune, Miss Morland. Will you next seek a husband to help you manage it all?"

Mortification coursed through Elizabeth at once, making her feel as though someone had poured a bucket of cold water over her head. It was so like her mother to say things best left unsaid, or to blindly embarrass herself and her family with impertinent questions.

Both Morlands colored, Catherine quite deeply; she looked down at her hands as she replied, "I do not think so, Mrs. Bennet. Marriage is not much on my mind at the moment, for I am still becoming accustomed to my having any fortune at all."

"Well, I advise you to accustom yourself very quickly, my dear girl, for as soon as word of that fortune gets out, there will be a great number of young men to come knocking at your door looking for a wife," said Mrs. Bennet.

Mr. Morland snorted. "We've already met one fortune hunter, ma'am, and that was before my sister came into her inheritance," said he in a bitter tone. "The Thorpes of the world are precisely the reason I shall be at my sister's side as much as I am able until she marries."

"It is most gentlemanly of you to look after your sister so diligently, sir," Jane observed.

"I thank you, Miss Bennet," Morland said, directing a smile her way that made her blush. "My sister means a great deal to me. There may be two brothers between Cathy and myself, but I do believe she is the best friend I have in the world, and I would be deeply grieved to see her taken advantage of."

"Oh James, you are too kind to me," Miss Morland with a smile; she reached over and laid a hand atop one of his. "You are the very best of my friends as well."

"I feel exactly the same about my sisters, Mr. Morland," Jane said then. "Among them I am admittedly closest to Lizzy, but I love them all so very much, I couldn't bear it if a man should take advantage of any of them."

Elizabeth watched this brief exchange with rapt attention, and though she and Jane had not yet spoken in depth of her dance partners—thus she had no real idea of her sister's true feelings— something about the way Jane smiled at Mr. Morland felt... significant. Could her sister's heart have already made its choice?

Had she fixed on a poor, not-yet-ordained clergyman rather than the wealthy young gentleman from the north?

If so, was Jane herself even aware?

Shaking her head minutely and setting her lips into a smile, Elizabeth turned her attention to the others and the conversation going on around her. Her mother was then talking of the ball, pointing out how fine Jane had looked dancing with Mr. Bingley.

"Though why Mr. Darcy did not ask you to dance, I cannot begin to comprehend," said the lady. "We all of us know you were the most beautiful girl in the room, so why would not the richest man ask you for a dance? He danced with Lizzy, you know, and she is nothing to you."

"Mamma," Jane admonished softly. "I assure you I am not offended that Mr. Darcy did not ask me to dance. There will be other opportunities for him to do so, should his stay in the country be lasting."

"I think I know why," piped up Lydia. "He is reckoned to be rather proud, Mamma—did you not see the way he walked about the room after his set with Lizzy? He was so stiff and haughty."

Her mother began to nod. "You know, my dear, I *do* recollect Mrs. Long saying she sat next to him for half an hour, at least, without his saying a word to her!"

"I do not think Mr. Darcy is proud at all, ma'am, at least not in a bad way," said Miss Morland. "He has always spoken very kindly to me, and I observed that he and Miss Elizabeth had a great deal of conversation."

"If I may so express it," added Charlotte, "if indeed Mr. Darcy is proud, then he has a right to be. One cannot wonder that so very fine a young man, with family, fortune—everything in his favor—should think highly of himself."

"What do you say, Miss Elizabeth?" pressed Miss Morland. "I daresay he did not speak with me near as much as he did with you."

Elizabeth drew a steadying breath. She'd not yet resolved her thoughts of the enigmatic Mr. Darcy, though recollection of their set together had plagued her long after she'd settled into her bed.

"I must admit," she began at last, "that I did make note of some degree of pride in the gentleman, but I could not speak as to the true depth of it. Though we did talk during our two dances, I do not believe it long enough a conversation for me to truly make out his character."

"Mr. Darcy is a quiet fellow," observed Mr. Morland. "But I think it more he is one of those people who find themselves discomfited when in unfamiliar company than that he is proud, and in my limited experience such a person prefers a small gathering of intimate acquaintances over a large party. He is also a rather intelligent man — despite having attended Cambridge — and from the little conversation I have had with him, he not only speaks well but he knows what he is talking about."

That Darcy was a learned man was no surprise to Elizabeth, as a university education would be essential to a gentleman who truly wished to maintain or even grow his fortune. She found herself wondering what subjects Mr. Darcy liked to talk about, as she recalled his saying that trivial matters bored him.

When the conversation turned from fortunes and marriage to gowns and fripperies, Mr. Morland's expression clearly showed it was a topic of which he was little educated and even less inclined to partake. Seeing this, and wishing to test the possibility of her favorite sister returning the interest of her admirer, Elizabeth stood and suggested taking the air.

"We should take advantage of the fine weather we're having while it lasts," she pointed out. "At this time of year, the warmth can turn to cold without any notice at all."

"Oh, we know all about that, do we not, James?" said Miss Morland, who jumped up enthusiastically. "Even in Fullerton — which is in Wiltshire, if you don't know, Miss Elizabeth — the weather can turn in but a moment."

"Jane, won't you join us?" Elizabeth asked her sister. "And you Charlotte. We can all of us have a cozy turn about the garden while our sisters and Mamma talk all the nonsense they like about lace and ribbons."

"It is not nonsense, Lizzy!" cried Kitty. "Mr. Bingley's sisters, and Miss Morland, were very finely dressed last evening!"

"Thank you, Miss Catherine — oh, how very odd to have to address another by my own name," said Miss Morland with a laugh.

"It is strange," agreed Kitty. "So you may call me Kitty if you like."

"And I am Catherine. Or Cathy, as my brothers and sisters like to call me."

Mr. Morland was then offering his arm to Jane as he said, "Shall we follow your sister's advice, Miss Bennet?"

"Taking a walk would be welcome, sir, as I've had no exercise yet today," said Jane as she laid her hand on his arm, a smile on her lips and a blush lighting her cheeks.

"Do not be too long in the sun, Jane," advised Mrs. Bennet. "I would not have you become too tan, which Mr. Darcy will surely not like at all."

Elizabeth just stopped herself rolling her eyes. While Mr. Darcy had likely admired Jane's beauty as much as every other young man at the assembly, he had shown no particular interest in her — or any other girl in attendance. After his dances with Miss Morland and herself, he had only danced with Miss Bingley; otherwise, he had spent his time walking about or sitting in silence.

Charlotte and Miss Morland joined her in following Jane and Mr. Morland out of the drawing room and through the back of the house. Elizabeth's purposely slow gate enabled the latter two to get some feet ahead of them when they exited into the garden, which was what she wanted.

"My dear Lizzy, I see what you are about," Charlotte said in a low voice. A glance at her friend showed that she smiled.

"I do not deny what you insinuate, my dear Charlotte," Elizabeth replied. "Mayhap I am wrong, but I believe I sensed a partiality in their looks to one another and so thought to provide an opportunity for them to decide if those feelings could become a true attachment."

"Upon my word, Miss Elizabeth!" Miss Morland cried softly. "If you mean to say that James admires your sister, I do not know that you are correct! Forgive me contradicting you, but my brother was greatly disappointed by a young lady only a few months ago, and I do not think him likely to risk his heart again so soon."

Elizabeth glanced at the pair before her, noting absently that Jane and Mr. Morland were almost equal in height; her sister was no more than four inches shorter. She then looked back to the young gentleman's sister. "May I enquire as to the circumstances?"

Miss Morland sighed. "Last Christmas, James was invited to stay with an acquaintance of his from Oxford. There he met with the sisters of this so-called friend, and he fell very much in love with the eldest girl, Isabella. The Thorpe family chose to holiday in Bath about the same time that dear Mr. and Mrs. Allen and I journeyed there at the end of January, though now I surmise their purpose was to find rich husbands for Isabella and her two sisters."

"Miss Morland, I beg pardon for interrupting, but that is hardly an uncommon occurrence," Charlotte observed. "Bath is much like London in that regard, drawing the marriage-minded and hopeful."

"Oh, do please call me Catherine! Or Cathy. Either will do," Miss Morland replied.

"I should be pleased to have the honor. Hereafter, I must be Charlotte to you."

Elizabeth echoed their mutual grins and added, "And you must call me Elizabeth, or Lizzy as my family so often does."

"Capital! We are such fast friends already, I am quite comfortable using your Christian names—I hope it is not wrong to feel so," said Catherine.

"No indeed," Elizabeth assured her. "When we are amongst mixed company, it would do to use proper address, but we are, as you said, among friends here and may thus dismiss such formalities."

Catherine smiled brightly for a moment, then it fell a little as she glanced again toward her brother. "Isabella claimed she had loved James from the moment they met, as he did her. But shortly after our quitting Bath following the death of Mr. Allen, I received word that my *friend* had been behaving most improperly with Captain Tilney, the eldest brother of another, more dear friend of mine. Eleanor Tilney really is the best, most delightful creature I have ever met, and her brother Henry was very charming and amiable. Their brother Frederick, however, is not nearly so good a person. He *knew* there was an understanding between my brother and Isabella, but he pursued her anyway—and she allowed his attentions! Eleanor and I believe she hoped to marry Captain Tilney, for he is, of course, his father's heir and they have a large fortune. Certainly greater than anything my father can give to James."

Elizabeth snorted softly. "I see where this tale is headed. I gather the Thorpes thought your family rich, given how well you lived in spite of there being a prolific number of children—or they expected Mr. and Mrs. Allen to provide for you."

"They did! Though at the time of our being in Bath, I had no notion at all that Mr. and Mrs. Allen had discussed naming me as their heir with my parents," said Catherine then. "I did not learn of it until nearly a fortnight after dear Mr. Allen was buried!"

The young heiress sighed again. "Eleanor herself wrote and told me of what she had witnessed passing between Isabella and her brother. She did not wish to speak ill of him, and was grieved to relay news that would surely make my brother unhappy, but she could not help but believe it right that James should know of his intended's conduct in his absence. He knew Isabella was distressed at having to wait two years for him to be old enough to take orders, but he did not think her character so weak as to be led astray by a meaningless flirtation."

"And so their engagement was broken, like your brother's heart?" Charlotte queried.

Catherine nodded. "It was. James has been so very melancholy since, and he used to be much like Mr. Bingley—all liveliness and good humor and happy manners. When it became known that I had been named as Mr. Allen's heir, he made it his purpose to see that no man would trifle with my affections just to gain my fortune as Isabella had done with him. He seeks to protect me from the Captain Tilneys of the world."

"It is a very commendable mission, Catherine," said Elizabeth. "Though I do not yet know you well, I most certainly would not want for so sweet a creature as you to fall victim to a fortune hunter. Mr. Morland told me something of his plan to watch over you, as well as to assist your father as much as he can, that when he is ordained he will be well-versed in his duties."

"Oh yes!" said Catherine. "And though I am surely biased in the matter, I daresay he could not find a better instructor in the duties of a clergyman than our father. Papa is so very well respected in Fullerton."

"Then I am sure you are right, and your brother has the best teacher he could get."

Her companion silent for a moment. "Though I do not know that my brother will even look at another woman in his present state, I should so much like for him to recover," said she. "He's a good man, I think. James has always been so very kind to me and our younger brothers and sisters—he really is my very best friend, and I am honored that he thinks of me as his. If he met the *right* girl, I am sure he would get over Isabella and never think of her again."

Another glance at the couple ahead showed Elizabeth that Jane was smiling—and blushing—at whatever Mr. Morland was saying to her. She thought it a very positive sign, and said so to the gentleman's sister.

"Lizzy is right, Catherine," Charlotte concurred. "If anyone could heal your brother's broken heart, I daresay Jane could. She's a beautiful girl, but she is not vain. She is not trifling or silly, and though I imagine she would like to marry a man with a fortune as much as the next girl, if her heart were to choose a poor man, then her only concern would be his ability to provide for her and their children."

Elizabeth nodded her agreement. "Very true, Charlotte. Though

Mr. Morland did tell me that the living he will have upon taking orders is worth four hundred a year, and that there is a small estate of equal value that will be his as well."

"Hmm... Eight hundred a year is no trifle, but you know your mother will never approve," said Charlotte. "She will insist that Jane make herself agreeable to Mr. Darcy or even Mr. Bingley."

"Jane is agreeable to everyone Charlotte," Elizabeth retorted. "That does not signify that either of the more wealthy gentleman will ever make her an offer. And even if they do, I am sure my sister will follow her heart—if it should choose the man who is relatively poor over the men who are maddeningly rich, then so be it."

"Surely your mother wishes for your sister's happiness?" said Catherine. "I am sure James would make her happy if they should like one another."

Elizabeth looked to her. "I am sure, in her own way, that she does," she replied. "However, my father's estate is entailed away from the female line, and when he is dead the cousin who will inherit may turn us out of the house as soon as he pleases. Thus, my mother is quite desperate that at least one of her daughters should marry a rich man who can afford to keep her and any unmarried daughters from starving in the hedgerows."

"If that is so, mayhap she ought look to you to take care of her," Catherine observed with a nonchalant air. "After all, you did get on with Mr. Darcy *very* well."

Fighting the heat rising up her neck that threatened to color her cheeks, Elizabeth lifted her chin and replied, "Yes, Mr. Darcy and I had some conversation during our dances. But that does not signify that he felt any particular regard for me, nor I for him. As already established, he is rather proud, and I made sure he was aware that my father's income is such that he can give his daughters nothing for their marriages. We have but a little beauty and our charms to recommend us, and if the truth must be known, I am not particularly inclined to marriage at present."

Charlotte laughed. "Elizabeth, my dear Catherine, long ago vowed that only the deepest, most abiding love would induce her into matrimony, and because there's not one young man in Meryton who has caught her eye, our Lizzy is sure she will end an old maid teaching Jane's ten children to embroider cushions and play their instruments very ill."

Catherine echoed her laugh. "Well, it is certainly possible that Miss Bennet would issue ten children if she *did* marry my brother, given the size of our family."

She then slipped her arm around Elizabeth's as she added, "As for you, my dear Miss Elizabeth, I would not discount Mr. Darcy as a potential husband just because you think him proud and are at present of no mind to marry. After all, you've only met him once, and you never know — on further acquaintance, he may just prove himself the very man who in talents and disposition is exactly suited to you!"

Chapter Five

That Bingley and his sisters would wish to discuss a ball the morning following the event was a matter of course.

That Darcy would wish to avoid being drawn into their dialogue was also; to ensure avoidance of it for as long as possible, when he rose he had his valet pull riding wear from the wardrobe. Thus attired, he was able to spend the hours until breakfast on horseback, in blissful silence and private rumination.

It both disturbed and pleased him that the prevailing subject of his solitary musings was Miss Elizabeth Bennet. The way she smiled and laughed with ease, the way she spoke to him and teased him... He'd never met another young woman quite like her. When first he had spied her across the ballroom, he had looked her over without any admiration. But even as he was settling within his mind that she had hardly a good feature in her face, Miss Morland and her bubbly disposition were dragging him over to be introduced, and on meeting Miss Elizabeth again after his second dance with the young heiress, he was struck with how intelligent that face was rendered by the beautiful expression of her eyes.

Darcy found himself mortified by this discovery and those which rapidly followed. His critical eye had noted more than one failure of perfect symmetry in her form, but as they danced he was forced to acknowledge her figure to be light and pleasing. Her manners—the impertinent wit and teasing nature—were not those of the fashionable world, yet he found himself caught by their easy playfulness.

He realized that he *liked* that she was so different from the young society maidens he was used to, and determined he should like to know her better.

On making this resolution, Darcy's mind turned to the course of action Miss Elizabeth had suggested he take for Miss Morland's benefit: bringing Georgiana to Netherfield. He had no doubt Bingley would agree should he ask, and the two girls were so close in age that they ought to make fast friends. The perpetual bubbliness of Miss Morland's personality might be just the thing to draw his sister out of the melancholy she'd fallen into after discovering the truth of Wickham's duplicity. Miss Elizabeth would also be a help in that regard, he acknowledged, and though the manners he had observed in the latter's mother and two youngest sisters left much to be desired, he could not but note the pleasing manners of the two eldest Miss Bennets as being such that marked them as proper companions for his sister.

Those two sisters were certainly better guides for an impressionable fifteen-year-old than Bingley's. All due credit to his friend, who was just what a young man ought to be—sensible, good-humored, lively—the elevation of his family by the acquisition of a great fortune had born in Mrs. Hurst and Miss Bingley a conceit of which even he could not approve. They were not deficient in good humor or the power of being agreeable when they chose; were sensible of the current fashions and handsome enough to do them justice. Their fortunes of twenty thousand each, however, had led to a habit of spending more than they ought, a desire of associating with no one but people of rank and wealth, and of thinking far too well of themselves and meanly of others. The family from which the siblings hailed was very respectable, but that was a circumstance which led to the sisters granting themselves greater consequence than they deserved, and a too-convenient forgetfulness as to the origin of their brother's fortune and their own.

Mrs. Hurst and Miss Bingley had, in essence, become the very model of a society woman which they believed they *should* be, and which Darcy thoroughly disliked.

Settled on deciding that yes, he would ask that Georgiana be allowed to join him, Darcy turned back for the house though he had not been gone but about an hour; there would be time for a refreshing bath and change of clothes, and time to write to his sister before breakfast should Bingley agree (and he hardly expected him to say no). He walked into the hall to find Miss Morland and her brother just coming in.

"Oh, good morning Mr. Darcy!" Catherine Morland greeted him

cheerfully. "I see you've been out riding—were your ears burning, sir?"

Darcy frowned. "I'm afraid I do not understand your meaning."

James Morland laughed. "It's a common saying in Fullerton, Mr. Darcy. I believe my sister was talking about you to her new friends, the Miss Bennets and Miss Lucases, and wonders if you are aware you were being talked of."

"Ah," said Darcy with a raised eyebrow. "I have heard the expression before, I believe, now you mention it."

To the younger man's sister, he said, "I do hope your raptures were all pleasant ones, Miss Morland. I should be disappointed in myself if I inspired harsh criticism of my character."

As she was then handing off her pelisse to a maid, it was a moment before the young lady replied, "I shan't prevaricate and say it was all good, sir—you have been reckoned proud and somewhat disagreeable. But there is hope! Miss Elizabeth enjoyed your dances with her, and your conversation. I do not think it presumptuous of me to say that she would not be disinclined to know you better."

That he was thought proud was no surprise, as Darcy was aware his discomfort in unfamiliar company gave him such airs. He had once forced himself to try and be pleasant, but his attempts came off as haughty and conceited, so he now chose to say nothing rather than embarrass himself.

Elizabeth's alleged pleasure in his company pleased him more than it should, and he smiled and nodded his head at the news. "Thank you for the insight, Miss Morland. I shall be sure to keep it in mind."

He turned to take himself to his room just as Bingley was coming down the stairs. "Good morning, Darcy—I see you've been for a ride, as usual. Miss Morland, Mr. Morland, good morning!"

Darcy nodded and they passed each other on the stairs as Miss Morland informed her host that she and her brother had been visiting at the Bennets' estate. "I was not aware you knew the way," his friend said somewhat stiffly, rousing his curiosity. A moment ago Bingley had been full of cheer as he greeted them.

"Oh, I got the direction from Miss Elizabeth last night!" Miss Morland replied, though the rest of the conversation was lost to his ears as Darcy reached the top of the stair and turned a corner.

An hour later, he was free of dust and perspiration and in fresh attire. Darcy went in search of Bingley to propose Georgiana's joining him and found him in the study, staring broodily into the low fire.

"Whatever is the matter, Charles?" he asked as he moved to sit in the opposite armchair.

Bingley blinked as he looked up at him. "Oh, Darcy, good morning. It's nothing, really. I'm just a little preoccupied."

"May I ask what about? Perhaps I can help you," Darcy offered.

His friend scoffed as he looked back into the fire. "I do thank you, Darcy, but I do not think so. I may well be making too much of it— 'tis only been one evening, after all."

Darcy then recalled a moment last evening when he had seen his friend strangely cast down. It was unlike Bingley's spirits to be dampened when he was at a party or a dance, and even less so that it should carry over. Comparing the younger man's behavior at the assembly and now, he began to suspect the cause.

"You are upset that Morland has been to see Jane Bennet, aren't you?"

Bingley groaned and threw back his head. "I shouldn't be, but yes!" said he. "She's an angel, Darcy—the most beautiful creature I have ever beheld. But she said yes to him—twice! And he has already called on her."

"I am sure he only went along as escort for his sister," Darcy suggested. "It would, after all, be inadvisable for Miss Morland to travel alone in unfamiliar country."

Bingley looked at him. "And that is to his credit, but he has already seen her again! Don't get me wrong, James is a capital fellow and I like him immensely, but…"

"But you'd rather he not be competition for Miss Bennet's attention." Darcy sat back comfortably in the chair and laced his hands together over his stomach. "Don't fret too much just yet, Charles—it is still early days of your being in the neighborhood. You may find yourself falling in and out of love with Miss Bennet as quickly as you are wont to do with the girls in Town. In the case of your actually seriously considering her, Miss Bennet may yet prefer you over Morland, or she may prove indifferent to the both of you."

He then sat forward again, and added, "Keep in mind, Charles, that you have a fortune that James Morland does not. I gather from my conversation with Miss Bennet's sister that while their father is a gentleman, his fortune is such that he has nothing to give his daughters for their marriages. Her mother's connections are an attorney and a tradesman. It would be a wiser course for Miss Bennet to accept a suit from you than one from James Morland."

"Wiser it may be, Darcy, but you know I have no wish to be liked simply for my fortune. And you feel exactly the same, I know you do."

Darcy conceded the point with a nod. "I do, indeed. However, I believe I can safely surmise that any young lady who married you for your money would eventually fall in love with you—you've too happy a disposition for the girl you marry to be at all miserable. As to Jane Bennet, I do not mean to suggest that she should or will desire your fortune more than yourself, only that she would be wise to consider how much more comfortable you could make her than Morland could."

"That is a good point, Darcy," Bingley mused. "After all, what is eight hundred a year to five thousand? Of course, your ten thousand would be an even greater inducement to the lady."

Darcy chuckled as he sat back again. "You have nothing to be concerned with on that score, Charles. I will own that Miss Bennet is very pretty, but she smiles too much."

"Pray do not say such things! I could never wish her to smile less, for her countenance is all radiance when she smiles," Bingley cried.

His words reminded Darcy of his own thought regarding Miss Elizabeth's smile, and he recalled his mortification that she had heard him speak it aloud. Forcing that feeling to subside, he recalled her suggestion regarding his sister and his own determination to do better by her.

"Charles, would you be at all opposed to my having Georgiana come to stay at Netherfield?" he asked. "I have of late been thinking that I fail in my role as a brother by so often being away from her, and something Miss Elizabeth said last night made me think that she might be a good influence on Miss Morland. I think Georgiana might be able to teach her the significance of being an heiress."

"Oh yes, I daresay she could, though I have met your sister but once in the years I've known you," said Bingley. "Even as a young girl, I thought her very well-mannered. Being an heiress herself, she could certainly convey to Miss Morland the importance of her role in society—but could not my sisters also be of such use?"

"I am sure they could," Darcy replied diplomatically. "But they are both of them older than Miss Morland, and Mrs. Hurst married besides. I thought perhaps someone closer to the young lady's own age might prove easier for her to form a connection with."

"Young ladies do tend to do that, don't they? Prefer company their own age, that is," said Bingley. "And whether she is of use to Miss Morland or not, that you feel even the least bit a failure as a brother is greater reason for you to have your sister with you, though I cannot imagine you actually failing at anything. Yes, Darcy! Do write and tell her she is welcome, for you know I love good company."

"Actually, I think I may just surprise her by making a trip to London, as then I can simply bring her back with me," Darcy said then.

"Now there's a capital idea—don't just tell her you want her with you, show her!" Bingley cried in a more cheerful tone.

"You might take your own advice, Charles," Darcy observed. "Though I urge caution in regard to Miss Bennet, when you are in company together, give her no reason to doubt your good opinion of her."

Bingley began to nod, and then to smile. "You are right, Darcy— absolutely right! Whatever would I do without you to point me in the right direction?"

❧❦

Miss Morland's visit to Longbourn was returned in due course. Her cheerful, pleasing manners appealed greatly to Elizabeth and to Jane—and with Catherine, at least, the former was delighted to become better acquainted.

Miss Bingley and Mrs. Hurst next paid call at Longbourn, and it was very soon apparent to the second Miss Bennet that the sisters thought her mother intolerable and her younger sisters not worth talking to. While she could—privately, of course—agree this was often the case, Elizabeth could not help but disapprove of their method of displaying their dislike. They literally turned their noses up in the air and outright ignored Mrs. Bennet and the younger girls unless they were directly spoken to. Their answers to questions were tight-lipped and short.

The visit was thankfully brief, though by its end, it was impressed upon Elizabeth that she and Jane were actually deemed worthy of the sisters' notice, as a wish of becoming better acquainted with *them* was expressed by Mrs. Hurst. Jane received this information with great pleasure; Elizabeth did not. She could only see superciliousness in their treatment of everyone they met, hardly excepting her sister, and simply could not like them.

Elizabeth did learn one very interesting piece of information from Mr. Bingley's sisters, however: Mr. Darcy had journeyed to London the day after the assembly, and he did not return alone. His sister and her companion were with him, and the fact that Mr. Darcy had taken her advice to heart gratified Elizabeth so much that she found herself almost eager to meet with the gentleman again no matter how proud he was thought to be. Surely he was, as James Morland had observed, a different person amongst his most intimate acquaintances.

Social intercourse between the Bennets and the Bingley party increased over the next few weeks as dinner invitations were issued and accepted by each house, and through parties held by Mr. and Mrs. Phillips as well as Sir William and Lady Lucas. Mrs. Allen did indeed prove to be a great talker. She became fast friends with a number of the local matrons—including Mrs. Bennet, Mrs. Long, and Lady Lucas—and when there was a party anywhere, those ladies could often be found grouped together chattering away. Miss Darcy proved even more shy amongst unfamiliar company than her brother, but Elizabeth—with the aid of Catherine Morland— was able to draw her a little more out of her shell with each visit, and an increase in the frequency of her smiles told Darcy that he had been right to introduce them.

It was soon very generally evident wherever they met that Jane Bennet had not one, but *two* admirers. Bingley and Morland each displayed a marked preference for her, and to her it was the most gratifying feeling to be desired by two fine young gentlemen. This much, at least, she confessed to her sister Elizabeth, though she could not—or would not—yet say which of the young men she preferred. They both made her laugh, they both made her smile, and each was a graceful dance partner.

Elizabeth stood with Charlotte, Catherine, and Miss Darcy observing Jane as she danced with Mr. Morland during a party at Lucas Lodge; Bingley, too, stood to one side and watched the pair.

"I cannot make it out," said Miss Darcy suddenly.

"Cannot make what out, Georgie?" asked Catherine.

Georgiana gestured toward the music parlor, where three couples danced—three of Elizabeth's sisters, with Morland and two young officers. Mary provided the jolly airs which guided their steps on the Lucases' pianoforte.

"Miss Bennet," said she. "It is clear that both Mr. Bingley and Mr. Morland like her, so why does she not make her choice?"

"Who do you think she should choose?" asked Charlotte.

"I should think it obvious—Mr. Bingley is the better choice." Georgiana then gasped softly and looked to the girl standing beside her. "Pray forgive me, Cathy—I mean no disrespect to your brother. He's a fine young man, to be sure."

"But Mr. Bingley has a fortune, and James does not," observed Catherine. "Do not look so surprised, dear Georgiana—I am not deaf to the whispers of our present neighbors. I know that the ladies and mammas hereabout think my brother very handsome, but not the most *prudent* choice given his lack of fortune."

"I sense that makes you rather bitter," said Elizabeth.

"Well, I suppose I am somewhat offended, for my brother's sake!" said Catherine. "He is a very fine young man in all respects, and though his income will be moderate, I am sure he could make a wife very comfortable. And happy—any woman lucky enough to catch my brother's eye would have no cause to repine."

She sighed then. "But I see more than you all, I suppose. He is my brother, and of course I want for his happiness more than anything. And any young lady who becomes attached to him must understand it will be near two years before he can take orders and command his own small estate—though if a young lady is truly attached, she will not mind suffering a long engagement."

"Jane may well have her choice made for her," said Charlotte. "She may yet lose the chance of fixing either one if she does not make her own preference clear soon enough. She has a composure of temper and a uniform cheerfulness of manner which guards her from the impertinent, but it is sometimes a great disadvantage to be so very guarded. If a woman conceals her affection from the object of it with great skill, she *will* lose him."

"You mean to say that they will both decide to give up their suit of her if Miss Bennet cannot or will not make up her mind?" asked Georgiana.

"Essentially, yes," said Charlotte.

Elizabeth suppressed a sigh as she looked again to where her sister danced, apparently quite satisfied with her partner, while the other gentleman in question looked on with a gaze both adoring and vexed. She recalled then that the scene had been much the same when the dancing had first started, when Bingley had been lucky enough to secure Jane's hand first and Morland forced to watch.

For someone whose heart was so broken only eight months ago, Elizabeth mused, *Mr. Morland sure has become quickly attached to another.*

But then, men seemed to find it so very easy to move on, whereas a woman who truly loved would love forever. Elizabeth knew that if

Jane's heart was engaged, she either had not yet determined which man she liked more, or that she would make her preference known in her own time. Charlotte's words came back to her, though, when the song ended and Bingley immediately stepped forward to seek another dance with Jane; it was again Morland's turn to watch and be vexed. Jane, of course, accepted the change of partners with a sweet smile.

It was the same sweet, gentle smile she always showed, and it suddenly struck Elizabeth that perhaps Charlotte had a point. The serenity of her sister's countenance was such that while it was obvious she received the attentions of the two gentlemen with pleasure, it might seem to others that her heart would not be easily touched—if Jane didn't make her choice soon, the two men might decide that waiting for her to choose between them wasn't worth the reward of securing her.

Elizabeth was snapped from her disturbed thoughts by a loud peal of laughter from Lydia. Excusing herself from her companions, she moved away with the intention of speaking to her sister about curtailing her volume lest their family be exposed to ridicule. She had taken only a few steps when she was waylaid by Sir William, who stood next to Mr. Darcy, when he asked her why she did not join the dancing.

"Mr. Darcy, allow me to present to you a lovely partner!" said the older gentleman. "Miss Elizabeth, though he detests the amusement so, I daresay our mutual friend here will not say nay to dancing a reel when such beauty is before him."

"Oh, you must excuse me, sir. I beg you would not think I moved this way to seek a partner—I have not the least intention of dancing," Elizabeth replied, fighting embarrassment. Sir William was a kind man, but a little too eager to see those younger than he enjoying themselves.

"I would be most gratified if you would do me the honor, Miss Elizabeth," said Darcy. "You are so often preoccupied with entertaining Miss Morland and my sister when we are in company together, I have not actually had the opportunity of thanking you for your attentions to the latter."

"Your gratitude is welcome, but entirely unnecessary, sir," Elizabeth replied. "Miss Darcy is a delightful girl and I enjoy her company very much."

Darcy smiled and bowed his head. "I am delighted to hear that you think so well of Georgiana. I would be doubly so if you would consent to a dance, though you did not come this way to beg for a partner."

Noting an uncharacteristic glint in his eye, Elizabeth realized that Mr. Darcy was teasing—*he* was teasing *her*! This was most unusual behavior indeed from so refined a gentleman, and she found herself returning his light smile.

"Well, when you put it that way, Mr. Darcy, how can I possibly refuse?"

Chapter Six

How could it have all gone so wrong?

Darcy scowled in the darkness as his carriage conveyed him and Georgiana back to Netherfield. One moment he had been dancing with Elizabeth, conversing easily—he'd been very much enjoying himself! Yet in the next moment, she was scowling and stalking away from him, and determinedly avoiding his eye for the rest of the evening.

What was it that had so drastically altered the ease with which they'd been getting along? Though it pained him, Darcy forced himself to review the last part of their conversation...

"I should like to speak to you, if I may, about your eldest sister," he had said as they departed the dance floor and began a turn about the room.

"What about her?" Elizabeth asked.

"It is clear to all, I am certain, that she is the object of admiration of both Bingley and Mr. Morland. Do you not agree that she should not entertain the attentions of both if she truly desires neither?"

Elizabeth frowned. "Why should you think she desires neither?"

Darcy drew a breath. "Well, Miss Bennet certainly enjoys the attention she receives from both, for she smiles prettily at each. However, I have often observed her interactions with my friend and his guest, and she shows no particular attachment to either gentleman."

"Jane is only behaving in the manner which she feels a proper young lady should."

"And that is to her credit, Elizabeth, but when a young lady is

50

being openly courted by two young men, she must at some point make her choice of them clear—especially to her admirers themselves."

His companion sighed, the sound of it bearing a note of exasperation. "My sister is shy and modest, and may not yet have come to know her heart's desire. She has, after all, only known Mr. Bingley and Mr. Morland a fortnight. And though they have often met, it is always in company—she has had no real time alone with either young man in which she might be sure not only of the gentleman's character but also her regard for him."

She looked up at him then. "If I may be so bold, why do you take such an interest in those gentlemen's affairs? Well, I can surmise why you would speak on Mr. Bingley's behalf, as he is your friend…"

Elizabeth stopped suddenly and Darcy was forced to turn that he could face her. She scrutinized him with an expression bordering on incredulity. "You believe she should choose Bingley."

He nodded. "I do," he confessed. "If she is indifferent to Bingley then she ought make it known to him, certainly, but I do not see any reason for uncertainty on her part. While Morland is an amiable and deserving young man, Bingley is quite clearly the better situated of the two. They would be able to marry directly rather than having to wait two years, and by merit of his fortune he is more than able to provide for her."

Elizabeth's brow furrowed and she crossed her arms. "I am surprised at you, Mr. Darcy," said she. "Had my sister been less well-mannered and made clear a preference for your friend, I daresay you would think her mercenary. After all, she has no fortune to make him richer, and what an *advantageous* match it would be for her. But because Mr. Bingley has a rival for her affections who just happens to suffer from genteel poverty, who must wait another two years before he can take up the profession for which he is intended, then she is instead indecisive and trifling with the affections of both."

Darcy frowned. "That is not at all what I said, Elizabeth—"

"*Miss* Elizabeth," she corrected him archly. "And though you used not the same words, that is the essence of your opinion. You believe Jane should choose your friend because he is the richer man and can make her life far more comfortable. Heaven forefend that a woman have the audacity to fall in love with a poor man."

Spinning on her heel, Elizabeth strode purposefully away from him, and for the last hour or two, Darcy had been forced to endure the acerbic wit of Miss Bingley as she remarked on his future felicity with the woman who had just turned her back on him.

Oh yes, that was it. Making it known that he believed Jane Bennet would do better to choose Bingley over Morland had ended his enjoyment of the evening rather abruptly. In spite of the overbearing solicitude of Sir William Lucas, the vulgar pretentions of Mrs. Bennet, and the improper behavior of the lady's two youngest daughters, Darcy had actually been at ease in company which would otherwise have made him feel distinctly uncomfortable.

A part of him began to wish he'd said nothing, as then he and Elizabeth would not have argued. Alongside that wish, however, was a little voice telling him it was all for the best. Elizabeth Bennet was as her sister—a young lady of genteel birth but no fortune. She had connections to trade. Neither she nor her sister were appropriate matches for himself and Bingley, and yet they were each of them in very real danger of becoming seriously attached.

"Brother? Are you well?"

Georgiana's timid-sounding voice snapped Darcy out of his reverie. "What makes you ask, dearest?"

"You're rather quiet, even for you," his sister replied. "I... I saw that you disagreed with Miss Elizabeth. Is that what troubles you?"

Darcy stifled a sigh. "In part, yes. But do not distress yourself, sister, I shall be well again. And pray do not allow the discord between Miss Elizabeth and myself to influence your affection for her."

"But why did you argue?" Georgiana pressed.

The carriage was just then turning up the drive to Netherfield. "Georgiana, I haven't any desire to revisit the disagreement anymore this evening. Perhaps in the morning we may speak of it, when I have rested and my thoughts are clearer."

He sensed more than saw his sister's nod of agreement. "As you wish, Fitzwilliam. Though I hope you will not mind my saying how much I have enjoyed myself this last fortnight. Being I am not formally out in society, it was very kind of you to allow me to pay calls and join you at parties amongst your new acquaintances."

Darcy smiled as a footman holding a lantern opened the carriage door and unfolded the step. "I am gratified by your pleasure, sister. I want to be a better brother to you than I have been."

Georgiana reached out to stop him as he moved to step out of the carriage. "You have always been a good brother to me, Fitzwilliam. Do not ever think otherwise."

Moved by the conviction in her voice, Darcy could only smile and incline his head. He then climbed out and turned to assist her, and tucked her hand in the crook of his arm as they made their way up the front steps.

Catherine Morland and her brother quickly caught them up and the two girls began immediately to chatter away about how much they'd enjoyed Sir William's gathering. Morland looked contemplative and spoke not at all. To his left, Bingley — who had just come abreast of him — appeared equally deep in thought. Behind them all were Bingley's sisters and Hurst, the former wasting no time in disparaging nearly everyone and everything they had seen at Lucas Lodge. Darcy decided to retire early, as he had no inclination to listen to their judgmental prattling, nor did he feel up to Bingley's engaging him again about what he should do about Jane Bennet.

He had his own concerns regarding a Bennet sister to occupy his thoughts.

☙❧

Elizabeth tried hard — in vain, as luck would have it — to avoid any discussion of the previous evening's party. She did not wish to relive her argument with Darcy, but the party was all Kitty and Lydia could be bothered to talk about at breakfast the following morning, as they had danced the evening away with their favorite militia soldiers.

She was grateful, for perhaps the first time ever, that her youngest sisters' self-centeredness prevented their speaking to *her* about the party, so Elizabeth was able to distract herself from vexatious thoughts by turning her attention to Jane. In spite of the opinions of Mr. Darcy and his own excellent sister, or perhaps because of them, she had determined to get Jane alone and speak to her on the matter of her two admirers. The only thing she agreed on was that it was best her elder sister make her choice clear, so that all the speculation of which man she would choose would end. Elizabeth had her suspicions as to whom her sister liked more, but vowed to keep that speculation to herself until Jane could be applied to.

A low roll of thunder led all the family to look toward the dining parlor window. Kitty and Lydia began to complain that they would not be able to go into Meryton to visit the officers if it rained. Mary was heard to remind them that there were plenty of more ladylike pursuits they could apply themselves to indoors. Mr. Bennet, much to the surprise of all, ruffled his newspaper in a huff as he turned

53

back to the table.

"Well, there go my plans for the day," he grumbled.

"Plans? You had plans, Mr. Bennet?" asked his wife. "What plans have you but to sit in your library and read your books, as you do every day?"

Mr. Bennet lowered his newspaper only enough to look over the top of it. "As it so happens, my dear, I was last evening invited by Sir William to join a shooting party. The gentlemen at Netherfield were also to attend, and after we were all to dine with Colonel Forster. You may be interested to know, Mrs. Bennet, that the local militia's top man is of a mind to marry."

"Colonel Forster is wanting to marry? How come we have not heard this?" posed Lydia. Kitty, as per usual, echoed her sentiments.

Perhaps if you spent less time flirting with his officers and more time attending to conversation, you might have done, Elizabeth thought peevishly.

"Well!" cried Mrs. Bennet. "Lydia, my dear, this is good news! He has not the fortune of Mr. Bingley and is a good deal older, but he has about three or four thousand a year, does he not?"

"Oh, yes, Mamma!" Lydia replied. "It is three thousand for certain, and I am sure Captain Carter mentioned only the other day that it is very likely he will have more in the next year or two."

"Oh, how wonderful for you my dear! Perhaps not as wonderful as Jane's sure match with Mr. Bingley —"

"Mamma, please," admonished Jane.

"Why is it wonderful for Lydia?" said Kitty. "She is only fifteen, and I am two years older!" She glared at her younger sister. "You don't even like Colonel Forster that much. You say he is old and ugly and too strict!"

Lydia stuck her tongue out at Kitty, then said, "But I am livelier than you, and prettier besides! If Colonel Forster had only the two of us to choose from in all the world, I am sure he would pick me!"

"Lydia, you are nowhere near mature enough to be any man's wife," observed Elizabeth. "You are silly, empty-headed, and vain, and you have flirted with so many of Colonel Forster's men I daresay he would not even look at you."

"Lizzy, how can you say such cruel things about your sister?!" cried Mrs. Bennet. "She is quite old enough to marry — in fact, women younger than she have been married in years past! And it is a great unkindness for you to think your sister silly and empty-headed."

"The past is not the present, Mamma. In the present, girls my sister Lydia's age are generally not even out in society," Elizabeth pointed out, "let alone married. And I say she is silly and empty-headed because it is true, for she has learnt next to nothing useful. I do not think you should put it into Lydia's head that she might be a match for Colonel Forster. I have observed him when in company and determined that he is a reasonably sensible man—and sensible men do *not* want silly wives."

Mr. Bennet chuckled and looked to her with a sideways glance. "Well said, Lizzy."

Mrs. Bennet and Lydia railed about the unkindness of Elizabeth's remarks and Mr. Bennet's agreement, Kitty complained about not being considered for Colonel Forster, Mary shook her head and quietly ate her breakfast. Jane looked to Elizabeth with a distressed expression, at which Elizabeth could only shake her head.

She was just determining that she'd had enough food and frustration to last her the whole rest of the day when a note was presented to her by one of the maids, who said it had just come from Netherfield. For the briefest of moments, Elizabeth wondered if Mr. Darcy had written to her, but she quickly dismissed the idea—he was too proper a gentleman to write to a lady not his relation.

"Why should anyone from Netherfield be writing to you, Lizzy?" her mother asked peevishly.

"You forget, Mamma, that I am closely acquainted with Miss Morland," Elizabeth reminded her as she broke the wax seal.

The note was not from Catherine, however, but Georgiana Darcy. It was a short missive that Elizabeth read aloud.

My dear Miss Elizabeth,

Cathy and I fully intended to call on you and your sisters this morning, but Mrs. Allen has taken her carriage to London for the day, and the gentlemen will be gone with the other vehicles for their shooting party. If you can, please do come and spend the day with us. Bring Miss Bennet or another of your sisters along if you should like, and we will have ourselves a merry little party!

Your friend,
Georgiana Darcy

"Well, what a kind young lady she is!" declared Mrs. Bennet. "And so good natured."

"I would like to go with you, Lizzy, if I may," said Kitty. Elizabeth looked up at her sister's subdued tone and noted an expression of vexation and disappointment on her countenance; it was clear she had not fared well in the argument with her mother and Lydia.

Feeling sorry for her sister, she opened her lips to agree but was interrupted when Mrs. Bennet cried out, "Absolutely not! If anyone should go, it is Jane—she was, after all, mentioned specifically by Miss Darcy."

"She also used the words 'or another of your sisters', Mamma," said Elizabeth.

"Nonsense, Lizzy! Would you have dearest Jane miss the chance of seeing Mr. Bingley today?"

The newspaper snapped and Elizabeth looked to see Mr. Bennet folding it. "I daresay, my dear," said he to his wife, "that our daughters would wish the carriage to convey them, but regrettably the horses are wanted on the farm today."

Mrs. Bennet scoffed. "They can go on horseback. In fact, it is ideal that they should! The rain will come and prevent their returning until tomorrow. Oh, Jane, can you imagine spending a whole night in the same house as so handsome a man as Mr. Bingley?"

"She might if she hoped to compromise him, Mamma, and I cannot imagine my sister applying herself to such an occupation," Elizabeth observed.

"Certainly not!" cried Jane.

"No," said Mr. Bennet. The family all looked to him. "Pray forgive me, girls, for I should not like to suspend any pleasure of yours. But I'll not subject you to the rain anymore than I would myself, even if it should manage to land one of you a husband."

Mrs. Bennet began to protest, leading to Mr. Bennet rapping his knuckles on the table. "Madam, you know very well how easily our Jane catches cold in damp weather—would you have her become ill from riding to Netherfield in the rain?"

Mrs. Bennet shook her head. "And very well she would be taken care of there, Mr. Bennet! All the while, she would have Mr. Bingley fawning over her, and I am sure by the end of her convalescence she would have an offer from him."

Jane's naturally pale cheeks were crimson with embarrassment, and Elizabeth's heart went out to her. Whether she liked Bingley better than Morland or not, such talk was clearly distressful to her sister. As much as she would have liked to spend the day with her young friends, she was pleased that her father had for once put his foot down and disallowed his wife's ridiculous attempts at matchmaking. Still, she was quick to write a note of apology and send it off with one of the footmen so that Georgiana and Catherine were not left no answer at all.

About half an hour after breakfast, all was as it usually was on a rainy day at Longbourn: Mr. Bennet was ensconced in his library, Mary was toiling away on the pianoforte, Mrs. Bennet lounged in a chaise pretending she'd not dozed off once, Kitty and Lydia were chattering away about the militia, Jane was working on embroidery, and Elizabeth was occupying herself with a book. The rain had started a quarter of an hour before and thunder rumbled every few minutes.

All the family were comfortably settled thus, and so were all of them rather surprised to suddenly hear a knocking at the front door. All the ladies were curious; Kitty and Lydia fought for position at the window, that they could espy who had come, but each complained that the heavy rain made it impossible to tell. As no carriage had been heard, and each occupant turned eagerly toward the open door as they heard the door to the library open. Moments later the front door was opened, then Mr. Bennet's voice carried to them when he welcomed the visitor.

"Such dreadful weather in which you have come in to call on me, sir," they heard him say.

"It is indeed, Mr. Bennet," said a very recognizable voice.

Elizabeth looked to Jane, whose eyes widened. "That is Mr. Morland, I am sure of it!" the latter cried softly. "Whatever is he doing here? I am sure the shooting party was canceled, as Papa did not go."

"I believe I can reasonably guess as to the reason for his coming all this way," replied Elizabeth with a smile, at which her sister blushed.

"I beg you would forgive me calling upon you in such a dreadful state, Mr. Bennet," Morland was saying. "I was out riding after breakfast and had intended to head directly to Lucas Lodge to take part in our planned excursion. I thought I could make it well before the rain started, but as you see, I did not. It came down so heavily from the start that I rather lost my way, and on recognizing Longbourn hoped I might beg to take refuge with your family."

"You may indeed, young man, but I daresay you would not wish to appear before my wife and daughters in such a state," said Mr. Bennet with a chuckle.

At this, Kitty and Lydia giggled and rushed toward the door. They were each of them stopped by a quick snag of the sleeve by Jane and Elizabeth.

"You will *not* go out there!" Elizabeth hissed. "Allow the poor fellow some dignity, for goodness' sake."

"Let us go somewhere that you might make yourself more presentable, Mr. Morland," they heard Mr. Bennet say next, to which their visitor readily agreed; the two men were next heard treading up the stairs to the first floor.

Kitty and Lydia twittered maddeningly as they returned to their seats, with the latter teasing Jane that Mr. Morland had come all the way to Longbourn in the rain just to see her. "I declare, Jane, that he surely has! He must have done in spite of their silly shooting party being cancelled to gain advantage over Mr. Bingley in your affections!"

Elizabeth noted that not only did color bloom in Jane's cheeks as she studiously concentrated on her work, but also that the corners of her lips turned up ever so slightly. To save her sister further harassment, however, she then turned to the youngest and said, "Now Lydia, we all of us heard Mr. Morland himself say that he merely lost his sense of direction in the rain; not an uncommon occurrence in such a deluge as pours outside. It is an unkindness to tease Jane so."

"Not to mention our Jane prefers Mr. Bingley. Do you not my dear?" said Mrs. Bennet.

Without even giving her daughter time to voice a reply, she launched into a monologue about what fine things Jane would have as Mr. Bingley's wife. When Jane sighed and her smile faltered, Elizabeth reached over and gently laid a hand atop hers, saying in a low voice, "Do not listen to her, dearest Jane. You and I know that a truly happy marriage does not need a lot of money."

Jane glanced sidelong at her before whispering, "No indeed, Lizzy. But it would make Mamma so happy to see me so well settled."

"Your choice of husband does not require you make your mother happy. It is your own happiness which must take precedence," said Elizabeth.

When Jane sighed again, Elizabeth decided to let the subject drop. She returned her attention to her book and was content to concentrate on the story until some minutes later, when Mr. Bennet escorted Mr. Morland into the room. She watched her sister's gaze as it roamed over the borrowed attire he wore before settling on his face, searching it as though to determine whether he was well.

James Morland beamed under her blatant scrutiny.

Chapter Seven

"**You really** must eat something, Cathy."

Darcy listened to the sound advice given by his sister to her friend as he carried his plate to the breakfast table. The three of them were, at present, the only members of the household to be up and about.

"I cannot. I am so very worried for James! It is not like him not to come home!" Miss Morland cried softly. "He could be injured on the side of some country road or kidnapped by highwaymen!"

What a fanciful imagination she has, Darcy thought as he sipped his coffee. He was about to offer her the assurance that her brother had surely taken shelter from the previous day's weather at the home of one of their friends when a note was brought in by a maid and delivered straight to Miss Morland. The young lady opened it eagerly as she exclaimed "It is my brother's handwriting!"

An relieved-sounding laugh escaped her as she started to read, followed quickly by the fall of her countenance into a worried frown.

"What is it, Cathy?" Georgiana asked.

"James is safe," Miss Morland replied absently. "He is at Longbourn, having lost his way to Lucas Lodge in the heavy rain. But he is ill! He developed a terrible cold overnight and has got himself a fever!"

She jumped up from her chair. "I must go to him at once!"

"But Cathy, Mrs. Allen has not returned from London. You have not your carriage."

"Then I shall walk," Miss Morland protested.

Georgiana looked to him in desperation. Darcy suppressed a sigh and said, "Miss Morland, do be reasonable. It is three miles' distance from Netherfield to Longbourn."

"It is no trouble to me, I like a long walk," she replied.

Georgiana looked aghast at her. "Three miles in all that dirt and mud? You'll not be fit to be seen!"

"I shall be fit to see James, which is all I want," her friend said, lifting her chin defiantly. "In any case, surely I needn't actually walk. Mr. Bingley has horses enough—James went off on one yesterday—I am sure he would not mind my borrowing another of them."

"I certainly should not," said Bingley as he entered the breakfast room. "But pray tell, why am I so willing to lend you a horse, Miss Morland?"

She waved the note in her hand and explained its contents. Bingley's smiling countenance fell when he heard his rival's location, but he quickly recovered and assured her she could have one of his horses to ride if she wished.

"Oh, but you needn't ride off on your own, Cathy," said Georgiana, who then looked to Darcy with a pleading expression. "Brother, might I not take her there in your carriage?"

"Our carriage," he corrected her gently; she still thought of everything that was theirs as his. "And you shall not take her alone. I will be the one to borrow a horse, that I may ride escort."

"Oh, Mr. Darcy, that is so very kind of you!" said Miss Morland. In brighter spirits now, she returned to her seat beside Georgiana and attended to her breakfast.

Darcy had offered her a nod of acknowledgment, then returned his attention to his own, though he was by no means unaware of the sullen posture Bingley had taken on when he sat himself at the head of the table. He picked at his food much as Miss Morland had done at first, and it was no trouble to guess the direction of his thoughts.

The girls finished eating in record time and rose to ready themselves; Darcy knew that not only was Catherine eager to see her brother, but that both were likely to be happy to be calling on their friends, for the weather had prevented their having any company other than Miss Bingley and Mrs. Hurst the day before, and through Catherine he had learned Georgiana wasn't particularly fond of either.

When they had gone, he turned his gaze to Bingley. "You are welcome to join us, Charles," said he softly.

Bingley sighed. "I think not," he replied. "I'm no fool, Darcy—I know when to admit defeat."

"Defeat?" Darcy said, confusion in his tone. "How are you

defeated?"

"Oh, come man! Do you really not see it?" Bingley said. "My rival for Miss Bennet's affections is not only a guest in her home but he is ill! Such circumstances are sure to do away with any hesitation such a kind-hearted lady as she might be feeling as to whom she admires more."

Silently, Darcy admitted he had a point. Women, in his experience, were always more sympathetic to the infirm than the hearty and hale.

"If you are sure you are defeated, Charles, then be gracious in it. Join us," he said at last.

"I will be gracious, Darcy, for I certainly could never be bitter in the presence of Miss Bennet," Bingley replied. "But I shall not join you in visiting today. I think it best that I spend the time of Morland's convalescence acclimating myself to the idea of having lost her to him."

He would still have a chance, Darcy mused, if he more firmly applied himself to the task, but given his proclivity for falling in and out of love, he suspected his friend would be himself again in only a few days. Still, in the time it took Bingley to recover his spirits, he would certainly be mopey and short-tempered. He acknowledged with a nod and stood, and after excusing himself, he went to go order his carriage and a horse be readied.

A quarter of an hour later, he and the girls were on their way to Longbourn. As he rode alongside the carriage, Darcy mused upon the fact that he could well have allowed them to go on their own—their destination wasn't far and he knew where they would be. He could rationalize that they were unmarried young women all he wanted, but there was no use denying—to himself, at least—that he had volunteered himself as their escort in the hope of seeing Elizabeth again and perhaps making his apologies to her.

Miss Elizabeth, he corrected himself, recalling with an amused grin how she had corrected him at Sir William's party.

The road, thankfully, was not nearly so muddy as he had secretly feared, and by the time their party arrived at Longbourn House, he had but to shake off some small spatters from his coat when he dismounted. He and his sister and Miss Morland were shown by the housekeeper to the drawing room, where all the ladies save Jane Bennet were gathered.

Mrs. Bennet welcomed them warmly and invited them to take seats. Catherine Morland demurred, saying she wished to see her brother.

"Oh, he's doing very well, I assure you," said the lady of the house. "My Jane and a maid are looking after him as well as the boy could hope, I am sure."

"I will take you to his room, Miss Morland," said Elizabeth with a smile. "Please excuse me, Mamma, I shall return shortly."

Discomfited by the departure of the only person of sense he could speak to, Darcy—instead of seating himself—moved to the window. He listened as Georgiana expressed her disappointment at not being able to see "anyone at all" the day before, to which Kitty Bennet replied she was also disappointed, for she had been sure "Lizzy would have brought me along".

"I should have been delighted to see you!" replied his sister. "I really liked the embroidery on your sleeves, on that gown you wore to Sir William's party the other night. I wonder, can you tell me where you had it done?"

"Why, it was by my own hand!" said Kitty with some pride.

"Oh yes, my dear girl, that was some fine handiwork," crowed Mrs. Bennet. "My Kitty can do very well with a needle when she applies herself."

Darcy listened with a disinterested ear as the ladies prattled on about embroidery and gowns and ribbons and the like, but he was immediately aware the moment he was not alone at the window.

"I cannot imagine you are thrilled by the conversation going on behind us," said Elizabeth softly.

He scoffed. "It is not my preferred topic of conversation, that much is certain."

A moment of silence passed, and then she said, "Mr. Darcy, I... It is not easy for me to speak thus... I do not imagine it to be easy for anyone, but..."

He looked down to find her looking up at him. "I am sorry for my temper the other night," she said. "I should not have spoken so."

Darcy shook his head. "Do not apologize for defending one you love," he replied. "Though I shall in turn offer my apologies for offending you to the extent that you were compelled to do so. It was certainly not my intention."

Turning his gaze back toward the window, he added, "I am full aware that sometimes, a woman will follow her heart even if it leads her into the arms of a poor man. And really, Mr. Morland will not be so very poor, if he is indeed her choice."

"But you cannot help thinking him the less prudent one."

"No, I cannot." Darcy sighed softly. "Bingley is somewhat despondent. He believes Mr. Morland being ill here will make your sister's choice for her."

"I am sorry for his disappointment, for your friend is a very fine gentleman, but..." Their gazes met again briefly. "I cannot say he is wrong to think so. Jane has been tending to Mr. Morland all morning."

"Is he so very ill?"

"Mr. Jones was summoned to examine him before breakfast," Elizabeth replied. "His fever is high, and he has been slightly delirious when conscious."

"I am sorry to hear it," Darcy said.

Elizabeth sighed as she wrapped her arms about herself. "It is only right," she said slowly, "that I do you the justice of acknowledging your point to be true. From an outsider's view, certainly, Mr. Bingley would be the more prudent choice for Jane—for all of us, if I am honest about it. Our father's income is enough to make us comfortable while he lives, but he cannot provide dowries for his five daughters and our estate is entailed—a cousin we have none of us even met will inherit Longbourn when my father dies. We have little, my sisters and I, but our charms to recommend us, and there is little chance of our marrying men of any consideration in the world."

She glanced up at him again, briefly, and he could tell she suppressed another sigh. "Though chances are slim, it is vital that one of my sisters should marry very well, that our mother and other sisters who are unmarried when our father leaves us should be provided for rather than forced to depend on the kindness of relatives who could not provide for all."

"One of your sisters?" Darcy queried, thinking her word choice an interesting one. "Do you not include yourself among those who ought to marry well if she can?"

Elizabeth laughed. "Who would have me, Mr. Darcy?" she rejoined. "Ask anyone in the neighborhood and they will tell you that I was surely *not* born to be a heroine like the lead in one of Mrs. Radcliffe's novels. My mother would say I am too sharp and impertinent and have no notion of when to hold my tongue. No, it is surely my lot to be..."

Who would have me, Mr. Darcy? she had said.

I would, his mind immediately replied, shocking Darcy to his core. So stunned was he that for several heartbeats, he could not even attend to what Elizabeth was saying.

Then he realized suddenly that she was not saying anything. His companion was, in fact, studying his countenance with a slight frown on her own. "Are you well, Mr. Darcy?" she asked.

He was touched by the genuine concern he noted in her voice. Forcing himself to relax, he drew a breath and offered a smile.

"Quite well, I assure you," said he, praying his voice did not sound as unsure as he felt. *What am I to do now?* he wondered. He had only the other day concluded that he ought to begin making plans to depart Bingley's company, lest the danger of becoming bewitched by Elizabeth Bennet's pert opinions and fine eyes be insurmountable.

"You appeared rather shocked for a moment, sir," Elizabeth replied. "I feared I had surprised you with my declaration."

"Which declaration was that?" he countered. "Forgive me, madam, for I was distracted by a thought that crossed my mind."

She grinned. "Must've been a heavy thought indeed, for you not to hear me declare I should be content to be governess to my sister's ten children, teaching them to embroider cushions, cover screens, net purses, and play the pianoforte very ill."

"I rather enjoyed your performance at Sir William's party the other night," Darcy said.

Surprise alighted in her expression. "You mean you attended me even after we had not so amicably parted ways?"

Darcy smiled. "Should I not have?"

Elizabeth laughed again. "Well, I suppose you could hardly help hearing me, but listening... that would be something else. Tell me, sir, what song did I play?"

He needed only a moment for his mind to recall the music, and he said to her with a smile, "I believe the song was *Light of Thiestledown*, was it not?"

Elizabeth grinned, though the slight widening of her eyes told Darcy he had surprised her further. "I am impressed, Mr. Darcy, that you paid attention."

Darcy held back a laugh. "Should I not have?" he repeated.

Her lips parted and she drew breath to reply, but was that moment distracted by the entrance of her sister Jane, who said, "Forgive my tardiness. I was assisting Sarah with Mr. Morland's care, then explaining Mr. Jones' instructions to his sister."

Georgiana stood from her place beside Kitty. "Is Cathy's brother really very ill?"

A look of alarm flittered across Jane's features, and though she informed his sister that the apothecary had declared Morland's condition only a "bad cold", something in her manner told Darcy that Bingley had been right to be concerned after all; the young lady looked as though she wanted to be back where she'd come from, her concern for Morland was so evident.

Bad luck for you, Charles, he thought as Jane at last moved further into the room and sat on the sofa between Kitty and Georgiana. Elizabeth watched her sister with some concern, then glanced sidelong at him and said in a low voice, "I do hope Mr. Bingley will not be so disappointed as to not be neighborly."

So, she saw it as well, Darcy mused. "There is no need to concern yourself on that score, Miss Elizabeth. He may need a day or two to accept your sister's choice, but I can assure you he will wish them both every happiness when their courtship is official."

Elizabeth sighed. "I do not know how Jane will bear so long an engagement as she will be forced to endure should Mr. Morland go so far as to make her an offer."

"Indeed," Darcy said. "I believe he has said it will be two years before he is able to take orders."

His companion turned back toward the window and wrapped her arms about herself again. "I must admit I fear for my sister's disposition to wait so long. Her constancy I know I can depend on, so long as she believes in any promise he would make, but it will wear on her. And I cannot help but wonder about *his* constancy—Catherine told us of his being engaged to another girl only about eight months ago. She claimed him despondent over the infidelity of this Miss Thorpe he'd hoped to marry and claimed he would not even look at another woman, his heart was so broken. Yet he has openly courted my sister."

She snorted softly. "How easily men forget the women they claim to love."

"I would not think so meanly of Mr. Morland, madam," Darcy said slowly. "Or men in general. I daresay it is not inconstancy that he displays, but that his heart sought solace from his disappointment and has found it in your sister."

Elizabeth glanced up at him. "Well, that is certainly a more pleasant way to think on the situation. Of course, nothing is certain and we have only our observations on which to base these assumptions. Still, I cannot seem to stop my mind coming round to those two years. How difficult it will be for both of them, and how it will surely wear away at Jane's natural strength. It would grieve me deeply to watch her bloom wither."

"Perhaps Miss Bennet and Mr. Morland will not have so long to wait to marry, though he will still have to wait to take his orders," Darcy suggested.

He felt a small rush of pleasure when she again looked up to him, her gaze curious. "How do you mean, sir?" she asked.

"Consider that Miss Morland is now very wealthy, and the mistress of a large house," Darcy replied. "Surely there is room enough for two more to take up residence there."

Elizabeth's countenance brightened. "That is true! And I have heard Catherine herself say she wished she could do more for her brother if he should indeed come to love Jane. I think it need only be carefully suggested that she offer them a place at Fullerton, if she does not think of it on her own."

Darcy smiled. "Quite so, Miss Elizabeth. Now you have a mission toward securing your sister's happiness: listen carefully and observe, and if necessary, implant the suggestion into conversation at the opportune moment."

Elizabeth laughed softly. "Listen to us, Mr. Darcy, standing here plotting intrigues. We've been conversing so long one might actually mistake us for being friends."

He brought a hand to his chest and effected a mock scowl. "Heaven forefend!" he cried. "We must part now, before it is too late and we are forced to keep up the pretense."

Elizabeth for a second seemed surprised that he had gone along with her jest; then her eyes sparkled and she tilted her head. "Very well, Mr. Darcy," she said as she began to turn away.

Darcy just stopped himself reaching out a hand to stop her. He let her go with only a nod and turned slowly to watch as she crossed the room and sat in the empty chair adjacent to her mother's, a position from which she could see everyone in the room, including him. And if he was not mistaken, when next she glanced his way she smiled; he felt emotion swell beneath his breast at the simple, sweet gesture.

And felt himself even more in danger of becoming seriously attached.

Chapter Eight

Mr. Darcy and Georgiana stayed only about half an hour at Longbourn.

Elizabeth was forced to admit that she was disappointed they had to go, for she'd enjoyed her conversations with both. Miss Darcy's seemingly inherent shyness was less present when in the company of Catherine Morland or Kitty and Lydia than it was when Miss Bingley and Mrs. Hurst were in the room. She had no trouble at all in discussing her accomplishments and all the other subjects young ladies her age liked to talk about when she was with her young contemporaries, but whenever Mr. Bingley's sisters were near, she tended to say little or nothing at all. Elizabeth suspected she felt intimidated by them, which was rather vexing as Georgiana Darcy was so much more what a young lady ought to be—she had seen after only one or two days why Mr. Darcy thought her a better example of a young heiress for Miss Morland than Bingley's sisters.

Darcy himself was… an enigma. She had liked him, thought him arrogant and insufferable, and found him surprisingly witty and thoughtful at different moments in the last fortnight—if she didn't know herself better, she might even suspect she *liked* him. Not that she did, of course, at least not in the way Jane admired Mr. Morland. It would not do at all for her to form an attachment to a man who would likely never see her as suitable wife material. After all, she had no dowry to make him richer and her mother's relations were a country attorney and a tradesman—as a gentleman's daughter she was technically his equal, but with her lack of fortune and low connections, an alliance between their families would be seen as a degradation on his part. Bingley, with his own connection to trade, could afford to be a little less scrupulous in his choice of wife, but Darcy could not.

So there was no point at all even considering entertaining such thoughts. Mr. Darcy was a delightful conversationalist and an impressive chess player, but good friends was all they were ever likely to be.

Catherine Morland refused to return to Netherfield when the Darcys made ready to depart, declaring she could not possibly leave her brother while he was still so ill. Elizabeth could tell her mother was vexed by having the Morlands in the house—especially Mr. Morland, who was a threat to her plans for Jane—but when Mr. Bennet was applied to for his consent, he readily agreed to Catherine staying, voicing his appreciation of "the young lady's admirable dedication to sisterly duty."

Elizabeth deduced, from the sidelong glance her father directed at Jane, that he was not unaware of his eldest daughter's growing admiration for the future clergyman who rested above stairs. Knowing Mr. Bennet's proclivities as she did, his second daughter suspected he would encourage the attachment simply to agitate Mrs. Bennet's "nerves" and amuse himself.

At this thought, she could only sigh and shake her head.

After dressing for dinner that evening, Elizabeth took herself to James Morland's sickroom, and knocked lightly on the partially open door.

"Come in," came Catherine's voice.

Pushing the door open further, Elizabeth was not much surprised to see her sister in company with the Morlands. "Jane, you'd best go and dress for dinner," she said to her sister.

Jane blushed and cast a glance at Mr. Morland. "I... Yes, I really should, I suppose."

"Do go and enjoy your dinner, my d— madam," said the patient weakly. "I should not like to be the reason *you* become ill."

Morland turned his gaze to his sister. "You really should go and eat as well, Cathy," he continued. "Mother and Father, and Mrs. Allen, would never forgive me if my foolishness led to your becoming ill."

"James, I can't leave you up here all alone! Besides, I haven't a dinner gown to wear," Catherine protested. She looked to Elizabeth then. "Could you perhaps have a servant send up a tray? My brother must have something as well. I do hate to ask, but I really must take care of him."

"Do not be silly, Catherine," Morland protested. "Go and have dinner with our hosts, it is the proper thing to do. I daresay they will not mind your not being appropriately dressed."

"Indeed not," said Elizabeth. "In fact, I really ought to apologize for not thinking of having your clothes sent for."

"Good gracious, why did we not think of it for either of them?" Jane asked as she stood suddenly.

Elizabeth laughed softly. "No need to be so alarmed, sister, for we shall certainly rectify our grievous error after dinner. Now both of you, do come. Catherine, you and Kitty are about the same size, and I am sure my sister will not mind lending you one of her evening gowns if you would not be averse to borrowing a dress for the evening."

Catherine shook her head. "I would not mind at all," she replied, then looked to her brother. "Are you certain, James?"

He nodded. "I am. You should go and be gracious, Cathy. But I would not mind a maid bringing me a bowl of soup or some such. I've only a cold, I'm not a complete invalid. I can feed myself."

His sister laughed and stood at last. "Very well, I will do my duty to Mr. and Mrs. Bennet. But you'd better not get any worse while I am gone!" she said, shaking her finger at him.

Mr. Morland chuckled, though almost instantly his mirth brought on a coughing fit. Distressed by this, Catherine sat again, but her brother waved her away. "No, go," he said when he could speak again. "Go on, Cathy, or Mrs. Bennet will likely be very put out by having to wait for her dinner."

Elizabeth grinned. "He's quite right, Catherine. Trust me when I tell you that it would not be wise to take the chance."

Catherine sighed and stood again. "Very well," said she, and in a moment, she was following Elizabeth to Kitty's room while Jane walked to her own. Kitty proved quite happy to lend her namesake a dress for dinner, and she and Elizabeth helped her select one that came close to matching her green eyes.

"If only one of your many admirers in Meryton could see you now, Cathy," Kitty said with a giggle.

Catherine rolled her eyes and groaned softly. "Pray do not remind me!" she cried. "In all my life, never have I been the object of such attention as I have been these few weeks. And to think, these young men would hardly have paid any attention to me at all were it not for Mr. Allen's fortune—John Thorpe only liked me because he believed me rich, and I wasn't then!"

"That is the way of the world, I'm afraid," observed Elizabeth. "Men who aren't rich themselves only want rich wives, and men who are rich only want wives who can make them richer."

The last she said with a pointed glance at her sister, who looked away with colored cheeks. Catherine protested that her declaration was not entirely accurate, for "James is not a rich man, and he does not seek a rich wife. Neither Isabella nor Jane has any fortune to speak of, and he formed an attachment to both."

"Indeed, dear Cathy—even young men have been known to imprudently throw themselves away on a poor woman," Elizabeth teased.

As the three girls then turned toward the door to make their way downstairs, the faint sound of carriage wheels and horses' hooves on gravel reached them. They heard it stop before the house as they reached the stairs, where they were joined by Jane, and by the time the four reached the ground floor, Mrs. Allen was being shown into the hall.

"Oh, dearest Catherine! Pray tell me, how is your brother?" the lady asked on sight of Miss Morland. "I have just returned from London, and at Netherfield I learned he is gravely ill!"

Sounds like something Miss Bingley would say, Elizabeth mused silently as Catherine assured her benefactress that James had only caught himself a bad cold.

"Well now, good evening Mrs. Allen," said Mrs. Bennet as she came into the hall. "Have you come to take Mr. Morland back to Netherfield?"

"Take him back!" cried both Catherine and Jane together. "Mamma," continued the latter, "you know very well that Mr. Jones said only this morning that Mr. Morland was too ill to be removed!"

Mrs. Bennet huffed and sniffed as she smoothed her skirt. "Mr. Jones was surely exaggerating, as he always does."

Seeing the mutual distress of her sister and her friend, Elizabeth took a step forward and said, "Now Mamma, do not be unkind. You know very well that Mr. Jones does not exaggerate."

She then looked to Mrs. Allen and added, "The apothecary prescribed plenty of rest, fluids, and fever powder as needed, and said that Mr. Morland might be well enough to return home by Saturday."

Mrs. Allen blew out a breath and offered a shaky smile. "Thank you, Miss Elizabeth. When that Miss Bingley told me of James's being

70

ill, I admit I feared what news I might have to deliver to his poor parents."

"Well, she has not seen Mr. Morland, so it is understandable her information would be somewhat inaccurate," Elizabeth assured her, wondering why neither Darcy nor his sister had been available to speak to the lady.

Mr. Bennet, Lydia, and Mary then appeared and Mrs. Allen was naturally invited to dine with them, which she happily accepted. After dinner, she went with Catherine to see James, and when the two joined the Bennet ladies in the drawing room a quarter hour later, they were both of them lighter of countenance and spirit.

"I am sure he will be just fine," said Mrs. Allen with a flutter of her handkerchief as she sat in the chair adjacent to Mrs. Bennet's; Elizabeth was forced to stifle a laugh, as the gesture reminded her so much of her mother. Mrs. Bennet almost immediately copied the behavior as she declared that "Of course he will be" and how happy she would be to see Mr. Morland up and about.

And out of your house away from Jane, Elizabeth mused.

Mrs. Bennet's unspoken wish was not, as it happened, to be granted. Mr. Morland's improvement in health was steady but slow, and he could not even leave his room until Thursday, when he was assisted into the drawing room after dinner by his sister. He sat with them only an hour before his seemingly ever-present fatigue overtook him, and spoke almost exclusively to Jane and Catherine. Later that night, after the family had all gone up to ready for bed, Elizabeth was just pulling down the counterpane when there was a light knock at her door.

Expecting it to be Jane, who often visited her to talk before retiring, she was surprised to find that Catherine Morland was her visitor. "Do come in, Cathy," she said, and gestured toward the two small chairs that sat before her fireplace. "What can I do for you?"

"You can tell me if I am being unreasonable," said Catherine as she sat down. "I... Well, you know as well as I that in spite of my belief otherwise, my brother has fallen in love with your sister Jane."

Elizabeth smiled. "Yes, it is clear indeed to anyone who sees them in company together. Jane certainly has made her heart's choice clear with how much she has attended your brother this week."

"Indeed she has, and I am immensely happy for them both," Catherine agreed, then sighed as her smile fell.

Elizabeth lifted an eyebrow. "If that is so, I wonder what brings you here to seek my discernment."

Catherine twisted her hands together in her lap. "Well, you know that James is to take orders, but that he must wait until he is four-and-twenty. That means that he and your sister would have to wait two whole *years* before they could marry, so that he is established in his profession and in possession of his estate that he can properly receive and support a wife."

"Yes," Elizabeth acknowledged as she sat back in her chair. "I am aware of his circumstances."

"And do you not think it most cruel? There cannot be anything more abominable to a young couple than a long engagement!" Catherine cried softly.

"It certainly will be difficult for Mr. Morland and Jane to suffer it, but what choice have they? If their attachment is genuine and strong, two years' time will not allow it to wither."

"Oh, most assuredly! I know James—when he gives his heart, he gives it all!" said Catherine with an enthusiastic bob of her head.

"As does Jane," Elizabeth said. "But again, what can be done?"

She suspected, given the direction of the conversation until then, that Catherine meant to suggest offering support to her brother and Jane. It seemed that she wondered if it was proper, or whether it would even be welcome.

Elizabeth's silent wonderings proved true in the next moment when her visitor espoused almost the exact thoughts she'd been having aloud. Sitting forward again, she smiled and said, "I think it entirely proper—not to mention most generous of you—that you would offer your assistance! And given your recent elevation in circumstances, I daresay it is your duty to aide your brothers and sisters in whatever ways you are able. Tell me, what form of assistance were you thinking of offering?"

Catherine was clearly much relieved by her words, as her worried expression changed immediately to one of delight. "I have been thinking of two ways I might help them, but I do not know which to offer. I know my brother's pride will be wounded by any offer of assistance, but surely I must do something! And surely he must see that I only want to see him happy at last. And I really must do something for dearest Jane, who has healed his heart after that wretched Isabella Thorpe broke it."

"What ideas have you for helping them on?" Elizabeth prompted.

Catherine reached up to the braid that hung over her shoulder and fiddled with the ribbon. "Well, I thought I might offer them an allowance or perhaps a modest compensation. I have also considered offering to have them live with Mrs. Allen and me at Fullerton Manor until James can take orders. Surely even his pride cannot be too hurt if he has options by which he can begin his happiness with Jane now rather than waiting for two years."

The latter was exactly the option Mr. Darcy had suggested. Elizabeth smiled. "I think, perhaps, that it would be less wounding to your brother's pride that you offer him and Jane a place to live rather than an allowance of any kind. He would still be benefiting from your inheritance, but it will be less obvious than if you simply offered him money."

"That is a very good point. I really do not want to offend James with offering any help at all," Catherine said then.

"When did you have it in mind to speak to him?"

Catherine bit her lip as she appeared to consider the question. "Well, having seen so much of his fondness for Jane these last few days, I thought perhaps tomorrow? Or should I wait until Saturday — perhaps I should wait until he has made his offer?"

"Given your brother's circumstances, and the fact that a two-year wait is what led to his former love's infidelity," Elizabeth began, "I do not think waiting until he makes an offer is the right course. Given his unfortunate failure with Miss Thorpe, he may be reluctant to speak for fear of rejection." *Or another abandonment*, she added silently, *though if he suspected Jane might leave him for someone richer, then he is a fool. After all, she has someone richer in waiting even now, and she didn't choose him.*

Her visitor began to nod. "Yes. Yes, you are right. James may not act at all for fear that he will get his heart broken again. Very well, I shall speak to him tomorrow."

Catherine stood then, and stepped forward to bend and embrace Elizabeth. "Thank you for listening, dear Lizzy. Somehow, I just knew you'd help me figure it all out."

Elizabeth laughed as she was released. "Thank you for that, Cathy, though I am hardly an expert in matters of the heart. I only know what I would do if our situations were reversed."

"Indeed, it is knowing that you love your sisters as I love my siblings that compelled me to seek your advice," Catherine replied. She then grinned and planted her hands on her hips. "Now that we have James and Jane all but settled, we must work on you."

Another peal of laughter escaped Elizabeth. "Me? My dear friend, whatever do you mean?"

Catherine sat again and leaned toward her with an eager

expression. "Why, you and Mr. Darcy, of course! Has he not called here every day?"

Elizabeth chuckled and shook her head. "Cathy, Mr. Darcy has escorted his sister to Longbourn that she may visit with us. He hardly comes here to see me."

"But he always seeks you out almost immediately upon arrival!"

"And how would you know that when you have spent the chief part of every morning with James in his sickroom?"

"Kitty said so," Catherine replied simply.

"Kitty sees only what she wants to see," Elizabeth retorted. "I am sure she is mistaken and that Mr. Darcy seeks only stimulating conversation when he is here, which he sadly will not find conversing with my younger sisters."

Catherine shook her head as she once again stood, a smile on her face as she said, "Oh, Lizzy, how can you be so bright and yet so dull at the same time?"

Following her statement with a cheerful goodnight and a wave, Catherine departed. Alone again, Elizabeth did not immediately go to her bed—instead, she remained in the chair by the fire, staring into the flames and mulling over the last few days. Darcy *had* almost immediately sought her company on each visit with Georgiana, but surely it was only because he enjoyed their conversations as much as she did.

But what if he does *feel something for you, Lizzy?* her inner voice asked. *What then?*

What then indeed.

Chapter Nine

Much to Mrs. Bennet's delight, James Morland was well enough to leave Longbourn and return to Netherfield on Saturday, as Mr. Jones had predicted.

As soon as Mrs. Allen's carriage carried him and Catherine away, Mrs. Bennet immediately pressed upon Jane the importance of paying a call to Netherfield as soon as propriety allowed. Her pretense would be to renew the acquaintance of Mr. Bingley's sisters, but the primary purpose of the visit would be to see their brother.

"You must be sure to make clear to Mr. Bingley that no attachment to that Mr. Morland has been formed during his unfortunate stay here," said the lady to her daughter.

Jane had colored deeply and Mr. Bennet had smiled a sly smile, and Elizabeth wondered if perhaps Mr. Morland had already asked his permission to seek her sister's hand in marriage. She wondered if Jane had accepted, and if Mr. Nelson would read the first of the banns at church the next day. It would certainly be like her father to say nothing and allow her mother to be surprised along with everyone else, though Elizabeth dreaded the chance of her making a scene.

Later that afternoon, Mr. Bennet actually left Longbourn—which he did so rarely—and rode his horse into the village. Elizabeth's suspicions about an offer being made were aroused again when, upon his return, her father summoned Jane to his bookroom. A moment after her sister emerged, she followed her into the garden.

"Jane?"

Her sister started and turned to her. "Lizzy! I... I did not hear you come out."

"I could see that your mind was in the clouds," Elizabeth observed. "Will you not share with me those thoughts? We have spoken so little this week, what with having guests in the house."

Jane stared at her a moment, her cheeks growing rosy, and then she simply nodded. Elizabeth stepped up beside her and linked their arms together as they had so often done, and the two began a slow, leisurely stroll. It was a few minutes, however, before her sister spoke.

"By now, I think, you must suspect the cause of my distraction," Jane said slowly.

"Is it Mr. Morland?"

Jane nodded. "Lizzy, I... I know you are aware, as is everyone, that both he and Mr. Bingley have expressed their admiration for me."

Elizabeth smiled. "I am aware, dearest, and feel that you have born their attentions very well."

Her sister scoffed softly. "And I am aware, believe it or not, that there are those who think I do not show enough of how I feel. It is only that I have felt I should not seem too eager to receive such attentions, especially from more than one gentleman, and that I needed to be sure of how *I* felt about each of them before being more openly expressive."

"You've no need to justify your behavior to me, I assure you," said Elizabeth. "I find no fault in such modest behavior—you've conducted yourself in a most ladylike fashion."

"Thank you for that, Lizzy," said Jane, looking to her briefly with a smile. "However, I know that the whole town is eagerly anticipating the revelation of my choice of suitors."

Elizabeth chuckled. "That they are—your dilemma has been the most exciting thing to happen in our little neighborhood for some years."

"I would be pleased to have made sport for our neighbors to laugh at had it not been so truly difficult for me to understand my heart's desire," said Jane in a tone that did completely away with Elizabeth's amusement.

"Forgive me, dearest," said she earnestly.

Jane dismissed her apology with a brief smile in her direction before she faced ahead again and sighed. "Mr. Bingley and Mr. Morland are both of them handsome and charming, and they are each of them blessed with such happy manners they are sure of being liked wherever they go. Though I have been courted in some manner before, never have I been so pointedly pursued, and though the attention has been flattering, it has also been overwhelming. Honestly, Lizzy, I did not know what to do!"

"I am sorry for your struggle, and for my part in making light of it," Elizabeth said. "As I have never been in your situation, I cannot say I know how you feel or that I would not be as overwhelmed."

She tilted her head and studied her sister for a moment. "Have... have you decided between them, or do you still struggle?"

Jane took a few more steps, then suddenly stopped and drew both hands to her face. Her shoulders shook and she made a noise which Elizabeth feared meant she was sobbing, but as she was slipping her arms around her sister, Jane turned to look at her with a tearful smile.

"Mr. Morland has asked for my hand in marriage, and Papa has given his consent to the match," said she as tears fell and a smile bloomed.

"That you smile makes me think you happy to receive his proposal, but your tears betray sadness, Jane," Elizabeth observed softly. "Why do you cry? Did you refuse him? Do you prefer Mr. Bingley?"

At last, Jane laughed a little, then sniffled and said, "I am happy, Lizzy, and I do care for Mr. Morland very much. My tears are of joy, for I shall soon be married; Catherine has invited us to live with her at Fullerton until James can take orders, and I think it the only reason our father gave his consent. But they are also of sadness. Mamma will be so disappointed, and Mr. Bingley as well, and I so dislike to be disappointing anyone!"

Now Elizabeth embraced her sister. "Oh, dearest Jane... How very *you* that you should be thinking of others on what should be one of the happiest days of your life," she said. "Your kindness and your affectionate heart—the sweetness of your disposition—are the very reasons, I do not doubt, that both Mr. Morland and Mr. Bingley have fallen violently in love with you. Now, if Mr. Bingley is truly the gentleman we think him to be, he will gracefully accept that your choice was not him, and he will wish you well."

"Oh, I do hope so, Lizzy. Mr. Morland told me after Papa had consented to our match that he would be speaking to Mr. Bingley in private about it. His hope was as yours, that his gentlemanly nature would not allow for bitterness."

"Mr. Darcy also told me that he believed his friend would bow out gracefully," Elizabeth mused. "Let us all hope that we are right."

The sisters started walking again, and Elizabeth went on with, "As for our dear mother... While she will indeed be disappointed that you did not choose Mr. Bingley's five thousand a year, I have little doubt that she will console herself with being the first of her friends to have a daughter well married. And really, Mr. Morland's prospects are not so very bleak, are they? In two years he will take orders and have eight hundred a year."

"Speaking of his being a clergyman," said Jane, "I wonder if I should spend the next two years actively pursuing some useful skill or other?"

"Jane, whatever do you mean? You already have many useful skills!" cried Elizabeth.

"Yes, I can sew tolerably well and follow a pattern, but... should not a clergyman's wife be able to do more? As I understand it, I will share almost equal responsibility for seeing to the needs of our parishioners."

"Your greatest asset, Jane, will be your generous, affectionate heart."

Jane smiled. "You have spoken of my affectionate heart already, and I am flattered you think of me so sweetly, sister. Still, I feel as though I should be able to... I don't know... Cook, or play the piano. Weave baskets, maybe?"

Elizabeth laughed. "Oh, Jane! If you are truly troubled you have not more accomplishments, then yes, use these two years until your husband has his parish to learn more. Apply yourself as you have never done before, and you will make him and our family proud."

Beside her, Jane now smiled and blushed prettily. "My husband..." she murmured. "Oh, Lizzy, how truly happy I am! When he asked for my hand this morning, James — that is, Mr. Morland — he told me he loves me. That his heart was so broken over his disappointment earlier this year that he did not think himself even capable of loving again, but that meeting me made him realize that not only *could* he love again, but that he *did*. That I made him feel so strongly almost from the first moment of meeting me is why he courted me so openly in spite of the competition of Mr. Bingley and his fortune."

"And your loving him in return is proof enough to my future brother that even a poor clergyman's son has a chance with the likes of Mr. Darcy and Mr. Bingley around," Elizabeth said. She then drew a breath and sighed. "I suppose the reason we've not yet heard Mamma's lamentations and exultations is Papa's doing. He went out this morning —"

Jane groaned softly. "Yes, to speak to Mr. Nelson about having the first of the banns read tomorrow. He told me before Mr. Morland and Catherine even left this morning to say nothing to Mamma, as he wishes to surprise her."

Elizabeth scoffed. "Papa and his foolish schemes… He finds it all very amusing to surprise our mother with such tricks, but I so wish he would take into consideration how wrong it is to treat her so! And further, I wish he would consider the risks."

"What risks, Lizzy?" Jane asked.

"Consider of whom I speak, Jane," Elizabeth replied. "At risk of sounding unkind, our mother—though she is two-and-forty—sometimes still behaves as an immature girl of Lydia's age. You know very well how much she thinks herself nervous, and how she reacts to surprises. That Papa means her to be informed of your engagement at the same time as everyone else is… Well, it is almost cruel of him! And her reaction will no doubt be overly dramatic and expose all of us to ridicule."

Jane was silent for a moment, then said, "Yes, I see what you mean. Do you think… Do you think that I ought to tell her? I would be breaking my promise to Papa, and I certainly would not like him to be angry at me for doing so, but neither would I wish public embarrassment on our family."

"I cannot tell you what to do, Jane, only what I would wish. But so you'll not be unduly influenced by me, I will only say that you ought let your conscience be your guide."

Jane nodded. "Yes. Yes, you are right, Lizzy. I must consider all the implications and do what I think is right."

Elizabeth slipped her arm about Jane's waist again and gave her sister an affectionate squeeze. "And I am sure you will. Now, let us talk wedding clothes…"

Later that day, as the family were all upstairs dressing for dinner, Elizabeth opened her door in time to see Jane entering their mother's room. Sure she knew what Jane had gone in to see her about, she said a silent prayer that Mrs. Bennet would not become hysterical. A part of her longed to be present for the conversation, but she understood that it was Jane's business and not her own.

That she heard little more than a single sharp squeal as she descended the stairs told Elizabeth that Jane had managed to exert at least some control over her mother's reaction—or perhaps Mrs. Bennet had simply been too incensed by her husband's desired outcome of tomorrow's events to be disappointed in Jane's choice of suitors. Whatever the case, when the two appeared in the drawing room some minutes later, she saw that her mother held her head high and her back stiff. She was angry, no doubt, but a look at Jane told her that it was not her daughter with whom the lady was displeased.

For that, Elizabeth said a silent prayer of thanks. It would certainly be one less burden for her sister to carry.

Throughout dinner Mrs. Bennet behaved as she ever did, chattering more with Lydia and Kitty than anyone else, and when Mr. Morland and his sister appeared with Mrs. Allen the next morning outside Longbourn church, she greeted the small party politely and inquired as to their hosts; Mrs. Allen informed them that Bingley, his family, and the Darcys had elected to attend services in Meryton. And when the first of the banns were read by Mr. Nelson, it was Mrs. Allen who emitted a muted screech of surprise. Mrs. Bennet merely preened and smiled.

Mr. Bennet was, to Elizabeth's discerning eye, rather disappointed that she did not react as he had expected her to. No doubt he suspected Jane of betraying the confidence he had demanded—indeed, he looked past his wife to his eldest daughter with one eyebrow raised. Jane colored, but pointedly turned her gaze toward her betrothed and smiled. Elizabeth knew her father would likely confront her later, though she hoped it would be in private so as not to cause Jane any further distress. Breaking her word to their father had surely caused her enough grief already.

After the service was over, Jane stood beside her mother with her hand on Mr. Morland's arm, accepting the congratulations and best wishes of their neighbors. More than one—Lady Lucas first among them—made a point of saying they were sure Jane would have chosen Mr. Bingley, "who has five thousand a year." Jane had looked to James and smiled, then politely replied to every person who brought it up that "Eight hundred a year, and very likely more, will be enough for me."

As she waited with her sisters, Catherine, and Mrs. Allen for the parade of well-wishers to end that they could all get home for breakfast, Elizabeth felt a tug on her arm and looked to a smiling Catherine, who leaned close and whispered, "James had a long talk with Mr. Bingley in his study yesterday. He told me that Mr. Bingley said he rather expected this would happen, and that he offered both sincere congratulations and best wishes for their happiness."

Elizabeth smiled. "I am glad to hear it."

"I believe he also means to call on your family tomorrow to offer his felicitations in person, to show there are no hard feelings,"

Catherine added.

"And we should be most happy to receive him," said Elizabeth, and then a glance at her father made her think of another. "Catherine, what of your parents? I know, of course, that your brother is of age and does not require your father's permission to marry, but I should think he would have at least sought their blessing."

Here, her friend's smile faltered a little and she sighed. "He intends to go to them tomorrow to tell them of his plans—I am to go with him that they will be assured of my pledge to aide him and Jane, and I believe we shall return on Wednesday or Thursday."

Catherine colored a little before adding, "He goes to them *after* securing your father's permission rather than before because he feared our parents would try to talk him out of it; 'tis also why I am to accompany him, to assure them of my assistance as well as confirm that Jane is *nothing* like Isabella Thorpe."

Elizabeth snorted. "I should think not!" she cried in muted indignance. "After all, my sister had the chance of marrying a man of five thousand a year, and she chose your brother. Her loyalty to those she cares for has always been absolute."

"I do not doubt you, Elizabeth," Catherine assured her. "I do not doubt you at all."

໑๏๑

The following morning, the Morlands and Mrs. Allen paid a brief call to say their farewells, with Mr. Morland pledging again and again to return to Jane. For the remainder of the hours before breakfast, Elizabeth remained near to her sister, having seen a hint of melancholy in her countenance though she was certain of her betrothed's return. Mr. Bingley also called as Catherine had said he would, with Darcy and Georgiana at his side, and offered his congratulations to Jane. She blushed and smiled, and thanked him for the kindness, though offered her apologies for any torment he would suffer as a result of her choosing another. Bingley assured her that while he could not say he was not disappointed, he genuinely wished her and Morland every happiness in the world, and hoped she would always think of him as a friend.

Elizabeth tried not to be disappointed in having no chance to speak privately to Darcy. He had greeted her, and offered the barest hint of a smile early in the visit, but the majority of his attention was on his friend and the conversation between Bingley and her sister.

When they were gone, she told herself it was just as well. A gentleman of Darcy's stature had to be careful how much attention he paid to a lady, lest he be accused of giving her false hope. And she was an intelligent, rational creature — she enjoyed their conversations but held no hope of more.

When breakfast came around, all the family were surprised by an announcement from Mr. Bennet: Mr. Collins, the cousin to whom Longbourn would eventually pass, was to visit them — and he would arrive that very day. He had written quite a long letter to Mr. Bennet, in which he lamented his not having written before his father's passing, and gave his assurances he had hopes of healing the breach between their families. He also spoke of his desire to make "every possible amends" to his cousins for his being the means of injuring them by inheriting Longbourn.

Elizabeth was struck by his pomposity, and asked her father if he imagined Mr. Collins to be a sensible man. Mr. Bennet answered that he rather hoped for "quite the reverse" and observed that there was "a mixture of servility and self-importance in his letter, which promises well. I am impatient to see him."

Mr. Collins was prompt in his arrival at four that afternoon, and was welcomed with all due politeness by the whole of the family. Mr. Bennet was content to be silent and observe his cousin's interactions with the rest of the family, who were ready enough to talk; Mr. Collins was likewise of no inclination to be silent himself. Elizabeth had noted that he was tall and heavy-looking, that his air was grave and stately, and his manners very formal. She found it difficult not to roll her eyes when he complimented her mother on the "fine family of daughters" she had been blessed with, as well as his certainty that she would soon see them all well-disposed of in marriage.

He and Mrs. Bennet then exchanged a short discourse regarding the entail, before Mr. Collins said something that gave Elizabeth pause:

"But I can assure the young ladies that I come prepared to admire them. At present I will not say more; but, perhaps, when we are better acquainted —"

There was only one thing he could possibly mean by his having come prepared to admire them, and with Jane already engaged, her mother was sure to direct his attention her way. Already Elizabeth knew that she and Mr. Collins would never suit — he was much too ridiculous! All his praising of his patroness, Lady Catherine de Bourgh, throughout dinner... She had already been struck by his deference to her in his letter, but oh! The way he spoke of her "affability and condescension" made her think he thought more highly of the lady than he did of the God he had vowed to serve.

She was reminded of her supposition regarding his means of making amends when he said to her father that Lady Catherine had advised him to marry as soon as he possibly could, provided he chose with discretion. The dread of being tied to such man made her shudder. Mr. Collins was not sensible at all, and the deficiency of nature had been little assisted by education or society; the greatest part of his life having been spent under the guidance of an illiterate and miserly father. Though he belonged to one of the universities, he had merely kept the necessary terms and had not formed any useful acquaintance there. The subjection in which his father had brought him up had given him originally great humility of manner; but it was now a good deal counteracted by the self-conceit of a weak head, living in retirement, and the consequential feelings of early and unexpected prosperity.

He was kind, yes, and his situation in life respectable, but Elizabeth could not imagine herself ever being happy with such a man as Mr. Collins.

After breakfast the following morning, all the sisters but Mary were to walk into Meryton—and much to Elizabeth's dismay, Mr. Collins was to attend them. She quickly learned that it was her father's wish, that he might have some measure of peace and privacy, for Collins had followed Mr. Bennet to his library immediately after their meal and talked of little else than his house and garden at Hunsford. She would, therefore, be forced to endure his company.

His discourse for the entire distance was little more than pompous nothings, and he seemed oblivious to the fact that the civil replies of his cousins were both indifferent and disinterested. Elizabeth, on turning down the main street with her sisters, was therefore greatly relieved to see Georgiana Darcy climbing out of a carriage some way ahead with her companion, Mrs. Annesley.

Turning to her cousin, she said, "My good sir, pray excuse me for a moment. I see before us a dear friend, and have a great desire to meet with her."

Elizabeth gave him no time to beg that she remain, hurrying away as quickly as politely could be done. She greeted Miss Darcy warmly, then said, "I do not recall if I had chance to ask you yesterday: how do you do at Netherfield without Miss Morland for company?"

Georgiana rolled her eyes, but smiled. "With dear Mrs. Annesley here," she began, gesturing to the older lady beside her, "I do quite well. Not that Mrs. Hurst and Miss Bingley are not good company, of course. But I do prefer Catherine and her brother, and dear Mrs. Allen. Oh, and you and your sisters, of course!"

Elizabeth smiled. "I prefer your company over that of Mr. Bingley's sisters as well, though *his* I shall always welcome."

"Are you in Meryton all alone, Elizabeth?" Georgiana asked then.

"Oh, no indeed. I have come with my sisters," she replied. "Our cousin Mr. Collins, who came to stay with us yesterday, walked with us."

"Capital! I should like to see them as well, and perhaps be introduced to your cousin."

Elizabeth had the mean thought that the younger lady could well do without meeting Mr. Collins, but refrained from expressing her distaste for the gentleman aloud. They had moved away from the carriage by then and Georgiana was casting her eyes about, and Elizabeth was quite surprised a moment later to see a look of great alarm overtake her features. Her young friend colored deeply and gasped, then began to breathe in rapid, shallow pants. She also began to noticeably tremble, and Elizabeth reached out a hand to her even as Mrs. Annesley slipped an arm about her shoulders.

"My dear Miss Darcy, whatever is the matter?"

"I... I cannot stay here. I cannot! I must go, I must go!" Georgiana cried, before she turned and hurried back to the carriage from which she had only moments ago climbed out.

"Do excuse us, Miss Bennet," said Mrs. Annesley as she made to follow her charge.

The concern on the lady's face and the distress on Georgiana's had Elizabeth hurrying after them climbing into the carriage as well. She simply could not take leave of her without discovering the cause of her young friend's torment.

Georgiana was now crying, her faced turned toward the door that faced the street, but when Elizabeth so quickly followed her companion, she sniffed and looked over. "Elizabeth, what are you doing? Your sisters—"

"My sisters will do very well without me, I assure you," Elizabeth said. "I could not bear to see you so overcome without knowing why. Will you not share it with me? Can I do nothing to bring you any relief?"

Georgiana looked to Mrs. Annesley, then to Elizabeth. "I... I can only tell you if you give me your word not to speak of it to a single creature—not even your sisters must know of my shame."

Elizabeth frowned. Her shame? she wondered. Now she knew that she *must* know all, and consented with a nod.

"Then let us be gone back to Netherfield," Georgiana said, and Mrs. Annesley knocked on the roof of the carriage.

As it began to move, Elizabeth glanced out of the window on the opposite side of the carriage. Though she had spoken to Mr. Collins of going to meet a friend, she could not simply disappear without some acknowledgement to her sisters, whom she now saw standing together with Mr. Denny, the officer Lydia had desired especially to see, and a rather handsome young man who appeared to be a gentleman. Propriety said she could not call out to them, but it did not prevent her sliding across the seat and waving to Jane as they passed. Her sister, she was sure, would recognize the carriage and know to where she was headed.

They were on the road out of the village before Georgiana deigned to speak, and in halting sentences told her of the wicked intentions of one Mr. Wickham.

Chapter Ten

Darcy was pleased to be enjoying a quiet moment to himself.

Bingley was in a meeting with the steward, his sisters and Hurst had followed Mrs. Allen's example and taken a day trip to London, the Morlands and Mrs. Allen would not return until the following evening or Thursday morning, and Georgiana had gone into Meryton with Mrs. Annesley.

He had sighed with pleasure when he sat back in a comfortable armchair by a window in the library with a favorite book.

Darcy was therefore rather surprised to hear a carriage approaching not half an hour later. Glancing out the window, he saw that it was his own, and wondering if perhaps Georgiana had forgotten something, he went into the hall to meet her. He was surprised again when his sister all but threw herself into his arms, sobbing, as well as to see that Elizabeth Bennet accompanied her and her companion.

"Whatever has happened?" he asked with concern as he wrapped his arms about Georgiana's slim shoulders.

Mrs. Annesley and Elizabeth glanced at one another, then the latter said, "Miss Darcy believes she saw a gentleman in the village with whom she says she dared not meet."

"It was Wickham!" Georgiana cried as she stood back and wiped at her eyes. "He is here, in Meryton! Why is he here, Fitzwilliam? Has he somehow followed us?"

"I do not know," Darcy replied, just barely keeping anger from his voice. "I cannot imagine he would, after our last meeting."

He then looked to Elizabeth, noted her countenance was full of concern and her gaze settled on his sister. "What was Wickham

86

doing when you saw him?"

Elizabeth blinked and looked up. "I... I cannot be sure. I only saw him as the carriage passed. He was standing with a militia officer of my family's acquaintance talking to my sisters and our cousin, Mr. Collins."

Darcy snorted. The militia—no doubt Wickham was in dire straits again and looking for easy employment to pay his way. Well, he would see to it that Colonel Forster was made aware of his old friend's proclivity for accruing debts he could not pay, though he had no idea how he would prevent the sure ruination of any number of young ladies in Meryton.

Theodore, he thought suddenly. Yes, indeed—his cousin could be of great service to him. Perhaps hearing the truth about his newest recruit, if indeed it was Wickham's intention to join the militia, would give Colonel Forster pause if he heard about his wretchedness from a fellow officer. He would send an express directly, but first...

"Mrs. Annesley, be so kind as to take Georgiana to her room, that she may refresh herself and rest."

Mrs. Annesley nodded. "Of course, Mr. Darcy. Come dearest," said she as she moved to slip an arm about her charge's shoulders.

Georgiana allowed herself to be led away, though she paused at the stair to bid a sniffly farewell to Elizabeth; in turn, Elizabeth wished her well. When the two were up the stairs and out of sight, Darcy looked to Elizabeth with a scrutinizing gaze and said, "Will you join me in the library, madam? I must speak with you regarding what happened."

"Of course, Mr. Darcy," she agreed with a nod.

Darcy turned and led the way, and being sure to leave the door open, moved across the room to the chair he had occupied before, though he did not sit. Nor did he speak until Elizabeth stood beside him.

"Doubtless my sister has told you the whole of our history with Mr. Wickham," he said.

"I could not say if it is the whole or no," she replied. "However, she did speak of their encounter in Ramsgate only this summer."

Darcy grimaced, and then proceeded to fill her in on the history of his family's connection with George Wickham. He was the son of his late father's steward, a year younger than himself, and in their youth they had played together. The elder Mr. Darcy's generosity had seen to it that Wickham was provided a gentleman's education, a generosity which was repaid in later years with gambling debts, drinking, and unspeakable behavior with women.

"All of this he carefully concealed from my father, of course, as well as his own, but I came to see him for what he really was," Darcy said with a sneer. "My father was so taken in by his charms, his appearance of goodness, that he left Wickham a legacy of one thousand pounds in his will. He had also made it known his hope that Wickham would make the church his profession, and told me of his desire that a valuable living in our patronage might be given over to Wickham when he was of age to take it."

"I assume you did not give it to him!" said Elizabeth. "With the picture you paint, such a man most definitely ought *not* be a clergyman."

Darcy looked to her with a wry smile. "Indeed, I did not. In fact, Wickham told me himself that he had no intention of taking orders, and asked that I grant him the value of the living instead. With a further three thousand pounds in his possession, he left Pemberley and we heard nothing from him for three years. It seemed, and I honestly thought it rightly so, that all acquaintance between us had been severed."

He went on to detail the first encounter with Wickham since their parting, by letter, when he had written two years ago to ask that he should grant him the living after all—and just at the time it was vacant. Darcy had naturally refused, citing his reasons why, and said that Wickham's response was full of such vitriol and strong language as could not be repeated. He talked of taking his sister from school that spring and setting her up at the family's house in London with a companion.

"In Mrs. Younge we were most unhappily deceived," Darcy said. "At Ramsgate—where she and my sister had gone for a holiday— after all was said and done and Wickham was gone, I learned of their prior acquaintance. She is apparently a relation of his by marriage."

"So his sudden reappearance in your sister's life after being out of it for some five years was undoubtedly by design," Elizabeth observed.

"Yes, and had I not decided to join her in Ramsgate a day earlier than planned, I should not have prevented the elopement," he groused. "Together they managed to persuade Georgiana that she was in love, so you can surely imagine her devastation when I revealed that only her fortune was his object, as well as some measure of revenge on me."

"What a wicked creature," said Elizabeth. "How can one man be so…so wretched?"

"By choice," Darcy replied immediately. "Like any man, he could achieve the riches he covets if only he applied himself more diligently. But Wickham's tastes are not what they should be, and he has inherited his mother's habits of extravagance."

He turned to face her more fully then, and crossed his arms as he said, "Miss Elizabeth, you now possess knowledge which could bring ruin to my sister—"

Her expression was at once indignant. "Mr. Darcy, I should think you know me well enough by now that you know I would never speak of such things! I have given Georgiana my word!"

"Will you give it also to me?" Darcy asked. "I beg your pardon, madam, that I must ask it of you, but so much damage has already been done to her impressionable mind. I could not bear it if gossip should ruin her chances of a respectable marriage."

Elizabeth's eyebrows lifted archly, and she fisted her hands on her hips. "As I said, *sir*, you ought know me well enough to know that I would never speak of a matter told to me in confidence, especially when my word has been given. That I have promised silence to your sister quite naturally means it is already promised to you by association and you have no need to ask that I do so again."

Darcy sighed and reached to pinch the bridge of his nose; he hadn't meant to anger her. "Please understand, Elizabeth," he said, "that I mean no offense to you, nor do I question your integrity."

"Were you not questioning my integrity, Mr. Darcy, you would not ask me to make a second promise of silence," she snapped in reply, and he looked up at the same moment she threw her hands up in the air in frustration, then spun about to walk away.

Her parting words stunned him to the core. At the door Elizabeth turned back, her gaze haughty, and said, "How Catherine can possibly believe that you admire me is beyond my comprehension—I can only imagine the poor girl's disappointment when I tell her that you most assuredly do not."

With that, she spun about and very quickly departed. Darcy stared after her, too shocked by her confession to have command of his feet. Catherine Morland was far more observant than he had given the girl credit for, if she had seen what he could hardly admit to himself.

But what was he to do now? Surely Elizabeth's reaction to the request he had made was evidence that he had been right to attempt concealment of his growing regard. She'd overreacted and stormed off rather than remaining and rationally discussing the matter.

Well, Darcy, you did insult her integrity, said his inner voice. *Is one promise given really not enough for you?*

Elizabeth had always been kind to Georgiana. Attentive. The exuberance of Catherine Morland and the wit of the second Miss Bennet had done precisely what he had hoped and drawn his sister out of the melancholy that had consumed her since Ramsgate. She was still reticent in the presence of Bingley's sisters, and some of the neighborhood parents such as Mrs. Bennet (she had confessed one night that the lady had an "exuberant" personality), but she had been more lively since coming to Netherfield than she had been in months.

He was also forced to admit that though he had often observed Elizabeth talking and laughing with her sisters, with Georgiana and Catherine, and her friend Charlotte, he had never heard her name spoken as being among the local gossips. The two youngest Bennet girls and far too many of the Meryton mothers had taken that post upon themselves. Elizabeth was more of a quiet observer of those around her, and if she did speak of what she saw it was all done behind closed doors.

Darcy dragged a hand over his face and sighed. He would have to apologize and let her know that of course, he trusted her to keep Georgiana's secret. They were, if memory served, engaged to dine at Longbourn on Thursday evening, to celebrate James Morland's return and his engagement to Jane Bennet. Bingley had been reluctant to accept the invitation when it had been issued by Mrs. Bennet during their call the day before, but Elizabeth had leaned close and spoken to him words Darcy had not heard. Bingley had then looked to her and smiled, nodded, and then happily accepted the invitation on behalf of himself and his sisters.

When he had asked Charles in private later that day what Elizabeth had said that made him agree, he'd replied, "She told me I should do it for Jane—for Miss Bennet. Though she has chosen Morland, she apparently frets over having disappointed me. That is… it is really very generous of her. And Miss Elizabeth is right, after all—she also reminded me that I should show my support of the match publicly to keep the gossip that I am a spurned lover to a minimum. And really, Darcy, I am truly happy that Miss Bennet is happy in her choice. I've no ill feelings towards her whatsoever."

"And towards Morland?" Darcy had asked him.

Bingley had laughed before replying, "Well, the gentleman is a visitor in my house, I can hardly display open hostility towards him.

And truth be told, I'm not even really angry. Just a little envious. Makes me wonder what it is he has that I haven't got."

Darcy had then proposed that the only real difference between his friend and James Morland was fortune, so it was all up to chance as to which of them Jane Bennet would choose. Bingley had agreed and declared his determination to put his affection for Miss Bennet in the past, where it belonged.

The dinner party was likely the first chance, Darcy knew, that he would have to speak to Elizabeth. Though because it was to be a party, he began to hope against hope that Wickham would *not* be invited — Mrs. Bennet took delight in entertaining officers at Longbourn, and if his nemesis had indeed come to join the local militia, his inclusion in the party was a possibility.

If only he could somehow make it known to Wickham that he would be there. Then the libertine would be sure to stay away. Or perhaps he should simply pack up his sister and return with her to London or Pemberley.

No! his inner voice cried immediately after the thought had occurred to him. *Do not let that wretch run you out of the neighborhood with his mere presence.*

Darcy snorted at his own thoughts. No, indeed. While he naturally desired to protect Georgiana's sensibilities more than he wished to avoid Wickham himself — and of course he wished that as well — it would send the wrong message to Wickham if he and his sister simply left. So no, they would stay. At least until he had consulted with Theodore on what was to be done.

With that in mind, he hurried over to a writing desk across the room and sat down to pen a letter. When he finished, he sent it off with his valet to have it posted express.

Georgiana stayed in her room much of the evening and came down only for dinner. She looked as withdrawn and subdued as she had when Wickham's duplicity had been revealed to her, and it did not go unnoticed by their host. Bingley gently inquired as to her health, with Georgiana replying that she was not feeling quite herself.

"I am sorry to hear it, but I do hope your ill-feeling does not last long," Bingley said, his expression full of sympathy.

"Miss Morland, her brother, and your aunt are due to return tomorrow evening or Thursday morning," Darcy observed. "And your sisters and Hurst due to return tomorrow. Surely the restoration of our full party will bring my sister cheer."

To his surprise, Georgiana's countenance brightened a little as he said this. "I do indeed look forward to having Catherine's company again," she agreed. "And her brother is very amiable, even if he…"

Her cheeks bloomed and she looked down at her plate as her voice trailed off. Bingley chuckled and said, "Do not distress yourself, my dear Miss Darcy—speak of Mr. Morland and his engagement to Miss Bennet as freely as you please, I am not bitter."

"It is very good of you to be so amiable," Georgiana observed. "I am sure it will ease Miss Bennet's worry of offending you."

"Well, I can't say I'm not disappointed that her heart didn't choose me, but I can hardly call myself a gentleman if I didn't wish the pair of them every happiness in the world," Bingley replied. "She is an angel of a lady and he a truly capital fellow, so I do not doubt I shall recover in time, or that we shall continue to be good friends."

That Bingley was so sanguine was a relief to Darcy; it bespoke of his spirit already being on the mend from his disappointment. Georgiana, though seeming to find it too difficult to look at him, nevertheless smiled and blushed at the attention from his friend.

As he observed their continuing intercourse, an intriguing prospect began to form in his mind; almost immediately, however, he dismissed it. After all, his sister might well form an infatuation for Bingley, but she was fair young yet to be married—she had not even had her debut in society. His friend, in turn, could hardly be expected to wait another year or more for Georgiana to mature further if he were truly of a mind to marry and settle down.

Pushing the thought of a match between Bingley and Georgiana from his mind entirely, Darcy turned his attention to the conversation so that he might join in.

৵৽

The return of the wayward members of the Netherfield party was complete by midday on Thursday. Morland and his sister were in the house not even an hour before they left it again, joined by Georgiana, as the young man was eager to see his betrothed. Mrs. Allen, who was content to remain and rest herself after the long journey from Wiltshire, had no scruple as to informing other residents of the outcome of their visit to the Reverend and Mrs. Morland.

Naturally, given his disappointment earlier that year, they were reluctant to give their blessing to James. The elder Mr. Morland had wondered if his son was acting imprudently—"He thought him on the rebound, I daresay"—but the fervent approbation of both

Catherine and Mrs. Allen herself, attesting to the forthrightness of Jane Bennet's character, at last convinced them. The Morlands were pleased for their son and proud of their daughter for choosing to use her recently acquired fortune to aid her brother, allowing him to marry sooner than he could otherwise.

"Catherine has no objection to sharing Fullerton Manor with James and Miss Bennet, and nor do I," Mrs. Allen told them with a fervent nod of her head. "The more the merrier, I say. The manor really is too large for only two people—I always told my dear Mr. Allen so. And since our Lord did not see fit to bless us with children, we were always having company over or hosting parties."

A lady such as she, Darcy mused, apparently could not bear the stillness of silence. For himself, he did not mind good company on occasion but in truth rather preferred times of peace and quiet that allowed for deep thought and reflection.

At almost the same moment the Morlands and Georgiana returned from their call to Longbourn, a horse and rider came up the lane. On catching sight of him through the library window, Darcy knew at once it was his cousin. The elder man was the second son of his uncle, the Earl of Disley, and had replied to his express with one of his own. There were some duties he could not simply discharge or hand over to another, but believed he could be at Netherfield to help him handle Wickham in only a few days.

He met Fitzwilliam as he was being let into the entry hall. "Theodore!" cried Georgiana as she turned away from handing her pelisse off to a maid. Walking over to him excitedly, she added, "What do you do here, cousin?"

"I am come to see you, of course! And your brother," he replied with a warm smile as he took her hands and bent to kiss her cheek.

Bingley was then coming down the stairs. "What do we have here, Darcy?" he asked.

"Charles, may I present my cousin, The Honorable Colonel Theodore Fitzwilliam," Darcy said. "Theo, this is my good friend Charles Bingley."

The two men bowed to each other, and then the Morlands—who were still in the hall—were introduced. "Forgive my intrusion on your party, Mr. Bingley," said Fitzwilliam genially. "My cousin has written me some once or twice regarding this fine house and the country hereabouts, and as I happened to have some business to tend to in the area, hoped to beg leave to join him here for a few days."

Bingley smiled. "Certainly, Colonel. As my aunt said only this afternoon, the more the merrier! I do love good company."

The group went then into the drawing room, and finding Mrs. Allen, Miss Bingley, and the Hursts there, another round of introductions were made. It was clear to Darcy that Caroline Bingley's interest was piqued on hearing his cousin's honorific. He watched her as she watched Fitzwilliam, who—on hearing that Morland had recently become engaged to a local young lady, and that they were to live with his sister at her new home—laughingly expressed his wish that *he* had a sister with a fortune who wouldn't mind sharing her house with him.

"My brother has a wife and children," he added, "so hardly has room at Rowarth Hall for a bachelor brother. Thus, I am forced by necessity to remain residing with parents who daily decry said bachelor status and harangue me constantly about finding a suitable wife to settle down with."

"I am sure that should be very easy for you, sir," said Miss Morland. "I cannot imagine the son of an earl has a want of money."

"Indeed," spoke up Caroline Bingley in a soft drawl. "Surely the younger son of an earl can know very little of *that*. Come now, dear Colonel, what have *you* ever known of self-denial and dependence? When have you been prevented by want of money from going wherever you chose, or procuring anything you had a fancy for?"

Darcy watched with increasing disbelief as she leaned toward his cousin and batted her eyes at him. *Good heavens*, he thought. *Whilst I am pleased it could mean she leaves me be, I would not wish to subject poor Theo to her attentions.*

"Perhaps, madam, I cannot say that I have experienced many hardships of that nature," Fitzwilliam conceded. "But in matters of greater weight, I *may* suffer from want of money. Younger sons cannot marry where they like."

He then laughed again. "My dear lady," he said next, his attention returning to Miss Morland, "Recall that I am the *second* son. Though my father is extraordinarily wealthy for one in his position, the vast majority of his fortune will go to my brother, who is the heir to the earldom. There are not many in my rank of life who can afford to marry without some attention to money, as our habits of expense make us too dependent on it."

Miss Morland's brow knitted in confusion. "So you will get nothing at all from your father due to order of birth? That hardly seems fair! My father has ten children and means to do what he can for each of us. Surely with only two yours can—"

"Cathy," her brother admonished her softly. "You know it is the way of things that the greatest portion of any man's wealth, if not all, goes to the eldest son. Consider my own situation: I get both a living and the little estate that goes with it, but Father can give nothing to our brothers except a small compensation and moral support in their chosen professions, unless by chance he should acquire another living somewhere."

"Do not despair for me, Miss Morland," said Fitzwilliam. "My father has promised me a sizeable inheritance, but sadly I shall not receive it until I marry. And even then, it would be best that the girl I wed come with a fortune attached, for the amount I shall receive will not sustain us in the lifestyle to which I am accustomed indefinitely."

Miss Morland scoffed and rolled her eyes, though she also smiled as she said, "Rich men and their rich habits. However is a poor girl to get by in this world when the only girl a man likes is a rich one?"

"Oh! But you are hardly poor, now are you, my dear?" offered Mrs. Hurst with a sly expression. "Being all but formally adopted by your good friend Mr. Allen and made heir to his fortune, you are *anything* but poor."

Catherine Morland blushed and looked away even as Mrs. Allen, in her particular naiveté, agreed enthusiastically with Bingley's sister that her young friend was "hardly poor."

"Indeed," said the lady, "our Catherine shall have her choice of suitors. There has been many a young man hereabouts who has paid her attention."

"Only because of the generosity you and dear Mr. Allen have shown me, ma'am," Miss Morland said. "Otherwise I should be nobody."

"It is good, then, that you have your brother here to look after you," observed Fitzwilliam. "I am sure he takes his role as your protector seriously, do you not?"

Morland nodded. "I do indeed, Colonel. I'll not allow my sister — any of my sisters — to be played for a fool."

Nor would I, Darcy mused, his gaze passing over Georgiana as she sat beside Catherine and listened to the conversation.

A few more minutes of being civil passed before he and Fitzwilliam could extricate themselves from the party. On the pretext of catching up on news of his cousin's family, Darcy went with him when the housekeeper — having been given an order by Bingley to prepare another guest room — announced that his room was ready. He waited until they were alone before broaching the subject of

Wickham.

"What do you plan to do?" he asked.

"First, I mean to determine what the blackguard has been up to hereabouts," Fitzwilliam replied. "You know his habits as well as I— it won't take him long to run up debt or ruin some poor shop-keeper's daughter."

Darcy scoffed. "And he's already had two days in which to do it. I also dread to think what rumors he may be spreading about me, for it is almost certain he has heard of my being in the neighborhood. It's bad enough that the locals think me haughty and proud."

Fitzwilliam grinned. "But you *are* haughty and proud, at least among those with whom you are unfamiliar."

His cousin clapped him on the shoulder. "Do not fret, my good man. I shall make it my secondary mission to improve the perception of your character."

Darcy could not help but think of Elizabeth. Could *her* perception of him be altered? And did he have any real wish that it should be?

Chapter Eleven

Jane was not the only one anxious about tonight's dinner party.

Elizabeth knew that her sister was nervous about showing too much affection for her "dear Morland" before Mr. Bingley, though she had told Jane she should not hide her feelings. It had been so wonderful to see Jane so happy these last few days, knowing she would soon be married. That Morland and Catherine had come to call only an hour after their arriving back in Hertfordshire was telling of his own eagerness to be reunited with his future bride. James had brought good news from his parents, which greatly relieved Mrs. Bennet's nerves.

For herself, she was not looking forward to seeing Mr. Darcy... and yet was intensely eager to at the same time. For a second time since their meeting, she'd found herself needing to apologize for her temper, and that made her more than a little uncomfortable.

But oh! What news she would have for him if they could manage to speak rationally... The night before, at a dinner party hosted by her Aunt and Uncle Phillips, she had been at last introduced to the infamous Mr. Wickham. Her sisters had all had nothing but kind things to say of him—Kitty and Lydia especially. He was "so handsome and so charming, and sure to be the best at everything."

Wickham did, admittedly, have a very fine person. His face was pleasing to look at and his smile charming, and he had the most excellent manners. Elizabeth would have claimed him to be one of the most amiable young men of her acquaintance if she did not know him for what he really was. Observing him from across the room at one point in the evening, she had thought to herself how very practiced his amiable character was, and she wondered if he ever found it exhausting to be so false all the time.

Shortly after making that observation, he had approached where she rested on a sofa and asked if he might join her. Elizabeth was not particularly willing to entertain him, but could hardly refuse without giving some reason; after her acquiescence was given, he sat in a chair adjacent to her. She wondered if he would speak of Darcy, if he even knew him to be in the country. Her curiosity as to whether he would mention his history with his former friend was soon satisfied when he began the subject by asking in a light, casual manner as to the distance betwixt Netherfield and Meryton. When she had given her answer he nodded once, then inquired as to how long Darcy and his sister had been staying there.

"About a month," said she, then unable to resist baiting him to see how much further he might take the subject, added, "He is a man of very large property in Derbyshire, I understand."

"Yes," replied Mr. Wickham. "His estate there is a noble one—a clear ten thousand per annum. You could not have met with a person more capable of giving you certain information on that head than myself, for I have been connected with his family in a particular manner from my infancy."

Elizabeth feigned a look of surprise. "From infancy?"

Again Mr. Wickham nodded. His gaze roamed over her countenance before he asked, "Are you much acquainted with Mr. Darcy?"

"As much as I ever wish to be," cried Elizabeth very warmly, her thoughts returning to their argument. "He can be very disagreeable."

"And his sister?"

She could not but be truthful, and said she liked Miss Darcy very much indeed.

Wickham smiled slightly. "I should have known it was she in that coach you rode past in yesterday; I did think the livery of the driver and footman very familiar. Your eldest sister informed us only a moment after it went by that she had just seen you in the Darcy coach and was certain she had glimpsed Miss Darcy as well. I must admit, I was relieved to hear it was Miss Darcy you were with and not her brother, for she is an amiable girl, though he…"

He looked around as he paused, then leaned forward. Elizabeth, sensing he might be about to reveal some confidence, sat likewise. Wickham went on to relate to her a rather different version of the circumstances regarding the living Darcy had told her of. He claimed himself both godson and favorite of old Mr. Darcy, and the object of intense jealousy on behalf of the younger.

"I cannot accuse myself of having really done anything to deserve to lose the living," said Wickham with a sigh. "Though I do have a warm, unguarded temper, and perhaps may have spoken my opinion *of* him, and *to* him, too freely. I can recall nothing worse. But the fact is that we are very different sort of men and he hates me."

Nothing worse indeed, mused Elizabeth, hoping that her expression did not betray her thoughts. *You only lied to an impressionable fifteen-year-old girl and meant to elope with her for her fortune.*

Lest she give away that she saw through his charade—and feeling no small measure of guilt in the doing—she then proceeded to abuse Darcy herself, to the point of accusing him of malicious revenge, injustice, and inhumanity towards Wickham. She spoke of his "abominable pride", to which Wickham replied "It has often led him to be liberal and generous, to give his money freely, to display hospitality, to assist his tenants, and relieve the poor. Family pride, and *filial* pride—for he is very proud of what his father was—have done this. Not to appear to disgrace his family, to degenerate from the popular qualities, or lose the influence of the Pemberley House, is a powerful motive. He has also *brotherly* pride, which, with *some* brotherly affection, makes him a very kind and careful guardian of his sister, and you will hear him generally cried up as the most attentive and best of brothers."

If nothing else he said had been true, Elizabeth knew herself that his last statement *was*. She had often observed Darcy with his sister and had witnessed firsthand their deep fondness for each other. And really, did he not truly care for Georgiana and wish to see her protected, he would not have gone so far as to demand a second promise of confidence.

On realizing this, Elizabeth felt her enmity dissipate. Though she still thought the request unreasonable, she understood the motivation behind it and so could forgive him the asking. Though after having such an epiphany, she'd found it increasingly difficult to join Wickham in speaking ill of Darcy. She began to hope—perhaps for the first time ever—that one of her younger sisters would give her reason to excuse herself, but though Lydia and Kitty laughed and talked a little too loudly, they were somewhat more restrained than was their wont. Elizabeth reasoned it was due to their needing to concentrate on the games they were then playing.

The discourse between herself and Wickham changed direction slightly when suddenly Mr. Collins, who sat to whist with her aunt at the nearest card table, mentioned his patroness, Lady Catherine de Bourgh. This caught Wickham's attention, and he had turned to Elizabeth to ask how intimately her cousin was acquainted with the family. She replied that Lady Catherine had recently given her cousin a living, though she knew not how they had been introduced and believed that he had not known the lady long.

It was then that Wickham revealed something astonishing: Lady Catherine was Mr. Darcy's aunt, and he claimed it generally believed that her daughter and Darcy would unite their great fortunes by marriage. Elizabeth had smiled, thinking of Miss Bingley and her vain attempts to gain Darcy's affections for herself...and was hard-pressed not to allow that smile to falter when she realized that being as good as engaged to his cousin meant he could not possibly be entertaining any thoughts of an attachment to *her*.

Catherine had to be wrong on that score, that was all there was to it.

"Mr. Collins," said she haltingly, "speaks highly both of Lady Catherine and her daughter; but from some particulars that he has related of her ladyship, I suspect his gratitude misleads him, and that in spite of her being his patroness, she is an arrogant, conceited woman."

"I believe her to be both in a great degree," replied Wickham. "I have not seen her for many years, of course, but I remember very well that I never liked her, and that her manners were dictatorial and insolent. She has the reputation of being remarkably sensible and clever; but I rather believe she derives part of her abilities from her rank and fortune, part from her authoritative manner, and the rest from the pride of her nephew, who chooses that everyone connected with him should have an understanding of the first class."

Elizabeth allowed that he had given a very rational account of it, and finding herself now thoroughly uncomfortable with the subject of Darcy and his family, began to wish that supper would soon be announced. In short order it was; cards were at an end at last, giving the rest of the ladies present their share of Mr. Wickham's attentions. Elizabeth was relieved to be free of him but found her mind so occupied with all they had talked of that she hardly said a word throughout the meal. The family's journey home gave her no moment to speak even had she wished to, for neither Lydia nor Mr. Collins were once silent. She had taken to her bed almost immediately on entering the house, feeling the pressure of a headache beginning behind her eyes.

And something akin to heartache beginning beneath her breast.

Now, in mere moments, the whole of the Netherfield party would be arriving to share a family meal. Colonel Forster and a few of his officers were already in the drawing room; thankfully, Wickham was not among them. Lydia, on questioning Mr. Denny as to where his friend was, learnt that Wickham had been ordered to remain behind by their commander.

"Colonel Forster had visitors, you see," Denny replied to her sister's enquiry. "That Mr. Darcy fellow, and a gent in regimentals like our own—I heard tell they were cousins. As it was, not as soon as they'd gone did the colonel call for Wickham to attend him, and when he returned to our tent—none too pleased, I might say—Wickham said he'd been given orders not to leave the camp tonight."

"Poor fellow!" Lydia cried. "How dreadful for him, for we will all have such a time together as we did last night!"

Elizabeth was intrigued by this revelation and wandered away to ponder it. Who was this cousin Darcy had been with, and what could they have said—without revealing the whole truth as regarded Miss Darcy, for surely *that* had not passed her brother's lips—that would lead Colonel Forster to restrict Wickham to the militia's camp?

The Lucases were the next to arrive, and Colonel Forster's attentions were immediately given over to Charlotte. The way her friend blushed and smiled and the way Sir William looked a little too pleased with himself led Elizabeth to begin suspecting that the colonel had settled on her friend for his choice of bride. Oh, how she hoped it were so! Charlotte was the most amiable creature she knew aside from Jane, and though not exactly young—as well as commonly thought to be plain—she was healthy and hardy, and to Elizabeth's mind perfectly suited to being a military man's wife. She had, after all, had the management of her younger siblings for many years, and the youngest Lucas boys could certainly be a rowdy bunch.

When the Netherfield party arrived at last, Bingley and Morland both were quick to offer their sincerest apologies for the lateness of their arrival. "Two horses threw a shoe, if you can believe that!" said Bingley.

"Indeed," said Morland. "One of his *and* one of ours!"

"Well, never mind all that," said Mrs. Bennet. "What's important is that you are here! Jane especially is so very happy to see you, Mr. Morland."

Jane blushed at her mother's words, while her fiancé grinned.

Bingley, much to Elizabeth's relief, did not seem at all distressed by the adoring expressions they favored one another with—either that, or he was more adept at concealing his emotions than he had heretofore led anyone to believe.

Darcy then begged the pardon of Mr. and Mrs. Bennet for adding an unexpected member to the party before he introduced his cousin, Colonel Fitzwilliam. "He came to call most unexpectedly, you see, and as we were engaged to dine with you all, I could not remain behind to entertain him."

"Truth be told, Mrs. Bennet," said Fitzwilliam with a grin, "I cannot stand to be alone in a strange house, so begged leave to join my cousin and his friends. Though we are not yet acquainted, I humbly pray you will grant me leave to join your most excellent company tonight."

Elizabeth bit her lip so as not to laugh at the way her mother blushed and giggled like a young girl, though her father had no such scruples and laughed aloud. "You are most welcome to join us, Colonel Fitzwilliam," said the latter, "though I daresay there may be some confusion should anyone here simply call out 'Colonel!'—you and Forster both will turn your heads!"

The two colonels laughed, as did several of the others. Mrs. Bennet then excused herself to go and check on the preparations for dinner and quit the room, and conversation between the various groups of guests resumed.

"My dear Elizabeth!" said Georgiana as she came up to her, Darcy and Fitzwilliam following a few steps behind. The younger girl leaned close as she took Elizabeth's hands and said, "I am so very *relieved* that a certain person is not in attendance tonight—I do not know that I could have borne it if your mother had invited him!"

Elizabeth smiled at her, and modulated her voice accordingly before replying, "In fact, she did. But I have it on authority from Mr. Denny—that officer my sister Lydia is at present latched onto—that Colonel Forster ordered him to remain at the camp this evening."

"I wonder why? But it does not matter, I am glad he is not here," Georgiana replied.

"It would be our doing, Georgie," said Fitzwilliam. "That ne'er-do-well is the reason I am in Hertfordshire, after all."

Georgiana narrowed her eyes as she gazed between her cousin and her brother. "You said you came to see me and Fitzwilliam."

"I regret that I spoke only a partial truth earlier, dearest, given your friends the Morlands were so close by. Now, will you do me the honor of introducing me to your pretty friend?"

"Oh, of course! Lizzy, may I present my cousin, Colonel Theodore Fitzwilliam. Theodore, Miss Elizabeth Bennet."

Elizabeth curtsied, then regarded the colonel with a discerning eye. "So... You must be the 'gent in regimentals' Denny spoke of."

"I am indeed," Fitzwilliam replied with a grin as he placed his hands behind he back. "And you are the Miss Bennet to whom I also owe gratitude for giving comfort to my cousin when she was so overcome on Tuesday morn."

He glanced sidelong at Darcy and lifted an eyebrow. "You didn't tell me, Darce, that she was so lovely a creature."

Elizabeth was certain Darcy was suppressing a growl when she glanced at him, and tried not to let that suspicion make her happy. Why should he be affected by his cousin's appreciation of her, if he was promised to another cousin?

"I did not consider the lady's beauty a factor in her assistance to Georgiana," he said stiffly.

"Whatever the case may be," said Elizabeth over Fitzwilliam's answering snicker, "I should like you both to know that not only was I happy to comfort her, as Miss Darcy is already a dear friend, but that I shall not speak of what I know to anyone. Miss Darcy's secret is safe with me."

The last she said with a pointed look in Darcy's direction; he acknowledged her offering the promise with an incline of his head.

A commotion across the room then caught Elizabeth's attention. Mr. Collins' expression had brightened on hearing the names Darcy and Fitzwilliam spoken by her parents on their arrival; he was now attempting to move their way, with Mary actively attempting to restrain him.

"But they are near relations of my patroness—oh, how wonderfully these sort of things occur! Who would have thought of my meeting with, perhaps, a nephew of Lady Catherine de Bourgh at such a gathering, let alone two—and her niece, besides! I am most thankful that the discovery is made in time for me to pay my respects to them, which I am now going to do, and trust they will excuse my not having done it before. My total ignorance of the connection must plead my apology."

"You are not going to introduce yourself to Mr. Darcy, his sister, or Colonel Fitzwilliam!" Mary cried.

"Indeed I am. I shall entreat their pardon for not having done so at once. I believe them to be Lady Catherine's *nephews and niece*. It will be in my power to assure them that her ladyship was quite well yesterday se'nnight."

Mary tried hard to dissuade him from such a scheme, assuring him that Mr. Darcy and Colonel Fitzwilliam would consider his addressing them without introduction as an impertinent freedom, rather than a compliment to their aunt; that it was not in the least necessary there should be any notice on either side; and that if it were, it must belong to the gentlemen who were superior in consequence to begin the acquaintance.

Mr. Collins listened to her with the determined air of following his own inclination, and, when she ceased speaking, replied that he believed there to be difference in the forms of ceremony amongst the laity and those which governed the clergy — and to Elizabeth's shock, equated his position as *equal* to the highest rank in the kingdom "provided an appropriate humility of behavior is maintained." He went on to say that he believed introducing himself to their guests to be a point of duty, excused himself for not following her advice, then thoroughly insulted her sister by suggesting that he was more fitted by his education and habits of study to decide on what was right than a young lady like herself.

Elizabeth was filled with angry mortification at such behavior; the subtle changes in the expressions of her companions told her they had likewise heard Mr. Collins' speech. Darcy was vexed, his sister shocked, and the colonel amused. And though she did not much care for her father's cousin, she could not but consider how his unsolicited attentions would reflect on her family, and determined to salvage the situation as best she could.

As he opened his mouth to begin introducing himself, she pretended to just take notice of him and gave him welcome. Collins' eyes widened, then his jaw snapped shut and his brow furrowed in a frown as she proceeded to present him to the Darcys and their cousin. A small part of Elizabeth was gratified to have thwarted his arrogance and self-gratification as she gave their names to him. Mr. Collins recovered quickly and offered his greetings, assured the three "honored guests" that their aunt was "in the best of health" when last he'd seen her, and that her daughter Miss de Bourgh — "Who I understand from my esteemed patroness is to be your bride, Mr. Darcy — "

Darcy's countenance immediately showed how displeased he was with this assumption, and was enough to make Mr. Collins fall silent. "Sir," he said stiffly, "whilst I have, of course, the greatest respect for my aunt and her daughter, I have none for those who bandy about the nonsensical idea of the former that I shall marry the latter. Miss de Bourgh and I are not engaged, nor shall we ever be. I trust that you will not speak of this matter further to anyone."

While Mr. Collins stuttered his apologies and attempted to assure Darcy that he would do as instructed, two thoughts occurred to Elizabeth: One, that he most assuredly *would* speak of it to Lady Catherine herself, either in a letter or when next he saw her. Two, that she herself was more pleased by the revelation that Darcy was not engaged to his cousin than she should be. After all, his not being engaged to Miss de Bourgh did not mean he had any designs of forming a serious attachment to *her*.

Besides, he had such an annoying habit of infuriating her. Being quite handsome and conveniently rich did not abate that unavoidable fact.

When at last the party sat to table, Elizabeth was greatly relieved that the seating was not formal; while her mother often followed the tradition of seating all the men at the hostess's end and all the ladies at the host's end of the table, as the party began to file inside the dining room, she happily said, "There are so many of us gathered together, I shan't presume to tell you all where to sit—please, choose whichever place that you like best!"

Having said that, she did take her usual place at one end while Mr. Bennet sat to the other. It was no surprise to Elizabeth that the couples—both confirmed and not—either sat next to or across from each other. Miss Bingley contrived to sit near to Colonel Fitzwilliam, but he placed himself between James Morland and Darcy; she could not sit next to Darcy as he pulled that chair out for his sister. Though she felt rather silly for behaving in such a manner, Elizabeth took Catherine by the arm and quickly walked around the table to sit, putting Catherine across from the colonel and herself across from Darcy—and much to her relief, Kitty quickly claimed the chair on her left.

As she scooted to the table, Elizabeth glanced up and saw that the corner of Darcy's mouth was lifted in a half grin; he knew what she'd been about, and confirmed this supposition by mouthing the words "thank you". She could not help the answering grin that turned up her own lips.

The dinner was splendid and the company most charming. There was very little else to distress or vex Elizabeth about the evening, and she was in a fair way of being immeasurably pleased. She and Darcy might not be suited to being more than friends, but she was certain they would remain friends even after he eventually left the country, for they conversed as naturally as ever they had before. His cousin she found to be a delight, and if she were not mistaken, his eye bore an appreciative glint for Catherine Morland. Her friend was fascinated by his tales of army life, which Colonel Fitzwilliam had a ready supply of.

She only hoped that the colonel appreciated Catherine equally, for herself and *not* her fortune, as so many of the young men in Meryton did.

Elizabeth was happy indeed, until suddenly Lydia cried out, "Mr. Bingley, you *must* hold a ball at Netherfield!"

Chapter Twelve

"A ball?" said Bingley.

"Indeed!" Lydia replied. "Do not you remember that you talked of having a ball when you first came into Hertfordshire? Kitty, don't you think it would be quite the scandal if he did not keep his word?"

Kitty nodded vigorously. "Oh, I do hope you will hold a ball, Mr. Bingley!"

"Just because one *talks* of holding a ball," drawled Caroline Bingley, "does not mean one will or one must. I am sure that my brother cannot possibly —"

"I should be delighted!" Bingley interrupted her. "Something a little more grand than the monthly assemblies in Meryton would be just the thing!"

"Oh, indeed it would be!" joined in Mrs. Allen. "My dear Caroline, I should be delighted to assist you with the preparations!"

Miss Bingley, seeing she was not to succeed in dissuading the scheme, acquiesced with disdainful civility. Conversation around the table then resumed, the prospect of a ball now the prevailing subject.

"A ball — how delightful!" said Catherine. "Colonel Fitzwilliam, do you dance at all?"

Elizabeth glanced across the table in time to watch the perpetual grin about the colonel's face grow. "Why, of course I know how to dance! Who do you think taught Darcy here everything he knows?"

Darcy scoffed. "My dancing master," he replied. "And my late honored mother."

Fitzwilliam sobered. "I shall concede to the latter, Darcy," said he. "My dearest aunt was indeed a fine dancer, and she taught us both very well."

He then looked back to Catherine, his grin returning. "Dare I presume to solicit your hand, Miss Morland, for the first two dances? We do not know when Bingley's ball shall be held, but I will definitely remain in the country for a time. Long enough to attend this ball, I assure you."

Catherine blushed scarlet, but she smiled and nodded her head. "I should be honored, Colonel. Thank you."

Elizabeth looked to her friend and smiled, happy for her to have already found a charming partner to open the dance with. Out of the corner of her eye, she noted Fitzwilliam jamming his elbow into Darcy's side; his cousin scowled at him, then cleared his throat.

"Miss Elizabeth," he said, and she looked up at him. "Might I have the honor of your hand for the first two dances?"

The first two dances. With Darcy. She would get to dance with him again!

Fighting to curtail her elation, for Elizabeth knew that his asking her was nothing more than a simple request to have an accomplished dancing partner, inclined her head and smiled. "I should be delighted, Mr. Darcy, provided I may be so bold as to suggest Colonel Fitzwilliam as my partner for the second set. After all, however will I know which of you is the better dancer?"

Fitzwilliam guffawed at her comment, and on Darcy's other side Georgiana giggled. Beside Elizabeth, Catherine also laughed. "Lizzy," said her friend between giggles, "do not you recall that James said one cannot tell other people whom they ought to dance with?"

"I do indeed, dear Cathy, and I am certainly not telling the colonel that he *must* dance with me—the choice is certainly his," Elizabeth replied. "But I think I should like to dance with him, if he is so inclined, and does not mind my impertinence in doing the asking. I simply must know if two men in the same family can really be equally accomplished at dancing."

Darcy's expression seemed a mixture of surprise and, if she were not mistaken, jealousy. Lifting an eyebrow, she challenged him silently to respond.

He cleared his throat. "I cannot speak for my cousin's acquiescing to your request; I will, however, warn you that should he grant it, you had best not care too much for your toes or your slippers, for they might both be ruined and you shall not dance again the rest of the evening."

"Oh, now that is throwing down the gauntlet indeed, Darcy!" cried Fitzwilliam. "Miss Bennet, your challenge is most readily accepted. I shall be glad to prove to you which of us my dear Aunt Anne taught best to dance."

"Brother, will I be allowed to attend Mr. Bingley's ball?" asked Georgiana then.

Darcy looked at her. "Of course, dearest. It would hardly be kind of us to hold a ball at Netherfield and force you to remain above stairs. I have but one caveat for you—you may only dance with the gentlemen who reside in the house."

"But what if someone else should ask me while you are all dancing? Theodore is already partnered for the first two sets," Georgiana protested.

"And I am only partnered for the first set, my dear," said her brother with a smile. "I should be delighted to dance the second with you, and I will talk to Bingley and see that he will save you the first."

Fitzwilliam looked around Darcy and added, "I have no wish to disappoint you, Georgie, but as you are not properly out, we must have some oversight as to your partners. Perhaps a compromise, Will? Should another young man wish to dance with your sister, it must be someone you have been introduced to."

"I should like to second that suggestion, if I may," added Elizabeth with a smile in Georgiana's direction. "I could name at least three young men you have met and conversed with, Mr. Darcy—in fact, you played a game of chess against William Lucas when last you attended a party at Lucas Lodge, and he is sure to attend the ball."

Darcy sighed and gave a curt nod. "Very well. If it is a young man with whom I have met and conversed, I will approve him."

"Oh, thank you, brother! I am so very excited to attend my first ball!" Georgiana cheered happily.

"Mrs. Annesley will chaperone you when neither Theo nor I are available," said Darcy. His tone, Elizabeth noted, brooked no argument.

Georgiana did not offer one—it was clear that she was ready to agree to anything just to be allowed to attend and to dance.

Although conversation throughout dinner was hardly lacking, a subject Elizabeth really wished to broach could not be across the dining table; there was too much risk others would overhear. Cards and entertainment were to follow the meal, and it was her hope she might get Darcy alone to backgammon or chess. Colonel Fitzwilliam, when talk of the coming ball was all but done, suggested making a table with himself, Darcy, and Georgiana for the first rubber of whatever game Elizabeth desired to play. This, she realized, was an even better situation—for she could relay Wickham's accusations to all concerned parties at once—and readily agreed. When Darcy cocked a curious eyebrow at her, she replied that she had some news regarding the gentleman he had spoken to Colonel Forster about earlier that day.

While the men were lingering over brandy and cigars, Elizabeth talked cheerfully with Georgiana, Catherine, Jane, and Charlotte; they spoke of the ball, Jane's upcoming marriage, and Elizabeth was at last able to ask her friend if indeed she were being courted by Colonel Forster. Charlotte blushed deeply and nodded.

"I am so very honored by his attentions, Lizzy," she said in a low voice. "I am not romantic, you know—I never have been. But ever since the colonel began to pay his addresses, I have begun to almost feel... I cannot really describe it except to say that my feelings make me think of romance. He has been so very kind and attentive when he has called on me. My only fear is..."

Her voice trailed off and Elizabeth reached for her hand. "What do you fear, Charlotte?" she asked softly.

Charlotte drew a breath. "My only fear is that he shall end up disappointed. I'm seven-and-twenty, after all, Lizzy. What if I cannot give him children?"

"Nonsense, Charlotte!" Elizabeth admonished her. "Women older than you have borne children. I am sure God will bless you with a dozen."

Her friend laughed and dabbed at her eyes with a handkerchief. "I should be happy if I only had one, I am sure!"

When the gentlemen at last rejoined the ladies, the servants were just behind bringing in the card tables. The doors to the music room were opened and Mary sat to the pianoforte to play for them. Elizabeth gestured for her party to join her at the table closest to the instrument, as the noise of the music would enable them to speak more freely. Once a deck of cards had been placed in Colonel Fitzwilliam's hand, she recounted her meeting with Mr. Wickham the night before.

Darcy was at once livid, and his cousin no less incensed. "Mr. Wickham is blessed with such happy manners," said the former bitterly, "that he makes friends easily."

"Whether he is capable of retaining them is less certain," said Fitzwilliam with a derisive snort.

"It...it wasn't all lies he said," offered Georgiana hesitantly. "After all, he *was* Papa's godson, and old Mr. Wickham was highly regarded by our father."

Darcy drew a breath and released it slowly. "Indeed, dearest, both of those statements are fact. But I am afraid that little else of what he said to Miss Bennet was truth. Father *did* once hope that Wickham would take the living, but—"

"It's quite all right, brother," said the younger Darcy. "I remember what you told me of it at Ramsgate."

"Might I ask what you said to Colonel Forster that led to his ordering Wickham to remain at camp?" Elizabeth asked then.

"Nothing less than the truth," replied Fitzwilliam. "We simply said that we had known the wretch since childhood, and knowing him to be in the neighborhood, could not in good conscience remain silent as to his deficits of character. Forster was informed of his habits of gaming, running up debt, and seduction of young women. I do not prevaricate when I say that it is likely only my connection to the nobility which led him to believe us, for the colonel himself regarded Wickham as a 'charming and amiable' fellow and said he was 'universally liked' among the regiment."

Elizabeth looked then to Darcy. "By the by, I feel compelled to apologize for my conduct last evening," she said. "I'm afraid I was for a time still vexed by our last conversation and I encouraged him to speak ill of you. It was unpardonable of me."

"On the contrary, Miss Elizabeth," said Darcy. "Although disguise of every sort is my abhorrence, your subterfuge has given us an idea as to what lengths Wickham is willing to go in order to sully my character. Think what he revealed to you only moments after first meeting you—who but one whose intent is to deceive would speak of such personal history to one whose acquaintance he has just made? *His* conduct was the unpardonable. At least you acted as you did only as a means of gathering information, and I am grateful that you were not swayed by his lies."

"As am I!" cried Georgiana softly. "Oh Lizzy, how mortified I am whenever I recall how thoroughly I was deceived in him—to think I was persuaded to believe myself in love with such a man is horrifying!"

"I would not be so hard on yourself, Georgiana," Elizabeth replied. "You are young and not much experienced in the world, and he is a practiced liar. Mr. Wickham took advantage of you for his own gain."

"In return for your clever use of feminine charms," spoke up Fitzwilliam, "I think I can safely speak for my cousin when I say I have no doubt at all as to your discretion in this matter."

"Theodore is correct," agreed Darcy. "As were you when you declared that a promise to my sister was as much a promise to me. I should not have asked you to swear another."

Elizabeth felt all the import of that statement as warmth bloomed in her chest and in her cheeks. All their disagreements thus far had led to *her* apologizing to *him*, so to have him also recognize that he had been in error felt momentous. She then remembered that, in fact, he *had* returned her apology once before, after their disagreement at one of Sir William's parties. His admitting to his own mistakes told her that Darcy respected her more than she had believed him to.

Smiling in return, she at last replied, "Thank you for that, Mr. Darcy. It may not have been necessary, but after my interaction with Mr. Wickham last evening, I understand why you did it. Your sister is as precious to you as mine are to me, and I would probably have done the same were our situations reversed. I am also relieved to have been told the truth of Mr. Wickham's character *before* meeting him, as I came to realize that did I not already know you as I do, his charming lies might well have thoroughly poisoned me against you."

Darcy's expression flickered, rousing Elizabeth's curiosity as to what he was feeling in that moment, but he said only, "Thank Providence, then, that you were not deceived."

After that statement, the four players readily altered their topic of conversation to the ball once more. Georgiana expressed her delight at being allowed to attend even if all her partners did have to be approved, and Elizabeth took the opportunity of asking questions of Colonel Fitzwilliam. He may have only just arrived in Hertfordshire, but she had seen him pay particular attention to Catherine already, much as the local boys had done—many of them only *after* learning she was an heiress. No doubt the colonel already knew of her fortune.

She found herself remarkably pleased with Darcy's cousin, and hopeful that his interest in her friend, whom she thought as well of as she did her own sisters—who would be as much as a sister when James and Jane were married—was merely an effect of his open and amiable nature.

Her concern was touched again when the first game was done and Georgiana offered to take Mary's place at the pianoforte. Her place at the table was taken by Catherine, much to her delight and the colonel's. Elizabeth could not help again wondering if he thought her friend pretty or if his charm was due to her wealth. Then she became rather angry with herself, realizing that her mistrust had been influenced by Wickham's attempted elopement with Georgiana. *Not all men are scoundrels, Elizabeth Bennet*, she told herself firmly.

Determined to enjoy herself, she forcibly pushed aside such morose thoughts as she had been having and concentrated on the game.

෧෮෯

Darcy became aware as soon as he stepped from his coach at Netherfield that Bingley and Caroline had been arguing. His friend was visibly vexed as he climbed the front stair, his sister trailing behind as she continued to harangue him.

His suspicion proved correct when he, Georgiana, and Fitzwilliam stepped into the entry hall, for it was in that moment that Bingley said, "That is quite enough, Caroline! If it is my desire to host a ball here at Netherfield, I shall, and if the prospect of an evening of dancing does not appeal to you, you are most welcome to beg that our sister and her husband take you to their home in London—or perhaps you would prefer our aunt and uncle's house in Scarborough?"

Beside him, Georgiana colored with embarrassment at having witnessed the scene; Fitzwilliam smiled his amusement. *No surprise there*, thought Darcy perversely, before he quietly encouraged his sister to take to her bed. Georgiana readily agreed, and after kissing both his cheek and their cousin's, bid a hasty farewell to the rest of their party. Catherine Morland quickly joined her in going up to the first floor.

"Darcy, Morland, Colonel Fitzwilliam," said Bingley then. "Would you all care to join me in a nightcap?"

"I would be delighted, sir," answered Fitzwilliam, and after divesting himself of his greatcoat and passing it to a waiting maid, followed after Bingley who was already on his way towards the study. Darcy and Morland were close behind, and when they were behind the closed door, Bingley turned to them.

"My apologies that you were forced to witness such a scene," he began, then he looked to Morland. "I also feel rather compelled to offer my apologies to you personally, James."

Morland frowned. "Whatever for?"

Their host went to the sideboard and poured himself a drink. "My sister thinks it an insult to host an evening of gaiety when you have robbed me of my heart's desire."

Morland scoffed. "Good gracious," he murmured. "It's not as if you were asked to throw Miss Bennet and I an engagement ball—that, at least, I own could be considered an insult."

He then stepped closer to Bingley and said, "Sir, you really have been most gracious regarding Miss Bennet and myself, and I cannot thank you enough for it. It cannot have been easy for you to allow me to return to your home or to witness our joy this evening."

"To be perfectly candid, 'twas not as difficult as I had imagined it would be," Bingley replied. "Seeing Jane—that is, Miss Bennet—seeing her happy pleases me. She's a good girl who deserves every happiness the world has to offer, and if she finds it with a capital fellow such as yourself, so be it. That she chose you and not me simply means that it is not yet my time to settle down."

"Your perspicacity in this matter is remarkably mature, Charles," Darcy said as he crossed the room and poured his own drink.

"Thank you, Darcy," Bingley replied. "I know that my history with the fairer sex, falling in and out of love and all that, might have given you reason to expect my feelings for Miss Bennet were just as flighty. I assure you they are not, but I think..." He paused and took a draught of his brandy, then sighed. "I think that being rejected by a girl I truly liked has pushed me to that greater maturity. I've learned that even the rich do not always get what they want."

"Speaking of the rich," said Morland as he poured two snifters and carried one over to Fitzwilliam. "You were most attentive to my sister this evening, Colonel."

Fitzwilliam's eyebrows winged up as he accepted the glass. "Miss Morland is a delightful girl," he replied slowly.

"She's also a very rich girl," Morland reminded him, "and you have said yourself that you cannot marry without some attention to money."

"Come now, Morland," said Darcy. "You don't seriously suspect my cousin to be acting a part when he has only just met your sister."

"It only takes one meeting, does it not?" Morland retorted.

Fitzwilliam, though surely amused by this turn of the conversation, nevertheless kept his expression sober as he said, "Mr. Morland, I have never been the profligate sort, nor have I ever used my noble connections to seduce young women as you may have heard my lot to do. I was brought up to treat women with respect no matter their station in life."

"That does not mean you've not as much an eye on Catherine's fortune as any of the fellows in Meryton who have tried to pay her attention," Morland asserted.

"Miss Morland's fortune is, at present, of no interest to me," Fitzwilliam rejoined. "What is of interest is becoming acquainted with a delightful, charming—if a touch naïve—young lady whose fine eyes and pretty smile I should like to see more of. I enjoy her company and conversation, and that is all."

They stared at one another for a long moment, then Morland nodded. "I would beg your pardon, sir, but as you have yourself acknowledged, it is my duty to see my sister protected."

"And it is to your credit that you are so vigilant, Mr. Morland," Fitzwilliam replied. "But while I can acknowledge such a fortune as hers is as attractive as she and would set me up quite nicely, the business which brings me to Hertfordshire all but precludes my pursuing any possibility of attaching myself, to Miss Morland or any other girl."

"And why *have* you come to Hertfordshire, if I may ask?" queried Bingley. "As charming as both your cousins are, Colonel, I suspect it was not Darcy's descriptions of the pastoral countryside which have brought you hither."

Fitzwilliam laughed. "No indeed, sir. I am here because a scoundrel of mine and Darcy's mutual acquaintance is in the neighborhood, and we wish to see all the local daughters' virtues protected."

Bingley scoffed. "Surely you don't follow this fellow everywhere?"

The cousins shared a look. "Certainly not," said Darcy. "However, this person is not only likely to run up debts and ruin shopkeepers' daughters, he is also about ruining my character to anyone who will listen. Only last evening he spoke to Miss Elizabeth about me and accused me of inhumane treatment, among other crimes."

"Impossible," said Bingley with a snort. "You're the most generous man I've ever known."

"It is kind of you to say, Charles," Darcy replied. "But suffice it to say, Morland is not the only one with a sister to see protected. Every brother in the neighborhood would want to keep theirs locked up if they knew about him."

"Then why not blast this man's true character to all and sundry?"

"Because despite what we know of him, it is not our intention to ruin him entirely," replied Fitzwilliam. "Only see to it that he behaves himself whilst we are all in the same neighborhood."

Morland scoffed, then said, "Something tells me you do not expect he will."

"For a time he may, but Wickham is too much a creature of habit," said Darcy.

"Indeed," agreed Fitzwilliam as he threw back the last of the amber liquid in his glass. "If there's anyone hereabout you ought to fear lusting after Miss Morland's fortune, sir, it's George Wickham."

Chapter Thirteen

Four days of successive rain followed the dinner party at Longbourn, restricting the ladies of that house — and all of the neighborhood — to remaining indoors.

Kitty and Lydia complained incessantly of not being able to visit with their aunt Phillips or their favorite militia officers. Jane, less vocal than her sisters, was sorry she could not visit with her fiancé. Elizabeth wished she could visit with Catherine and Georgiana and Charlotte, and even missed Mr. Darcy's company a little — not that she could admit as much to anyone but herself.

The only one of the sisters to have no complaint was Mary, who used the time to practice more. Longbourn was almost never silent amidst her playing and the youngest girls' complaints.

Shoe roses and other "absolute necessities" were purchased by proxy on Saturday, a servant being sent out with a list after a letter from Netherfield brought with it an official invitation to the ball to be held there. Tuesday was to be the day, shorter notice than Elizabeth had expected, but she was certainly not displeased. It gave the whole house something to look forward to.

Even Mr. Collins expressed some delight in the prospect of attending a ball and declared he would be extending his stay that he could. Elizabeth was rather surprised that he neither entertained any scruple on joining in such an evening's amusement nor dreaded a rebuke either from the Archbishop, or Lady Catherine de Bourgh, by venturing to dance. He went so far as to say that he was by no means of the opinion that a ball of this kind, given by so amiable a young man as Mr. Bingley to respectable people, could have any evil tendency.

"I am so far from objecting to dancing myself," he added, "that I shall hope to be honored with the hands of all my fair cousins in the course of the evening; and I take this opportunity of soliciting yours, Miss Elizabeth, for the two first dances especially."

Kitty and Lydia twittered madly at this, and Mrs. Bennet declared it quite the honor for her to be so singled out. Elizabeth, therefore, could not but be gratified in explaining that not only were the first two dances already claimed, but the second two also. Collins colored with embarrassment, and Mrs. Bennet sputtered with surprise.

"Who, Lizzy? Who have you promised these dances to, when our dear Mr. Collins has been so very attentive to you during his visit?" her mother demanded.

"Ma'am, with all due respect to Mr. Collins," said Elizabeth with forced civility, for she hoped to avoid dancing with her clumsy cousin entirely, "you would not have me reject the offers of Mr. Darcy and Colonel Fitzwilliam when I had no guarantee that my cousin would even attend Mr. Bingley's ball, would you?"

"Why would such gentlemen as they ask *you* to dance, Lizzy?" queried Lydia. "I'm a far better dancer and more interesting than you — and I am certainly fonder of officers than you are. Mamma, was not Colonel Fitzwilliam so very fine in his regimentals last evening?"

"He was indeed, my dear, but Lizzy," said Mrs. Bennet, "why *did* they ask you to dance? Our family owes the proud Mr. Darcy no particular civility, and his cousin, though an officer, is unknown to us."

"I believe it a personal challenge between the gentlemen, ma'am," Elizabeth replied. "Each of them spoke of Mr. Darcy's late mother having taught them to dance, and because Miss Morland and I were in conversation with them at the time, we were each of us asked to dance, that they might prove to us which of them was the better dancer."

Mrs. Bennet regarded her with narrowed eyes, no doubt wondering whether her least favorite daughter had somehow attracted the richest man in the neighborhood or the son of an earl — or if she could, given the "proper encouragement". Elizabeth feared these were her mother's thoughts as she sat back suddenly with a satisfied smile upon her lips.

"Mr. Collins, I am sure Mary will be delighted to dance with you," said the lady. "And did you know that she is as much a student of Mr. Fordyce as are you, sir? Mary dear, perhaps you and Mr. Collins might spend some time together today reading from your book."

Elizabeth stifled a groan and pitied her sister for being manipulated into spending time with her cousin. Mrs. Bennet was not at all subtle in her designs of having him take an interest in one of her daughters; if he married one of them, she would never have to leave the house that had been her home for more than twenty years. Elizabeth had been her first object and his, as Jane was engaged. Now, it seemed she believed her to be the object of affection to either Mr. Darcy or Colonel Fitzwilliam, and had thus suggested Mary.

It was perhaps unchristian of her, but Elizabeth began to hope that they were both of them disappointed, and that he was forced to return to Kent without having succeeded in his quest.

The day of the ball arrived, bringing with it brighter skies and no rain. This was a great relief to all the ladies at Longbourn, who had each in her own way feared the ball might be cancelled. Mrs. Bennet insisted that each of her daughters have a bath, putting the maids to a great deal of work hauling buckets of water up and down the stairs. They were none of them allowed to eat very much, for she was certain that Bingley would have a grand feast.

Elizabeth had chosen to be a little bold with her ensemble, pairing a white satin gown she had worn several times but was still remarkably in excellent condition with a sleeveless open robe made of red Indian muslin. The material had been a gift from her aunt Mrs. Gardiner, but she'd had no idea as to what to make with it until now, and had spent the majority of the four days turning the material into a garment that might be paired with any number of her evening gowns. Jane had kindly helped her to add some ready-made gold embroidery to embellish the piece.

The hours we spent making this had better be worth it, Elizabeth thought as she slipped her arms through and secured it at her bustline. It was her hope to dance half or more of the night away, to be far too busy enjoying herself to remember that she would soon be losing her most beloved sister to marriage. One more week was left for Mr. Nelson to read the banns before Sunday service, and then Jane and James would set a date. The rest of the Morland clan would come to Hertfordshire to attend the wedding, and then Jane would be taken away to Wiltshire to begin her life as Mrs. James Morland.

She wondered as she sat at her dressing table and began to set her hair how soon she might be able to go and visit her sister. Wiltshire was delightful country, according to the Morlands and Mrs. Allen, and she would be more than happy to spend several weeks there with her sister.

"Oh, Lizzy, you look lovely!" cried Jane when she entered the room some minutes later. "You will surely stand out from all the rest in that red."

Elizabeth frowned. "Do you think it too bold?"

"On the contrary, it's wonderful! I think it brings out the highlights in your hair," her sister replied.

"Well, in any case, it is not I who must shine brightly tonight," Elizabeth went on. Admiring her sister's soft peach frock, she said, "That gown looks really lovely on you, Jane. Your dear Morland will not be able to stop smiling from the moment he catches sight of you."

Jane smiled and blushed, then said, "And I am sure a certain gentleman from Derbyshire will not be able to stop smiling when he sees you, Lizzy."

Elizabeth waved away her words as she set down her brush and stood. "Do not you start on that nonsense, Jane. I have enough of Catherine's foolish hopes that he admires me."

"But he does! Surely you are not blind to it—oh Lizzy, I am surprised at you!" said Jane with a laugh. "Mr. Darcy speaks to almost no one but you whenever he calls here, and even when he is in conversation with another, his gaze finds you wherever you are. It is the same anywhere we are in company together."

Elizabeth felt her emotions begin to swirl but fought to rein them in. "I am sure you are mistaken, dearest. While I have had conversation with Mr. Darcy, and have danced with him—will dance with him again this evening—I am sure our acquaintance is nothing more than a pleasant diversion to him."

Jane tilted her head to the side as she regarded her. "Who are you trying to convince of that, Lizzy? Me, or yourself?"

"You, of course, for I am already convinced of it," said Elizabeth as she picked up her gloves and brushed past her sister. She would not tell her the truth—could not, as she had hardly been able to admit it to herself. In spite of her every intention otherwise, she had begun to feel an attachment forming for Darcy. But it was one she knew in her heart had no hope of being furthered, for he was a rich man with noble connections, and her father could give him nothing.

It would be difficult, but she would enjoy their evening together and then say her goodbyes when the time came. For no doubt he would soon leave the country to spend the winter in London—is that not what men of his station did?

In time the Bennets were arrived at Netherfield, and took their place in the line of guests moving into the house. Soon enough they were the next to be greeted by their host and his sisters; Bingley was as amiable and welcoming as ever, and his sisters as sneeringly civil as they usually were. Elizabeth was determined not to allow the contempt of the sisters to dampen her spirits or her enjoyment of the evening. There were candles everywhere for light, and displays of flowers and ribbons to catch the eye. Whether Caroline had accepted Mrs. Allen's assistance, done the work herself, or put it all on her aunt, the décor was splendid.

"Elizabeth, you look stunning!" cried Catherine as she and her brother approached; the latter's eyes were, of course, only for his fiancé. In fact, James offered his arm to her sister and in moments he and Jane drifted away from them.

Turning her attention to Catherine's violet-colored gown, she said, "I think stunning is a word that better applies to you, Cathy. What an extraordinary dress you are wearing."

"I am sure Mr. Darcy will disagree," said Catherine with a grin.

"You are no doubt mistaken. Mr. Darcy and I are only friends."

"Oh, Elizabeth, how can you be so blind!" said Catherine, then she frowned suddenly and added, "Do you not like him at all? Is that why you deny any attachment?"

Elizabeth shook her head. "My dear Cathy, I deny there being an attachment because none exists," she said. *At least not on his side, I am sure*, she added silently.

Catherine snorted softly and laughed. "I don't know what county you've been living in these last weeks, dear Elizabeth, because I can assure you that Mr. Fitzwilliam Darcy *definitely* admires you a great deal. I do not know how you can have talked with him so much and not noticed."

"Not noticed what, Cathy?" said Georgiana as she and Darcy stepped up to them.

Elizabeth pasted on a smile. "How very lovely you look this evening, Miss Darcy!" she said brightly.

If at no other time that they had met, she could then most definitely feel Darcy's eyes on her, and she endeavored to meet his gaze with equanimity. "Mr. Darcy," she greeted him with a bow of her head and a curtsey.

Darcy bowed. "Miss Bennet."

She turned her attention to Georgiana. "You really do look splendid this evening, Miss Darcy. That white gown suits you very well."

Georgiana blushed and fingered the folds of her skirt. "White looks good on everyone," she replied. "But you! Oh, I do not know that I could look as well as you in red."

"You are very kind to say so," said Elizabeth.

Fitzwilliam approached them then, offered his own compliments on her ensemble, then held out his arm to Catherine. "I figure we might as well stick by each other, as we are to dance the first dance together, Miss Morland. What say you, Darcy? Shall we take a turn about the room with our lovely partners?"

As his sister held his right arm, Darcy wordlessly turned and offered Elizabeth his left. She took it in equal silence, and they strolled lazily about the perimeter of the ballroom together with Fitzwilliam and Catherine providing the majority of the conversation.

It was not until the first dance of the evening had begun that Darcy spoke more than her name. "You look beautiful this evening, Elizabeth."

His voice was so soft that she nearly did not hear him, though when his words registered, she felt color fill her cheeks. "Thank you, Mr. Darcy," she replied.

Darcy's grip on her hand tightened a fraction, leading her to look up. "I mean it," said he. "I... I think you one of the handsomest women of my acquaintance."

Were the dance not a familiar one, Elizabeth thought she might have stumbled, so stunned was she by the confession. Could Catherine—and Jane—be right about him? Did he admire her more than she realized?

"I am honored by your praise, sir," she managed at last, offering a tentative smile.

Darcy's posture immediately relaxed, and he answered her smile with one of his own. For the rest of the set conversation flowed more naturally between them, and when their two dances were over, he seemed rather reluctant to hand her over to his cousin.

"So, Miss Elizabeth," Fitzwilliam said as soon as the dance had separated them from Darcy and his sister, who were now to dance together. "I have you to myself at last."

Elizabeth laughed. "And why should you desire that, sir?"

"Because now I can beg you to end my cousin's torment."

She frowned. "Whatever do you mean, Colonel?"

"Darcy! He's wild about you, I'm sure of it," Fitzwilliam replied.

Elizabeth scoffed to cover her shock at his words. "Good gracious," said she. "Whatever is in the water here at Netherfield?

Catherine, too, has suggested that Mr. Darcy admires me, and I will tell you as I have done her that I am sure you are mistaken."

"On the contrary, madam," said her partner. "You do not see how he looks at you, watches you, when you are unaware. You do not see the way he has glared at some of the other young men here when they have turned their heads to admire you."

"Even if that were true," said Elizabeth, endeavoring to ignore the thrill that coursed through her, "just because your cousin thinks me pretty does not mean he desires an attachment. He has known me for the same length of time that Mr. Morland has known my sister Jane, and has made no overtures of courtship."

"That's because he's shy!" the colonel retorted.

"Impossible," she argued.

Fitzwilliam shook his head. "Nay, it is true—he's afraid you will reject him, I am sure of it."

I think you one of the handsomest women of my acquaintance.

No. It was as she had said—just because the man admired her beauty did not mean he was in love with her. Catherine, Jane, Fitzwilliam—they had to be wrong!

Who are you trying to convince of that, Lizzy? Me, or yourself?

Jane's words from earlier came back to her, and it was then that shock began to course through her. What if they were *right*?

"Miss Elizabeth, are you well?" Fitzwilliam asked then.

"I am quite well, I assure you," she replied. "I just… How can he love me? I am sure your family would never approve a match between us."

"And why should we not? You are a gentleman's daughter, he is a gentleman. Does that not make you equals?" Fitzwilliam said.

"But who is my mother? Who are my aunts and my uncles? Surely you are not ignorant of their situation—my uncle Phillips is an attorney in Meryton and my uncle Gardiner owns a warehouse in Cheapside. Would not your father the earl disdain such connections?"

"My dear Miss Elizabeth, Darcy's choice of bride is his own—my father may give his opinion, but ultimately the decision of whom he takes to wife is his," Fitzwilliam told her.

Elizabeth stubbornly shook her head. "That may be so, but I am sure Mr. Darcy has no more wish to marry me than I have any wish to marry my father's cousin. He has given me no indication that he cares for me as more than a friend, and I am intelligent enough to know that to expect more would be folly. A man of his station would be far better off marrying a girl from a family as rich as his."

Fitzwilliam looked at her with incredulity. "You don't think you are good enough for him, do you?"

Elizabeth bit her lip. "Sir, I really think we should speak of something else."

"Forgive me, madam," the colonel said. "I have no wish to distress you, of course, but I hope you will at least consider what I have said. I do believe that Darcy truly admires you, and I do not think you could find a better man than he. My cousin has never cared as much for the opinion of the *ton* as others of our circle."

"Perhaps not as regards himself," said Elizabeth. "But he must think of his sister. Even if he were to decide a country squire's daughter with no dowry is good enough for him, his marrying me could sully *her* prospects, and I know he loves her too much to take the risk."

Feeling suddenly quite overwhelmed, Elizabeth broke away from her partner and excused herself. She made her way across the ballroom and walked through the music room to the garden doors, which were quite thankfully standing open. Yes, fresh air was what she needed, and room to think. Why was everyone so suddenly sure that Mr. Darcy liked her? What did it matter if he did? It was as she had told his cousin—he had given her *no* indication of feeling more than friendship for her other than the compliments he had given her earlier that evening. If he could not *show* her how he felt, how was she to know his words had meaning?

"Lizzy, are you all right?"

Elizabeth turned to find Catherine behind her. Forcing a smile to her lips, she replied, "I am quite well, Catherine. I think I became overheated, is all—there's quite the crush at this much-anticipated ball of Mr. Bingley's."

Catherine seemed relieved, though also as if she did not quite believe her. *She's an observant one*, Elizabeth mused, as the younger girl came closer and put a hand on her shoulder.

"Are you certain you are well? Mr. Darcy thought perhaps the colonel had said something that upset you."

"Why should he care?" Elizabeth countered as she turned back to gaze over the lawn.

"Dear Lizzy, why must you be so obtuse?" said Catherine as she stepped up beside her. "I own that I am certainly no expert in matters of the heart, but I cannot help wondering why you do not acknowledge the truth when it is plain before you."

Elizabeth drew a breath and sighed deeply. "I suppose that… Oh, Cathy, for all my wit and impertinence, it would seem I am just as vulnerable at heart as any other girl."

She looked to her friend with a weak smile. "I am afraid, you see, of you all being right about him, because it would mean risking my heart. I *want* you to be right and am afraid you are wrong. I am afraid he would choose me only to regret his choice."

Catherine once again put a hand on her arm in a comforting gesture. "But why should he regret you, Lizzy? You are so very kind and amiable, witty and charming…"

"And certain members of my family are utterly ridiculous," Elizabeth rejoined. "You have seen how Kitty and Lydia behave with the officers, receiving encouragement instead of correction from our mother and indifference from our father. A man of his station would never connect himself to such a family."

"A man of what station, pray?" said a voice from the shadows.

Elizabeth was startled and Catherine gasped; alarm shot through the former to see Mr. Wickham stepping out of the darkness and into the light.

Chapter Fourteen

"**Mr. Wickham!**" cried Elizabeth, hoping that her step back did not make her appear to be retreating from him.

Though desperately she wished that she could.

He came up the steps at a lazy gait, a genial smile on his face. "Good evening, Miss Bennet," he said with a slight bow. "My, do you look lovely. And your friend, as well."

"Sir, what are you doing here?" Elizabeth asked. "Mr. Denny told us that you had been restricted to the camp until further notice— though sorry I was to hear it, as I cannot imagine why."

"It was Darcy's doing," Wickham replied, his gaze flitting between her and Catherine. "He and his cousin, Colonel Fitzwilliam, visited the camp the other day and spread more of their mutual hate for me to Colonel Forster. I cannot imagine why he should have believed their lies."

"Perhaps he means to protect you from them?" she suggested. "After all, even Denny has said you are universally liked."

Wickham smiled again. "Denny is a capital fellow and a very good friend," said he. His eyes once more shifted to Catherine. "Speaking of friends, will you not introduce me?"

"Oh, of course," Elizabeth replied, and performed the introductions quickly.

"So this is the Miss Morland I have heard so much of since my coming to Hertfordshire?" said Wickham with a grin. "I am very pleased to meet you, madam. Miss Bennet's sisters Kitty and Lydia have told me so much about you, I feel as if we are friends already."

"I... I am obliged to you, sir," replied Catherine in a halting voice.

Wickham then glanced toward the house. "To answer your question, Miss Bennet, I am come to see what all the fuss is about. My fellow soldiers have talked of little else these last few days but this ball I have been so meanly left out of. Rather unfair of Darcy, do not you think, to not put aside his enmity for one day and allow me as much enjoyment of an evening of pleasure as the rest of the regiment?"

"Most certainly," Elizabeth replied, then turned in what she hoped was a casual manner toward Catherine and said, "Miss Morland, I think it best we return to the party, or your brother will come looking for you."

"Not to mention the gentleman you spoke of earlier may come looking for *you*," suggested Wickham. "Pray rest my worries and tell me you were not speaking of Darcy."

Elizabeth forced a laugh. "Certainly not! You know I dislike him as much as you. We were talking of Mr. Bingley. My good friend here thinks he admires me, but I am sure she is wrong about him. Mr. Bingley's fortune has been acquired through trade, you see, and if he is to be accepted by society he must distance himself from it as much as possible. I have an uncle who happily works in trade, though it is a respectable line, and as such it makes me an unsuitable candidate for his bride."

"No doubt he would be poisoned against you by Darcy in any case, who would do his best to convince him of the evils of such a connection," observed Wickham. "And though I would greatly wish to remain in your company, ladies, I would not have you get into any trouble by lingering too long."

"Y-yes, we…we only came out for a breath of fresh air," managed Catherine. "Quite the crush in there."

Wickham smiled. "I do not doubt it, for near the whole of the regiment was invited to attend. I bid you *adieu*, dear ladies, and hope to see you again very soon."

His gaze as he spoke the last lingered on Catherine, and Elizabeth began to feel a second wave of alarm course through her. Taking her young friend by the arm, she turned away from Wickham and forced a casual stroll through the house toward the ballroom.

Catherine leaned close to whisper, "Lizzy, who was that man? I sense you did not like him at all, and you lied about Mr. Darcy and Mr. Bingley."

"I had to, Cathy," Elizabeth replied. "I do not think I can explain all, as it is not my place, but suffice it to say that Mr. Wickham is *not* a good man. I must find Mr. Darcy and Colonel Fitzwilliam at once."

She did not have to go far into the ballroom to find them, as both lingered close to the door separating the ballroom from the music room. Darcy walked up to Elizabeth and looked into her eyes.

"Miss Bennet, are you well?" he asked.

"Madam, if the matter of which I spoke to you earlier in any way grieved you, please accept my sincerest apologies," added Colonel Fitzwilliam.

"That is neither here nor there, Colonel," Elizabeth said. "Cathy and I just met Mr. Wickham."

A scowl descended over both gentlemen's faces. Darcy looked to his cousin, who nodded and moved into the music room. Darcy then took Elizabeth by the arm.

"Come, Elizabeth, let me find you a chair. You look dreadfully pale," said he.

Elizabeth allowed herself to be led, with Darcy on one side and Catherine on the other. They found, by happenstance, an empty sofa set against a wall between two statues.

"I am quite well now, I assure you," said she as she sat down. "I was simply so very surprised to see him."

"Mr. Darcy," said Catherine as she sat beside her. "May I ask how you are acquainted with the gentleman? He was most unkind to you, and Elizabeth said she *had* to lie to him."

Darcy's searching gaze captured hers, and so Elizabeth explained the brief encounter. Her own gaze then fell on Catherine as she added, "I fear now that Kitty and Lydia may have spoken too freely of Cathy's fortune and he has now set his sights on her."

Catherine frowned. "Wait, do you mean to say he is a fortune hunter? Like John Thorpe?"

Darcy grimaced. "I know nothing of this Mr. Thorpe, but the answer is yes. Mr. Wickham has long had hopes of either swindling a lady out of her fortune or marrying a girl of fortune—not that he would keep it long in either case, as his gaming habits and other vices would lead to his wasting it all away."

Fitzwilliam returned then, his expression dark. "No sign of the bugger, Will."

"Should we tell Colonel Forster, do you think?"

His cousin glanced at Catherine and Elizabeth. "Nay. By the time he sends anyone to check on him, the lout will have returned to camp and will be able to deny the whole thing."

Darcy's nod of acquiescence was clearly reluctant. "Very well.

Still, I would have Mrs. Annesley keep a close watch of Georgiana, and we must look after Miss Morland to the best of our ability."

Fitzwilliam's gaze flickered. "Miss Morland? What has that scoundrel done to you?"

Catherine shook her head even as Elizabeth replied, "He did nothing, Colonel—to either of us. He only said that he hoped to see us again very soon and… Well, the way he looked at Catherine made me wonder if he knew about her fortune."

"He won't get it," said Fitzwilliam forcefully. "Have no fear, Miss Morland, I'll not let that libertine get near you."

"Please, let us not speak of such things tonight," replied Catherine with what Elizabeth sensed was forced cheer. Her friend was clearly still confused about Wickham, but not insensitive to their alarm where he was concerned. "Let us remember that we are at a party and should be enjoying ourselves!"

Fitzwilliam's patented grin made a triumphant return as he stepped up to Catherine and offered his arm. "You are absolutely right, Miss Morland. Might I escort you to your next partner?"

She smiled at him. "Why, thank you, sir," said she as she stood. Turning back to Elizabeth, she said, "You are sure you are well?"

Elizabeth offered her own smile. "I am, I assure you. I was just startled, that is all."

With a nod, Catherine allowed herself to be led away. Darcy, who had sat next to her, stood and held out his hand. "Allow me to follow my cousin's example and lead you to your next partner."

Elizabeth placed her hand in his and stood. "I actually have no partner for this third set," she confessed. "And though I had some hope earlier of dancing half the night away, at present I rather think I would like a glass of wine and a stroll."

Darcy inclined his head, then moved her hand to the crook of his arm. "I should be happy to oblige you, madam."

They soon found a servant carrying a tray and procured themselves a glass of wine each. Elizabeth sipped the beverage, feeling its warmth soon radiating through her and calming her nerves. They spoke little at first as they walked about the room, but soon enough he asked her if, indeed, Fitzwilliam had upset her.

"After all," said he cautiously, "you did not finish your set with him."

Elizabeth felt more than the wine warming her cheeks then. Drawing a breath, she replied slowly, "My sister Jane, your cousin, and Miss Morland are all of the same mind."

Darcy frowned. "The same mind about what? I do not understand."

She chuckled. "Something I once told you was beyond *my* understanding. I shouldn't worry yourself over it, Mr. Darcy."

His unexpected pause made her turn and look up at him; Darcy now stared at her in wonder.

"Sir, I feel compelled now to ask if *you* are well," Elizabeth said, half-jokingly, as she regarded the curious expression now set upon his countenance.

"Quite well," was his only reply, and they continued on.

Though difficult at first, Elizabeth managed to push thoughts of Wickham, Darcy as a possible admirer, and all other unsettling thoughts from her mind. She had been determined to enjoy herself at this ball before it started, and she meant to reclaim that mindset for the rest of it.

Everything else could wait.

❧

The morning after the Netherfield ball began the same as that which followed the assembly only a month prior: Catherine and Georgiana were determined to visit their friends at Longbourn to talk over the dancing, the food, the gowns, and the men they were fortunate enough to dance with. James Morland and Mrs. Allen accompanied them, and upon arrival the latter was shown by the housekeeper to her mistress's bedchamber, for she had complained of her nerves since waking.

"The truth is," said Elizabeth to her visitors after Mrs. Allen had been taken away, "Mamma is vexed that Colonel Forster announced his engagement to Charlotte last evening."

Lydia, who sat across the room with Kitty—each of them attempting to redress a bonnet—looked up with a sour expression. "I can't imagine why he picked her! She's an old maid, and not even pretty!"

"Charlotte Lucas may not fit society's standard of conventional beauty, Lydia, but clearly she possesses some natural charms which Colonel Forster finds attractive," spoke up Mary.

"I bet he just wanted someone who his officers wouldn't flirt with," said Kitty with a snort, which led to both her and Lydia giggling madly.

"Catherine Bennet, that was most unkind!" admonished Jane.

"And unjust," said her fiancé. "I think Miss Lucas to be a fine-looking girl."

Jane smiled at him. "Thank you, James, for admiring our friend."

Morland returned her smile and gave the hand he held an affectionate squeeze.

"Oh, Lizzy!" Georgiana was saying then. "Did you notice how everyone was looking at you in wonder last night? That bold red robe you wore over your gown was very eye-catching!"

Elizabeth hoped that her countenance did not show her emotions, as Colonel Fitzwilliam's remark about Darcy scowling every time some gentleman looked at her came to mind. "I am glad you approved of it, Georgie. And you! I daresay you were very admired as well. Did not you dance nearly every dance?"

Georgiana smiled dreamily. "I did, yes! Though it was a little disconcerting with Mrs. Annesley or my brother so near all the time. And Cathy!"

Catherine raised an eyebrow at her friend's impish grin. "Why do you smile like that, Georgiana?"

"I think a certain gentleman, also a colonel, showed quite a marked interest in you last night."

James Morland cleared his throat and stood. "Miss Bennet, might we take a turn about the garden? There is a slight chill in the air this morning, but I am sure a warm cloak will do you good."

Jane chuckled. "And not having to listen as your sister talks of her partners will do *you* good, I am sure," she said, standing and allowing him to lead her from the room.

Catherine, meanwhile, was blushing. "I... I am sure you are mistaken, Georgiana."

Now who's being obtuse? Elizabeth wondered with a small grin. Fitzwilliam may have been primarily concerned about Wickham, but it was quite plain—to Elizabeth as well as Georgiana, at least—that her welfare was not the only reason he had hovered in Catherine's vicinity the whole of the evening. Elizabeth had noted on a number of occasions how intently he watched her as though fascinated—and more than once, Darcy's cousin had frowned when the gentleman Catherine was dancing with got a little too close or made her laugh.

"And I am sure I am not!" Georgiana was saying. "I am sure Theodore likes you. I know you have been disappointed that your friend Mr. Tilney did not pursue a closer acquaintance with you, but if your brother can get past his first love being unfaithful, surely you can move past not having had a romance at all!"

"It's not that, Georgie—at least, it is not *only* that," replied

Catherine.

"Well, what else is there?"

Catherine turned an imploring gaze to Elizabeth, who lifted an eyebrow to prompt her to continue. Sighing, Catherine went on, and said, "Colonel Fitzwilliam is a charming and amiable gentleman. But he is already almost thirty! I am only a month over eighteen, and he barely knows me besides. He has seen much of the world whereas I have never set foot outside of Fullerton until this year. Such a man could not possibly wish for so young and naïve and inexperienced a person as myself for his wife!"

"In my limited experience," began Elizabeth, "it is natural for a man to wait longer to marry than it is for us ladies — he waits until he is established, either at his estate or in his career, while women are expected to be ready for marriage by the time they are sixteen, when their parents begin to parade them about the marriage mart during the Season in London or Bath or somewhere. All so that they can be free of the burdens they placed on themselves by having children in the first place."

"Charlotte is not sixteen," Kitty pointed out. "Colonel Forster apparently doesn't want a young bride."

"Charlotte Lucas is level-headed and sensible, Kitty," said Mary. "It is likely that Colonel Forster desires a wife who is mature enough to deal with the nonsense and follies of his soldiers — many of whom, I have noticed, act much like spoiled, undisciplined children."

"You take that back, Mary Bennet!" cried Lydia indignantly. "Denny and Carter do *not* act like spoiled, undisciplined children!"

"Nor Chamberlayne, either!" added Kitty.

"In any case," broke in Elizabeth, hoping to stave off any further argument, "what my experience has taught me is that no matter their own age, men tend to prefer wives that are young and pretty, and healthy enough to bear them several children."

She cast her gaze quickly towards her youngest sisters and leveled a stare at them. "And before either of you makes another unkind remark about Charlotte's age, perhaps I should remind you that Mamma was the same age as she when she bore Lydia."

This piece of information seemed to surprise Kitty. "Was she really?"

Elizabeth nodded. "She was. In fact, women in their thirties have born children before, so I do not despair of my friend being able to provide Colonel Forster with heirs."

"I believe another point that Elizabeth was intending to make,

Miss Morland," Mary interjected, "is that the disparity in your ages has little bearing on whether or not Colonel Fitzwilliam admires you. Men of thirty have married women of only eighteen years before."

"Indeed so, Mary," Elizabeth agreed, rewarding her sister's insight with a smile.

"I do not know," said Catherine. "I like Colonel Fitzwilliam, to be sure, but I do not know if I like him in that way."

"Well, it's as you said, you hardly know each other—the colonel has been in the neighborhood what, only a week?" Elizabeth pointed out. "Though I cannot disagree with his dear cousin Georgiana's assessment, as I *do* believe he admires you, I would not vex yourself over the possibility. Simply enjoy his company as you have done thus far, and let things happen as they may."

"And what about you, Lizzy?" Catherine rejoined. "Do you intend to let things happen as they may with Mr. Darcy?"

Kitty and Lydia twittered across the room as Mary raised one eyebrow and Georgiana grinned. "Oh, I should like it above all things, Lizzy, if you should become my sister! You are so very witty and lively, and so very kind to me that I feel almost as though we are sisters already!"

Elizabeth suppressed the urge to groan. Though she had all but confessed her feelings for Darcy to Catherine the night before, she had no desire at all to revisit the subject. Yes, she liked him very much and would be immeasurably gratified were he to reciprocate her regard, but her assessment of the man himself remained firm—he had given her no indication that he felt more for her than he ought, so there was little to be gained by expressing her own interest.

"Really, I would have you all put the very idea out of your minds," said she at last. "I am sure that Mr. Darcy has no intention at all of making a match with me."

Even if I do wish that he did.

❧

Elizabeth decided to repay Catherine and Georgiana's visit by calling on them at Netherfield the next day; the two were almost always calling at Longbourn due to having access to a carriage, which of course made traversing the three-mile distance much easier for them.

She did not take her father's carriage, nor even a horse. Feeling a need to get out and experience nature as she had not done for some weeks, soon after rising she had donned warm outwear and sturdy half-boots to begin the trek on foot. Elizabeth was often jokingly referred to as a "great walker" by her family because she liked to ramble about the countryside wherever her feet would take her — indeed, she could walk for hours and not feel the least tired. And so used to a long, solitary ramble was she that she had traversed the distance in little more than half an hour.

A carriage stood waiting at the steps and Catherine was coming out of the house with Mrs. Allen as she approached.

"Why, good morning to you, Miss Elizabeth!" said Mrs. Allen with a cheerful wave.

"Lizzy, did you walk all this way?" asked Catherine with a little laugh as the two ladies came down the steps.

Elizabeth smiled. "I did, yes, but it's no trouble to me at all. I like a good, long walk. Clears the mind and refreshes the soul."

"I feel exactly the same! Eleanor and I — that is, my friend Miss Tilney — would take long country walks almost every day when we were at Bath. Her brother Mr. Tilney joined us often."

"You know, Catherine, I used to think that you had made a conquest of young Mr. Tilney," said Mrs. Allen then. "Mr. Henry Tilney was a very agreeable young man, Miss Elizabeth — he understands muslin ever so well and is not at all like that brother of his, who had the audacity to pursue a young lady already engaged to another."

Catherine leaned closer to Elizabeth as she said, "Mrs. Allen takes it very personally that Isabella was lured away from James in the manner that she was."

"Indeed I do! How a young lady can behave so abominably toward so deserving a young man as your brother, I shall never understand," Mrs. Allen replied. "And for what? Mere promises that rascal Captain Tilney had no intentions of keeping whatsoever."

Elizabeth bit her lip to keep from laughing at Catherine's amused expression, though she knew her friend felt much the same as her benefactress. She then glanced between them and the waiting carriage and said, "Well, I shan't keep you from your outing any longer. I'll just go in and visit with Georgiana."

"Oh, but she's got herself a bit of a cold," said Catherine. "Her brother and Mrs. Annesley have encouraged her to stay abed today."

Recalling that Georgiana had complained of fatigue and a bit of a headache the previous morning, though she had professed it no more than having worn herself out with dancing at the ball, Elizabeth sighed and turned her gaze to the house. "I shan't disturb her, then. I suppose I will just return home, as the two of you are going out."

"Nonsense my dear, you will join us!" said Mrs. Allen as she positioned herself between her and Catherine and hooked her arms with theirs. "We are for Meryton, as Catherine here has some packages to post for her family, and I some letters to send to friends."

"I have been very lax in my duties as a daughter and sister," said Catherine as the three started for the carriage. "James and I have been here a little over a month now, and I have sent no presents to my parents or my younger brothers and sisters! I have bought them all, of course, on previous trips into Meryton, but have been waiting until I had some trinket or other for each before posting them."

Elizabeth grinned and told her it was a logical plan of action, and happily accepted the footman's assistance into the carriage when it was her turn to get in. The three of them chatted away, talking more of the ball at first, before Catherine also recalled that Mr. Bingley had gone to London that morning to take care of "some business or other" that would keep him there at least until Friday.

"Mrs. Hurst and Miss Bingley have talked of joining him there and convincing Mr. Bingley that he ought not return to Hertfordshire," Catherine went on with a sour expression. "I do not think they realize how loudly they whisper, those two."

Elizabeth laughed. "Indeed they do not," said she. "And even if their endeavors should be successful, I am sure that Mr. Bingley would not simply abandon you here. It was his idea that you come for a visit, after all, and I think him too much a gentleman to not give his guests some degree of warning should he decide to quit the place."

What she did not say was that she would understand if Bingley *should* decide to quit the neighborhood and give up Netherfield entirely. He might not have come into Hertfordshire with the intention of finding himself a wife, but he had developed strong feelings for a local girl, and she could imagine it being difficult for him to remain even though Jane's marriage to Mr. Morland would take her to Wiltshire.

Chapter Fifteen

When they had arrived at the post office, Elizabeth helped Catherine carry in the parcels she intended to send off. After she had paid, and Mrs. Allen had paid the postage for her letters, the three made their way down to the haberdasher's. Catherine said she had been working to embroider a handkerchief for Mr. Bingley as a gift for his kindness, but she had run out of thread and needed another spool to finish it.

"Had I any idea I would be coming into the village, I'd have brought my reticule," Elizabeth murmured. "I've another gown I have some idea how to trim afresh, and a hat that will match spleendidly once I've remade it."

"Whatever you like, I shall get it for you," said Catherine.

Elizabeth shook her head. "Oh, no, Cathy, I can't have that. I can wait to get the materials."

"Nonsense, Miss Elizabeth," said Mrs. Allen as they entered the shop, which in truth housed both a haberdashery and a milliner — Hilton's Haberdasher and Hats, the proprietors, Mr. and Mrs. Hilton, had called it.

"You have become a very good friend to my dear Catherine, such as Miss Tilney was to her in Bath," Mrs. Allen continued. "I should be quite happy to purchase anything you like, if you'll not allow Catherine to do so."

"It is very kind of you, but I really can't ask you to—" Elizabeth started to protest.

"Nonsense, my dear girl," said Mrs. Allen firmly, taking her by the arm again and guiding her over to the racks of ribbons. "You are not asking, I am insisting. Now, choose whatever you like."

Elizabeth sighed in resignation, though she also smiled. It would be nice, she mused, to spend the time she needed to look over the selections carefully, rather than feeling rushed as she usually did when accompanied by her sisters or her mother. While she and Mrs. Allen talked over ribbons and buttons and what she hoped to do to her dress, Catherine completed her own purchase, and announced she would be heading to the bookshop just two stores down the street.

"If I have not returned by the time you are done, that is where you will find me," said she as she went out the door.

Beside Elizabeth, Mrs. Allen chuckled. "Indeed she will not return—that child is a voracious reader of novels. I expect we shall have to go and drag her away when we are done here."

Elizabeth smiled. "Does Fullerton Manor have a well-stocked library?" she asked.

Mrs. Allen nodded. "Indeed it does! My Mr. Allen was much like your father and Mr. Darcy in that way."

This was a surprising comparison of the three gentlemen in question, Elizabeth thought. "How so?" she asked.

"Well, I have heard Mr. Darcy say that his library at Pemberley is the work of generations, and that he cannot abide neglect of a family library," Mrs. Allen replied as she moved to the next rack of ribbons. "And your father, as Mrs. Bennet has often said, can always be found in his book room. Mr. Allen was a mixture of the two: he rather enjoyed reading, and was always buying new books for our library at the manor—Catherine was forever borrowing books from us. Now they are hers to enjoy for the rest of her life."

Elizabeth offered the lady a smile when melancholy crept into her features. "And I am sure Catherine appreciates the generous gesture of now having her very own library, even if she has yet to tell you so. I know that I would certainly appreciate having a library of my own. I can go into my father's bookroom and borrow any book that I like, to be sure, but they are all *his*. I have very few books that are truly mine alone."

"Well then, when it is your turn to marry—and I am sure it will be very soon, now your eldest sister is to marry dear James—you be sure, Miss Elizabeth, to fall in love with a man who has room enough in his house that you may have a library of your very own."

Elizabeth laughed as her eye caught sight of the very color of ribbon she wanted for her project. "And enough money, I daresay," said she, "to keep it well-stocked!"

Mrs. Allen insisted on purchasing the whole spool of ribbon as well as some lace that Elizabeth had noticed; the latter insisted she would repay her the money when she could. Mrs. Allen assured her there was no need as her purchases were wrapped up for her by Mrs. Hilton. As they walked from the haberdasher's to the bookshop, the elder lady jokingly wondered how many more books her protégé would be adding to the Fullerton Manor library.

"This time, for she has already purchased two books since our coming to Netherfield."

Much to their mutual surprise, however, Catherine was not in the bookstore when they arrived. Elizabeth walked to the counter to speak to Mr. Laraby, who owned the place, asking if he had seen her.

"Oh, I seen the young miss all right. Well, I seen her through the window, as she ne'er came inside," replied the shop owner. "One of the militia officers—I don't rightly know his name—met her outside the door, and they walked away together toward the tea shop."

Dread filled Elizabeth's stomach, though she prayed her alarm did not show. Thanking Mr. Laraby, she took Mrs. Allen by the arm and headed out of the shop, turning to the left. There was immediately before them an alley that ran between the buildings—Mrs. Martin's tea shop being just on the other side—and as they neared it she heard a man's voice...

...a very recognizable man's voice, the very one she had prayed was *not* the one to lead her friend away.

"I hear someone coming this way, my dear," said Wickham. "Let us make this look good."

Elizabeth heard only a squeak in reply, but she was certain it was Catherine who had made the noise. Quickening her steps, she rounded the corner to find Wickham pressing Catherine into the outside wall of the book shop, holding her by the shoulders as he kissed her.

"Good gracious!" cried Mrs. Allen when she came around the corner just behind Elizabeth.

Wickham's head snapped up and he grinned widely; Catherine looked utterly frightened.

"I'm afraid you've caught us in a compromising position, Miss Bennet," said Wickham. "I told Miss Morland we ought not be alone together, but when we met only a few minutes ago, she insisted she must speak to me at once. And just as you were coming around the corner, she kissed me!"

"That—that's a lie!" Catherine stammered. Elizabeth noted her face was bright crimson and her eyes were filled with tears. Her breathing was shallow and she looked on the verge of swooning.

"Come, Miss Morland," said Elizabeth, holding out her hand. Catherine ran to her immediately; Elizabeth gave her hand a reassuring squeeze before she passed her over to Mrs. Allen.

Glancing once more at Wickham, she lifted her chin and glared at him with as much *hauteur* as she could muster. "I am surprised at you, sir. You claimed that Darcy's and his cousin's words to Colonel Forster were lies, yet here you are forcing yourself on an innocent young woman. This is scandalous behavior indeed, and all of your own doing. No doubt you will be hearing from Miss Morland's brother very soon."

Wickham did not look in the least bothered by her dressing down; in fact, he grinned lasciviously. "Oh, I am looking forward to it, Miss Bennet, especially as we are drawing quite the crowd. Do not distress yourself overmuch, my dear Miss Morland, for I am certain to be fair when our marriage settlements are drawn up."

Elizabeth looked over her shoulder as he spoke—dread for Catherine's fate flooded her veins to find that indeed, four people had stopped to observe their confrontation. Catherine fell into Mrs. Allen's arms and began to sob.

"Let us get Catherine home, Mrs. Allen," she said to the lady, refusing to acknowledge Wickham any further.

ða∽ó

A cry for help in the hall brought Darcy, Fitzwilliam, and Morland to their feet at once. None of them expected to find Catherine Morland collapsed on the ground, cradled in the arms of Elizabeth Bennet.

"Thunder and turf!" cried Fitzwilliam as Catherine's brother ran to her side and dropped to his knees.

"Cathy!" said he as he took up her hand, then turned an alarmed visage to her friend. "What happened?"

"Oh! Oh, I hardly know!" said Mrs. Allen, who was now fanning herself. "There was a man and Catherine, we were in an alley—"

Miss Bingley and Mrs. Hurst were then appearing at the top of the stairs. Darcy stepped forward and said in a low voice, "Ma'am, you may wish to speak no further on the subject until a conference may be held in privacy."

Mrs. Allen glanced at her nieces-by-marriage. "Oh, yes. Yes, of course, Mr. Darcy."

He turned to his cousin. "Theodore, ring for Mrs. Nicholls. Tell her we need Mrs. Annesley to attend Miss Morland in her room."

Fitzwilliam stepped closer. "You and I both know who is to blame, I expect," he whispered.

Darcy only nodded, then his cousin moved away to the nearest bell pull. Looking to Mrs. Allen, Darcy asked her if she had any salts.

"Oh, oh yes, of course!" she replied, and hurried to pull the item out of her reticule. The small bottle was handed to James, who quickly pulled the cork and held it under his sister's nose. In a few seconds, as Mrs. Nicholls was walking into the hall, Catherine Morland revived.

"James! Oh James, what shall I do?!" she cried at once, tears spilling from her eyes as she rose and clung to him.

"Mr. Darcy?" called out Miss Bingley. "Whatever has happened to poor Miss Morland?"

"She has only fainted," he answered, knowing better than to say anything more.

Caroline looked to Louisa; both of them wore expressions of obvious curiosity, but thankfully they knew him well enough not to press further. Darcy suspected one or both would try to get the story out of the servants, but if he had anything to say about it, the servants would have nothing to tell.

As quickly as could be managed, Mrs. Annesley was fetched by the housekeeper, and Catherine was taken to her room by Mrs. Allen and his sister's companion. Darcy then looked to Elizabeth and tilted his head, and she nodded in silence; he led the way to Bingley's study while she, Fitzwilliam, and Morland followed. Near as soon as the door was shut, James turned to her and demanded a second time to be told what had happened.

Elizabeth told a story which Darcy had feared from the moment he'd heard of Wickham's appearance at the ball two nights before— he had forced a compromise of Miss Morland, orchestrating it so that his behavior would be witnessed.

"I feared such a thing would happen, that he knew of her fortune and would try something to get his hands on it," Elizabeth said at last, echoing his thoughts. "Only I did not think he would take such a drastic step so soon—I thought he might try to court her first."

"Wicky must be desperate, Darce, for him to take such a step so soon after meeting the girl," Fitzwilliam observed.

"I'll kill him!" cried Morland, whose countenance was colored puce with his rage. "Where is the bloody militia camp? I'll go there at once and call that wretched knave out!"

"Don't be a fool, Morland," said Fitzwilliam, whom Darcy noted was wearing an angry scowl. "You can't face him."

"The ████ you say!" Morland yelled back. "That reprobate has compromised *my* sister—I'll see him dead rather than hand her over to him!"

"James. Dear brother-to-be," spoke up Elizabeth in a soft, pleading voice. Morland looked to her, as did Darcy and Fitzwilliam. "Believe me when I tell you that I understand your anger. But while he has not been with the militia long, I am sure Mr. Wickham has had more training with a pistol or sword than you have."

Fitzwilliam snorted. "He's had to learn long before joining the militia, I do not doubt, to protect himself against angry fathers and husbands."

"Indeed, Colonel," Elizabeth agreed, then she walked over to Morland and took his hands in hers. "I know you want to see justice for Catherine, but if harm should come to you in the doing, neither Jane nor Catherine would forgive you. You are soon to be married, sir—you cannot risk your life and chance making my sister a widow before she becomes your bride."

Anguish overcame his expression. "Then what am I to do, Lizzy?"

That he had addressed her so was a sure sign of Morland's torment, Darcy noted, as he had only ever been formal with her before. He felt for the other man, whose pain was one he knew all too well.

"Nothing," Fitzwilliam said. "I'll challenge him."

Morland looked to him. "You? Why should you stand against him when it is my sister whose virtue has been compromised?"

"Because he'd more than likely kill you," Fitzwilliam replied bluntly.

"But not you?"

"No," Darcy put in. "Theodore is an expert marksman—it is but one of many reasons the army will feel the loss of him whenever he chooses to settle down."

Fitzwilliam stepped closer to where Morland and Elizabeth stood together. "Sir, I'm sure you will forgive me the observation, but you strike me as the sort who has never harmed another human being in all his life. Taking the life of one of your fellow men is something that stains your soul whether he is deserving of death or not. It haunts you—I should know, I live with many ghosts. Also, I daresay you would not wish to take up the cloth in two years' time to preach

141

before a God whose covenant you have already broken. Allow me to stand for you, that you do not take your orders with such guilt upon your conscience."

Darcy watched Morland as he stared at his cousin, then he glanced at Elizabeth before giving her hands a squeeze and turning to pace away from her. He ran a hand through his hair and over his face a number of times, muttering under his breath, before he turned back to say, "What if you are successful, and this villain is killed? Will that save my sister from ruin?"

Fitzwilliam turned his gaze to Darcy, who sighed and said, "No one can say for certain, I'm afraid. Even if Wickham's death is covered up—even if no one who saw the confrontation knows precisely who Catherine was with, they still know that *something* happened. Those who witnessed the altercation have likely already spoken of it to others."

"They will also know that it happened to her and not myself, given her reaction and his words," said Elizabeth, "especially since he made a point of raising his voice that they might hear him."

"Good God, what are we to do?" Morland muttered. "Oh, how I wish my father were here to advise me!"

If his father were here, the decision as to what action to take would not be up to James. Darcy considered that he might offer to send for the Reverend Morland, but by the time of his arrival, Wickham would likely be dead and the damage to Catherine's reputation irreversible.

"Miss Bennet," said Fitzwilliam, breaking the somber silence.

"Yes, Colonel?" she asked.

"What was Wickham wearing when you met him?"

Elizabeth blinked in confusion. "Why does it matter?"

Fitzwilliam turned to her. "Because much as it pains me to admit it, Wickham and I are of a similar build and coloring. Thus, anyone not intimately familiar with both of us might mistake one for the other—from a distance, at least. For that matter, if Wickham was wearing his uniform, it could have been anyone of like appearance in the militia."

Understanding dawned in her eyes, and if Darcy were not mistaken, something akin to pride as well.

"He was indeed wearing his regimentals, sir," said she at last.

Fitzwilliam next turned to Morland and stood to his full height. "Sir, I respectfully request permission to seek Miss Morland's hand in marriage."

Again, Darcy watched as Morland studied his cousin, seeking he knew not what in the latter's countenance. Reassurance, perhaps, that he was making the offer for the right reasons.

But what could there be that was right about any of it? An innocent young woman's reputation had been tarnished by one man's evil actions, and his cousin—honorable fool that he was—was sacrificing his chance at a love match to save her.

"I will not commit to an answer until my sister is recovered enough that we may discuss the circumstances in which she has found herself rationally," Morland said at last. He then loosed a ragged sigh and added, "Though I do offer you my sincerest gratitude that you are willing, Colonel."

"I do not make the offer lightly," Fitzwilliam returned. "As I have said to you before, your sister is delightful and charming. She is pretty, sweet tempered, and not unintelligent. I do not think it an assumption to say that I believe she enjoys my company as much as I do hers. I understand that I have known her only a week's time, but given our interactions in the last se'nnight, I have every reason to believe we will do well together—and before you even ask, my proposal has nothing to do with Miss Morland's inheritance. I would offer for her even if she were poor in order to save her from the ruin Wickham has forced upon her."

"That I believe you to be sincere in your regard for Catherine is the only reason I am even contemplating granting your request," Morland replied. "Though if she agrees, we would, of course, still need to speak to my father."

Fitzwilliam nodded. "Of course," said he, then he looked to Darcy. "I don't need a second, but I should like to you come all the same. I want at least one witness who will not question my motive in seeking a duel with the blackguard."

Darcy nodded, having already expected to join him. He then looked to Elizabeth and said, "Miss Bennet, I will have my carriage ordered to take you home."

"Pray do not trouble yourself, Mr. Darcy," she replied. "At least, not until your safe return. I should rather like to stay with Catherine a while, if I may."

"Of course," Darcy agreed, at the same time as Morland said, "Thank you, Elizabeth. I am sure Catherine will be comforted by your presence."

Elizabeth smiled at him, then said to Darcy, "If I may use Mr. Bingley's desk, I should like to write a note to my family, that they do not worry for me when I am not home soon as expected."

"Certainly." Darcy turned and gestured to the desk behind him. "When you have finished, any one of Bingley's footmen will convey it for you."

Elizabeth replied with a nod, then moved to sit in Bingley's chair. Morland stayed with her while he and Fitzwilliam took their leave. It was not until they were on horseback and cantering toward Meryton that either ventured to speak again. Naturally, Fitzwilliam had to say something smart...

"'Not until your safe return,'" said his cousin with a snarky grin. "And you think she doesn't like you."

"It was a general statement—" Darcy began.

"She didn't say it to *me*, Will," Fitzwilliam interjected.

"—which I do not doubt was meant for both of us," he finished stiffly.

Fitzwilliam shook his head. "I shall never understand why two people so obviously in love with one another fight so strongly against it."

Darcy stifled a growl. "Theo, I have already explained myself to you. It matters not what I think of Elizabeth when she does not care for me."

His cousin scoffed. "And yet your feelings have not changed in spite of your belief that the lady does not return your affections. Heavens, the two of you really are perfect for one another."

"I am afraid to ask your meaning," Darcy replied in a droll tone.

Fitzwilliam glanced over. "You are each of you so bloody certain the other does not feel the same that you spend all your time denying how you feel to everyone who talks of it and absolutely none whatsoever talking about how you feel to *each other*. Maddening, you are."

With a sigh and a shake of his head, his cousin kicked his horse into a gallop, leaving Darcy to catch up.

Chapter Sixteen

Darcy and Fitzwilliam arrived at the militia's camp in record time.

That they galloped through drew many stares, and as he dismounted before the largest of the tents, Darcy could hear murmuring from those soldiers milling about nearby. He barely had the time to tie his horse's reins to the hitching post before following behind his cousin as he stormed through the flap of Colonel Forster's dwelling.

"To what do I owe the pleasure of this visit?" said the man sitting behind the desk as he looked up at them. "Or have you come to regale me with further tales of Mr. Wickham's misdeeds? I can assure you lads that he's been a model officer, though he has hardly had chance to do any of what you accused him on Thursday last as I've had him restricted to camp."

"You are either lying or a trusting fool," Fitzwilliam declared.

Forster stood, a scowl on his face. "You dare come into my camp to blacken *my* name now, do you?"

Darcy put a hand on Fitzwilliam's arm. "Colonel Forster, I am certain my cousin means no insult to you," said he. "However, we have reason to believe Wickham has twice left the camp—on Tuesday evening and this morning. Today he took advantage of a young lady of fortune in the hopes of forcing a marriage. Miss Elizabeth Bennet of Longbourn was a witness to both incidents."

He hated having to involve Elizabeth—even just by name—but Darcy felt certain that only his mentioning one person surely known to Forster, whose character was irreproachable, would convince the man of their own sincerity. Recognition, indeed, sparked in Forster's eyes, and he drew a deep breath through his nose.

"She is a trusted, intimate friend of Miss Lucas," he murmured. "I have had no reason thus far in our acquaintance to doubt her honesty."

Forster then picked up a bell on his desk and rang it. Seconds later, an officer Darcy recognized—Denny, the one who'd brought Wickham into their midst in the first place—stepped inside. His commander ordered him to fetch Wickham from their tent and bring him back at once. Denny glanced between Darcy and Fitzwilliam, swallowed, and then hurried away to carry out the task.

They waited nearly ten minutes for their return, during which time Darcy began to wonder if Wickham had escaped and deserted, or was given the opportunity to run by his friend. A perverse sort of relief coursed through him when at last Denny appeared with Wickham in tow.

Wickham merely stared at them on first entering the tent, a telling sign that Denny had warned him who he was to be meeting there. He then crossed his arms, lifted one eyebrow, and said, "To what do I owe the displeasure? Have you come to spread more of your lies to Colonel Forster?"

Fitzwilliam's face darkened with anger, and he stepped across the short space between them to stand toe to toe with Wickham. "On behalf of Mr. James Morland, for whom I stand proxy, I demand satisfaction for your offenses against him and the honor of his sister."

For the briefest of moments—and perhaps only to Darcy himself, who knew Wickham better than the rest—his old friend's countenance showed his alarm. He hid it well, and quickly, proving what a fine actor he was.

Wickham laughed. "You can't seriously be challenging me to a duel, sir! It is illegal in this country."

"Are you refusing to answer my challenge?" Fitzwilliam retorted.

"You'll be tried for attempted murder," said Wickham.

Fitzwilliam scoffed. "Oh, there will be no *attempt*, of that I can assure you. Should the witnesses here gathered report me for taking your worthless, wasted life, the charge would be murder. But then, you seem to be forgetting who my father is—not that I would need the earl's assistance in avoiding a trial."

Wickham's eyes widened a fraction. He then looked past Fitzwilliam to Forster and said, "Colonel Forster, sir, surely you do not condone this willful invocation of illegal action!"

"On the contrary, Wickham," Forster replied gravely. "In spite of that declaration of law, as a career military man I recognize that, oftentimes, a duel is the only way for one gentleman to settle his dispute with another—especially so when the offense regards the honor of a female relation. I've met Mr. Morland and he's a slight little thing; the boy's probably never swatted a fly in the whole course of his life. That he should seek a proxy to issue a challenge on his behalf does not surprise me."

At this, Wickham's face darkened. "Oh yes, because the weak little prig of a would-be parson knows very well he'd lose against me," he said with a sneer. His eyes then returned to Fitzwilliam.

"By no means do I admit to whatever you accuse me of—" he began.

"Admission of your guilt is not required," Fitzwilliam snapped. "Do you accept the challenge, yes or no?"

"I accept," Wickham replied, his tone full of derision. "And we shall see which of us is to escape trial for murder."

He swung away to look at Denny. "I should like you for my second, Denny. I know I can trust you."

Denny looked as though he'd rather do anything else, but nodded his acceptance in silence. Behind them all, Colonel Forster huffed, calling their attention to him.

"Seconds, when and where should you like to do this?" he asked.

Darcy looked again to Denny, then said, "Have you not a shooting range for target practice here at the camp?"

Denny swallowed, then replied, "We do, sir."

"And it is restricted? No access is granted to visitors to the camp?" Darcy pressed, thinking then of Elizabeth's youngest sisters and the other young ladies in Meryton who liked to move about the camp flirting with the officers.

Denny nodded. Turning his eyes to Forster, Darcy said, "Your shooting range will suffice, as it eliminates the chances of non-military personnel witnessing the event."

"Agreed," said Forster. "And the time?"

This Wickham answered himself. "A quarter of an hour, unless it takes Fitzwilliam here longer to acquire a pistol. Might as well have done with it, eh? And we shall see which of us comes out the victor."

"That we shall," Fitzwilliam replied.

Forster then nodded to Denny, who took Wickham by the arm and guided him back out of the tent. Forster then blew out a breath.

"I meant what I said, gentlemen—I stand by a duel of honor no matter what the law says," he began. "But as I am, in essence, sentencing a man to die today—regardless which of them it turns out to be—I would have you explain to me *why* I have agreed to allow it."

Darcy and Fitzwilliam shared a look, then the former relayed to Colonel Forster what Elizabeth had told him, both of Wickham's appearance at the ball as well as his compromise of Catherine Morland only about an hour since.

"I can hardly believe it of him," said Forster as he dropped into his chair when Darcy had finished. "I swear to you, he's been a model officer. I've had no reason to question him—his manners or his behavior—except for what you told me of last week."

"Wickham's appearance of goodness has been carefully crafted over the years, Colonel," Darcy told him. "Many have been fooled by it."

Fitzwilliam turned to Forster and said, "Upon my honor, sir—as a soldier and as the son of an earl—I would not challenge him did I not know him to be a knave of the worst sort. Truth be told, I should have done ages ago. Then dear Miss Morland would not be faced with the potential destruction of her character."

Dear Miss Morland, was she? Darcy mused, and found himself suddenly wondering if there was more to his cousin's offer to marry Catherine than even he realized.

In precisely a quarter of an hour, it was all over. Wickham lay dead on the dusty ground of the militia's shooting range, having received Fitzwilliam's shot directly between his eyes. Darcy's cousin did not escape unwounded, however, as they had expected; he and Wickham had fired at the same moment, though the latter's shot was wide and grazed Fitzwilliam's shoulder.

Darcy's only concern was what Wickham's friends might say, for there was no way they might have kept the matter entirely secret. Several of the enlisted men and a few officers were present at the range when their party appeared, and by their behavior none of the soldiers could be clueless as to their purpose. His concern was somewhat mollified by Forster's announcement beforehand, ordering his men to silence.

"I will not have any of you sullying the name of this good Company by alluding to any illegal action taking place here. This is a dispute between gentlemen, soldier to soldier. Whatever the outcome, it shall not be spoken of *to anyone*. Is that understood?"

His men could do little but agree. Next, the combatants paced off, turned, and shots were fired. Darcy had sighed in resignation—they could return to Netherfield with the report that James Morland's honor was satisfied.

Darcy stood now with Fitzwilliam in the medical tent while the militia's surgeon stitched up the gash on his shoulder.

"I bet that bugger is laughing in whatever section of Perdition he now resides in," said his cousin through gritted teeth. "'You might have killed me, but at least I didn't miss entirely.'"

The surgeon grunted and Darcy shook his head. "You are fortunate it is only a flesh wound," said he.

His cousin snorted. "Surely you didn't expect I would lose?"

"No, but I know Wickham even better than you," Darcy replied. "I own that I feared whatever damage he managed to cause would be worse."

The surgeon had finished tying off the last stitch and was now covering the wound with a bandage. When he had completed that task, he began packing away the articles of his work. "Keep it clean and dressed. Should be able to remove the stitches in a fortnight, minimum."

Fitzwilliam glanced at the dressing on his arm. "Thank you, sir. It is good work."

"Of course it's good work!" snapped the gruff old man, who was the oldest member of Forster's regiment. "I'm a doctor, not a butcher!"

Fitzwilliam chuckled as the surgeon moved away from them. He winced as he lifted his arm to have Darcy help him put his shirt, waistcoat, and jacket back on. When he was dressed, they made their way back to Forster's tent to collect their horses. No one spoke to them; in fact, anyone in their way moved out of it. In silent agreement exchanged in a glance over their saddles, the two simply mounted and rode away.

The journey back to Netherfield was made at a walk, and remained silent until Fitzwilliam suddenly said, "Bugger! I shall have to tell my father about this, won't I?"

Darcy nodded. "I do not imagine you can avoid it, if Miss Morland accepts your offer. Lord Disley is not likely to believe you fell in love with her in only a week."

"Indeed, Darcy," Fitzwilliam agreed.

They were silent again for a minute or two, and then, "You think me a fool, don't you? For offering to marry her."

Darcy looked over at him. "I must own that I do, to an extent."

"Whatever do you mean by that?"

"Theodore, your parents' match was not for love. It was for money and politics, and you have known it most of your life," Darcy replied. "You have told me for as long as I can remember that you wanted a different relationship with your wife than they have."

Fitzwilliam inclined his head. "And I still desire it, Darcy, but at least in my situation there is mutual admiration. My father and mother did not even like each other when they married, and though now they do, there is still little more than respect for a fellow peer between them. The only true love either of them feels is for Philip and I, and my brother's children."

"Precisely my point," Darcy rejoined. "Why would you take the chance of having a loveless marriage when it is what you desire most in your life?"

A sigh escaped his cousin as he turned his gaze forward. "Will, you and I both know how these things work. Gossip spreads like the plague, especially when the rich are involved, and though Catherine is not likely to be known among our circle at present, her name and this nasty business will eventually reach Town. There is little doubt that Mrs. Allen intends to eventually take her there, to introduce her into high society, because that is what wealthy widows do with their unmarried daughters."

"Catherine Morland is not her daughter," Darcy felt compelled to point out.

"She's as good as," Fitzwilliam replied. "Catherine has been named Mr. Allen's heir, she now owns the house he once did, and his widow is her companion. Besides which, you know perfectly well that ladies in Mrs. Allen's situation often take on the task of introducing young ladies of wealth and consequence into society when they have no other capable of doing the office for them."

"Be that as it may, Theo, why—"

"Because I like her!" Fitzwilliam declared. "Catherine is the most charming, unaffected young lady I have ever met, besides your Elizabeth, and I really do enjoy spending time with her. I meant what I said to Morland earlier—I've every reason to think we would do well together. My parents are proof enough that a successful marriage can be made on less, but again, at least Catherine and I like one another already."

Darcy then recalled his thought on hearing Fitzwilliam refer to the young lady as "dear Miss Morland," his suspicion that perhaps his cousin felt more than he let on, and then felt his own argument fall rather flat.

With a sigh, he inclined his head. "Indeed, Theo. At least you have mutual admiration between you, should Miss Morland say yes."

"There's just something about her—I cannot properly put it into words," Fitzwilliam went on. "I have lain awake these last six nights wondering what it is that draws me to her as a moth to a flame. I wonder if it is the way her eyes sparkle when she's excited, or the brilliancy of her smile, or if it is even how little she knows of the world—"

"Placing you in the position of being her educator, in more ways than one," Darcy observed.

His cousin frowned. "It's not like you to be crass, Darcy."

"It was not my intention to imply anything of the sort of which you are thinking. I only meant that there is much you can teach Miss Morland—things about the world in general, learned from your travels; how to navigate high society; your love of history may be of interest to her. I have noted in her a great desire to learn and improve herself, something which her fortune now makes possible that her family's circumstances could not. You've also already two interests in common: you both enjoy dancing and riding on horseback."

"Aye, I've noted we have common interests," Fitzwilliam said. "Such will certainly come in handy for the first awkward nights of our union, provided she sees reason and agrees to the match."

"You have already noted she is not without intelligence, Theo," said Darcy. "I should think that when the facts are presented to her— that it is either marriage to you or the ruin of her reputation—Miss Morland will agree."

He sighed softly, then added, "Though I have said I would wish for you to wed a woman you love, I am also proud of you for being so kind to our young friend. There are sadly few in the world who would be willing, and that you have offered for her is a mark of genuine good character."

"There are few who would be willing even where she poor," Fitzwilliam corrected him. "No doubt her five thousand pounds per annum would be inducement enough to any one of those canting prigs back there, were they to learn she was seen with a soldier." He snorted derisively, shook his head and squared his shoulders, then continued with, "I'm rather proud of being the sort of gentleman who would do as much for the lady—or any other lady I liked so well as I do Catherine—had she nothing at all to bring to the marriage."

"She would have brought three thousand pounds without her inheritance from Mr. Allen, as I understand from something her brother told us," said Darcy, "so even she would hardly have brought nothing. However, since her elevation to fortune, she has told her father to split that equally among her three sisters. Her generosity has thus increased their fortunes to four thousand pounds."

Fitzwilliam grinned. "Do you see, Darcy? I shall be marrying a girl with a most kind and generous nature."

"If she says yes," Darcy reminded him.

The colonel's grin disappeared. "Indeed. *If* she says yes..."

As they were then turning up the lane to Netherfield, Darcy found he could not help reversing their roles—usually his cousin was the joker while he was the more serious of the two. But in sensing that Fitzwilliam was actually nervous and afraid that Miss Morland would reject his proposal, he found he could not help teasing him about how mortifying it would be were she to do so.

"Shut it, Darcy," his cousin growled as he dismounted his horse before the steps of the house. As the words were accompanied by a wince and a slight roll of the left shoulder, Darcy decided he had made him suffer enough.

They entered the foyer as Miss Bingley was crossing from one room to another. She stopped and looked to them with a coy smile, then suddenly gasped and drew a hand to her lips.

"Colonel Fitzwilliam, whatever happened?! Please, sir, tell me that is *not* blood on your jacket," she cried softly. "Oh, I am sure I shall go faint."

A sidelong glance at Fitzwilliam showed Darcy that a muscle twitched in his cousin's jaw. "Then I strongly advise you to turn your eyes away, Miss Bingley," said the former as he continued across the floor toward the stairs.

Darcy followed, their pace briskly taking them away from the lady, and each went in silence into their guest rooms to freshen their attire. As his man helped him exchange his dusty clothing for clean garments, Darcy could not help wondering if Elizabeth were still in the house. Had she remained all this time to comfort her friend, or had she at last made her way home, too impatient to await his return?

And why should it matter either way, old boy, if you are so sure the lady does not care for you? he mused as Vincent was tying his cravat.

When he had dressed he rang for a servant, asking the maid who responded if she knew where Mr. Bingley's aunt and her friends might be.

"Mrs. Allen and Mrs. Annesley are in the breakfast room with Mr. and Mrs. Hurst and Miss Bingley, sir, but Mr. and Miss Morland,

Miss Darcy, and Miss Bennet elected to take breakfast in the library."

Heavens, he'd forgotten all about breakfast. No doubt Caroline was both vexed by the four young people not wanting to share the meal with their host's family and yet pleased she did to not have to make the effort of being polite to them all—she'd been rather out of sorts by not capturing Theodore's attentions beyond polite and indifferent replies the last week. Darcy thanked the girl and sent her on her way, then went to his cousin's door and knocked. Fitzwilliam came out almost at once wearing a slight grimace.

"I think I shall have to see if Bingley has a remedy chest," said he as he slowly rotated his left arm. "Wretched shoulder is aching now."

"I believe he has. Mrs. Nicholls will know where it is kept," Darcy said, then turned to lead the way downstairs.

As they neared the library door, Fitzwilliam paused. Darcy turned back to him as he shook himself, mumbling about how he was a soldier and had faced down hordes of Frenchmen. "One tiny slip of a girl should not make me so bloody nervous," said he as he drew a breath, squared his shoulders, and moved to open the library doors himself.

Chapter Seventeen

Elizabeth and the others heard the return of Darcy and his cousin; Catherine and Georgiana both expressed their relief verbally, while she had remained silent...though no less relieved they were back again. She knew that seconds could be called upon to act in the stead of the challenger or challenged in a duel, and though she detested the necessity of the barbaric practice, her certainty that Darcy would have no need to go so far was strong. Still, when the two men stepped through the library door, she breathed her relief that he appeared unharmed.

Catherine stood immediately and took a few steps toward them.

"Colonel Fitzwilliam," she began tearfully. "My brother—he said... he said you..."

Fitzwilliam walked up to her, stopping a little more than arms' length away to bow from the waist. "You need not fear you will be forced into marriage with that scoundrel, my dear Miss Morland. He is the ███ problem now."

Elizabeth watched with no small amount of surprise as Catherine then threw her arms about him; a soft cry of pain from the colonel led her immediately to pull away. Beside Elizabeth, Georgiana stood and moved toward the pair.

"Theodore, are you hurt?" said Miss Darcy.

Fitzwilliam's eyes remained on Catherine as he replied, "'Tis just a scratch."

"You mean he shot you?!" Catherine cried. "You... You took a bullet for my brother. For me! You are hurt because of my foolishness!"

She turned away from him but Fitzwilliam stopped her by reaching for her hand. He held it pressed between his and waited through her sniffles until she at last raised her eyes back to him.

"My dear Miss Morland, do not ever blame yourself," said the colonel softly. "Whatever he said to you, whatever he did to you, I can assure you that *you* are not at fault for any of it. George Wickham was a villainous libertine who would have sold his mother to pay a debt, had she still been alive."

"Is George really dead, Fitzwilliam?" queried Georgiana, her question punctuated by a sneeze.

"He is, yes," her brother replied. "You need no longer fear him either, dearest."

Darcy then moved past his cousin and Catherine to take his sister by the arm. "Come, Georgiana, and sit by the fire. You are still unwell and should be in bed."

James stood from the table and went to stand next to his sister as the colonel at last released her hand. "I am truly sorry you were injured facing that wretch in my stead, sir. I hope it is nothing too serious."

"His shot grazed my arm, that is all," Fitzwilliam replied. His gaze at last turned to James. "Did you also speak to your sister of what else we discussed?"

At this, James looked to Catherine. She sniffled again and said, "H-he did say that even should you be the victor in the duel, my character might still be destroyed. James said that...that a marriage of convenience might be my only salvation. But who would have me after what that man did to me?!"

Fitzwilliam looked to James with a frown. "You didn't tell her about...?"

"No," said James with a shake of his head. "I thought... Well, I rather thought it should come from you."

Elizabeth cleared her throat in a delicate manner as she at last pushed to her feet. "Should we all give you some privacy, Colonel?"

"No, Miss Bennet, I should think not—all of you but Georgie already know what I mean to say," Fitzwilliam replied.

He held out his hand and waited until Catherine took the hint and placed one of hers into it. "Miss Morland—Catherine, if I may... We do not know each other well, but we have got on rather splendidly, I think, from the first moment of our meeting. I have very much enjoyed talking with you, laughing with you, and dancing with you. These circumstances are wretched—there can be no denying that—

but I cannot bear to see so amiable a young lady as you cast down, nor could I stand by and do nothing while the cruel and cowardly try to bring you down further. *I* will have you, madam, if you will have me."

From her place by the fire, Georgiana gasped. Darcy cautioned her with a soft *shh* to remain silent.

Elizabeth slowly took a few steps to the right, that she might get a look at Catherine's face. She was in awe of Darcy's cousin for his kindness to her friend, and as much as she would have wished circumstances to be different—that their coming together was due to want rather than need—she could not but think that this moment was incredibly special. She felt privileged to have been allowed to be a part of it, and was compelled to sate her curiosity as to how Catherine was feeling about it.

Catherine's expression at first seemed one of confusion. "You... You can't mean it," said she. "How can you ask me to marry you on so short an acquaintance as ours?"

Fitzwilliam looked for a moment at their joined hands, then back into Catherine's searching gaze. "I am asking you because I care what happens to you. I cannot abide the wont of society to degrade someone's character when they have done no wrong. I understand that Meryton is not a large town, that one might think that if you should leave it, all will be well again. Unfortunately, gossip has the means of spreading beyond even a small, idyllic hamlet such as this. There are people here who make regular sojourns to London, to Brighton, to Bath... These are places you may go, where you have been. You may not be known in them now, but by the time you go to them or return, it is sadly possible that your name and the terrible situation caused by Wickham's greed may have been spread about."

"Cathy," spoke up James. "If you are married soon, anyone you meet who has heard of this unfortunate business will merely assume you were two young lovers who were caught in an assignation. For that matter, who is to say you did not know Colonel Fitzwilliam before his coming to Hertfordshire?"

"But why him?" Catherine demanded. "Why not Mr. Bingley or Mr. Darcy? Why does Colonel Fitzwilliam give up his chance to marry for love? If matters are as you say, and marriage is all that will save me from ruin in the eyes of society, why can I not marry one of them, or anyone I choose?"

On hearing these words, the colonel grimaced and let go her hand. He took a step back as he said, "I shall not press you, Miss Morland, if the thought of marriage to me is so reprehensible to you. But you must know that, having been seen in the presence of a man in regimentals, your options are sadly limited to one serving King and country."

Fitzwilliam took another step back, then suddenly turned about and started for the door. He had taken but two steps when Catherine hurried to stop him, reaching out to take his arm.

"Colonel, please wait," said she, drawing a ragged breath as tears began to spill down her cheeks. "I beg you not to think ill of me, for I do not at all find the thought of marriage to you reprehensible. It's just that it pains me deeply to consider what you would be giving up — what we should both of us be giving up — if we should marry."

Turning partway back, Fitzwilliam asked, "And what do you think that is?"

"Why, the chance to be married to the person we love."

Fitzwilliam took the hand on his arm and once more pressed it between his own. "I like to think — that is, I sincerely hope — that our mutual respect for one another might one day grow into love. As there is some measure of fondness between us already, have we not as much chance of a happy life together as a marriage that begins with love?"

"I... I do not know, really," Catherine said. "I have never been in love. I only know that I want to be, someday."

The colonel nodded, then reached into his pocket and pulled out a handkerchief. He held it out to Catherine, who took it and quickly dried her face.

They still held hands, Elizabeth noted, which she felt was a very good sign.

"If you will accept me, Miss Morland," said Fitzwilliam after a moment, "I shall make you a promise."

"Oh? And what shall you promise me, sir?"

He smiled. "I will give you my solemn promise to do all that is within my power to make you happy, that you do not regret saying yes."

Once more, Catherine looked to her brother for guidance. "James, what do you think? What do you imagine our father will say?"

James drew a deep breath and released it slowly. "Cathy, you must know that I shall ever only want what is best for you, and I do not doubt that Father would say the same. In an ideal world you *would* be allowed to marry for love, as I will do, but regrettably you have not the choice because that wretch Wickham stole it from you.

Now you have but to decide whether you are willing to accept a man who is sacrificing his own chance at a love match to preserve your reputation, or to risk the censure of the *ton* that you will surely be amongst one day and possibly any chance at all of being respectably settled."

Catherine sniffled once more, then drew a breath and squared her slim shoulders. She looked to Fitzwilliam and offered a teary smile. "It seems I have little choice, really, but to accept you and pray that you keep your promise. So you'd best be good to me, Colonel Fitzwilliam, as I've three brothers older than myself who will call *you* out if you are not."

Laughter escaped the colonel as well as her brother, then the former lifted her hand and pressed his lips to the back of it. A faint blush colored Catherine's pale cheeks, then she turned suddenly to Georgiana and made a sweeping gesture toward her.

"Go on, Georgie. Say it if you must."

Elizabeth knew instantly to what she referred, and a grin alighted on her face.

Georgiana sneezed again, then grinned widely as Fitzwilliam looked between the two. "Dare I ask to what it is you refer?" he asked.

Elizabeth moved forward and stood next to Catherine. "Your dear young cousin made an observation of you yesterday," said she, "in which she expressed her belief that you admired our friend Miss Morland."

Fitzwilliam raised an eyebrow as he looked to Georgiana and said, "Is that so?"

Georgiana giggled. "I did, and Lizzy agreed with me," she replied. "We were right, Cathy! Theodore would not have offered to help you did he not admire you."

"I must beg to differ, Georgiana," spoke up Darcy. "You and I both know our cousin to be a genuinely good man. I believe he would have offered marriage to Miss Morland even without his present admiration for her."

Catherine and Fitzwilliam looked to one another; he smiled and she blushed again, and then a silent agreement was made by all at once to return a semblance of normalcy into their lives. Elizabeth and Catherine were encouraged to take seats near the fire, with the gentlemen offering to bring the food nearer, that Georgiana did not need to get up again. Breaking their fast commenced in silence for a few moments, until Catherine broke it by saying,

"James, we shall have to go to Fullerton again, won't we?"

Her brother inclined his head. "I believe we must," said he. "Such delicate news as this cannot be written of in a letter."

Catherine's answering nod was reluctant. "I do not think I can bear to even imagine how distressed Mamma will be. To think that I have gone from innocent girl to compromised to engaged, all of a single morning!"

Elizabeth reached over and laid a hand to her shoulder, as her friend had done at the ball when she was feeling her own emotional turmoil. "Cathy, I am sorry for all the pain you have felt in these last hours. I can only imagine how overwhelmed you must be feeling, but surely God will have His say in making things right for you."

Catherine smiled weakly. "You know the people here the best of us, Lizzy. Do you really think they will gossip about what they saw? There were only three or four ladies, I think, who stopped to look."

"There were four," Elizabeth clarified. "And unfortunately, I cannot give you a certain answer. My neighbors are at heart good people —as are most in the world, I imagine—but as Meryton *is* a small market town, anything that happens outside of the normal routine of a day is like to be talked of."

Catherine groaned, then glanced at Fitzwilliam. "I own that I had some small hope we might not need to marry, but it seems I am to hope in vain. It's just not fair that either of us should be forced to make a decision we'd not have done otherwise just because that hateful man kissed me."

Both James and Fitzwilliam's expressions darkened. "What is unfair is that he has forced the necessity upon you, Cathy," said James. "But I pray you would not distress yourself over what our parents will say, as I am certain that Father and Mamma will be most grateful to the colonel for the offer he has made you."

"As regrettable as our circumstances are, Miss Morland," began Fitzwilliam, "you must remember that yours is not the only reputation at stake. You have three sisters whose chances of a good match would suffer should your character be damaged by Wickham's misdeeds. Even your brothers' chances would be lessened."

Catherine frowned. "Do you mean that my entire family could be made to suffer?"

"It is most unfortunate—and unfair—but Theodore is right," offered Darcy. "In such cases as these, society likes to shun all in a family for the actions of one, because the rest are believed to be tainted by association."

At this, Catherine snorted. "If that is the way of society, then I want nothing to do with it! I should be quite happy to stay always at Fullerton."

"Even the citizens of your beloved Fullerton would behave so, madam, should they hear of what was done," Fitzwilliam said. "I truly dislike laying so much upon your shoulders, my dear, but you really must think of others and not just yourself. You stand upon the precipice of change for your entire family — the reputation of all those you love most rests in your hands."

"Much as I am loath to agree, Colonel Fitzwilliam is right," said James. "By accepting his offer of marriage, you not only save yourself, you also save the rest of us from ruin."

"Mr. Bennet would be within his rights to revoke his permission for your brother to marry his daughter," the colonel went on. "You might consider that as well."

The expression which overcame the faces of both Morlands was one of horror; Elizabeth knew she needed to speak up. "That may be true, Colonel, but I believe I may safely venture that my father would not take such an action. He would believe the truth, that Catherine was not a willing participant in what happened."

She turned to her friend then and added, "However... Though it pains me to burden you with more responsibility, in marrying your brother, Jane links my family's reputation to your family's, and scandal would then not only harm yours but ours as well. Regrettable as it is, you must consider all who will be affected by your choice."

Catherine emitted an unladylike groan as she set her plate aside and stood, pacing away from them with her hands on her hips. "All right, I get the point!" she said, her voice tinged with anger and frustration. "I am Atlas, with the whole of the bloody world upon my shoulders!"

Fitzwilliam hurried to stand and stepped to where she paced. He stopped her movement in taking her by the shoulders. "Catherine, I am sorry," said he. "It is assuredly not anyone's intention to make this situation any more difficult for you to endure than it already is. We only want for you to understand how even one action not of your doing, and how you respond to it, can affect more than yourself."

Catherine's eyes filled with tears. "You're telling me that it is up to me to save my family, but nobody who had ever seen me in my infancy would have supposed *me* born to be a heroine," she said morosely.

Fitzwilliam smiled. "I rather like the idea of being wed to a heroine."

"You said I would need to marry a soldier. It does not have to be you," Catherine said then.

"Why do you resist the idea of marrying me?"

"Because… Because I think too well of you to want such a burden as saving my family to be yours," she replied. "And I fear you will come to regret the choice you make now, and will resent me for it later."

Fitzwilliam lifted a hand to brush away the tears that fell over her lashes. "I hardly think I ever shall, knowing now that you wish to spare me your burden. But while you want to save me, I want to save you. So let us save each other and carry the burden together."

The brief silence that followed his words was broken by a sigh from Georgiana. "Oh, how romantic!"

Her statement was followed by laughter from all. Even Catherine laughed through her tears, and at last was escorted back to her chair by Fitzwilliam.

When they were both of them seated, he said, "I should like to go with you when you make your journey, though I would make a slight alteration to the plan of going to Fullerton directly."

"What sort of alteration?" asked James.

"My parents are by now be arrived in London for the winter," said Fitzwilliam. "I should like to introduce Catherine to them when I inform the earl and countess that I am to marry."

"Oh, heaven save me!" cried Catherine. "I had forgot that your parents were peers! Are you truly certain, Colonel, that you want to marry me? Would they allow you to when there is such a risk of scandal?"

For the first time, Elizabeth noted some concern creeping into the colonel's features. "In all honesty, they will not likely be pleased by the circumstances," Fitzwilliam admitted. "But then, at risk of sounding indelicate, I've no doubt that the size of your fortune will appease them. One or the other of my parents is likely to exaggerate the truth a little and claim a prior acquaintance between us, especially if the Allens are known to them."

"Oh, that is a good point, Colonel!" said Elizabeth. "It may well work in your favor be there even a remote acquaintance, I should think."

"But would not Mrs. Allen have spoke of it already, if she knew your parents?" asked Catherine.

Fitzwilliam tilted his head in thought. "Perhaps, if she had met either since their marriage."

"It is possible, however," said Darcy, "that either my aunt or my uncle may have known Mr. or Mrs. Allen before their marriage. They could have known the earl when he held his father's lesser title, as Theodore's brother does now."

"There is one way we may find out," said Georgiana. "Let us call Mrs. Allen in here to ask her."

Chapter Eighteen

"**Oh yes,** let us do that," said Catherine.

Elizabeth smiled at her friend and rose to go and give the bell-pull a tug. The maid who responded was given direction to find Mrs. Allen and bring her to the library; they did not wait long for her appearance.

"Oh, Colonel Fitzwilliam, I am glad you are come home safe!" said the lady upon closing the door. "James told us you were to fight that perfidious man who accosted my dear Catherine — tell me he has been done away with!"

Fitzwilliam gave a slight bow. "Though I regret the necessity of my actions, yes. Mr. Wickham is deceased and Miss Morland is saved from him. However, it does not free her from the possibility of scandal, I'm afraid, as Miss Bennet has stated there were witnesses other than she and yourself."

"Oh yes, there were — Mrs. Long was one, if I recall, and dear Miss Elizabeth, you know how *that* one likes to talk, I am sure!" said Mrs. Allen as she came closer. Stopping behind Catherine's chair, she laid one hand to the top as she lifted her handkerchief to her lips, reminding Elizabeth of her own mother.

"Oh, my good sir, have you or Mr. Darcy any idea as to how we may save dear Catherine from ruin?" Mrs. Allen asked. "I have been in society many times, but so little in recent years as to have hardly been at all. You young gentlemen have greater understanding of the *ton* than even I, I am sure. What can we do?"

Fitzwilliam looked to Catherine, who drew a breath and gave a slight nod. On looking back to Mrs. Allen, the colonel said, "Ma'am, as the person who accosted Miss Morland was in regimentals, we have determined that marriage to a soldier is regrettably her only choice."

"Will you do it?!" begged Mrs. Allen, stepping around to grasp his hands. "Please, sir—you are a soldier, are you not? And you are single. I know I have not the right to ask you such a thing, given how little we are acquainted, but I should be eternally grateful, as I know my dear friends Reverend and Mrs. Morland will be, if you might be so kind as to marry their daughter that her reputation is preserved."

She gestured to Catherine. "I am sure she and James will forgive me the liberty, and I pray you will also, but Catherine is very dear to me, you see. She's a very good girl, sir. And pretty, as you see here. She's full young yet and has much to learn, but I am sure she will do you credit."

"Mrs. Allen," Catherine interrupted her. She stood and drew a breath, then said, "Colonel Fitzwilliam has already made me an offer of marriage. I have accepted him."

Mrs. Allen looked between them. "He has? You have, sir? Oh, bless you, my dear boy!" She stood on her toes to kiss Fitzwilliam's cheek. "Thank you! Thank you! Oh, Catherine, how worried I have been for you! Your reputation—your family's reputation!"

Catherine's expression soured. "Believe me, Mrs. Allen, I am full aware of the implications. My friends have made sure of it."

"The reason we asked you here, ma'am," said Fitzwilliam, "is because Mr. Morland and Miss Morland have determined to journey to Fullerton to inform their parents—"

Mrs. Allen swiveled to encompass the sister and brother in her gaze. "Oh, yes! Oh, you could not tell your poor mother such news in a letter!"

"Indeed, Mrs. Allen," said James.

"As my betrothed and her brother must inform their parents," Fitzwilliam went on, "so must I inform my own. So we shall be traveling first to London that I may speak to them, as well as introduce Miss Morland to them."

"Oh, what a fine idea!" agreed Mrs. Allen. "Catherine, my dear, you will soon be the daughter of an earl and a countess—how grand!"

"Mrs. Allen," spoke up Darcy. "The incident of this morning will no doubt be the cause of some concern for my aunt and uncle, but we have discerned that their worry might possibly be abated by some...exaggeration of the relationship between Miss Morland and

Colonel Fitzwilliam."

The lady frowned. "Exaggeration? What do you mean, exaggeration? I won't allow you to lie about Catherine—"

"Mrs. Allen, Mr. Darcy does not mean that anyone should lie about me," said Catherine. "What we were wondering is if, by chance, you might have met either of Colonel Fitzwilliam's parents."

Mrs. Allen looked to Fitzwilliam. "Who are they again, sir? I remember you saying they are an earl and a countess, but I am afraid I do not recall your father's title."

"My parents are the Earl and Countess of Disley, ma'am," Fitzwilliam replied. "Before taking up the earldom, my father would have been known by his secondary title, Viscount Rowarth. My mother, before her marriage, was known as Lady Frances Booth. Her father was the Earl of Warrington."

A look of concentration came over the lady's features; after a moment, she shook her head and said, "Those names and titles are all unfamiliar to me, I'm afraid. But Mr. Allen may have known them. I seem to remember that he knew some peers in his youth—he did say he went to school with several young men of rank in his day."

"If my father knew him, and thought well of him, then it will certainly make his acceptance of my marriage all the easier," said Fitzwilliam. "I need not his permission, for I am nine-and-twenty, but I should like his blessing."

"Yes, indeed… Oh! I understand now what Mr. Darcy meant by exaggeration!" Mrs. Allen crowed. "If my dear late husband was known to one or the other of your parents, then one could easily assume that, through their acquaintance, you might have met Catherine months or even years ago. What happened today could then be easily turned to your advantage, as a secret assignation by two young lovers who simply were not careful enough!"

"That is the idea, Mrs. Allen," said Catherine in a droll tone as she returned again to her chair.

Elizabeth moved away from her friends, as they talked more of going to London, to stand at the window. She sighed as she wrapped her arms about herself, wondering just how much of today's events she ought to reveal to her family, if Mrs. Long had not yet made her way to Longbourn to spread the gossip.

She was joined there a moment later by Darcy. "Are you well, Miss Bennet?"

"Quite well, sir," she replied. "I am just…"

"Wondering about the effect this news will have on your family?"

her companion ventured.

Elizabeth nodded. "Yes. I truly do not believe my father will rescind his blessing of my sister's marriage, but there will undoubtedly be some concern as to how it will affect the prospects of my sisters."

From my mother most of all, she added silently.

"Your parents will surely be appeased on hearing that Miss Morland and my cousin are to marry, thereby giving them some degree of connection to the nobility via the marriage of their daughter to her brother," Darcy suggested.

Elizabeth chuckled. "You know my mother so well, Mr. Darcy."

"Forgive me, I should not have —"

"You'll come too, won't you, Lizzy?"

Elizabeth turned at the question Catherine asked. "Come where?" she queried.

Catherine laughed as she moved across the room to stand before her. "Why, to London, of course. And Fullerton. James means to ask your father if Jane may accompany us, that he can introduce her to our parents before their wedding."

Elizabeth glanced briefly at Darcy, whose expression showed no emotion other than mild curiosity. She could not but wonder what he was thinking, if he would want her to join the party — for surely he and Georgiana would at least accompany their cousin to Town.

Looking to Catherine, she said, "Will not your coach be rather too full if Jane goes along?"

"Oh, but you can go with us — can she not, brother?" said Georgiana, her question once again followed by a sneeze.

"Certainly, if Mr. Bennet should grant his permission that Miss Elizabeth may accompany Miss Bennet," Darcy replied. "Now, sister, that is the third or fourth sneeze of the last half hour. I should like you to get back into bed and rest."

"Oh yes, my dear girl," said Mrs. Allen, who moved to assist her. "Come, we will stop in the drawing room for Mrs. Annesley, that she may accompany you."

Georgiana sighed as she stood. "I am rather tired. Good day to you all. I hope to be well enough to join you for dinner."

When she and Mrs. Allen were gone from the room, Elizabeth glanced around, then said, "I believe I should also take my leave. I must speak to my parents about what has happened, if Mrs. Long has not done so already."

"Indeed," said James as he stood. "I must join you, that I may speak to your father regarding our journey."

"And I shall go as well," said Catherine.

Elizabeth did not miss the brief flicker of pain in Colonel Fitzwilliam's eyes when Catherine spoke but her friend did, as she had already turned away from him. Though she knew their relationship was now irrevocably changed—she believed for the better—Elizabeth vowed that if given the chance while they were at Longbourn, she would encourage Catherine not to behave any differently towards the colonel, lest she sow the seed of the resentment she already feared he would come to feel.

She might even speak to her on the way, she mused as James went to call the carriage. At least then Catherine might not feel so embarrassed, when there would be no one else to offer an opinion but her brother.

❧

Darcy's eye was on Fitzwilliam, whose own eyes followed Catherine as she trailed after her brother and Elizabeth on quitting the room.

"Have I made a mistake, Will?"

Darcy suppressed a snort. "*Now* you ask the question?" said he. "Not even an hour ago you were telling me all the reasons you had for wanting to marry her. Have you changed your mind?"

Fitzwilliam turned to him. "No, of course not!" he retorted. "It's just... She seemed so eager to get away from me. I wonder if I might have pushed her too hard to accept me because it's what *I* wanted, not just because marrying a soldier is what she needs."

"I surmise that Miss Morland is only overwhelmed, not that she no longer desires your company," Darcy said. "Remember, Theo, that you have the benefit of eleven years more life in the world than she has. She was also probably frightened out of her wits by what Wickham did, as well as the knowledge of how damaging it could be to herself and her family. Give her time to adjust to her new circumstances."

"From innocent girl, to compromised, to engaged. All of a morning," Fitzwilliam mused, repeating Miss Morland's own words.

"Exactly so."

Fitzwilliam sighed, then rubbed a hand over his face. "When do you think we might take this trip? I don't believe it should be put off long."

"Agreed. Though I do not imagine it will, we should endeavor to reach your parents before the story has the chance to," Darcy said then. "That way, when your engagement to Miss Morland is announced, the narrative can be controlled."

"Especially if either of them was acquainted with Mr. Allen," his cousin noted.

"Quite so," Darcy conceded. "Though now I think of it, I almost dread the meeting with your mother and father."

Fitzwilliam frowned. "Why should you fear it? I'm the one that must tell them I'm to marry a girl because she was compromised by that rat Wickham."

Darcy snorted. "Think about it, cousin: Philip is married and has children. You're soon to be married."

"At last, my mother will no doubt say," Fitzwilliam mumbled.

"Precisely. Now, who do you think she will focus on next in the family?"

After a moment of staring at him, his cousin began to laugh. "Oh dear, I see now what you mean. Once it is firmly established that I am no longer in the running for all those silly girls in the *beau monde*, she will look to you."

"I'm so pleased you now take pleasure in my imminent torture," Darcy drawled.

"Oi, weren't you mocking my fear of Catherine saying no when we were coming up the drive?" Fitzwilliam challenged.

Darcy nodded with a chuckle. "*Touché*, cousin."

When the Morlands returned from Longbourn later that morning, Darcy and Fitzwilliam had removed from the library into the billiard room. The game, which was at an even score, was abandoned upon their entrance. Jane and Elizabeth, announced Morland, would be joining them in going to London and Fullerton.

"Mrs. Long had already been to Longbourn to share the 'news' with her good friend Mrs. Bennet," Morland groused. "Fortunately— if that word can even be applied this mess—it is as we figured: the lady knew *something* had happened, but not precisely what. As soon as we stepped foot in the drawing room, Miss Lydia asked Catherine which one of Colonel Forster's soldiers she'd been meeting with—she thought it 'very wrong' of her not to have shared she had a favorite. Her remark was followed by Mrs. Bennet telling us that Mrs. Long had come by to ask if she had heard that 'Miss Morland was caught in an assignation with one of Colonel Forster's men' by Elizabeth, Mrs. Allen, herself, and three other ladies whose names I have already forgotten."

Darcy shook his head in disbelief at the impertinence of their queries. How such intelligence as existed in the eldest three Miss Bennets—as Miss Mary had proved to be near as sensible as Jane and Elizabeth—had developed alongside such foolishness as existed in their mother and youngest sisters, he was at a great loss to understand.

Miss Morland colored, but lifted her chin. "I told the truth, or at least a limited version of it, as Lizzy advised me to do. She thought it a good idea, and James and I heartily agreed, that we should take as much control of the story as we can. We decided that—because there *were* witnesses—if asked any questions, I should be honest and admit having met someone, but to say nothing of who it was or what actually took place between us. Anything else that is said can be dismissed as gossip and speculation."

Fitzwilliam smiled at her. "Miss Elizabeth is very wise. I agree that it will help, though I caution you it is not likely to do away with the gossip entirely. The people here will still talk and wonder over those details you refuse to specify."

Miss Morland moved to one of two chairs before the fireplace and dropped indecorously into it with a groan. "Ugh! I *hate* prattling gossips! May God strike me down if I should ever engage in such tittle-tattle ever again!"

"Mr. Bennet, who was on our arrival reading a newspaper, asked to speak to me privately," her brother went on. "I knew I would need to tell him the entire truth if I hoped to retain the privilege of marrying his daughter, so I told him everything that transpired this morning. You may imagine my relief when he was not as disturbed by the news of my sister's situation as I had feared."

Mr. Bennet was likely more amused than bothered, thought Darcy sourly. He felt for Elizabeth, Jane, and Mary for having a father who was not unintelligent, but who cared more for his own comforts and needs than those of his family, and who took delight in the follies of his neighbors.

Fitzwilliam looked at James. "He could have withdrawn his blessing, Morland, that is true, but as Miss Bennet is over the age of majority…"

He allowed the remainder of the sentence to go unsaid. Morland appeared to consider the notion, then shook his head. "No. No, Jane would never go against him like that."

"And she is a good girl to not want to displease her father," said his sister. "I certainly have no wish to displease mine."

"Miss Morland, I am sure your father will not blame you for what has happened," Fitzwilliam said.

Miss Morland looked to her brother for a moment, then back at him. "No, he will not," said she with a weak smile. "Still, I cannot help despairing of my parents' displeasure with the lot of this nonsense."

"It is only natural that they should be concerned for you," said Darcy. "But even having not met them myself, I imagine they will be pleased for you to have met a gentleman of such steady character as Theodore, who is so willing to bear the burden of your troubles with you."

Color came to her cheeks and she glanced down at her hands, which she now twisted in her lap. "I am so nervous," she said then, "to be meeting with an earl and a countess."

Fitzwilliam crossed to sit in the chair opposite her and leaned forward, bracing his elbows on his knees as he looked to her with an earnest expression. "Pray do not make yourself uneasy, my dear Miss Morland. My mother and father will think you as delightful as I do when they come to know you."

"Are you certain they will not be disappointed by your choice of bride?" she asked. "I have a fortune, yes, but no connections worth speaking of, and then there is this dreadful business which is the only reason we are marrying to begin with."

Fitzwilliam reached over and took up one of her hands, which Darcy noted looked so very small and fragile in his cousin's.

"My dear, you will have all the connections you shall ever need when we are married. And if it pleases you to remain always at Fullerton, then I am sure I shall be content with that."

Miss Morland laughed. "You cannot mean that. A gentleman as worldly as yourself, staying always in the country?"

"If it makes my lady happy, I will do what I must."

A full smile was his reward. "Already you are too generous to me, sir. I would not keep you from your friends and relations in any city if you should want to go and see them."

"I'll not go anywhere without you once we are married," Fitzwilliam insisted.

The two began to argue good-naturedly over whether he should stay with her at Fullerton, if she would join him in visiting his friends and relations, or if he should go visiting alone. Darcy felt some relief in seeing her now more relaxed, and behaving towards his cousin in the same manner she had been before Wickham pulled that wretched stunt of his.

James Morland sidled up to him, and said in a low voice, "What to say if asked questions is not the only thing Elizabeth gave her opinion of to my sister on the way to Longbourn."

Darcy lifted an eyebrow in curiosity; Morland was no longer using proper address in regard to Elizabeth—but then, she had used his Christian name earlier, and they were soon to be brother and sister.

"Did she? And what other wisdom did she pass on?"

"Elizabeth mentioned Catherine's behavior between the time of your return and the time of our departure, noting that she seemed to have altered her manner. Elizabeth said that, while she understood the situation to be overwhelming, the fact that Cathy and the colonel are going to be married should have no affect on how she behaves towards him. She said quite plainly that Cathy ought to think of him as she ever did, and allow the relationship to progress as it would naturally have done."

"They are wise words," Darcy noted, then he raised his voice a little and suggested they begin making plans for their journey. As there were two carriages between them and a total of nine travelers, he and Fitzwilliam would go on horseback. Mrs. Annesley, Georgiana, and Elizabeth would have the Darcy coach, while the Morlands, Mrs. Allen, and Jane would take the Allen carriage.

As to accommodations, Darcy immediately offered his London townhouse. There was plenty of room for everyone, he assured Catherine Morland when asked, though some of the party would have to share rooms. Her brother reminded him that the Bennet sisters had relations who lived in London and said they might wish to stay with them, to which Darcy replied he would certainly see them conveyed to Gracechurch Street if that was their wish.

Mrs. Allen was next informed of the plan they had settled on; she agreed readily with everything. A note was then dispatched to Longbourn to convey the plan to Jane and Elizabeth; a reply was brought back to Darcy stating they would be honored to be his guests, though they expressed a wish to spend at least a full day in the city that they might have opportunity to pay a call on their uncle's family.

He and the others had no issue with acquiescing to the request; in fact, as they were not to depart until after breakfast the following day, it was no trouble to delay going on to Fullerton until Saturday.

Bingley surprised the house by returning earlier than expected;

he'd believed he would not be back until Friday morning, but he returned shortly before dinner was called. After greeting everyone and giving assurance that his business affairs were settled—and dismissing his sister Caroline's complaint that she had just been suggesting to Louisa that they join him in London, thereby negating a reason for his returning to Hertfordshire at all—he pulled Darcy aside and said in a low voice,

"I stopped in Meryton to pay on my accounts there, and you'll not believe what nonsense I heard!"

Darcy grimaced, and then as quickly and quietly as he could, explained that morning's horrid events and their aftermath.

Chapter Nineteen

If the Darcy townhouse was any indication, Elizabeth mused, the estate in Derbyshire must be very grand indeed.

The furniture and decorations were all clearly expensive, but of a somewhat understated elegance. To her mind, instead of being an obvious attempt to not exaggerate the family's wealth, it seemed rather to make it all the more prominent by its tastefulness.

After Darcy showed all the public rooms to his guests, everyone was taken by a maid to their private chambers. Elizabeth and Jane were to share a room, which suited the sisters very well. When alone, Jane confessed that she had felt some concern over the propriety of both herself and Catherine being under the same roof with the men they were to marry, but said it surely could not be questioned when they were each sharing a room with another person.

Elizabeth could not help but laugh. "I do not imagine Mrs. Allen has shared a room with anyone but her husband since she was a girl! But yes, with an older companion for Catherine, and my own diligence, the virtues of both of you will be protected."

She was a little surprised when her sister then blushed deeply and turned away from her. "Jane, what is it?"

Jane drew a breath, then turned to her with her eyes still cast down. "I... We have *not* anticipated our vows, James and I—let me be clear on that, Lizzy. But I... I can hardly believe I shall confess this, but I think—had I my own room—I might have been sorely tempted."

Elizabeth could not but stare in open-mouthed shock. "Jane Bennet, I am astonished!"

At last her sister lifted her head to meet her gaze. "You would not think it, I believe, to look upon the slightness of his build, or by his impeccable manners, but James is a very passionate individual. The very few times we have been alone together, when he has kissed me... Lizzy, I do believe I could literally *feel* his desire for me. His need, if it can be described as such. It... It was dizzying. Overwhelming. I am in awe that any woman should have such power over a man that she can all but undo him with only a kiss."

Elizabeth shook her head. "I must say, I did not know even you could inspire such a reaction in a man. His self-control and yours are to be commended."

Jane's sigh was clearly one of relief. "Thank you, sister, for not passing judgment upon me for my behavior. I know it is highly improper, but..."

Holding up a hand, Elizabeth said, "You need say no more, dearest. What you do in privacy with your betrothed is your own concern. Though just so you know this, if you and my soon-to-be brother *had* anticipated your vows, I do not imagine I could pass judgment. Firstly, it is not my place but God's to do so; secondly, I know that the two of you truly love one another, so sharing yourself with him would only be natural. And surely the wedding will be soon enough that if you *were* to go so far, no questions would be asked if your first child came only eight months and a half or so after the ceremony took place."

Jane blushed even deeper and covered her face with her hands, but when she looked up again at last she wore a smile. The two then set about changing their traveling attire and attending to their hair, that they would be more presentable when calling on their aunt in Gracechurch Street after the luncheon Mr. Darcy had arranged to be served, as the party had missed having a proper breakfast.

On entering the dining parlor, they found everyone but Mrs. Allen already arrived. Upon inquiry, Catherine said that her friend had been fatigued by the journey, though it was fairly short, and had requested a tray in her room.

"She means to prepare herself, she said, for tonight's 'very important event' as she described it," Catherine finished.

Elizabeth knew instantly to what she referred: the dinner party that Darcy and Colonel Fitzwilliam hoped to arrange, in which Catherine would be introduced to the latter's parents. While she and her brother would be accompanying the Bennet sisters to Cheapside, their host and his cousin were set to call on Lord and Lady Disley in

Bolton Street.

Catherine, who was a bundle of nerves over meeting the earl and countess, was glad to have some distraction from it in joining Jane and Elizabeth's visit to their aunt, uncle, and young cousins. When they had finished dining, the Allen coach was called for and the four took their leave.

"I do hope the colonel's meeting with his father goes well," Catherine mused when the carriage was underway.

Her brother, who sat beside her, reached over and took her hand to give it a squeeze. "Cathy, pray do not distress yourself. Theo is sure—"

"Since when do you call him that?" she interjected. "I can't even bring myself to use his full Christian name, though he has told me I may."

James chuckled. "Sister, he shall soon be my brother—we have mutually agreed that formality is hardly necessary between us."

Catherine snorted softly. "How lovely for you. I'm to be the man's *wife*, yet I cannot even picture a time when I shall address him as Theodore, let alone shorten his name to Theo."

"Cathy," said Elizabeth with a warm smile, "I am certain such intimate familiarity will come to you in time. Your engagement was sudden and under distressed circumstances—it is only natural that you should wish to stick to the comfort of formality for a time."

"I am trying to be as comfortable in his presence as I was before, as you advised me, Lizzy," said Catherine, "but at times I find it rather difficult when I think of how we are soon to be very intimately connected."

From the corner of her eye, Elizabeth noted Jane and James glancing at one another; he smiled, she blushed. Then, drawing a deep breath, Jane said, "I am sure every newly betrothed young lady feels as you do. I know I have been made nervous many times when I think of the life I shall soon be leading."

Catherine huffed as she looked out the side glass. "I just... I think it also in part because I honestly never thought of the colonel in that way—I may have done in time, though I can't be sure of it. I only know that all that was on my mind the whole week of his being at Netherfield was that I thought him amiable and charming. I enjoyed his company; as all I had hoped for was to find new friends and amusement in Hertfordshire, I thought I had done very well for myself. Though I am certainly of an age when young women begin turning their minds to serious thoughts of marriage, I..."

She shrugged her shoulders and sighed. "I'm just not one of them. I've only had hope of enjoying myself, and now I must remember I am soon to be a wife."

Elizabeth smiled. "I feel exactly as you do on that score, my friend. I am two years older than you, and still have no thoughts of matrimony. Well, none beyond the occasional thought of hopefully marrying well one day, but then, I have also given equal thought to never marrying."

Catherine giggled. "I remember when we first came to Hertfordshire, and you said you would be content to be governess to Jane's ten children."

Her smile widening, Elizabeth replied, "And that is still as true today as it was a month ago. Only once in my life have I ever entertained the idea of an attachment to a particular gentleman, but I have had to accept it will never be. I intend to focus all my energies on seeing my sister and my friend most happily settled."

Catherine, she sensed, would have liked to press her for more — or perhaps to argue again that she was being foolish, as Elizabeth had little doubt they all knew to whom she referred. She was grateful when, as her friend's lips parted to speak, her brother squeezed her hand again and shook his head.

Upon arrival at Gracechurch Street, Mrs. Gardiner welcomed her nieces with a wide smile and open arms. "What a pleasant surprise!" said she as she embraced Jane, adding when she held Elizabeth to her, "How came you to be in London?"

"First, dearest aunt, may I present our companions — two people who are very dear to us," said Jane. "This gentleman is my betrothed, Mr. James Morland. With us is his sister, Miss Catherine Morland. Mr. Morland, Miss Morland, my aunt Mrs. Edward Gardiner."

Marjorie Gardiner's expression lit up on hearing the name of the young man that stood with them, whom she knew of only from letters. "Well, this is a gift I am sure your uncle will be sorry to miss, for he is at his warehouse toiling away — and the children too, as they have just gone to the nursery for their naps. But please, do let us sit down to some tea."

"Please, do not trouble yourself, Aunt," said Elizabeth as Mrs. Gardiner led them to the drawing room. "We have just had a luncheon, as we skipped breakfast that we could start our journey early this morning."

"Very well. Do be seated," said her aunt.

When all were settled, she asked again how and why they were in town. Elizabeth told her only of the purpose of their journey — no mention was made of Wickham or the compromise.

Mrs. Gardiner was in raptures, and congratulated her nieces' friend on making such a fine connection. "I do not know them personally, of course, but I have heard of the earl's family — they are related to the Darcys of Pemberley. That estate is but five miles from, Lambton, where I grew up. But pray, you have not said where you are staying. Does Mrs. Allen have a house here in Town?"

Jane and Elizabeth exchanged a glance. "Aunt," began the latter, "we are all of us guests of Mr. Darcy."

"Oh," said Mrs. Gardiner softly, followed by an increase in volume as she said again "Oh! Upon my word, I should have realized — you did just say that he had also been staying at Netherfield with Mr. Bingley. Oh Jane, Lizzy… How extraordinarily fortunate you are, to have made such friends!"

"All the gentlemen have been very kind and agreeable, yes," said Jane. "And Mr. Darcy is generosity itself in having us all to stay at his house in Grosvenor Square."

"We shall only be staying the one night, as Colonel Fitzwilliam is eager to obtain my father's permission for us to marry," Catherine offered.

"Well, I wish you every happiness, Miss Morland, as I do my dear niece and your brother," Mrs. Gardiner said, then she turned her gaze to Elizabeth. "It will be your turn soon, my dear."

Elizabeth laughed. "Aunt, whatever do you mean?"

"Why, to be married, of course!" replied Mrs. Gardiner. "Have you never heard that going to one wedding brings on another? Here soon there will be two — nay, three, as did you not write in your last letter that your friend Miss Lucas was also to be married?"

Fighting to contain the warmth that rose up her neck, Elizabeth replied, "Indeed, Aunt, but that does not signify that I shall be the next to march to the altar. For all we know, it could be Mary."

"Yes. I have heard from your mother as well," said her aunt. "She has high hopes of Mary securing an offer from your father's cousin."

"Yes," said Jane with a nod. "He is to return to Kent tomorrow, but as far as I am aware, he has not spoken."

Elizabeth scoffed. "I'm surprised we've heard nothing from the infamous Lady Catherine," said she. To her aunt, she added, "Mr. Collins had the audacity to speak of a supposed engagement between Mr. Darcy and the lady's daughter, which was summarily refuted by him. I had the suspicion, based on how often he speaks of his 'noble patroness', that Mr. Collins would write to her of the matter or return to Kent and tell her in person of the incident, but neither has occurred so far as I am aware."

"It is possible, is it not," said Catherine, "that Lady Catherine has written to Mr. Darcy and he has simply not mentioned the letter in your hearing?"

"A very good point, Miss Morland," observed Mr. Gardiner. "And Lizzy, my dear, whatever should happen in that quarter, I daresay it is of no consequence to you. Unless, of course, you have formed an attachment to the young man."

Catherine and Jane both grinned. Elizabeth, certainly not wanting to visit *that* subject—though she might have done were she seeing her aunt alone—shook her head firmly and replied that there was no chance at all of her forming an attachment to Mr. Darcy.

༺༒༻

During luncheon, Georgiana had asked Darcy if he and Fitzwilliam wished her to accompany them to Bolton Street. Fitzwilliam replied that it was not necessary for her to go, as he did not wish to distress her with talk of Wickham. She had agreed it was for the best she remain at Darcy House, for she had already heard all she ever wished to hear about "the abominable scoundrel" and his actions towards her friend.

As the carriage carried them to his uncle's London home, Darcy watched his cousin carefully. He suspected Fitzwilliam was nervous—telling his parents he planned to marry would be nothing, but telling them *why* he was suddenly so set upon the endeavor... He knew his cousin did not want to argue with his father. He would keep his word and marry Catherine regardless of the outcome of this visit, but it would pain Theodore if his choice were to cause a breach in the family.

"Right then, here we go," Fitzwilliam muttered as the carriage drew to a stop before Disley House. He alighted first and Darcy followed in silence.

A benefit of being family—and known to the butler—was being admitted immediately to the earl's presence. His uncle, aunt, and even Theodore's older brother Philip, Viscount Rowarth, were present in the drawing room when they entered. The three looked up in surprise and greeted them warmly.

"Is Sophia here with you?" Fitzwilliam asked his brother.

Rowarth shook his head. "She and the children are spending the day with her parents."

"It is good to see you again so soon, Theodore," said Lord Disley.

"Indeed," said Lady Disley. "Whenever you say you are going to join Fitzwilliam somewhere, you are gone for at least a month."

"And I might well have been this time, Mamma, but for some news I am come to share," Fitzwilliam said. "It will gratify you, I believe, to know that I have met someone I intend to marry."

A sharp cry emitted from his mother, while expressions of astonishment overcame the faces of his father and brother.

"I am pleased that you have turned your mind to marriage at last, son," Lord Disley began, "but this is a rather sudden scheme, is it not?"

Fitzwilliam nodded. "It is, yes. However, there is some little urgency that the young lady marry, lest her reputation forever be destroyed."

The expressions facing him changed from surprise to confusion and concern. "Theodore, as I know you too well to suspect you of ungentlemanly behavior, I believe some explanation is in order," said his father.

Darcy began their story, explaining that he had written to his cousin for advice on how to manage Wickham being in the same town as his sister; his relations all being aware of the near-disaster at Ramsgate led them to nod or verbally agree with his seeking counsel. Fitzwilliam then picked up the narrative, explaining that his cousins were not Charles Bingley's only charming guests. He spoke of Mrs. Allen and the Morlands, emphasizing Catherine's beauty, temper, and other amiable qualities, before mentioning her having been named as heir to Mr. Allen's sizeable fortune. Darcy then spoke again and gave the account of Wickham's attempted compromise, followed by Fitzwilliam telling them about the duel by proxy, then saying,

"I could not, in good conscience, allow that reprobate to ruin Miss Morland's irreproachable character. Knowing she had been witnessed in the presence of a soldier, I felt it my duty to give relief to the young lady's distress, and so offered myself in marriage to her. She has accepted me."

Lord Disley had risen to pace during the recital of events; he paused with one arm resting on the mantle over the fireplace, and turned his gaze toward them as he said, "I commend you for being honorable, Theodore, and am relieved you were not more seriously injured. But marriage to a girl who could bring scandal on the family?"

Darcy watched Fitzwilliam scowl, then school his features. "Sir," said he, "I do not come to ask your permission, as I have no need of it. I would, however, appreciate having your blessing—though should you deny your approbation, be aware that I will proceed without it."

Fitzwilliam took a step toward his father. "She is a good girl, Father. Her sweetness of character, her gentle spirit, would be crushed beyond recovery should the story spread beyond Meryton—I can't let that happen. I *won't* let it happen."

His brother startled them all by laughing. "You *like* her, Teddy."

"I do, yes," Fitzwilliam replied immediately, for once ignoring the nickname he so despised. "While it's true I've only known her a week's time, I honestly believe we will do well together. I can't explain it, I just feel it to be true."

"You mentioned a Mr. and Mrs. Allen, son," spoke up Lady Disley. "Tell us about them."

Darcy shared a glance with his cousin—it was the opening they had been hoping for. Sharing all they knew of the Allens, they were both of them relieved when a glint of recognition came into Lord Disley's eyes.

"Fullerton, did you say?" he asked.

Darcy and Fitzwilliam nodded in unison.

The earl took his arm from the mantle and raised his hand to his chin. "I do seem to recall an Arthur Allen from when I was at Cambridge. He was heir presumptive to a sizable estate, if memory serves—his uncle had daughters, but they were still hoping for a son at the time—and I believe he was from Fullerton. In Wiltshire, yes?"

Again, Darcy nodded. "It is in Wiltshire, yes."

"If it is the same fellow, my dear, we may be able to turn this to our advantage," Lord Disley said to his wife. "We have only to say that Theodore and Miss Morland were introduced some time ago, and on meeting again they formed an attachment. Their assignation in that alley may have been an imprudent choice, but then they were going to marry anyway."

"That was our very idea, Father, if chance should prove you knew the gentleman," said Fitzwilliam. "Admittedly, these are not ideal circumstances upon which to build a life together—neither Miss Morland nor I are very sanguine about it. But as I cannot bear to see her disgraced and she cannot support the idea of damaging her younger sisters' prospects or her family's reputation, we have agreed to the match."

"But what if the story should remain within the borders of that little market town?" asked Lady Disley. "Are you certain you wish to forsake the chance of marrying a young lady from a good family?"

Fitzwilliam frowned. "The Morlands *are* a good family, Mother. Granted, I've not met Reverend and Mrs. Morland as yet — we go on to Fullerton tomorrow, that I may seek her father's permission to marry her — but I believe I can safely say that they are eminently respectable, if their eldest son and daughter are anything to judge by. The gentleman has two or three other livings under his oversight, one of which is to be given over to his son in two years, and he has enough fortune that his four daughters were to have three thousand each; the younger three now have four, as Miss Morland has abdicated her claim to her father's money in light of the amount she inherited from Mr. Allen."

"And just how much is that?" Lady Disley pressed.

Fitzwilliam looked to her. "Miss Morland's income is five thousand a year."

Lord Rowarth laughed again. "Well done, Teddy!"

The colonel shot his brother a sour look. "I'm not marrying her for her money, Philip," he snapped.

The viscount waved off his words. "Yes, yes, I know. You've offered to marry her because you're the epitome of a gentleman, rescuing a lady in distress."

"Exactly."

"As you are so determined," said Lord Disley in the same 'that's enough' tone he'd used when his sons were boys — Darcy had even heard it directed at himself a time or two in his youth — "I will conditionally grant you my blessing, Theodore."

"Conditionally, sir?" Fitzwilliam countered.

"I want to meet her — and Mrs. Allen, if possible, to determine if her husband is indeed the gentleman I remember."

Fitzwilliam turned to Darcy with an expression that bespoke of his relief. "It is good that you ask, Father, as we had hoped to have you over to Darcy House for dinner this evening that I may introduce you to Miss Morland."

"They have traveled with you?" asked Lady Disley.

Darcy nodded. "Mrs. Allen, Miss Morland, Mr. James Morland, his betrothed, and her sister. And Georgiana and her companion, of course. As it was necessary that he escort his own sister to Fullerton, young Mr. Morland desired his lady accompany him, that she might

181

meet his parents before their wedding. Her younger sister was invited by Miss Morland to join them. As there was not room enough in Mrs. Allen's carriage for all—and because Theo asked me to lend him my support in his address to you—I offered my carriage for their comfort."

"My lord?" said Lady Disley to her husband.

Lord Disley inclined his head. "We have no engagement for this evening. I should like to meet this Miss Morland and judge her worth for myself."

Seeing that his cousin was about to argue with his father, Darcy reached forward and touched a hand to his arm, hoping that he was able to convey with his gaze that he should not press the point. His cousin looked over, and after a moment he nodded.

"Blast and botheration," said Rowarth then. "My curiosity is piqued, but I cannot join you, for I am to dine with the Talbots this evening."

"And you can't risk upsetting the in-laws, now can you?" Fitzwilliam said with a mild sneer at his brother.

Darcy glanced at his uncle, who sighed and gave a mild shake of his head. Theodore and Philip, though they respected one another as men and were loyal to each other as family, simply hadn't the same close, brotherly relationship that the former had with their cousin. Darcy had always supposed it due to he and Theodore being closer in age; they had played together more as children, while Philip had been consumed with the importance of his place as heir to the earldom. His arrogance had mellowed a great deal as he matured, but the brothers had yet to cease trying to one-up each other and could hardly be in company together without sniping at one another.

"We had a luncheon upon arrival, Uncle, so dinner will be a little later this evening—about six," Darcy said.

Lord Disley nodded. "Very well, Darcy. Your aunt and I will be there."

Offering a nod, Darcy then touched Fitzwilliam's arm again; the latter bowed to each of his parents, issued a terse farewell to his brother, then about-faced and marched from the room. Making his own farewells, Darcy quickly followed.

"Judge her worth for myself," his cousin mumbled as they descended the front steps toward the carriage. "Even without her inheritance, Catherine is worth ten girls from those so-called good families Mother admires so much."

As is Elizabeth, Darcy added silently.

"And Philip, that wretch," his cousin went on as the footman opened the carriage door. "Why does he always have to bait me so?"

"Why do you always rise to it?" Darcy countered. "As I have said many a time, Philip needles you because he knows it bothers you. If you would stop reacting to his childishness—"

"Yes, yes, I know. If I'd stop letting him get to me, he'd stop pestering me," Fitzwilliam said with a dismissive wave.

When the carriage was underway again, Fitzwilliam took a deep breath and sighed. "Well, at least my father didn't object outright," he said.

Darcy nodded. "Indeed."

"And I am sure once they have got to know Catherine a little, there can be no objection at all," his cousin went on.

Offering a smile, Darcy nodded again. "Surely not," said he... then found himself wondering if, perhaps, it might be a good thing after all that the Disleys were coming to dinner.

After all, they would also be meeting Elizabeth.

Chapter Twenty

"**Oh, Lizzy,** what shall I wear?!"

Elizabeth smiled with warmth as she entered the room Catherine shared with Mrs. Allen. Her friend stood at the side of her bed in her underclothes; her trunk was open at the foot of the bed and what looked like every dress she had brought on the trip was laid out on top of it.

"Oh, do please help her decide, Miss Elizabeth," spoke up Mrs. Allen. "For she will not listen to me!"

Stepping up beside her friend, she glanced over the selection of dresses and pointed to a pale green frock made of chiffon. On it were sewn small crystal beads the color of emeralds, set in the shape of flowers.

"This one, for certain," said she. "I believe it very pleasantly compliments your eyes, Cathy."

Mrs. Allen looked from Catherine to the gown and back again. "Why, indeed it does! Oh, Catherine, you shall make such a fine impression on Lord and Lady Disley, I am sure of it."

Catherine picked up the dress and held it to herself. "I certainly hope so, Mrs. Allen. I should be so very distressed for Colonel Fitzwilliam if his parents do not think me good enough for their son. He says he will marry me even without their approval, but I know he desires it very much."

"He is a good boy to want his parents to like his choice of bride, and a good man, I daresay, to be willing to go forward with the match even should they not," said Mrs. Allen.

She came around to stand by Catherine and Elizabeth, and

touched the former's cheek softly. "I pray you would not think so little of yourself, my dear. I am sure they will adore you as much as I do."

Catherine took a deep breath and nodded, though her smile remained small and showed that her nervousness was not abated. Elizabeth helped her don the gown and finish setting her hair, then Catherine grabbed a pair of white satin gloves and put them on. The three met Georgiana and Jane in the hallway and the ladies went down to the drawing room together.

The three men were, of course, already gathered there. Fitzwilliam stepped forward to take Catherine's hand and bowed over it.

"You look remarkably lovely this evening, Miss Morland," he said.

Catherine blushed, but her smile grew and she replied, "You flatter me, sir."

"Nay, 'tis not flattery—it is the truth!" Fitzwilliam insisted. "That gown is very becoming, and I daresay it matches your eyes."

Elizabeth smiled when Catherine glanced at her and said, "That is almost exactly what Lizzy said to me."

Fitzwilliam then looked over at her and winked, a grin splitting his lips as he said, "Miss Elizabeth has a very discerning eye."

His expression then sobered and he drew a breath. "I should like you to know, Miss Morland, that I have always thought you a beauty."

Again Catherine blushed, but her smile grew a little wider. "That is most kind of you to say, Colonel."

She then drew her own fortifying breath and looked at her betrothed more squarely. "When do you expect your parents to arrive? I believe Mr. Darcy said dinner would be at six."

Elizabeth glanced at Darcy, who was then looking at his watch. "It is twenty minutes to six now," said he. "I expect the Disleys will arrive shortly."

'Shortly' was but another five minutes. When the bell rang, Catherine—who had been seated—stood and began to wring her hands. Elizabeth stood as well and moved to her side as Darcy and Fitzwilliam moved toward the drawing room doors.

Placing an arm about Catherine's shoulders, she whispered, "Remember to breathe, Cathy. Just be your sweet, charming, amiable self and they will adore you as much as the colonel does."

Catherine looked to her. "Do you really think he adores me already?"

Elizabeth smiled and nodded. "I really do—after all, he thinks you a beauty and is willing to marry you even if his lofty parents do not give their blessing. And as he has danced with you, I should think he may be half in love with you already."

"Do not be ridiculous, Lizzy," Catherine said as voices were then heard in the hall. "Adoration I might be willing to entertain as true, but certainly not love."

"Why not? According to my mother, dancing with someone is a sure step to falling in love, and Colonel Fitzwilliam has danced with you several times."

Catherine had not a moment to reply to this remark, as the doors were opened by the butler and a footman, and Fitzwilliam's parents were announced. Darcy and his cousin bowed in greeting, then led the elegantly dressed pair over to where Catherine stood.

Fitzwilliam held out his hand to her and when she had placed hers in it, drew her forward. "Mother, Father, it is my honor to present my betrothed, Miss Catherine Morland. Miss Morland, my parents, the Earl and Countess of Disley."

A bow and curtsies were exchanged, then Lady Disley said, "It is a pleasure to meet you, Miss Morland. A very great pleasure, as you are the first young lady to lead my son to serious thoughts of marriage."

"It is a pleasure to meet you also, my lady," Catherine replied.

Lady Disley looked her over, then said to her husband, "My lord, is she not a pretty little thing?"

"She looks just as she should, my dear," Lord Disley replied.

"Your gown looks especially well made, Miss Morland," Lady Disley went on. "Was it done here in London?"

"No indeed, my lady," Catherine replied. "Mrs. Allen commissioned this gown for me during our stay in Bath earlier in the year."

As this brought the attention of the earl and countess to the others in the room, Darcy then performed the duty of introducing everyone. Lord Disley—when all names, curtsies, and bows were given—moved further into the room to stand before Mrs. Allen.

"My son tells me there is some small chance your husband and I may have known one another," said he. "Pray tell me, Mrs. Allen, was Mr. Allen's Christian name Arthur and did he attend Cambridge?"

Mrs. Allen's expression brightened. "It was, sir, and he did! Mr. Allen always spoke very fondly of his time there, and the gentlemen he met with."

"And did he inherit his estate from an uncle?" the earl pressed.

The lady nodded vigorously. "Oh, yes. I remember he said that his aunt and uncle had been hoping for a son even though the years for such a blessing were passing his aunt by. Mr. Allen's uncle passed and he inherited only a year or two before our marriage, and I enjoyed the comforts of that beautiful house with him for two-and-twenty years."

Catherine stepped away from Fitzwilliam's side to stand at hers, and laid a comforting hand on her arm as she said, "Remember, Mrs. Allen, that you shall always enjoy Fullerton Manor's comforts, for in Mr. Allen's will you were granted lifetime residency there. And even had you not been, you know I could never turn you out of your beloved home."

Mrs. Allen smiled at her and patted the hand that rested on her arm. "It is very sweet of you to say so, my dear."

Lord Disley glanced between his son and the girl he hoped to marry. "Is the Fullerton estate a large property?" he asked.

Mrs. Allen blinked. "Well now, I do believe it is. Though Mr. Allen was the principal landowner of the parish, you see, so he had not only the estate grounds but many tenants."

"And his income was five thousand a year?"

"It was, yes. Now it is Catherine's income—and *that* after all regular expenses and taxes are paid, mind you," Mrs. Allen replied.

Lord Disley looked to his wife, who smiled and nodded. *Well, at least they approve of Catherine's fortune*, Elizabeth mused sourly. *No doubt they are mightily pleased for their son to have landed himself such a rich bride in spite of the slim chance for scandal, for once they are married, all that income will legally be his.*

She then glanced at Darcy, and on finding his gaze was on her, blushed and looked away. Would he be so willing to take the risk of censure from his noble relations, as his cousin was? Elizabeth had not the possibility of a scandal hanging over her head, but neither did she come with a fortune attached as Catherine did. Would the earl and countess be willing to overlook her lack of dowry as they seemed so willing to overlook her friend's compromise?

Oh, why was she torturing herself with such thoughts?! Surely if the man admired her, as so many believed of him, he would have declared himself by now.

Elizabeth fought to push the idea of herself and Darcy together to the back of her mind, as she had so often had to do of late. A moment later, the butler announced dinner, and for the first time she hoped not to be seated too near him. It would be best, she began to believe, that she begin distancing herself from Darcy as much physically as she was trying to do mentally. The time would soon come, she was sure, when they would be parted permanently, and it was best she begin preparing herself.

Her hope was not entirely in vain—the seating was formal and she sat to his end of the table rather than Georgiana's, but as Mrs. Allen had precedence over her, the widow sat to their host's left. Jane was to Mrs. Allen's left, then herself, and then Lord Disley, who was on Georgiana's right. On her left was Colonel Fitzwilliam, with James across from Elizabeth herself and Catherine across from Jane; Lady Disley was on Darcy's right.

They were through the soup course before Lady Disley began an inquisition of her prospective daughter-in-law, asking pointed questions that bordered on impertinent. The countess asked as to the size of her family, had the children a governess, and did she or her sisters play, sing, or draw. Lady Disley asked how many livings were in Reverend Morland's oversight, the amount of his income, she wanted to know if Catherine's younger sisters were out... Elizabeth could hardly believe the impudence of the woman, and wondered if all noble families were so snobby and arrogant. She was thankful that Lord Disley seemed more interested in speaking to his niece, his son, and even James than herself.

"And you, Miss Bennet?" said Lady Disley suddenly, drawing Elizabeth from her brief reverie. "How many is your family?"

"I am the eldest and Elizabeth the second of five daughters, ma'am," Jane replied.

Lady Disley's eyes flicked to Elizabeth, then back to Jane. "Do you play and sing, Miss Bennet?"

"I am afraid I do not, but Elizabeth does."

The countess looked to her again and Elizabeth smiled archly, recalling the same query being made to Catherine only moments ago; she'd seemed disappointed that Catherine was not musical, but praised her professed desire to learn some instrument now she had the means to pay for instruction.

"Only a little, and very ill," she said in reply to Lady Disley's silent query.

"Oh! Then after dinner we shall be happy to hear you. Darcy's instrument here is a capital one, second only to the one he has at Pemberley for my niece. Do your younger sisters play and sing?"

Elizabeth nodded. "One of them does."

"Why did not you all learn?" Lady Disley asked. "As I said to Miss Morland about her and her sisters, you ought all to have learned—of course, now she has the fortune to supply proper instruction, and I am sure my son will see to it all her sisters are as well educated as she. Do you draw?"

"No, not at all," Elizabeth replied.

Lady Disley's gaze returned to Jane. "Do any of you, Miss Bennet?"

Jane shook her head. "Not one."

"That is very strange," observed the countess. "But I suppose you had no opportunity. Your mother should have brought you here every spring for the benefit of masters."

Jane's countenance was flushed now, and Elizabeth began to feel the indignity of being judged with a harsh eye. "My mother would have had no objection," said she, "but my father hates London."

Lady Disley arched an eyebrow. "Has your governess left you?"

"We never had any governess."

"No governess! How is that possible? Five daughters brought up at home without a governess! I never heard of such a thing. Your mother must have been quite a slave to your education."

Elizabeth could hardly help smiling as she assured her that had not been the case.

"Then who taught you? Who attended to you? Without a governess, you must have been neglected."

Once again Elizabeth exchanged a look with her sister, then she said, "Compared with some families, I believe we were; but such of us as wished to learn never wanted the means. We were always encouraged to read, and had all the masters that were necessary. Those who chose to be idle, certainly might."

Lady Disley then went on a short tirade as to the benefit of a governess preventing idleness, adding her belief that nothing could be done properly in education without steady and regular instruction, which of course a governess would have provided.

"If I had known your mother, I would have advised her most strenuously to engage one," she said at last. "Are any of your younger sisters out, Miss Elizabeth?"

"Yes, ma'am, all."

"All! What, all five out at once! Very odd! And you only the second. The younger ones out before the elder ones are married! Though at least Miss Bennet is to be married in a few weeks, and I am gratified that Mrs. Morland was not so foolish as to allow her second daughter out as yet... Your younger sisters must be very young."

"Yes, my youngest—like Miss Darcy—is not sixteen," said Elizabeth. "Perhaps Lydia *is* full young to be much in company, but really, ma'am, I think it would be very hard upon younger sisters that they should not have their share of society and amusement because the elder may not have the means or inclination to marry early. The last-born has as good a right to the pleasures of youth as the first. And to be kept back on such a motive! I think it would not be very likely to promote sisterly affection or delicacy of mind."

"Upon my word," said her ladyship, "you give your opinion very decidedly for so young a person. Pray, what is your age?"

"With three younger sisters grown up," replied Elizabeth, smiling, "your ladyship can hardly expect me to own it."

Lady Disley seemed quite astonished at not receiving a direct answer; and Elizabeth suspected herself to be the first creature who had ever dared to trifle with so much dignified impertinence.

"You cannot be more than twenty, I am sure, therefore you need not conceal your age. Miss Bennet," she said, looking once more to Jane. "What is your age?"

Jane swallowed nervously. "I am two-and-twenty, my lady, and Elizabeth is but twenty years."

"Lady Disley," said Darcy, speaking up at last. "Might I enquire as to the point of these questions? Miss Morland I can understand your desiring to know more of, but Miss Bennet and her sister are not soon to be your relations."

His aunt sniffed and lifted her chin a fraction. "Perhaps not directly, Darcy, but Miss Bennet *is* to marry Miss Morland's brother, which creates some degree of relationship between her family and ours."

"That may be so, ma'am, but you hardly need know every minute detail of their lives," Darcy protested. "Besides which, they are my friends, and I can plainly see that your line of questioning is distressing to Miss Bennet. Kindly cease this interrogation and be more civil to your fellow guests."

It was all Elizabeth could do not to turn a gloating smile towards Lady Disley, who reacted to the none-too-subtle emphasis on the last two words first with an astonished expression—as though she could not quite believe her nephew had spoken to her in such a manner—and then a haughty sniff and a lifting of her nose even higher into the air. Keeping her head bent slightly toward her plate, Elizabeth glanced sidelong at Darcy and flashed a quick smile, hoping that he would interpret it as the gratitude she intended it to be.

Her hope was satisfied when Darcy met her gaze and almost imperceptibly inclined his head, before drawing his aunt into a discussion about the improvements to Disley Court which she had mentioned when last they had seen one another.

After the meal, when the ladies retired to the drawing room to allow the four men to enjoy their port and politics — or whatever it was men talked of when alone together — Catherine waited to walk by Elizabeth, leaning over to whisper,

"I cannot tell if Lady Disley liked me or not."

"I am sure she liked you more than me, Cathy," Elizabeth whispered back.

"Indeed, though I can't imagine why she spoke to you as she did," Catherine said. "Her questioning me I well expected, but for her to ask such things of you and Jane seems — "

"Miss Bennet, Miss Elizabeth."

Catherine and Elizabeth drew up short; Lady Disley had turned to address the latter and her sister just as the two girls entered the drawing room.

"Yes, my lady?" prompted Jane.

Fitzwilliam's mother looked between them with a haughty gaze. "I pray you understand my reasoning for asking you such questions as I did while we dined."

"As a matter of fact, ma'am, I'm not certain I do," said Elizabeth, drawing an alarmed gaze from Jane.

"Why, it is all about connections, Miss Elizabeth," Lady Disley replied. "In society, one must be certain of making the *right* connections. Take your friend, for example — Miss Morland was born to a mere clergyman, but her parents wisely cultivated a relationship with the Allens, thereby drawing the attention of their wealthy neighbors to the eldest of their daughters. The young lady's amiable qualities led to their selecting Miss Morland as heir to the estate, and she is soon to be wed to the son of an earl."

She turned what Elizabeth believed to be a practiced smile at Catherine. "You are a good girl, I think, as you know when to show deference to those of higher rank than yourself. What accomplishments and manners you lack can be improved upon by dedicated study with masters — I am sure my son will see to it you have only the best."

"I thank you, ma'am," Catherine replied demurely, as she seemed not to know what else to say.

"I am afraid, my lady, that I still do not understand why you made such inquiries of my sister and I as you did," Elizabeth pressed. "While it is true there will be *some* connection between our families when Mr. Morland and Jane are married, it is peripheral at best—one you need hardly concern yourself with, I should think, as the chances of our families meeting with any regularity are almost non-existent."

The expression on the countess's face was one of disdain, though she hid it well behind another false smile. "'Almost' is not 'entirely', Miss Elizabeth. There is at least *some* chance of my meeting Miss Bennet again, and any of her family that visits her."

"But you would be meeting us in the country and not here in Town, I am sure, therefore if the connection to a country family whose patriarch earns only two thousand a year is so disagreeable to you, I am sure you need not acknowledge it at all."

"Lizzy!" cried Jane softly.

Elizabeth felt a small dose of shame as she observed her sister's distress.

"Pray forgive me, dearest," she said in a soft, placating tone. "I am sure that you—and Lady Disley—know I intend no disrespect. But you know how my courage always rises at any attempt to intimidate me, and though it may not have been Her Ladyship's intention to insult, my innate loyalty to our family would not allow me to say nothing in our defense."

"Well, at least you have *that* in your favor, Miss Elizabeth," said Lady Disley then. "Family loyalty is of near as much importance as having proper connections."

With that, she turned her attention entirely onto Mrs. Allen. The four young women moved to sit together across the room from the matrons.

"Oh Lizzy," whispered Georgiana. "I simply cannot believe you spoke to my aunt in such a manner!"

Elizabeth, though still incensed by the countess's attitude, began to feel the impact of her own behavior. "Oh, do please forgive me, my friend! I have been rather too outspoken this evening, haven't I? It's just that I cannot seem to help myself when I imagine my relations are being insulted, no matter how foolishly some of them behave."

"Lizzy, you know how much I love you, and how greatly I esteem both your loyalty and willingness to defend our family," Jane began. "But Lady Disley is a countess! She could very well speak to all her acquaintances about your behavior this evening, and they will speak to theirs... Lizzy, recall the reason that Catherine and Colonel Fitzwilliam are marrying: people talk, and gossip spreads."

"I think I see what you mean, Jane," said Catherine. "If Lady Disley feels insulted by Elizabeth's manner, and talks of it to her friends, then the gossip could damage your family's reputation as much as my compromise might have done mine."

Real shame now began to course through Elizabeth, and she wished she could groan aloud. But that would be unladylike, and give Lady Disley even more reason to despise her.

One day, Lizzy, some young man will catch your eye — and then you'll have to watch your tongue, Jane had once said to her.

Well, if there had been any chance of a match between her and Darcy before, there was certainly none at all now... and all because Elizabeth didn't know when to keep her pert opinions to herself.

Chapter Twenty-One

Darcy's expectation of hearing his uncle's opinion was not long held.

As soon as the port was poured, and his uncle had lit a cigar, the earl looked to him and said, "Fitzwilliam, I did not speak at table as you had handled the matter, but I must have a say now."

Darcy set his glass on the table. "By all means," he prompted.

"Dressing down a countess before commoners is simply not done," Lord Disley replied. "The distinction of rank must be preserved—you would have better handled the situation to have reminded Miss Elizabeth of her place."

"I rather thought it best to remind my aunt of hers—she is a guest in my home, as Miss Elizabeth is," Darcy replied stoically. "More than that, sir, while the latter's replies were impertinent, the former's questions were insolent. Miss Elizabeth may indeed give her opinion very decidedly, but Lady Disley gives hers too freely."

"I did not hear all that was said," put in Fitzwilliam, "but what I did reminded me uncomfortably of Aunt Catherine. Has Mother been spending time with her of late?"

His father frowned at him. "That is neither here nor there, Theodore. The point I am making is that the young lady did not show proper respect to a countess—it is she who ought to have been corrected, not your mother."

"And that countess did not show proper respect to a gentlewoman by prying into the intimate goings-on of her family unnecessarily," Darcy replied, his tone sharp. "Her rank does not excuse rudeness."

His uncle studied him over the rim of his snifter, through the smoke of his cigar, with a narrowed gaze. After a long, silent moment of scrutiny, he cried out and pointed at him.

"Ha! You're in love with her, aren't you? That's why you defend her so," said he.

"What I think of Miss Elizabeth is not open for discussion," Darcy replied. "One of my guests was rude to another, I set her down for it. If you disagree with how I handle disputes in my home, you are free to take your leave."

Fitzwilliam looked between them and then snorted. "And here I thought I might be about to sow discord in the family," he muttered.

Lord Disley stared at Darcy for another silent half minute, then turned to his son and said, "Speaking of, Theodore, I will grant that Miss Morland seems a good sort of girl. She was properly demure, and she is a pretty little thing—your children certainly won't want for handsomeness."

"Good heavens, Father, I've barely got her to accept me—I've no intention of pressing her for children right away."

His father scoffed. "You speak as if you won't be consummating your marriage on the wedding night."

James Morland stood abruptly. "Pray excuse me, my lord. Colonel, Mr. Darcy. I am afraid that the present topic of conversation is not one in which I wish to partake."

He bowed his head to each before picking up his glass, downing its contents, and then exiting the room.

Lord Disley laughed. "You'd think the boy doesn't intend to do the same with that pretty blonde girl he is to marry."

Darcy stood, drawing surprise into his uncle's expression. "Whether or not that is so is of no concern of yours, my lord."

Fitzwilliam downed the remainder in his glass and stood as well. "Nor is it when I choose to consummate my marriage, sir. I'm rather disappointed in you, Father—you've always been arrogant and classist, but you've never been so vulgar as tonight. Pray excuse me."

He bowed and then started for the door; Darcy bowed also and was close behind. Stepping into the hall, he spoke to the footman waiting there, telling him to have the earl's carriage brought round, as he did not expect he and the countess to remain much longer. He was not wrong, for within minutes of his and Theodore's entering the drawing room, Lord Disley appeared and announced to his wife that he wished to set off for home.

Lady Disley seemed surprised by this, but in taking note of the refusal of her son to even look at his father, and Darcy's own angry countenance, she nodded and stood to join him. She turned at the door and said, "I expect when next we see you, Theodore, you will be married — unless we should be invited to the wedding. In that case, we will see you then."

Fitzwilliam turned and nodded. "Once I have acquainted myself with Reverend and Mrs. Morland, and received approbation to proceed, Miss Morland and I will discuss our wedding. You'll be among the first to know our decision."

Lady Disley nodded once, then followed her husband into the hall. In only a few moments, they heard the front door open and shut.

Elizabeth stood and approached Darcy and Fitzwilliam, who stood together by a window. "Mr. Darcy, Colonel Fitzwilliam... I feel that I am responsible for the turn this evening has taken. I beg you would forgive my rudeness to Lady Disley —"

Darcy held up a hand to halt her words. "While you may have been a little more blunt that was strictly necessary, madam, my aunt was no less at fault with her line of questioning. It is no concern of hers how you and your sisters were brought up, as the connection between our families will be peripheral at best."

"Be that as it may, sir, I am your guest and have been rude to another," said Elizabeth. "I beg your pardon."

That she felt the weight of her own responsibility in the conflict and begged his pardon was more than he would get from either his uncle or his aunt, who were likely to act as if nothing had happened when next they were in company. It was their way. Darcy thanked Elizabeth for acknowledging her conduct was not without fault before smiling and telling her to think no more of it.

Georgiana then stood and timidly suggested some music. Fitzwilliam heartily agreed and begged her to play something jolly.

"I feel like a dance is just the thing to liven the mood!" he declared.

Darcy was not particularly in the mood to dance, but he would not discourage the others. He followed them all into the music room at a sedate pace, and though he helped move a few pieces of furniture to make room for dancing, was content to sit and observe. Elizabeth, at first, sat with Georgiana at the pianoforte, turning pages for her, though a time or two he glanced up to find her watching him. She looked quickly away each time; the third he smiled at her, and she blushed.

After Georgiana had played two songs, Elizabeth offered to play, though also apologized for her skill not being to the same degree as that of Georgiana. Though she did make a few mistakes, Darcy still found pleasure in listening to her, and on thinking she would play better if only she cared to practice more, found himself suddenly imagining her sitting to the grand pianoforte at Pemberley to do just that. He could even hire a master for her, if she wished more instruction.

Good heavens, one would think I planned to marry her, he mused, then began to think that perhaps having Elizabeth Bennet under his roof had not been so great an idea. It was dangerous to want someone whose regard for him did not match his own for her.

It would be best, he thought at last, that he and Georgiana not go on to Fullerton with the others in the morning.

ক্ষূপ্ত

Elizabeth, on emerging from her room the next morning, asked a passing maid whether she knew where her master was. The girl replied that she believed Mr. Darcy to be in the study with Colonel Fitzwilliam. This was perfect for her purpose, as she had hope of asking Darcy if she might borrow a book to pass the time in the carriage. They were leaving rather early in the day in the hope of reaching Fullerton that night, which meant many hours of sitting in the rocking vehicle with nothing to entertain but conversation with her fellow travelers—and while Elizabeth very much enjoyed that particular activity, she also had a great love of silence.

As she turned a corner on the ground floor to go down the hall where she recalled the study to be, Colonel Fitzwilliam was coming out of it.

"I still think you're being a fool about her, Will. Just tell—"

She did not hear all of Darcy's response, but it sounded like he said his mind had been made up. Elizabeth tried to step back around the corner without drawing attention to herself as Fitzwilliam was closing the study door, but she was not fast enough. He caught sight of her and called out her name.

Pasting a smile on her face, she turned back and greeted him with a cheerful, "Good morning, Colonel."

The grimace he wore was quickly replaced with a smile. "And to you, madam," said he.

Elizabeth glanced down the hall toward the study, then back to Fitzwilliam. "Pray forgive me if I am prying, but is something wrong with Mr. Darcy?"

The grimace returned. "Nothing but his own pigheadedness," he said sourly. Drawing a breath, he then added, "By and by, Darcy has elected not to go on to Fullerton with us—as there is no real duty or service for him to perform, he sees no reason to continue. So he and Georgiana will be staying here."

"I see," Elizabeth replied. "I am sorry to hear it, for they will be missed."

She turned away from the colonel but stopped to turn back once more when he asked, "Was there something you needed, Miss Elizabeth?"

"I had thought to ask Mr. Darcy if I might borrow a book to pass the time on our journey, but if he is not to attend us, then I would have no chance of returning it to him. So I shall make do with conversation with my companions."

Elizabeth walked determinedly away then, fighting the sting of tears behind her eyes. There could be no doubt as to the reason for Darcy's sudden decision to stay in London—regardless of the pardon he had offered her for her conduct, he had been offended by her behavior towards his aunt and could not bear to be in her company.

A serving of pastries, cakes, coffee and chocolate awaited her in the dining parlor, where she found Jane, James, and Catherine already seated. Georgiana soon followed her cousin into the room, and none were remiss to the look of sadness on her face.

"Georgie, are you well? Does your cold still linger?" Catherine asked her.

Though she sniffled, Georgiana shook her head. "No. It is my brother—he has said we are not to go on to Fullerton with you."

Elizabeth felt all eyes turn to her, but she determinedly focused on her plate and hoped that her feigned indifference was more convincing to the others than it felt to herself.

"But why?" Catherine pressed. "There is room enough for Lizzy in our carriage, to be sure, but I don't understand. I thought we were all going?"

"Fitzwilliam said he had some business matters to attend to that he had been putting off too long," Georgiana replied.

"In that case, Miss Darcy," said Jane slowly, "I can understand your brother's needing to remain."

"But surely it does not mean that she must do so as well!" Catherine insisted. "Did you not tell me once, Georgiana, that the colonel was also your guardian? Can he not take responsibility for you—that you, at least, may join us?"

"Indeed I do share guardianship of my cousin, Miss Morland," said Fitzwilliam. "But I am afraid that Darcy's authority takes precedence over my own, given their closer relationship. And as he is...out of sorts this morning, I'm not sure it would be wise to challenge it. Otherwise, Georgie, you know I would not mind in the least having charge of you that you could go with us."

Georgiana offered a teary smile to her cousin. "I know, Theodore, and I thank you. Please forgive my silliness. It's just that I was rather looking forward to meeting all those brothers and sisters Cathy has—ten children in one family is almost more than I can imagine!"

"Well, they won't all of them be there, of course," spoke up James. "Our brother William is out to sea with the navy, and Edward is at Oxford studying law."

Catherine grinned. "Only everyone younger than myself will be there."

"I should have liked to meet them just the same, as I have no younger siblings," Georgiana said. "Perhaps another time. After all, we are to be cousins, are we not?"

When Mrs. Allen at last came into the dining parlor, she was immediately made aware of the change in plan. Like Catherine, she lamented that Georgiana could not go with them to Fullerton, but at the same time assured Elizabeth that there was "quite room enough" for her in the carriage.

"I know how we can make things a little more comfortable," said James suddenly. "Do you think, Colonel, that I might borrow a horse? It is no trouble to me to ride on horseback. With Elizabeth going in the carriage, her trunk will need to be secured to the footman's post, which means his having to ride with the driver on the box, otherwise I should have been glad to sit and help drive."

Fitzwilliam nodded. "There are horses here for the grooms as needed. I do not think Darcy will protest, as I can see it returned easily enough."

The new arrangements were quickly made, and it was not long after that trunks were brought down and outerwear was put on. Elizabeth, Catherine, and Jane all shared an embrace with a tearful Georgiana before going out the door to the waiting carriage. As James was handing her in, Elizabeth could not help glancing toward where she believed the study window to be, and if she were not mistaken, she saw the curtain move as though someone had been watching.

I hope he feels sorry for disappointing his sister, she thought. *No matter his feelings towards me, it is wrong of him to upset her so.*

The carriage was soon pulling away from the pavement, and though there was some speculation on Mrs. Allen's part as to what business Darcy might have that would prevent his continuing on to Fullerton, Jane deftly managed to change the subject to Catherine's family by asking again after all the names and ages of the children. Catherine was more than happy to speak of her siblings and all their different personalities, which took some considerable time, as she and Mrs. Allen often went on tangents about each regarding some misadventure or other anecdote.

Elizabeth was grateful to Jane, who perhaps had taken some notice of her distress regarding Darcy's choosing to stay behind, though she endeavored to conceal her pain.

Not well enough, it would seem, she thought with a sigh, and was only a little forced to feign cheerfulness as she listened to Catherine and Mrs. Allen wax eloquent about the many Morland children.

❦

About an hour after the departure of his guests, Darcy remained ensconced in his study, brooding over his decision. Georgiana's displeasure at being forced to stay behind was evidenced not only by the tears he had witnessed, but also the melancholy tunes she had chosen to play on the pianoforte.

Though he could not tell her so, he felt her sadness. Perhaps it had been rude of him as their host, but he could not make himself leave the study to see Fitzwilliam and the others off. If he'd looked into Elizabeth's eyes for even a moment, her indifference to him would not have mattered—his resolve would have crumbled and he'd have told Georgiana to send for her trunk.

No, he had to be firm. It was time to put this infatuation out of his head…and his heart. The only way to do that was to give up the acquaintance entirely.

He was startled by an unexpected knock on the door. A moment later, his butler entered, carrying a note on a tray.

"This note is addressed to Colonel Fitzwilliam, sir," Tolliver said as he held the little tray toward him.

"Thank you, Tolliver," Darcy said as he took the folded paper, noting it was addressed in Lord Rowarth's handwriting. Wondering what the viscount could have to say, and knowing his cousin would excuse his taking the liberty, Darcy waited until the servant was gone again before he broke the seal.

Disley House
30 November

Theodore,

I've no idea when you mean to depart for Wiltshire, so it is with the hope of your still being in Town at this hour that I write this.

Father has just received word by express from Lady Catherine that she means to be in London today. She intends to confront Darcy about his allegedly denying his engagement to Anne — apparently, he met the Hunsford parson recently and disavowed any engagement existed. Of course, we all know it to be a fantasy of hers that our cousins would marry one day, and our aunt is nothing if not persistent. On the other hand, Father suspects Darcy to have formed an attachment to some bit of muslin he met in the country that he says is a most imprudent match, so has actually pledged to lend his support to Lady Catherine's cause.

I know you think me uncaring, but even I cannot abide shackling poor Darcy to a sickly thing like Anne, even though it would greatly increase his fortune. So, if this note reaches you in time, I suggest you hurry yourselves out of London as quick as may be. I do not think our father or our aunt will follow, but you never know.

Your brother,
Philip

Darcy stared in shock for near a minute before folding the note and shoving it into a pocket as he stood. Quick steps took him to the music room, where Georgiana looked up with some surprise at his hurried entrance.

"Brother, whatever is the matter?" she asked.

"Do you still desire to join your friends in Fullerton?" he countered.

Georgiana stood from the instrument and stepped around it. "Of course I should like to have gone, but they departed more than an hour ago. What's happened?"

"Remarkably, Lord Rowarth has done me a favor," Darcy replied. "He sent a note for Theo warning that Lady Catherine means to speak to me about marrying Anne, and that his father intends to support her. She will be here sometime this morning, and I have no desire to engage in intercourse that cannot but end with bitter feelings on all sides."

It was, perhaps, cowardly to run, but better to not be home when they came to attempt forcing his hand than to sow further discord in the family by fighting with them.

Georgiana grinned. "I shall have my trunk packed in a trice!" she said as she hurried past him, all traces of her earlier disappointment gone in but a moment.

So will I, Darcy thought, as he followed her from the room.

Chapter Twenty-Two

"**Lizzy, are** you well?"

Jane asked the question about an hour into their journey. Elizabeth realized she must make some effort to appear cheerful, lest her sister or their friends begin asking questions she was in no frame of mind to answer. Forcing a smile, she replied that she was only tired, then leaned her head into the squab with a soft sigh.

She could feel Jane's eyes on her, and Catherine's, but was grateful that neither pressed her for conversation. They both of them were content to go from speaking of Catherine's family to wedding clothes—Catherine might still be nervous about her forthcoming marriage to Colonel Fitzwilliam, but it did not dampen her enthusiasm for fashion, which had been "woken" in her only that year when she and the Allens were at Bath. Elizabeth listened with only half an ear as she and Mrs. Allen spoke of the shops and dressmakers in Bath they had patronized during their short time there, and the widow talked of knowing a number of fine linen drapers and modistes in London where they could begin having their new wardrobes put together.

Elizabeth could only think of the pain she was feeling. Darcy might well have been indifferent to her before, but he must truly despise her now, if he were so willing to keep his sister from a journey so looked forward to. He couldn't even be bothered to farewell his own guests!

Blast my wretched impertinence! she chastised herself, though she knew it was not only her inability to *not* speak her mind that had led to the break-up of their party. She reasoned that was only the final straw for Darcy, who must have been gathering a list of imperfections and reasons to find fault with her—not least of which was the situation of her family.

They had no fortune—Mr. Bennet could give his daughters no dowry, and their only inheritance would be the equal distribution of what dowry their mother had been given, on the event of Mrs. Bennet's death. Her youngest sisters behaved inappropriately, her mother encouraged rather than checked their often outrageous decorum, and her father did even less to properly manage his family. He seemed not to care that his wife and children would literally be left with almost nothing when he died. They had no "proper connections" in society and were linked to trade.

How anyone could have thought Darcy interested in her was truly beyond Elizabeth's comprehension. It was a wonder he had not tried to talk Mr. Bingley out of his pursuit of Jane.

Later in the afternoon, as the countryside passed outside the windows of the carriage, she found herself cheering somewhat on seeing scenery that, while not so full of color as in the spring and summer months, nevertheless held beauties to catch the eye. Elizabeth was able to participate in the discussion of books Catherine had engaged Jane in; it was thus her sister's turn to fall silent, as Elizabeth had a greater enthusiasm for reading for pleasure as well as discussing those books she had read.

They stopped for dinner in a market town that reminded Elizabeth very much of Meryton. There were two inns, and Colonel Fitzwilliam inspected both before declaring the larger of the two best suited for bringing ladies into. A private dining room was quickly secured and their dinner ordered.

"I must say," said Mrs. Allen as she took a lazy stroll about the room, "that I am grateful, Colonel, that you chose to stop. With the chill of winter encroaching the environs even this far south, we could not leave the side glass in the doors down lest we wished to freeze!"

"Not to mention it is rather nice to be able to get up and walk about to stretch our legs," offered Elizabeth.

Fitzwilliam shared a look with James; both men smiled, then the former said, "I am happy to be of service, ladies. Though not only did we weary travelers need the rest, so did our horses."

"I regret to observe, however," said James, "that I do not think it likely we will reach Fullerton tonight. The colonel and I have talked of it, and should like your opinions as to whether we ought to take rooms here, if there are any available, or if we ought to press on a while longer, stop for the night at another inn, and continue to Fullerton tomorrow."

"But tomorrow is Sunday!" said Mrs. Allen.

Fitzwilliam smiled kindly at her. "I know that travel on Sunday is not generally done, ma'am, but it will only be a short journey. I think, given our purpose, the Almighty will forgive us taking the liberty."

When the lady blushed under his gaze, twittering that of course he was right, Elizabeth found herself hard-pressed not to laugh. Colonel Fitzwilliam certainly knew how to pour on the charm.

The four ladies looked at one another. "I should really like to go on," said Catherine. "As the colonel said, it will be a short journey."

"I concur," said Jane. "The light may go in an hour or so, but the carriage has lanterns by which the driver and horses might see the road."

Elizabeth and Mrs. Allen readily agreed to press on, so as soon as the bill was paid after their meal, the ladies took to the carriage and the gentlemen their saddles. It was well and truly dark, with few stars peeking through the inky blackness of the night sky, by the time they reached a town James said was "less than two hours from home".

The whole party was much relieved that a respectable establishment was found with enough rooms available, though consideration for other travelers meant sharing two to a room. The weariness of the ladies led to their retiring almost immediately, though James and Fitzwilliam elected to have a nightcap in the public dining room. The two were contemplating a second drink before retiring to their room when they were both of them astonished by the entrance of two other weary travelers.

"Darcy!" cried the colonel, rising from his chair at a table near the door with unabashed surprise. "I can hardly believe it! How did you find us?"

Darcy's brow was as furrowed in surprise as his cousin's. "We did not, precisely. It is chance that brought us to the same establishment as yourselves."

Georgiana was then looking about the dining parlor. "Where are Elizabeth and Jane and Catherine and Mrs. Allen?"

"The ladies were understandably wearied by many hours in a carriage," said James. "They have already gone to bed."

"How did you catch us up—and why?" pressed Fitzwilliam.

"First let me see if there are rooms for Georgiana and myself," Darcy replied.

Fitzwilliam nodded; Darcy then went to the innkeeper and took the last two rooms he had for himself and his sister. He saw Georgiana to her room before returning to the dining room, where he ordered his own nightcap after rejoining his cousin and Morland at their table.

He took a drink of bourbon as he pulled Rowarth's letter from his pocket and handed it to Theodore. His cousin snorted as he read, then said aloud, "No wonder you're here when you were so adamant about staying."

Morland was understandably confused, so Fitzwilliam quickly filled him in. "I see," said the former. "So you're here because you wished to avoid this aunt of yours who wants you to marry her daughter?"

Darcy nodded. "In part," he confessed. "However, the larger reason is that I know my refusal will lead to harassment and resentment on the part of my aunt and her brother. There will be anger and bitterness cast about that I'd simply rather not expose myself or my sister to."

"Did you stop at all?" Fitzwilliam asked. "You must have got this note fairly soon after we left; we stopped for maybe an hour around five this afternoon for dinner."

"Rowarth's note arrived little more than an hour after you'd gone," Darcy replied. "We stopped only once, to rest the horses. I own that I was hoping to catch you up, but was not entirely sanguine about it, given the lead you had."

"Well, whatever your reasons, I am glad you are come," said Fitzwilliam. "I'm like to need a character witness when I meet with Reverend Morland on the morrow."

The gentleman's son laughed. "I'd not vex yourself over meeting with my father and mother, Theo. They will surely be pleased to know you, especially after learning of your kindness to Catherine."

Fitzwilliam drew a breath. "I do hope that I am able to convey that I marry her not because of her money, but a genuine desire to see her safe from the damage gossip can do to one's reputation. I've seen it happen, James, and it's no trifling matter."

Morland studied him for a moment, then asked, "Do you care for my sister—is it more than gentlemanly character that presses you to help her?"

Fitzwilliam looked at him squarely. "I cannot say that I love Catherine as you do Miss Bennet," he began, "but yes, I care for her. As I said to Darcy, there's just something about her that draws me."

After another moment of staring at him, Morland smiled. "That is good enough for me, and I am sure it will be for my father also."

Fitzwilliam acknowledged the approbation with a nod. The three then finished their drinks and mutually agreed it was time to retire. Darcy's cousin walked with him to his door, at which time he said, in a low voice,

"I believe Elizabeth will also be pleased to see you—no, do not speak. Just listen. Catherine confided to me that her friend appeared utterly miserable on our departure from Grosvenor Square this morning. She said Miss Elizabeth spoke no more than a word for well over an hour."

Darcy drew a breath. "At risk of offending, Theo, Miss Morland oftentimes has a rather active imagination, no doubt influenced by her preference for Gothic novels."

"That may be true, but ladies also know how to read the emotions of other ladies far better than we do," Fitzwilliam countered. "Are you truly certain that Elizabeth is indifferent to you?"

"Theo, in the near six weeks of our acquaintance, Elizabeth has displayed no particular regard for me," Darcy said. "I do not know how many times I have said this."

"But have you ever displayed your regard for her? Have you given her any indication that you feel more for her than friendship?" his cousin rejoined. "Think about that before you give up on her entirely."

"And what of our family? You know what your parents and our Aunt Catherine will say should I choose Elizabeth for my wife," Darcy pointed out.

Fitzwilliam sighed and shook his head. "Cousin, while any breach of family harmony will no doubt be distressing, you are not required to marry to make *them* happy. Marry the woman you love because you know she will make *you* happy."

With that, his cousin turned and walked back down the narrow corridor to his room. Darcy entered his, readied for bed, and laid awake considering Fitzwilliam's words long into the night.

Elizabeth, on stepping out of the room she shared with Jane, was greatly surprised by the person she met in the hall.

"Miss Darcy! How…? When…?"

Georgiana laughed and reached for her hands. "Last night, and very late I think. You and the other ladies had all gone to bed by the time we arrived."

"We?" Elizabeth queried.

"Fitzwilliam and I, of course! I could hardly come all this way on my own."

A little laugh escaped her. "Of course. Forgive me, I must still be half asleep to not have thought of that. Catherine will be so very happy to see you, and Mrs. Allen and Jane as well."

Catherine and Mrs. Allen were, in that moment, coming out of the room they had shared. "Georgie!" the former exclaimed, running up to her friend and embracing her. "I am so happy to see you! Though I can't imagine how you caught up to us—I assume your brother is with you?"

Georgiana nodded as Jane now emerged, and happy ejaculations were once again shared. "Let us go down and join the gentlemen," said Mrs. Allen, "and then I am sure we will hear everything."

Elizabeth and the others agreed, though Georgiana chose to fill them in as they walked down to the private dining parlor. Darcy hadn't chosen to follow her, Elizabeth thought—of course he hadn't. He followed simply because he wished to avoid arguing with his relations.

"He could have taken you back to Pemberley," she heard herself observe at one point.

"You know, I did consider that," Georgiana replied. "But then, I begin to think he was afraid they would simply follow, and Fitzwilliam wouldn't want that at all."

"Could they not also follow you to Fullerton?" Catherine asked. "I mean, the colonel's father had remembered Mr. Allen and where he was from."

Georgiana paused outside the door to the dining room. "I suppose that is possible, though I cannot imagine Uncle Richard taking the trouble."

Catherine had just opened the door when she spoke; the elder girl whirled in surprise. "The earl's Christian name is Richard?!"

The three gentlemen had stood on their entrance. "Yes, my father's name is Richard," said Fitzwilliam. "Why does that surprise you so?"

Catherine looked to James, and the brother and sister laughed. "But that is *our* father's name as well!" said she.

"Ha! That is a capital surprise," Fitzwilliam said with a smile. "Come, ladies, do be seated."

As chance would have it, Elizabeth found herself seated to Darcy's right. She acknowledged him with a polite nod when he held out her chair for her, not expecting him to speak in return.

"How was the journey from London, Miss Elizabeth?" he asked.

She poured herself a cup of chocolate from the carafe sitting before her. "It was pleasant enough, I suppose, Mr. Darcy."

"I am pleased to hear it," he replied.

"And your journey, sir?" she asked, still amazed that he and his sister had managed to meet them.

"Fast," Darcy said with a wry half smile. "Though I had not much of it given your party's lead, when I was motivated to join the excursion after all, I admit to some hope of catching you all up."

"Georgiana mentioned that you had received some word from Viscount Rowarth—I believe that is your elder cousin's address— regarding an engagement that, if memory serves, you denied existed."

She watched him grimace out of the corner of her eye. "I did deny it, because it does not," Darcy replied. "Lady Catherine and my mother bore children within a few months of each other. When one had a son and the other a daughter, the two made a joke of saying that perhaps one day we might marry and unite our great fortunes. At least, it was a passing fancy on my mother's side; since her death, my aunt has held firm in her belief that it was my mother's dearest wish as well as hers."

"Even were it truly what your mother wanted, it does not mean that you are required to follow through, does it?" Elizabeth asked.

Fitzwilliam guffawed at that moment, and joined their conversation saying, "Indeed not, Miss Elizabeth! Though Darcy is an honorable chap who might well have done if it were truly his mother's wish, I am sure you know that a gentleman is not obligated to comply with the desires of his mamma or his aunt. He can and will do as he pleases."

If only doing as he pleased might include marriage to a girl with vulgar relations and no fortune...

Stop it, Elizabeth! she admonished herself. *He's not here because he wants to marry you, he's here because he does not want to marry someone else.*

Conversation flowed freely as they consumed their early repast, though Elizabeth could not help noting that Darcy was tense. Why, she could not imagine—unless he feared his aunt and uncle might follow him after all. And though she continued to remind herself that he had not come out of a desire to see her, she was nevertheless pleased to have him near. She felt both pain and pleasure to be in his presence again, though she knew that, eventually, the pain would be greater.

Soon enough they were on the road for the last leg of their journey. Georgiana had once again offered to share her carriage with Elizabeth, who was not averse to being eminently more comfortable than the day before, as she would have an entire seat to herself. Her only fear was that Darcy's sister would renew her hope of their one day being sisters, but that fear was for naught, as Georgiana was far more preoccupied with meeting the six brothers and sisters still at home with Reverend and Mrs. Morland.

"I just can't imagine it!" she said more than once. "A family of ten children! I should have liked to have younger brothers and sisters, but it was not to be. Poor Mamma suffered greatly in birthing me, I have been told, and never quite recovered her health. She died when I was but three years."

"My mother's labor with Kitty was difficult," Elizabeth shared. "With Lydia more so. She still believed she could give my father a son, but with the complications from my youngest sister's birth, they were advised not to try again."

"I am sorry for your family not to have the assurance of a son, who would surely provide for his sisters' comfort and protection as my brother does me," Georgiana observed. "It is too bad, perhaps, that Mr. Collins could not have grown up with you. He is not your father's son, of course, but he could have been raised as one, seeing as he is to inherit the estate."

Elizabeth smiled. "An interesting idea, that," she said. "It is not likely to have happened given the discord between my father and his, but with your having suggested it, I will now wonder what life might have been like to have Mr. Collins as a brother."

Georgiana giggled. "I am sorry—perhaps I should not have suggested it," said she. "I dread to think what living with him would be like."

"Well, I would hope that both his manner and his person would be much improved under my father's influence. In fact, I daresay that having a son—even an adopted one—would likely have generated greater interest in my father for managing his income better," Elizabeth replied. "My sisters and I might well have had at least *some* dowry by this time."

The two talked on as the Darcy coach followed Mrs. Allen's on into Fullerton, arriving within the promised two hours. Elizabeth was a little surprised to find Darcy immediately at the carriage door when at last they were stopped before the stone edifice of Fullerton Manor, his hand waiting to assist her to the ground.

"Oh, it's magnificent!" said Georgiana as she was handed down. "Theodore, don't you think so?"

Fitzwilliam was examining the structure before him when his cousin asked her question. "It is a handsome building indeed."

"It was built during the early Tudor dynasty," said Mrs. Allen with pride. "My late husband's family has owned most of the land hereabouts since that time."

"It is regrettable, then," said the colonel, "that there are none of them left to whom he could have passed his estate. I am a firm believer in that properties which have been long in a family should be kept in it."

"Oh, indeed, sir!" the lady agreed with a vigorous nod. "But though Mr. Allen's family legacy has sadly ended, I can think of no one I should like better to have the guardianship of this house than Catherine, who I know will preserve its history for a new family legacy, one that she will share with you, Colonel."

Elizabeth watched as Fitzwilliam looked down at Catherine and smiled. She blushed, and thanked Mrs. Allen for her generous praise. They moved on then into the house, where the party was introduced to Perkins, the butler. He welcomed his mistresses warmly, informing them both that per the instructions sent by express, all the guest rooms had been aired and were ready.

At this moment, James Morland turned to the party and said, "As I will not be spending my nights here, I shall go on to the rectory and give Mother and Father the news of our arrival, Catherine. They should be returning from morning service about now."

"You'll not be staying with us?" his sister asked.

"Cathy, you know our father does not believe a gentleman should share residence with his betrothed before they are married, except when it is absolutely necessary," he said.

"Oh. Oh yes, I had not thought of that," Catherine replied. "But then what shall we do for the colonel before they are introduced?"

"The dower house!" cried Mrs. Allen. "It's small, I'm afraid—only a four-bedroom cottage—and hasn't been used for many years, since Mr. Allen's dear mother left us. But he was not lax in its upkeep, I can assure you. Colonel Fitzwilliam can stay there to observe propriety, and James as well, should he not want to stay at home with your parents."

James and Fitzwilliam looked to one another and laughed. "They'll be calling it the bachelor house 'ere long," said the latter.

"Perhaps so, if Mr. Darcy should stay there with us," James said.

Darcy nodded. "I have no issue sharing the cottage with my cousin and yourself."

"Then it is settled!" said Mrs. Allen, who immediately called Perkins back to her side and instructed him to send the housekeeper and a few of the maids to the dower house to prepare it for the gentlemen's residence.

She turned back to the others as he went off to carry out her instructions, clapping her hands gleefully. "We shall have us a merry little party of ladies the next few nights."

"Well, since we men are to reside in the dower house," said Fitzwilliam, "I expect we ought to go there now, with the servants. A note can be sent to the rectory to inform Reverend and Mrs. Morland of our arrival and desire to meet with them."

"Y-yes," said Catherine, whose nervousness, Elizabeth could see, was back in full force. "We need only meet with Mamma and Papa for now, I should think, though my brothers and sisters will want to meet you, of course."

"We must have a dinner party!" said Mrs. Allen. "All but the youngest three children can attend, which would give us…thirteen at table."

"Can food enough for so many be arranged in only an afternoon?" asked Catherine.

Elizabeth could not help but grin at the determined expression which overcame Mrs. Allen's countenance. "Come with me, my dear Catherine. Watch and learn."

Chapter Twenty-Three

Though he attended Fitzwilliam and Morland back to the manor for the meeting with Reverend and Mrs. Morland, Darcy elected to stay with the ladies while the brother and sister, and his cousin, met with the former's parents in the library.

Theodore had been near as nervous as Miss Morland appeared, and Darcy had quietly wished him success before taking his leave at the door. Mrs. Allen suggested they pass the time by her showing them the house, to which the Bennet sisters and his own agreed. It was, he had to admit, a magnificently appointed home — the entirety of it was original 15th century stone and wood, and there were some pieces of furniture from that time in remarkably like-new condition. He could well understand the lady's pride in the house and its furnishings, as well as imagine Caroline Bingley's envy should she have known what the house and its contents alone were worth. His cousin, should all go well with the Morland parents, would not be uncomfortable taking command of such a house.

They were just returning to the drawing room when those in the library emerged. It was obvious that at some point in the proceedings therein that Catherine and her mother had both cried, but their faces were dry now, and as the three men seemed to be at ease, Darcy suspected that Fitzwilliam's point had been carried.

In fact, he smiled as he looked down at Catherine, whose hand was on his arm, then back to Darcy and the other ladies and said, "It is now official. Miss Catherine Morland and I are engaged."

Georgiana squealed with delight and rushed over to embrace her friend. "I am so happy we shall be cousins!" she said.

Catherine laughed. "So am I, Georgie," she replied as she returned the hug.

"Congratulations, Theo," said Darcy as he shook his cousin's hand.

"Miss Sarah shall be inordinately pleased now you are to be married, Catherine," said Mrs. Allen then. "She can now be introduced into society!"

"Let us, perhaps, see James and Catherine married before we think of that, Mrs. Allen," said Reverend Morland with a smile.

His wife smiled as well and Mrs. Allen laughed. "Of course! You know, my dears," said the latter to Catherine and James, "you might consider having a double wedding. It would save much of the expense—though we simply *must* do as I told you before, Catherine and Jane, and go to London to have your wedding clothes made, for that is where you will find the best muslins!"

"I should like that, Mrs. Allen—though Mamma, I would like very much to take Sally with us. She should have something new for the wedding," Catherine said.

Mrs. Morland's next smile was an indulgent one. "Perhaps, Cathy. But let us talk over what *you* will need first, my dear."

The women all moved to sit on the sofas and armchairs to talk of wedding clothes. Darcy joined the other men at a smaller seating arrangement on the far side of the room.

Mr. Morland sighed as he watched them. "It is almost too difficult to believe that both my eldest son and eldest daughter are soon to be married," he said. Looking to Fitzwilliam, he added, "I know I have said it already, Colonel, but I really must thank you again for being of such moral character as to think of Catherine's reputation after that person assaulted her. She might not herself have considered the possible damage to her respectability had you not pressed the point."

Fitzwilliam inclined his head. "I must own that I feared we might have pressed it too hard," said he, "for she was very distressed when we explained the need for her to marry."

"Do not think that Catherine is without intelligence," said her father. "She is a smart girl, but she *can* be somewhat scatter-brained. I regret that I have often thought over these last months—before she and Mrs. Allen went into Hertfordshire to visit with her late husband's nephew—that Catherine did not quite fully grasp the

impact her having a fortune would have on those around her. Even
with the sad example of James's disappointment earlier in the year, I
do not think it occurred to her that she would be *more* of a target for
schemers and scoundrels than before. Suspecting she had a fortune is
one thing, knowing it is another — and we all know that word gets
out. Yet, my daughter still believes there is good in everyone, until
that belief is proven unjustified."

Fitzwilliam nodded again. "I know that how our engagement has
come about is not what she would have wished for, but I am hopeful
of ours being a happy match."

"Oh indeed, my boy!" said Mr. Morland. "There may not be love
between you now, but there is mutual admiration and respect, and in
the absence of love I can think of no better cornerstones for the foun-
dation of a lasting marriage. But do not despair of her never loving
you — my Catherine has such a generous, caring heart that I do not
doubt she will in time. And she will be such an excellent, doting wife
that I am sure you will one day love her."

Fitzwilliam smiled. "I can assure you, sir, that I look forward to
feeling for your daughter as she deserves."

The ladies were given about half an hour to talk before the
reverend suggested to his wife it was time to take their leave. He and
Mrs. Morland would, of course, be delighted to join the party for
dinner with the elder three of their younger children, said he, with
his lady thanking Mrs. Allen for the suggestion of including them.

"Sally, Thomas, and Robert will be thrilled with the novelty of
dining away from home," she said. "We've not done since…"

Mrs. Allen smiled. "It's quite all right, Mrs. Morland, you can say
it. Your family has not dined at the manor since before we went to
Bath." She paused and drew a breath, and her smile became a little
sad. "I know that I was a wretched creature those first months after
my husband passed so unexpectedly, but I am much better now. Our
dear Catherine, especially, has helped remind me that I still have
much to live for."

"You are too kind, Mrs. Allen," the young lady replied.

After Reverend and Mrs. Morland's departure, it was noted by
Fitzwilliam that a few of their female companions appeared weary.
Mrs. Allen remarked that she was a little tired, and given that
Georgiana had so recently had a cold — however brief it had been —
Darcy seconded his cousin's suggestion that perhaps they ought all of
them to rest before dinner. Thus, he, Fitzwilliam, and Morland bid
the women a good afternoon and took themselves back to the dower

house. On the way, Darcy was filled in by the other two on some of the details of the discussion in the library, and how the Morlands had reacted.

"Father truly is grateful to Theo for being willing to marry Catherine," said James. "When we told him she had been compromised by a man hoping to marry her for her money, his first concern was whether any gentleman would have her at all. He feared that her fortune alone would not be enough to secure her a husband should it get out that she had been touched, even if it was without her consent."

"Indeed, James," Fitzwilliam replied. "However, had I seen what was described to us with my own eyes, I would do precisely what I have done. What happened to Catherine was not by her choice, and she should not be punished for it."

As they were entering the dower house, Morland took a glance around the drawing room and said, "You know, I'd all but forgotten this cottage even existed until Mrs. Allen mentioned it. It's a fair size, and while I greatly appreciate my sister's offer to reside at the manor with her and Mrs. Allen, I do not think she has considered how... different it might be now she's to marry also. I've a mind to suggest Jane and I live here, that you might properly establish yourself as master of the manor, Theo."

Fitzwilliam inclined his head. "That is generous of you, James," said he. "And you're right, this is a good-sized house, I think. You've a drawing room, dining parlor, study, four bedrooms, and a large attic for the servants to make their beds in. I daresay any couple just starting out would be quite pleased to have such a place as this — were Catherine and I not set to live in the manor, and Mrs. Allen were to offer the dower house to us, I'd not turn up my nose."

"Really?" said Morland with some surprise. "I would have expected it, to be honest. I mean, you *are* the son of an earl, and have never wanted for any of the comforts of life."

Darcy found himself grinning as he recalled the discussion from when his cousin had first appeared in Hertfordshire. "Despite his proclaimed habits of extravagance, Theo has rather simple tastes."

His cousin turned to him. "Yes, Will, I do. My simple tastes, however, tend to have some air of expense and elegance about them — I enjoy fine clothes, fine horses, fine furniture, fine wine, and fine food. Those cannot be had without money. However, even though the furnishings here are rather modest, I can see they are well made. The bed in my room is comfortable. All the rooms are a fair size, so I don't feel crammed in. Yes, I am sure I could be comfortable here, until a larger house could be acquired."

"And there we come to it!" said Morland with a laugh. "You'd be content here, but only temporarily."

Fitzwilliam grinned. "But of course! I *am* the son of an earl, after all, and the image must be maintained!"

Darcy did not much care for gatherings where he did not know everyone—as he had told Elizabeth on the night they met, he simply had not the means of conversing easily with strangers. This was especially true when in the company of young people, so he was very much surprised to find himself in conversation with Thomas Morland, who was but fifteen. The two were seated next to one another during the meal, and after the boy had hesitantly asked him if he liked horses or history, Darcy felt relief in having two subjects in which he was greatly interested offered as topics for conversation.

Putting himself and the boy at ease, he nodded and confirmed that he liked both, after which followed an animated discourse over which horse breeds were best and which kings of England were the most effective at government. He found himself not only surprised by the young man's intelligence, but also ashamed at his having assumed that the number of children in the family meant that their education had been neglected. He then recalled that James Morland had studied for the clergy at Oxford, and that his younger brother Edward was there now to study for the law.

It disturbed Darcy a great deal to suddenly realize he was no less guilty of arrogance and classism than his uncle and his aunts.

The other regret he found himself subject to at dinner was having no real opportunity to talk to Elizabeth. She sat directly across from him, which would have made conversation easy, but was as caught up with those on either side of her as Darcy was with Thomas Morland on his left and Fitzwilliam on his right. It pleased him very much to see her enjoying both food and friendship with her companions, but to not be able to speak to her himself—to have little chance of attempting to recapture the ease with which they had begun their friendship near six weeks ago—was more distressing than he cared to admit. If he could not have her affection, he wanted at least her friendship. On being in her presence again, he'd found that he could not, after all, simply give her up, and would take whatever of herself she was willing to share with him.

He thought that he had kept his observation of Elizabeth to

himself—that he had been careful not to glance her way too often—but when the ladies retired to the drawing room after the dessert course, taking twelve-year-old Robert with them (much to the boy's dismay), Darcy's attention to Elizabeth was addressed by the last person he would have expected.

When each adult male had poured a glass of port for themselves, and Thomas had been allowed a glass of watered sherry, Reverend Morland turned his attention to Darcy and said, "I noticed, Mr. Darcy, that you paid special attention to Miss Elizabeth Bennet this evening, though you said nary a word to her."

Fitzwilliam scoffed. "Darcy pays attention to her whenever they're in the same room, though he'll deny it until he's blue in the face."

"Theodore," said Darcy.

His warning was not to be heeded. Fitzwilliam knocked back a good swallow of his port, then continued with, "I keep telling him to just confess his admiration, but he will not!"

"Why don't you speak, if I may ask, Darcy?" queried James.

Darcy sighed as he pinched the bridge of his nose. "I'd rather not discuss it," said he.

"Fine, *I* will," declared Fitzwilliam. "Scowl at me all you like, Will, but *something* has got to knock some sense into that stubborn head of yours!"

He turned toward Reverend Morland. "I believe my cousin to be in love with Miss Elizabeth, sir, but he will not speak because he believes her indifferent to him. Why, I cannot imagine. She smiles at him, has had several lengthy conversations about who knows what with him, she has expressed concern for his welfare, and she has danced with him!"

Reverend Morland chuckled. "And dancing is a sure step to falling in love, is it not? My Catherine very much enjoys dancing, Colonel, so there's another blessing in *your* favor," he said.

He then looked to Darcy with a contemplative expression, and after a draw of breath and a drink from his glass, the gentleman said, "Sir, pray forgive me speaking on a subject which obviously brings you some discomfort, but if I have learned anything at all over the long years of my life, it is that one must take a chance before that chance is taken away from them."

"That's what I keep telling him!" said Fitzwilliam with a wave of his hand. "If he doesn't say something now, some other lad will snatch the girl up and then he'll be miserable."

Darcy set his glass down, a little harder perhaps than he had intended. "And what would you have me do, Theodore? Walk up to her and declare myself, only to be humiliated by her rejection? Yes, we have conversed; yes, we have danced—but I would do the same with any other young woman of my acquaintance. Her willingness to engage with me when we are in company does *not* signify that she returns my regard!"

"But if you do not speak, Mr. Darcy, how will you ever know the truth of that?" said Reverend Morland softly. "Perhaps the courtship practices of the wealthy are somewhat different than they are for those of us with less fortune, or perhaps they have simply changed from the norm of my youth. But as I recall, a young lady waits for the gentleman to speak first, that she does not appear too forward and— dare I say it—risk her reputation."

Darcy blanched as though he had been struck. *No*, he thought. *It cannot be so bloody simple as that.*

"If the young lady truly does not return your affections," Reverend Morland went on, "then at least you will know for certain. I should think it best a young man speaks and is hurt by a refusal than to torment himself with uncertainty. Once you have been assured of affection or indifference, then you will know how best to proceed thereafter."

Darcy sighed and took a long pull of his drink before he could bring himself to speak. "You might think that a young man who is educated, who has lived in the world, who has managed a vast estate and the upbringing of his younger sister for years would have little experience with being afraid, but... I have, since meeting Elizabeth Bennet, never been so terrified of not being wanted. I have never desired any woman as I do her, and it paralyzes me to think that she may laugh at me, or even just look me in the eye and tell me she does not share my feelings."

"I've not been in your position before, cousin, though I daresay I came close when I feared Miss Morland might reject my offer," said Fitzwilliam, his tone now bereft of the jollity it had held before. "It is humbling to witness the truth of your internal struggle, and I am sorry for all my teasing. But I second what Reverend Morland has said to you: *say something*. At least if you do, you will at last know the place you hold in her regard."

Thomas Morland cleared his throat. "Pray forgive me, sir, if I speak out of turn," he began, "but is it not also possible that Miss Elizabeth is just as afraid of rejection as are you? Perhaps she has not spoken or given you any indication of her regard because she believes you are as indifferent to her as you think her to you."

"Very wisely spoken, son," said Reverend Morland as Darcy's gaze once more found his cousin's. Fitzwilliam had said much the same to him, and he had dismissed it as nonsense. He'd believed his regard for Elizabeth was clear, at least until he suspected her to be indifferent, but… could he truly have judged her, and himself, so ill?

Dragging a hand over his face as he groaned, Darcy gulped the last of the alcohol in his glass before saying, "I've been rather a fool, haven't I? One tiny slip of a girl should not make me so nervous, but I have only to look at her and I am weak."

"Did you ever feel that way about Mamma, Father?" Thomas asked Mr. Morland.

His father smiled. "I could not have married your mother, Tom, did she not make me weak with but a glance—and I do not think there would be ten of you did she not make me feel so still."

"I regret that I never before considered whether you and Mamma loved each other, Father," said James. "But then, I think I have always just *known* that you did. I've felt it in the way you behave to one another, how you have treated my brothers and sisters and myself with such kindness."

"I am pleased, then, that we have been such an example to you, James. May God bless you and your sister with the same degree of happiness that I have had with your mother these three-and-twenty years."

He had raised his glass to them as he spoke, then brought it to his lips to drink; the vicar paused as they touched the rim of the glass, and—looking to Darcy—said, "And may He bless you as well, Mr. Darcy, in granting you the courage to say what is in your heart to the woman you love."

Chapter Twenty-Four

Elizabeth was delighted for her sister.

Mr. and Mrs. Morland had greeted Jane warmly earlier in the day, made the usual remarks about her beauty, and praised her for healing James's wounded heart. After Catherine's engagement to Colonel Fitzwilliam became official, and the ladies had sat together talking of wedding clothes, Elizabeth was certain that Mrs. Morland was impressed by Jane's simple tastes.

Now, she and Mrs. Allen were having a discussion with the two soon-to-be brides about household budgets. Catherine's mother seemed further impressed with Jane's suggestions for economy, and her willingness to learn what household skills she currently lacked in order to have more money for hiring servants.

"You'll not need many, given the size of the dower house," said Mrs. Allen, who had—after hearing James's suggestion at dinner that he and Jane live in the dower house instead of the manor—chastised herself for not thinking of it before.

"Your chambermaid can double as a lady's maid, Miss Bennet, if you need assistance dressing," said Mrs. Morland. "My son is used to dressing himself, so he'll not need a valet. I would imagine, with there being only two of you, you'll not need more than a man of all work, a cook, and two maids."

"I agree, ma'am," said Jane.

"And you'll not have to concern yourself with paying the wages of your servants while you live at the dower house," said Catherine. "No, please do not protest—it is my gift to you and my brother."

Jane shook her head. "But Catherine, you already give us gift enough by granting us leave to reside in the dower house, that we may marry now instead of waiting until Mr. Morland can take orders."

"My paying your servants is an extension of that gift," Catherine insisted. "You'd have had the benefit of servants staying here with us in the manor, after all. You have servants at Longbourn. And it will hardly be anything to pay them for you—less than a hundred pounds a year, I am sure."

Elizabeth suspected then that Catherine would also attempt giving her brother and Jane a living allowance for their food and other needs, unless James found some work that paid well enough to cover those expenses. It really was kind of her to be so generous with her new fortune as to be willing to assist her brother and his new wife in starting their lives.

The gentlemen did not linger too long over their port and were with the ladies again in only half an hour—much to the relief of Robert, who'd sulked over not being allowed to remain with the other males. Elizabeth was instantly aware that there was something different about Darcy. There was an expression of determination on his face, though he smiled as he moved directly toward where she sat somewhat away from the other ladies, taking the chair adjacent.

"Had you pleasant conversation while our party was divided?" he asked her.

An unusual question, she mused, but nevertheless replied, "In truth I had very little, Mr. Darcy. The prevailing topic was household budgeting, and as your sister and I are not soon to be married, we were both of us content to listen and observe."

"Have you no interest in learning to manage a household budget?" Darcy queried. "Would it not be useful information for when you do marry?"

Elizabeth grinned. "I *did* listen, Mr. Darcy, even if I did not participate in the lesson," she replied. "Besides, I have some aptitude with numbers and already know how to balance a ledger."

Darcy nodded. He then looked about the room; she followed his gaze, and felt a small thrill of pleasure when he gestured to a chess board and suggested they play a game or two. The board was set up on a small table between two chairs on the opposite end of the room from the main conversation area, giving the arrangement something of an air of intimacy.

Do not see more than there is, Elizabeth, she chastised herself even as she went with him toward the game. On closer inspection of the game pieces as she sat, she noticed for the first time that they were all made of glass—one set clear and the other frosted.

"How interesting," she observed, picking up one of the frosted knights to examine it more closely. "Usually chess pieces are painted or stained wood, or polished stone."

"Interesting you should mention stone," said Darcy, who had sat on the side of the clear pieces. "I've a set at Pemberley with one side carved in black and white marble and the other in malachite."

Elizabeth looked up at him. "The pieces must be almost too beautiful to play with."

Darcy smiled. "I have often felt so, though I have some obligation, of a sort, to make use of them, as my grandfather carved them himself."

"Did he now?"

He nodded. "At first it was simply to pass the time when he was once indisposed with a broken leg, using some malachite my father, who was but ten or so at the time, had found in a small cave in one of the surrounding foothills. And of course, having carved enough pieces for one side of the board during his invalidity, my grandfather felt he could do no less than make a complete set. The board is also hand-made, though it was stained and put together by a woodsmith in Lambton. He gave the set to my father for his birthday that year."

"I think I should like to see it sometime," Elizabeth confessed, surprised she had spoke the thought aloud.

Darcy smiled again. "I should be most pleased to show it to you."

A different sort of tension than she had felt before in his presence Elizabeth became aware of then, and feeling the need to regain some sense of balance, lifted an eyebrow and made a saucy rejoinder. "Will you be as much pleased to lose when you do so?"

Her companion chuckled. "Win or lose, I imagine I shall be happy just to be sharing the moment with you."

Heat suffused Elizabeth's neck and cheeks, and she found herself trapped in the warmth of his gaze.

After a moment that seemed the breadth of a second and an eternity at once, Darcy blinked and looked down at the board. "Ladies first," he said softly.

Elizabeth made her first move; Darcy made his. The first few minutes of the game were passed in silence, though they could hear the conversation going on across the room. She was vaguely aware of cards being suggested, and as there was a spinet at one wall, while a footman was sent for card tables, Georgiana was asked by Catherine to play for them.

She began with a soft piano sonata, and after the first strains had gone by, Darcy said, "You may recall, Miss Elizabeth, my aunt having mentioned the pianoforte we have at Pemberley."

Elizabeth did recall, and said so to her companion. "What made you think of it?" she added.

"Georgiana. Having heard her play on not only the pianoforte, but also harpsichord and spinet, I can tell that Mrs. Allen's instrument needs tuning."

Tilting her head to listen, Elizabeth could not but agree, and she suspected she surprised Darcy that she could tell; she explained by informing him that as Mary played the pianoforte at Longbourn every day, she'd soon learned the difference between a finely tuned instrument and one that was in need of service. "Though I still do not quite understand why you should think of your instrument at home, unless you remark not only that this one needs tuning, but that yours is superior."

"Yes and no," he replied as he took one of her pawns. "Superiority in manufacturing is a matter of opinion in nearly every case, and without closer inspection I could not tell you whether Mrs. Allen's is finely or cheaply made. We've a Broadwood and Sons in Pemberley's music room at present, and I am attempting to secure an Erard with a Viennese action because my sister's favorite composer prefers them over English models—though I'd much rather support an English manufacturer, as Erard once made a piano for Napoleon."

That he should do anything for his sister that made her happy did not much surprise Elizabeth, but that he would attempt to purchase a specific model musical instrument for such a fanciful reason as that which he had given was delightful. She smiled and said, "It is unfortunate, then, that these action things—whatever they are—are not available on English models. Could you perhaps have one custom made with it?"

Darcy looked up with a smile. "English pianos do have them, but they are made somewhat differently than the Viennese action. Georgiana, who learned the history of her own favorite instrument from one of her masters, has told me the latter has a lighter sound than the English version. And I may have no choice but to try having one custom made here in England as I've had no success thus far with acquiring a genuine Erard piano—rather vexing, that—and I hope very much to have a new instrument for Georgiana's sixteenth birthday."

"When will she be sixteen?"

"In May."

"She is but a month older than Lydia—her birthday is in June."

Another few moves were made in silence, then Elizabeth ventured to ask, "Who is Georgiana's favorite composer?"

"Mozart."

Smiling, Elizabeth said, "I rather like his music myself, though I fear the gentleman would be affronted to hear my poor attempts to copy his genius."

"I would hope that any composer would be more pleased a person would want to play his music than he is affronted by imperfect performance," Darcy observed.

Elizabeth smiled as she took another of his pieces from the board. "Perhaps you are right," said she, "but then, I've never met a composer so I could not speak the truth of it either way."

Their conversation then returned to Pemberley. Darcy casually began to talk of the house, some of the rooms, and the grounds that surrounded it. He spoke of its history, how the building had become synonymous with his family "almost as if Pemberley were a Darcy in itself," and how there were some families in the *ton* who had been longing to see the place for years.

"Why can they not go and tour it, as I have heard the owners of some great houses allow people to do?" Elizabeth asked.

Darcy chuckled. "The house *is* open for viewing in the spring and summer months, but that is an activity for common people, so they would say. No, my dear Miss Elizabeth… No one from the so-called good families would dare to lower themselves to going on a public tour. They must be invited by the master or mistress of the estate— for there is prestige in being invited."

A thrilling little shiver twittered down her spine when Darcy said "my dear Miss Elizabeth," but though it pleased her to hear the words put together, she forced herself to remember that they were merely friends having a game and conversation. Sometimes she wished she could stop hiding that she cared for him, but to confess her heart's desire to a man who had given no indisputable indication that he felt such affections himself would be a breach of propriety. Her mother had always stressed that a young lady may smile at a gentleman she liked but could do no more, as it was his place to speak first.

It was one of the few lessons on decorum Mrs. Bennet had taught her elder girls that, after Lydia had come along, she had given up stressing as important to remember (now she very much encouraged outrageous flirtation, as if that was any better). Yet Elizabeth had followed the direction in her youth and continued to follow it, as it was a guideline for behavior that she actually believed in. A young lady's reputation was a precious commodity—as Catherine had so recently learned—one that simply could not be risked on what might turn out to be an infatuation.

Of course, Elizabeth was full aware by now that this was no infatuation she felt. Against every inclination to the contrary, she had fallen in love with Darcy. But she could not tell him so, no matter how much pain she suffered at not being able to reveal her truth. She wished she could, just to be able to say it, even if he rejected her.

She realized suddenly that Darcy was staring at her, his expression one of concern. "Are you well, Miss Elizabeth?" he asked.

Elizabeth forced a smile. "Oh, quite well, I assure you. I beg your pardon for my wandering thoughts. Now where were we?"

"It is your move, and I was espousing the virtues of Derbyshire."

Elizabeth studied the board, then made a move which cost Darcy a rook. He chuckled, and she noted that he was just then realizing how few of his pieces remained in play.

"What are these virtues of Derbyshire you wish to tell me of? I am pleased that they appear to be distracting you from the game, but I warn you, Mr. Darcy, that my Aunt Gardiner has already initiated an interest in me to see the country, as she was reared in Lambton—which is but five miles from your estate, I believe. Should you tell me anymore than she has, I will have no choice but to see the place for myself one day."

Darcy looked up again and smiled. "I sincerely hope that you will."

It was difficult throughout the evening to remain steady in her belief that Darcy's behavior was not indicative of a change in his regard. By the end of it, however—the Morlands had decided to depart after only two rounds of card games, but the others continued to play after they'd gone—Elizabeth's reason began to give way to hope. Maybe his feelings were new and had startled him, or maybe he had always liked her and really was just as shy as Colonel Fitzwilliam had claimed at the ball. Whatever the case, this more open—almost flirtatious!—Darcy had caused Elizabeth's own feelings to surge so high that she almost could not contain them.

After a light soup for supper, the three gentlemen departed for the dower house. Darcy's good night to Elizabeth included a gentle smile and a press of his lips to the back of her hand. She was all amazement, and had stood staring at the closed door for several seconds until Mrs. Allen had yawned rather loudly.

"Well, my dears, I must say I am thoroughly worn out by the excitement of today," said the lady, before she walked up to Catherine, cupped her cheeks, then leaned forward to kiss one. "I am so very happy for you, my dear. The colonel is a fine man, and I just know he will be good to you. Think of that, of all the potential there is of your being happy together and falling in love together, rather than *why* you're marrying. Do that, and I am sure you will be content."

Catherine seemed almost too emotional for words, though she managed to give her thanks to Mrs. Allen, who then bid goodnight to the rest of them before starting up the stairs. When she had turned out of sight on the landing, Catherine drew a breath, then swirled toward Elizabeth and grabbed her hand. "Oh Lizzy, what a night you've had!"

Elizabeth laughed. "Whatever do you mean, Cathy?"

Beside Catherine, Georgiana grinned. "I think she means you and Fitzwilliam," said the younger girl. "My brother was very attentive to you this evening."

Not wanting to raise their hopes anymore than hers had been—and Darcy's behavior had raised them indeed—Elizabeth laughed again and said, "So we talked of Pemberley and Derbyshire while playing two games of chess. I should think that merely a pleasant way to pass an evening."

"Lizzy, I must say that Mr. Darcy did seem more… I don't know, more open, I think," said Jane. "More relaxed even."

"I cannot help but wonder what my father, James, Tom, and the colonel may have said to him when they were having their port together," Catherine said then. "I am sure they said something, for there really was something rather different in his manner after they returned to us. As Jane said, he seemed almost relaxed."

"Yes, Mr. Darcy does give off a constant air of tension," Elizabeth mused.

"I know many mistake his stiffness of manner for arrogance and pride, but I do not think he has ever *meant* to appear so," said Georgiana. "But for all his intellect and confidence, my brother has never quite mastered being comfortable among strangers, unless he can rely upon the companionship of someone he knows very well to help put him at ease. Truly, I am the same in that regard — people I don't know just make me so nervous! Fitzwilliam, however, is definitely most at ease among his intimidate acquaintances, as am I."

"I have noted that about him, and you, Georgie," observed Elizabeth. "But I do not want for you all to think his geniality towards me this evening means more than it does. It is difficult enough for me to gird myself against disappointment."

She had turned away toward the stairs as she said the last, but was stopped by a hand on her arm. Catherine's expression was one of gleeful amazement, which was mirrored on Georgiana, and Jane looked to her with a knowing smile.

"Elizabeth Bennet, are you at last admitting that you admire Mr. Darcy?" Catherine asked.

Elizabeth smiled. "I have never said that I do not admire him, Catherine, only that there was no attachment between us and that I did not think there likely to ever be one. I said that because it is true, and because I did not wish to develop hopes in myself or others that I could not expect to be furthered. I will now only say that I still do not, but that sometimes he does make it very, very hard not to."

With that, she turned determinedly toward the stairs and started up them. Behind her, she heard Catherine say, "Very well, we shall just have to hope for her, until such time as Mr. Darcy declares himself."

Elizabeth was grateful that the very pleasant end to her day did not keep her long from sleep, and when she woke as the sun was rising the next morning, she found that, while she could recall no details of her dreams, they had left within her a feeling of joyful contentment. It was always nice to wake from dreams that were pleasant, save for when she wished she could have seen more — or just remembered what she had seen. To her, it meant good tidings for the day to come.

As she'd had no chance the last three days to go for a good, long walk, Elizabeth dressed quickly and slipped on her half boots. Because it was now December, there was a decided chill outside — frost still lingered on the grass and mist in the air — and she was grateful for the foresight to have brought her wool pelisse on this journey. Because she was unfamiliar with the grounds of Fullerton Manor, Elizabeth decided to walk with the house to her back, where it would always be in sight should she turn her head.

She'd not walked far when a figure appeared in the mist some distance ahead. At first, she could make out nothing from the shape of the figure except the certainty that it was a man. Elizabeth paused but was not yet alarmed, for the gait of the approaching man was smooth and steady, and this was an hour at which many farmers and servants were already about their morning tasks.

When the mist at last began to clear, she realized that the person coming toward her was familiar: it was Darcy! A little surprised to see him up and about — much less walking across a wet, misty field — Elizabeth could not stop herself feeling a little thrill of delight at the possibility that he had come specifically to see her.

As he neared, she could see a pleased expression on his countenance. His pace quickened a little, and in only another minute or two he was before her, bowing his head.

"Good morning, Miss Elizabeth," Darcy greeted her. He smiled. "I thought you might be up walking before the others are awake."

Elizabeth grinned. "Know me so well do you, Mr. Darcy?"

He chuckled. "I recall you mentioning once or twice that you enjoyed a good walk each morning, when you could manage one. And… I confess that I hoped today would be no different. I thought to join you in taking the air, if you would not mind the company."

Her grin bloomed into a smile. "I do not mind at all, sir."

Moving to her side, Darcy offered his arm; she took it and they continued in the direction of the dower house. After a minute or so of silence, he drew a breath and said, "Madam, I've a matter of some import on my mind that I should like to speak to you about, if I may."

"Certainly, Mr. Darcy — I won't even argue with you about promising confidence, if you should require it."

"I hope very much that such a promise will not be necessary, or desired, on either side," Darcy said. "You see… I have wished to speak of this particular matter to you for some time, but I have not had the confidence of being well-received."

At once, Georgiana's words from last night came to her; reflexively, Elizabeth gripped his arm tighter in nervous anticipation. "I will hear anything you have to say, Mr. Darcy."

Darcy glanced down at her, smiled, and looked ahead again. "You once said to me that you were at a loss to understand how Miss Morland could imagine that I admired you. At the ball, after Wickham had come and gone, you said that she, your sister, and Theo were all of the same mind concerning something that you'd told me was beyond your understanding. In that moment I did not take your meaning, but later it became clear to me."

Elizabeth felt herself blush. "Ah... Yes, I..." she said hesitantly, trying and failing to think of a good reply.

"They are not wrong," Darcy said suddenly, stopping and turning to look at her.

Chapter Twenty-Five

Elizabeth blinked. "I beg your pardon?"

He took a step toward her, making the space between them all but disappear. "Elizabeth, I…"

"You cannot truly like me sir. I-I have no fortune. I have no connections of which your noble relations would approve," she spurted, both needing and dreading to have the failings of her family addressed once and for all.

"I cannot deny that is true, but nevertheless, I *do* admire you, Miss Elizabeth Bennet," said Darcy in a husky voice. "Very much so. In vain have I struggled against my inclinations otherwise, for the reasons you state and others. But it will not do. My feelings will no longer be repressed."

The breath she did not realize until that moment she'd begun to hold escaped her. Elizabeth gulped and drew another. "Oh, Mr. Darcy…"

"Have I any chance of succeeding? Any at all?" he pressed. "For some weeks now I have felt myself falling hopelessly in love with you — hopeless, I say, because despite our many amiable meetings, I came to believe you utterly indifferent to me. Others have proven wiser than myself advised me to stop being a fool, to lay myself before you in the hope of securing your hand, if not your heart. As Theo does with Catherine, I have great hope that I may be able to earn your love in time."

"Sir," said Elizabeth, who was now fighting the sting of joyful tears. "I am honored you think me worthy of your love, that you would desire my own to be yours. For the same many weeks, I have thought *you* indifferent to *me*. I have believed that you despised my family's circumstances for being so decidedly below your own, that you thought them—and myself by association—too vulgar to be connected to you."

"I own that I have thought lowly of some of your family, and for that I am duly ashamed," said Darcy. "At the same time, how can I not respect your good parents for raising such a fine daughter as yourself? As are Jane and Mary?"

He smiled then. "Even Kitty and Lydia are not without hope of remedy, should they be given proper instruction. I should be glad to assist your father in that respect, if you think it would not be too wounding to his pride that I should offer."

Darcy gave her hand a gentle squeeze. "I pray you do not think I suggest a governess or finishing school for your sisters because I feel any embarrassment I may be soon related to them. I do it only for you, so that you understand I would do anything to help better the lives of those you hold most dear."

And so that I am less embarrassed by my own connections, I do not doubt, Elizabeth thought wryly.

"And what of your noble relations, Mr. Darcy?" she asked then. "Given the less than amiable feelings I no doubt stirred in the earl and countess, you will still have me, when I lack the ability to know my place and hold my tongue?"

Darcy laughed. "While there *are* occasions in which it would be advisable to think before you speak, my dear, when we are among our friends or alone together, I would have you be as impertinent and witty as ever. To confess the truth, I think those same decided opinions to which my aunt took exception one of your most refreshing characteristics."

Elizabeth had to laugh. "Oh, you may regret saying so one day, Mr. Darcy, when my pert opinions are your old friends after some twenty years, at least."

He reached for her hands and lifted them, holding them to his heart. "Then you will have me? You will do me the honor of becoming my wife?"

Joy—pure, unadulterated happiness—suffused Elizabeth then, and so overcome was she that for a moment she had no voice with which to speak. She could only nod her head as tears spilled down her cheeks.

Darcy raised her gloved hands to press his lips to her knuckles. "Oh, dearest, loveliest Elizabeth... For how much longer might we both have been in misery had I not been at last prompted to speak?"

"I dread to think on it, sir," she managed at last. "I don't know that I would ever have found such courage, as I was taught to let the gentleman speak first—though you would not think it on observance of my youngest sisters."

"That was suggested to me—that you were simply behaving modestly," Darcy said. "It does you credit, my love, and is certain proof that you *can* keep that sharp tongue of yours behind your teeth. Oh, but I should have known, or been more clear in my own behavior as to the strength of my affections."

"But you said you believed me indifferent," Elizabeth rejoined. "And I believed the same of you—oh, Mr. Darcy, we are cast in the same stone, you and I! Both of us falling so helplessly in love and both of us too afraid to speak our truth to each other."

"Fitzwilliam. I should like above anything to hear you say my name."

Heat flushed her neck and cheeks again as Elizabeth smiled. "I should be delighted to say it…Fitzwilliam. And I should say, I think I have earned the privilege of doing so at least once, as you have done my own name."

A hearty, happy laugh escaped him, and after reaching into a pocket to draw out a handkerchief, Darcy handed it to her before he turned to tuck her hand at his elbow once more. They continued on to the dower house, where his cousin and James were just coming down from their rooms. The two were, to Elizabeth's eye, wearing hopeful gazes as they saw who their housemate was with, and their joy was almost a match for that of the couple when their news was shared.

"Do our sisters know?" James asked.

Elizabeth laughed. "No, indeed! It has only just happened as we walked together."

"Then we must tell them at once!" said the colonel. "The ladies at the manor will be made as happy as we are that the two of you have quit dancing around the truth and admitted your affection at last."

"You just want to boast that you were right all along, Theo," said Darcy in a droll tone.

"Well, I was!" said Fitzwilliam with a laugh. He turned to Elizabeth and added, "Now we are to be family, Miss Elizabeth, I should be honored if you would use my Christian name. Might save you some confusion, given his is the same as my family name."

Elizabeth smiled. "I shall warm up to it, Colonel, in time."

James and Fitzwilliam soon donned cloaks and hats, and the four departed together to walk to the manor. When they arrived, Elizabeth removed her pelisse and hat before the gentlemen and went on into the drawing room, leaving them in the hall. She found Catherine there at the writing desk, the younger girl's pen stilling on her entrance.

"Lizzy," she greeted her with a smile. "I thought I heard you moving about earlier. I've just been writing to my friends, the Tilneys — well, to Eleanor — to tell them I am to be married. Who is in the hall — have my brothers and sisters come to call?"

"One of them has," said Elizabeth with a grin. "But not from the rectory. No, our visitors so early this morning are your betrothed, my sister's betrothed, and my own."

"Your own?" queried Catherine, just as Darcy was leading the others into the room. She jumped up with a squeal of delight and ran to throw her arms around Elizabeth. "I knew it! I knew you loved each other!"

Elizabeth laughed and returned the embrace. "Yes, we did — we do. And now we are to be married."

"Once Darcy here has secured your father's permission," quipped Fitzwilliam.

"As much as my father will not want to lose me, I daresay he will not withhold his approval," said Elizabeth. "And even should he be inclined to do so, my mother would never hear of his saying no to my dear Mr. Darcy's ten thousand a year."

"I pray you would forgive my saying so, Elizabeth," began Darcy, "but your father would be a fool indeed to decline my offer. The benefit to your mother and sisters upon the event of his death is almost immeasurable. You must know that I could not allow their suffering for want of a home."

"Yes, when the melancholy event occurs, Darcy is sure to find some place for your mother and younger sisters, be they unmarried at the time," said Fitzwilliam. "But it is likely not to be anywhere too near Pemberley."

Darcy shot his cousin a scowl, but Elizabeth could only laugh. Catherine declared that they simply *must* tell the other ladies the joyful news, and so ran out of the room to fetch them. She, Jane, and Georgiana entered the room together a few minutes later; greetings were exchanged before Darcy and Elizabeth shared the news of their engagement. Georgiana reacted much the same as Catherine, first embracing her brother and then Elizabeth herself. Jane was a little more sedate in her expression of happiness, but in her eyes Elizabeth could see that she felt it a great deal.

"I am so very happy for you, Lizzy," said she as she stood back from a warm embrace. "You are going to bring so much more joy to our mother than did I with my engagement."

"Jane, Darcy's income may far outdistance that which your James will have, but our mother will surely be delighted to have not just one, but *two* daughters married."

"Whatever do you mean, Miss Elizabeth?" said Mrs. Allen, who was just then coming into the room. "Two daughters married?"

Darcy moved to her side and held out his hand. Elizabeth laid hers in it with a smile, then looked to her hostess and once more shared the news of their engagement. Mrs. Allen was in raptures; she believed Mrs. Bennet would indeed be overcome with happiness to have her two eldest daughters married, and remarked how they would all of them soon be "such a fine family of young people."

Georgiana was just saying how remarkable it was that they would all be connected to such good friends when they all of them noted the arrival of a carriage. Moments later, the door bell was rung—and it continued to ring until the door was answered.

"Who the " muttered James as he, Darcy, and Fitzwilliam stood.

"Where is he? Where is my nephew? No, I will not wait!"

Darcy and Fitzwilliam looked to one another, the latter saying, "Speak of the ..."

࿇

It was an effort for Darcy to school his expression as his late mother's sister, Lady Catherine de Bourgh, noisily made her way to the drawing room. Perkins had barely got the door open to announce her when she bustled past him.

Darcy need not have bothered concealing his irritation, as his aunt certainly had not concealed her own displeasure—her aging, lined face was set in an angry scowl.

"Fitzwilliam Darcy, I demand you attend me at once!" Lady Catherine barked.

"I am standing right here, Aunt, there is no need to shout," Darcy replied in a softer, more controlled tone.

"I will shout if I like, sir!" she countered. "I am your superior in rank and in family, and you have most seriously displeased me!"

"I am sorry to hear it, ma'am, but that does not excuse your ill-bred behavior in the home of a lady you have not even met," Darcy pointed out. "Kindly lower your voice and allow the proprieties to be observed. Then, perhaps, I may deign to speak to you on the matter which has brought you hither."

Lady Catherine rapped her walking stick on the floor as she sniffed and lifted her nose. "Very well, get on with it, then. I have not the patience for dilly-dallying."

As Catherine Morland was the legal owner of Fullerton Manor, Darcy introduced her first, as the lady of the house and as his cousin's betrothed. Lady Catherine looked her over with a satirical eye, but nodded her head. Darcy next introduced Mrs. Allen, stating she was the widow of the late master of the estate, then introduced James Morland before coming last to Jane and Elizabeth Bennet. All of the ladies unknown to his aunt stood and curtsied as they were introduced then sat down again, except for Elizabeth.

"La! So this is the strumpet which has caused you to forget your duty," said his aunt with a sneer in Elizabeth's direction. "Do not have any hope of your attachment to my nephew being furthered, young lady, for no marriage can ever take place. Mr. Darcy is engaged to *my* daughter!"

"No, he is not," replied Elizabeth calmly. "Mr. Darcy is engaged to me — we have declared our intention to marry just this morning. I am very sorry if your daughter is disappointed, my lady, but as I understand it, the hope of his marrying her was but a passing fancy —"

"Passing fancy, indeed! What nonsense! It was the dearest wish of his mother as well as of hers," Lady Catherine interjected.

"No, Aunt, it was not," said Darcy firmly. "It may have long been your greatest desire, but it was never my mother's. She told me this herself. In fact, my dear mother told me the day she died that she hoped I would do as she had done, to follow my heart and marry a woman I loved. I have heeded her instructions and engaged myself to the only woman I have ever or could ever love."

Lady Catherine snorted. "Love! Pah, what good is love without connections or fortune? This girl has none! Lord Disley says that her father can give her nothing — he is but a country gentleman with an income hardly worth noting. Her mother's relations are a country attorney and a tradesman."

"Did my father have the Bennets investigated?" asked Fitzwilliam indignantly.

"Of course he did, as soon as he had any idea that this *person* sought to quit the sphere in which she'd been brought up!"

"Lady Catherine, in marrying your nephew I should not consider myself as quitting that sphere," said Elizabeth. "He is a gentleman, I am a gentleman's daughter. So far, we are equals."

Lady Catherine tossed her head. "Equals, indeed. You bring *nothing* to any marriage you enter. A lady's duty is to improve the reputation of her husband, and that you shall *never* do. Oh, Darcy, are the shades of Pemberley to be thus polluted? Will you not see that she has deluded you with her arts and allurements to forget your duty to family and station?"

"Lady Catherine—" Darcy began.

Her fury remained focused on Elizabeth. "You would ruin him in the eyes of society? For none of his friends or family will take notice of you—neither your name nor his will be mentioned by any of us. You will both of you be shunned for the disgrace of the connection. And my niece! Would you destroy her prospects for an advantageous match?"

"I beg your pardon, madam," spoke up Catherine, standing again, "but I have heard quite enough. I cannot abide such rudeness! You have now insulted my good friend by every possible method, and can surely have nothing further to say."

Lady Catherine looked to her with some surprise. Then her gaze narrowed as she said, "Oh, but I have a great deal more to say, young lady, and I shall say it—"

"No, ma'am, you will not," said Darcy. He stepped toward her, moving purposely into her personal space so as to be more imposing. "Lady Catherine, as my hostess has observed, you have said quite enough. Your displeasure is noted, but my resolve remains firm. And as I am both a gentleman of independent means as well as some years over my majority, no one can force me into a connection I do not desire. Really, I wonder at your taking the trouble of coming so far on so pointless an errand. You must have known that your opposition—and my uncle's—would not sway me. Your daughter Anne has all my respect and affection as a cousin, but no more. I share Elizabeth's sentiments, in that I am sorry if she is disappointed. But I was never going to marry her, and it is time that was accepted by all the family."

"Oh, but think of what you are giving up if you continue on this course: you would have Anne's fifty thousand pounds—you would have Rosings!"

"And they are prizes indeed, Aunt, but I have no desire to claim them. Let some other gentleman have those rewards—I already have mine."

Again his aunt's gaze narrowed. "You are resolved, then, to pursue this folly?" she asked.

Darcy moved back to stand at Elizabeth's side. He smiled down at her as he took her hand in his, then looked back to Lady Catherine. "To pursue one of life's greatest rewards is never folly, Aunt. I regret that my choice is not agreeable to you, but it is made."

Lady Catherine sniffed disdainfully. "Very well, I shall know how to proceed. I take my leave with no compliments to you, sir, for you deserve no such attention. You are henceforth unknown to me."

She turned then to Fitzwilliam. "I would advise you, young man, to throw off your unworthy cousin—and make certain you take a firm hand with this one," she said, jerking her thumb at Catherine, "lest she become outspoken and opinionated. A young lady of low birth ought to remember her place, especially one who has been elevated from obscurity."

"And that really is enough," snapped Fitzwilliam, who moved to take his aunt by the arm. "Lady Catherine, it is past time you deprived us of your unwanted company. Allow me to show you the means of doing so."

Lady Catherine sputtered and spewed righteous indignation the whole way, but Fitzwilliam was not to be deterred in escorting her to the door. There was something of a finality in the sound it made when he shut it behind her.

Darcy noted that Georgiana was on the verge of tears. Going to his sister, he sat beside her and took her hand in his. "Pray, do not be distressed, dearest. I am sure you understand that such a confrontation was inevitable."

Georgiana, who trembled slightly, drew a deep breath and blew it out slowly. "Yes, I know. You have long denied any attachment to our cousin. But knowing an argument was inevitable does not make witnessing it any less troubling."

"I'd put it out of your mind, Georgie," said Fitzwilliam as he returned to the drawing room. "Lady Catherine is only angry she didn't get her way. Be thankful that now she's cast Darcy off, you'll never have to be bothered with her."

He stepped up to his fiancée and cupped her cheek, causing Catherine to blush. "You were rather remarkable, Catherine, standing up to her like you did."

The rosy color of her cheeks deepened, and she blew out a breath before saying, "I am obliged to you, sir, for being so kind. I rather feared that I had spoken out of turn."

"No indeed, dear Catherine," said Mrs. Allen. "You are the mistress of Fullerton, and it is within your right to speak up in defense of one of your guests."

"I confess I so often forget, as in my mind I still think of you as Fullerton's mistress," Catherine replied.

Mrs. Allen stood and stepped up to her. "No, my dear," said she. "Now that title belongs to you. While I have given it up rather sooner than I expected, I am most pleased to pass it on to one so very worthy of taking it. As a matter of fact..."

She drew a breath and set her shoulders back. "As a matter of fact, I think it is time I removed from the mistress's bedchamber."

"Oh no, Mrs. Allen! It is your room!" cried Catherine.

Mrs. Allen took her hands and gave them an affectionate squeeze, and she smiled as she said, "No, my dear. It is *your* room, and it is time you should have it. I will go and see to it that our chambers are reversed, while you visit with your dear colonel and your friends."

The lady then moved off toward the door, where she stopped and turned back with an almost sad expression. "You know, I feel quite sorry for your aunt, Mr. Darcy, Colonel Fitzwilliam... She must be so very lonely to be so disagreeable to everyone. I am glad to know I shall never have to suffer being friendless."

The lot of the young people stared after her even after she had quit the room. Georgiana broke the silence by saying, "Do you suppose that is possible, brother? That our Aunt Catherine is lonely? I confess I never thought if it that way, when she has Anne for company."

Darcy shared a look with Fitzwilliam, who sighed and said, "While she does have Anne with her, Georgie, our cousin is more often than not in her room. Since our uncle passed, Lady Catherine has rather been much alone in that house."

"Now I think on it," said Darcy, "I believe Lady Catherine's arrogance and officiousness, disagreeable as those traits were, worsened when my mother died—and became unbearable when she lost Sir Lewis only a few years after. With Anne being so often confined to her bed, I suppose it is no wonder that she attempts to assert her authority where she can, as she travels out of Kent so little because of her daughter."

"Such as around her parish," observed Elizabeth. "Mr. Collins has told us, has he not Jane, that she is often about the place giving her advice and opinions, though it is more often than not unsolicited."

"He did also say that she likes to be of use where she can, so that is at least one redeemable quality in the lady, is it not?" Jane countered.

"My aunt does not like to be trifled with, nor does she brook refusal to do as she says," Darcy mused. "I can, therefore, understand her behavior, if it truly stems from loneliness and a lack of varied society. But I cannot condone it when her unladylike conduct does no credit to her upbringing and causes embarrassment to her family."

Fitzwilliam snorted. "We're the only ones to be embarrassed by it, I imagine. Clearly my father has little handle on her, if she were not patient enough to wait for our return to London."

"Speaking of London," said Catherine with a grin at Elizabeth. "Now we are *three* of us in need of wedding clothes—Mrs. Allen is sure to be thrilled with taking three to the linen drapers and modistes in Town!"

Elizabeth smiled and laughed. "She will be happy indeed, as will my mother," said she. "But before I can dare to arrange any dress fittings, my dear Mr. Darcy has a task to complete."

"Oh?" Darcy said. "And what, pray, is that?"

Her lips lifted into that saucy little grin he had come to adore almost from the first moment he'd seen it. "Why, you must go to my father and ask his permission to marry his favorite daughter!"

Chapter Twenty-Six

The group of friends stayed at Fullerton until Wednesday, giving Jane Bennet and Colonel Fitzwilliam a chance to get to know the six younger brothers and sisters they would soon be acquiring.

The eldest of them, Sarah, was a very pleasant girl—pretty and cheerful—and though she also enjoyed novels, she was somehow not quite as naïve as her elder sister. She liked to be called Sally, and at present was a most invaluable helpmate to her mother and the nursemaid in looking after the youngest children, now that Catherine was moved to Fullerton Manor.

Thomas, the next youngest, was smart, athletic, and expressed great interest in learning about the army from his future brother-in-law. He needed some profession, after all, and while he respected the choice of his father and eldest brother, had no inclination for joining the clergy. As he had reached fifteen only four months prior, there were another eight in which he could resolve to join or change his mind, as one had to be sixteen to purchase an ensign's commission. His next sibling, Robert—though he had protested being made to sit with the ladies after dinner on Sunday—was still very much a boy, and had been described by both his parents as being "not quite ready for manhood or responsibility."

The youngest three Morland children were all of them under ten years, and Fitzwilliam had confessed to Darcy in private conversation his pleasure and relief that his future in-laws had income enough to afford not only the minimum number of servants for a house the size of the rectory, but also a nursemaid to help care for their children, that it was not all left to their sister to do. In turn, he had gotten on so well with them all that Reverend Morland said to Darcy one afternoon that he was certain of his cousin's being "a most excellent father, when the time comes."

Darcy could not but agree, as Theodore had always had an affinity with children. His naturally charming manner and oftentimes gregarious personality—not to mention more than a decade in the army—had made him a natural at getting others to listen, and his willingness to join in fun and games endeared him to those younger than himself. In fact, if Darcy was not mistaken, he had witnessed some increase in admiration on the part of his cousin's future bride, as she watched him playing with the youngest Morland, who was a boy of but four years.

Sally was overjoyed at being granted permission to join her sister on the return trip to Meryton, as Catherine had promised to purchase her a new gown for the wedding. She had not been outside of Fullerton before, and looked forward to having a "grand adventure," though her stay in London would be only a day and Meryton was much like Fullerton. She would be leaving home for the first time, and that was enough for her.

Because Catherine was now officially engaged to Colonel Fitzwilliam, her father requested that Mrs. Allen—who would once again be going along as chaperone—find some manner of lodgings where she and his daughters could stay together, rather than the three staying at Darcy House in London or at Netherfield in Meryton. Mrs. Allen said she would be happy to take rooms in a hotel for herself and the girls in Town, and Elizabeth and Jane declared they would lodge with their aunt and uncle for the night. As to where Mrs. Allen and the Morland girls would stay in Meryton, it was some relief to all when Elizabeth mentioned that Purvis Lodge, a handsome but small estate, was available to rent.

"Oh yes!" Jane had said. "Mr. Bingley once told me he had considered the lodge, but was convinced by his sister's inclinations for a large house to take Netherfield instead."

There was another impromptu dinner party on Wednesday evening for last moments of togetherness between Catherine, James, and their family—at least for another week. James and Jane had decided on 10 December for their wedding date, seeing no real reason to delay beginning their life together—so long as the marriage articles were quickly written up and agreed upon. Reverend and Mrs. Morland would come up with the six children still at home so that Jane could fulfill her mother's wish to be married at Longbourn

Church. Catherine vowed to hire two carriages for the trip for their comfort, as well as giving her parents some money for a night of lodging on the road.

Fitzwilliam and Catherine had also set a wedding date: 1 January. In order to fully secure her comfort in marrying, the colonel was more than happy to allow for the banns to be read rather than acquiring a common license. The last of their banns would be called on 22 December, and like her brother, Catherine had agreed that there was little point in delaying the marriage long after. However, she and the colonel would be marrying at Fullerton, and would begin the new year together as husband and wife.

𝕒𝕖

Elizabeth and Darcy once again sat together over the chessboard the night before their departure. For the first time they were on the verge of a stalemate in the game, so he decided something of a break was in order and sat back, looking to Elizabeth with a warm smile.

"All this talk of weddings these last three days has me thinking of our own," said he.

Elizabeth returned his smile. "I like that you are thinking of our wedding, Fitzwilliam. I've been thinking of it myself," she replied.

"And I am pleased you have been thinking of it as well. Pray tell me your thoughts on the matter," he said.

"Something Mrs. Allen said on Sunday about a double wedding. Though I hesitate to ask it of you, I was wondering if you would mind sharing a wedding day with James and Jane," said Elizabeth.

Darcy sat forward and held out his hand. When she had put hers into it, he said, "Never hesitate to ask me for anything, be it a need or a desire. If your sister and Mr. Morland agree to the scheme, I would be delighted to share the day with them. I would marry you to-morrow if only I had a license."

She grinned his favorite grin then, and teased him with, "Well, we *are* to pass through London, Mr. Darcy. You might acquire it then."

He chuckled. "I shall have to, if you wish to share the day with your sister."

In the morning, when the two carriages departed from Fullerton Manor, Jane rode in the Darcy carriage with Elizabeth and Georgiana. She confessed that James had told her not to worry over the future as her mother so often did, as he intended to see to it the small estate he would inherit would be hers should anything happen to him. The

243

only reason he did not take it now, she said, was that the present parson of the living James was to have had been granted leave to live in the house, as the village where his living was had no dedicated rectory.

"You know, Jane," said Elizabeth, "Mr. Darcy has a number of livings in his purview that are of greater income. Perhaps one of them will come available at the time my brother is to take orders—I am sure he would be happy to assist you both, especially if there is a child by then."

"Oh, he absolutely would!" agreed Georgiana. "And it would be so pleasant to have one of your sisters near you, I am sure."

Jane blushed. "Though you know I would be happy to have as many daughters as our mother, I do hope that James and I should have a son. At least one, so that worry would be off my mind. For all her fancy of nerves, Lizzy, you know that Mamma's concern for us all is very real."

Elizabeth nodded. "I do know it, but with my marriage to Mr. Darcy, she'll not have to worry anymore. You know he has already vowed to see to her comfort and that of our younger sisters when our father is gone."

"Yes, and what a relief to her it will be," said Jane. "Though you know what else she will think when she has learned you are to marry a man of ten thousand a year."

Laughing, Elizabeth replied, "Oh yes! She will expect me to wake up our sisters' ideas of a husband and throw them in the path of other rich men!"

The three ladies continued chattering amiably until their party stopped for a luncheon and they were happily reunited with their friends in the other carriage. When they set off again, Elizabeth traded places with Sally, who wished to further her burgeoning friendship with Georgiana. Riding with Mrs. Allen and Catherine, Elizabeth was subject to talk of muslins and gowns and how much they were looking forward to their day in London.

They stopped for the night at a very respectable inn, relieved that there were enough rooms for their large party, though as before there was a need to share. The travelers were up again at dawn for the last leg of their journey to London. On arrival, their first objective was to find a hotel for Mrs. Allen and the Morland girls. Elizabeth and Jane were then escorted to their aunt and uncle in Gracechurch Street; the Gardiners were absolutely delighted by the news that Elizabeth was to be married.

"And to Mr. Darcy of Pemberley, of all people!" her aunt exclaimed.

"You must come and see us in the spring when you take your annual holiday, Aunt," Elizabeth said.

Mrs. Gardiner, who had been standing when she spoke, stepped back and almost fell into her seat. "I am to see Pemberley at last! It has been a dream of mine since I was a girl to go inside that beautiful house!"

While the ladies spent their afternoon shopping for wedding clothes, Darcy and Fitzwilliam had debated whether they ought to notify the earl they were in Town for the day. Darcy decided that he would at least send his uncle formal notice of his intention to marry, expecting either a scathing reply or none at all. He was surprised when a reply did come, bearing a more positive message than he had imagined: *Congratulations. I hope you will be happy.*

Darcy, Fitzwilliam, and Morland were not idle with their time otherwise—while the women were concerned with clothes, they saw to more practical matters regarding their marriages. Darcy met with a bishop of his acquaintance to acquire a common license. They went also to a carriage maker where new carriages were ordered by all three; James had at first protested Darcy paying for a carriage for himself and Jane, remarking that it was his own responsibility, but Darcy insisted on doing the kindness.

"You may consider it a wedding present, if you like. You and Miss Bennet will require your own transportation, as you cannot always depend upon Mrs. Allen and your sister, nor should you."

"Though Catherine is likely to insist on purchasing the horses to pull it," quipped Fitzwilliam.

At last James relented, saying, "If I cannot dissuade you from the expense, then make it only a chaise. I will save for a larger carriage."

Darcy agreed and the money was paid, and they all went on to other shops, purchasing gifts for their brides and new mothers.

A family dinner was once again had that evening at Darcy House, to which Mr. and Mrs. Gardiner were invited. Elizabeth got the impression on introducing her aunt and uncle to Darcy that he was relieved she had at least *some* relations of sense and fashion. Mr. Gardiner's manners were those of a gentleman, Mrs. Gardiner's those of a lady. When it was mentioned that Elizabeth had invited them to visit Pemberley for their yearly holiday, Darcy readily agreed that they should come.

By midday on Thursday, the whole party was once again in

Meryton. After seeing Mrs. Allen and the Morland girls to Purvis Lodge, which had been rented by proxy via an express sent to Mr. Phillips on Monday to engage the place on their behalf, they went next to Longbourn. As Jane and Elizabeth were being welcomed back by their mother and sisters—Mr. Collins, they learned, had gone home to Kent with no wife at all—Darcy sought the necessary interview with Mr. Bennet, that he might secure his permission to marry Elizabeth. The matter was settled rather quickly, and a time was set the next day for both he and James to sit down with the gentleman and Mr. Phillips to draw up marriage articles.

After near an hour at Longbourn, Darcy, Fitzwilliam, and Morland at last made their way to Netherfield. On arrival, they learned that Caroline had at last carried her point, and Bingley was planning to go to London for the winter.

"I'm immeasurably happy for you and Miss Elizabeth, Darcy!" Bingley said. "I'll send Caroline on with the Hursts, so I can be here for your wedding."

"And I'll be glad to have you, Charles, but will you be able to tolerate watching as Jane Bennet marries another? We are to marry on the same day," Darcy said.

Bingley looked to James, but he smiled as he said, "I shall be well, Darcy—I have parted with my feelings for the lady, and wish her and her betrothed nothing but happiness."

"You are very kind to say so, Charles," said James. "I truly hope we shall remain friends, and that you will soon find another beautiful lady to love."

Bingley nodded. "I should like that very much."

The next week was a flurry of activity at the three estates around Meryton where the interested parties resided. Dinners and card parties were held at each, and there was so much talk in town of the double-wedding of the eldest Bennet sisters that very little was said of the compromising situation in which their friend Catherine Morland had found herself. What little *had* been said—according to Lady Lucas and Mrs. Phillips—was that she had been seen speaking to an officer quite alone and they *might* have kissed. When it was shared that Miss Morland was engaged to the cousin of Mr. Darcy, the townspeople naturally shifted from thinking it had been one of Colonel Forster's men to certainty it had been Colonel Fitzwilliam all along—and what two eager young lovers did not seek a moment alone together?

Gossip also had been spread—purposely by Forster himself—that

Wickham had died in a "tragic training accident" at the militia's shooting range. It was a sad business, said he, but such things happened. He and Charlotte Lucas were set to marry in January also, about the middle of the month.

$\approx$

Elizabeth woke early on the day of her wedding. After putting on a petticoat, stockings, and a walking dress, she hurried to Jane's room, pleased to find that her sister was awake also.

"Come Jane, and dress quickly. Let us take one more solitary stroll about the garden together as single ladies."

"I should like that," said Jane as she rose from the chair at her dressing table. "Oh, Lizzy, I'm so nervous! We have both of us woke to this day as a single young woman, and in only a few hours, we shall both of us be wives!"

"Indeed. It is time to grow up, I suppose," said Elizabeth. "But do not be too nervous, dearest. James will be there at the altar waiting for you as promised, as my dear Fitzwilliam will be waiting for me."

Jane finished pulling a walking dress over her head. "It's not that I fear he won't come, or that I may swoon during the ceremony—it's tonight! I am so nervous about the consummation of our vows."

"I will own that I am somewhat nervous in that regard as well," Elizabeth admitted. "But remember what our Aunt Gardiner told us last week—do not go into it with fear. Relax as much as you can, and be sure to tell your husband what you do and do not like. Soon enough, if we are fortunate, we may find joy in the bedding."

Jane sighed and looked to her. "I am holding that advice close to my heart, Lizzy."

Together the sisters made their way downstairs, donned cloaks and hats, and went out the back door into the garden. After they had walked around it, they extended their walk to circumvent the house itself, the wilderness beyond the wall, and then walked once more around the back garden before re-entering the house. The whole of their walk was spent in contemplative silence, Elizabeth feeling certain that her sister must be thinking much the same things she was: about how their lives would be changing once they signed their maiden names to the register, for after that moment they would be Bennets no more. They would be wives with a household to manage, and both of them elder sisters to new siblings acquired through their new family ties.

And, perhaps in the early autumn, one or the both of them might become a mother.

"Girls!" they heard their mother screech as soon as they stepped into the house. "Where *have* you been?! You are both to be married today—you cannot go ruining your complexions with chilly air!"

Elizabeth suppressed a sigh. "Mamma, a walk in the cool air of the morning will not ruin our complexions.

"You could have caught a chill! Do you think your Mr. Darcy will be happy to have a sick wife the first week of his marriage?!" Mrs. Bennet argued. "Never mind—go to your rooms and warm yourselves by the fire. I've got the maids set to bring you bathing water—make sure you add the scented oils so that you smell like the beautiful girls you are. No run along, run along! You must bathe and have your hair set, you must dress..."

Elizabeth turned with her sister toward the stairs, rolling her eyes at Jane, who blushed and smiled. Over the next couple of hours, the eldest Miss Bennets were washed, primped, curled and pinned, and dressed in one of the new gowns purchased for their trousseaus. After Mrs. Bennet had approved their appearances, she went ahead with the younger girls to the church, to which Mr. Bennet would convey Jane and Elizabeth via the family carriage.

As the small coach began to trundle the short distance to Longbourn church, Mr. Bennet drew a deep breath. "I am glad to have this moment alone with you girls," said he. "I want to take this opportunity to tell you how very happy I am for you both. You have each of you used good sense in your choice of husband, while also managing to follow your hearts. I am sure you will each of you do very well indeed."

Elizabeth, fighting tears, reached across the carriage to take her father's hand; Jane echoed the movement by taking the other.

"Thank you, Papa," said Elizabeth. "I know it is difficult for you to let us go, though it was always to happen—or so our mother hoped."

Mr. Bennet chuckled. "Yes. Sadly there will hardly be a word of sense spoken at Longbourn with the two of you gone. Well, Mary has shown rather a good deal more sense of late, so perhaps I shall be content with her company."

"I think you should endeavor to spend more time with her, Father," said Jane. "I do think Mary only needs a little more recognition to encourage her intellect. Poor girl has been so lost, being in the middle of two pair of best friends."

"Perhaps she has, dear Jane," said her father.

They were just then pulling up outside of the church, where many of the Longbourn villagers and some of their friends from Meryton were gathered. Inside the building, Elizabeth had eyes for no one but Darcy, and Jane no one but James. The ceremony was long and full of formal language, but when it was done, they were presented with the marriage register, each of the couples signing their name to it with the Bennet parents and the Morland parents as witnesses.

A wedding breakfast was held at Netherfield, as it had a ballroom large enough to fit all the family and friends who were attending. There was much food, much joy, much laughter and good cheer to be had and felt by all. Mrs. Bennet, to the surprise of none who knew her, boasted of the benefits of Elizabeth's marriage to Darcy, and how it would surely further her new son James in his career as well as throw the younger girls in the path of other rich men. Elizabeth, seeing how uncomfortable the notice and attention made her husband, attempted to shield him from her mother's joyous effusions, as well as Mrs. Phillips' vulgarity, by steering him to conversations with those of her family and friends with whom he could speak without mortification.

When the party was over, the couples took their leave to begin their lives together in their new homes. James and Jane went into Wiltshire to set up in the dower house of Fullerton Manor, and Darcy was able to at last show his beloved Elizabeth the family home of which he was so proud. When she saw the place for the first time, and had taken a long moment to appreciate its handsomeness and surroundings, Elizabeth looked to her husband and said,

"Upon my word, Mr. Darcy... Seeing our home at last, I truly begin to feel that to be mistress of Pemberley might be something!"

About the Author

Christine, like many a JAFF author before her, is a long-time admirer of Jane Austen's work, and she hopes that her alternate versions are as enjoyable as the originals. She has plans to one day visit England and take a tour of all the grand country estates which have featured in film adaptations, and often dreams of owning one. Christine lives in Ohio and is already at work on her next book.

Want to let Christine know what you think? Then be awesome and go post a review on the purchase page at the retailer where you bought your book! Reviews don't have to be long—just a few words will do—and they can totally make an author's day. You can also contact her on Facebook, visit her website, or send her an email. She would love to hear from you!

https://www.facebook.com/AuthorChristineCombe

allthattheydesire.blogspot.com

authorchristinecombe@gmail.com

Also by Christine Combe

What Might Have Been Series:
The Correction of Folly
Choice and Consequence

Standalone Novels:
The Reintroduction of Fitzwilliam Darcy
A Promise of Forever

Austenesque Must Reads

Hello book lover, Christine here! I like to close out every novel with a list of other Austen variations that I found enjoyable. Check out these fabulous authors and their *very* entertaining books:

Beth Massey
Duty and Deceit

Maria Grace
The Dragon Keepers' Cotillion

Jennifer Redlarczyk
A Very Merry Mix-Up

Joyce Harmon
Mary Bennet and the Bingley Codex

Jayne Bamber
Five Daughters Out at Once

Made in the USA
Monee, IL
12 May 2022

96312881R00152